Praise for *Finlay Donovan Is Killing It*

"Part comedy of errors, part genuine thriller... Deftly balancing genre conventions with sly, tongue-in-cheek comments on motherhood and femininity, Cosimano crafts a deliciously twisted tale."

—*Booklist*

"Suspenseful, funny... More, please." —*Kirkus Reviews*

"Amusing... pleasingly absurd... [a] romp from a skilled comic writer." —*Publishers Weekly*

"[A] fun adult debut... Readers will enjoy this breezy romp." —*Library Journal*

"If you love thrillers but wish the genre would lighten up a little, then you absolutely must read *Finlay Donovan Is Killing It*."

—POPSUGAR (Best New February Books)

"Part screwball comedy, part morality tale, the amusing *Finlay Donovan Is Killing It* is also a tale about parenting, bad divorces, reinventing oneself, rising above misery, and, well, becoming a hit woman. It's a solid, thoughtful, and funny-yet-poignant mystery that never once becomes a one-note story."

—*South Florida Sun Sentinel*

"Smart aleck-y and shrewd, tense and twisty, *Finlay Donovan Is Killing It* portends serial success for Cosimano and additional adventures for Finlay."

—*The Free Lance-Star*

"This story is terrific." —*The Florida Times-Union*

"Vero and Finlay's escapades together reminded me of a Lucy and Ethel skit, in a good way. If you need a laugh (and who doesn't?), you can't go wrong with this one." —*Mystery Scene*

"Reminiscent of Janet Evanovich's Stephanie Plum character, but with a fresh feeling. The ending packs a wallop and leaves us at a truly surprising cliff-hanger . . . already anticipating Book #2 in what I hope will be a long-running mystery series."
—*Mystery & Suspense Magazine*

"A delicious, funny, and smart story . . . I loved this book and can't wait for more from Ms. Cosimano."
—*CrimeReads* (12 Must-Read Laugh-Out-Loud Mysteries)

"Read in a single night, applauding along the way. For anyone who's ever wished to turn her life around, Finlay Donovan is the master. From failing everything to succeeding brilliantly, she proves you only need to get mistaken once for a contract killer to solve all your problems." —Lisa Gardner, #1 *New York Times* bestselling
author of *When You See Me*

"Funny and smart, twisty and surprising—Finlay Donovan is a character to root for. This suspenseful romp made me laugh but also kept me on the edge of my seat with its many surprises. I can't wait for the next book!"
—Megan Miranda, *New York Times* bestselling
author of *The Last House Guest*

"Edgar-nominated author Elle Cosimano's adult debut has everything I love—a plucky protagonist, perfect plot twists, and Panera! Finlay Donovan is not only killing it—she just may be my new favorite character. You won't be disappointed."

—Kellye Garrett, award-winning author of *Hollywood Homicide*

"Clever, perfectly plotted, and laugh-out-loud funny, *Finlay Donovan Is Killing It* is one of those books that will make you smile long after you've turned the last page. This series is pitch-perfect and will be devoured by fans of Janet Evanovich. Elle Cosimano hits it way, way, way out of the park!"

—Wendy Walker, bestselling author of *The Night Before* and *Emma in the Night*

"Fresh, fast-paced, and darkly fun with a deeply flawed but compulsively likable heroine, *Finlay Donovan Is Killing It* is a madcap thriller that will keep you flipping pages long past your bedtime!"

—Katherine St. John, author of *The Lion's Den*

"Elle Cosimano came up with one of the freshest, most fun, and interesting premises for a mystery this reviewer has ever seen. Her writing is terrific, the characters well-rounded and completely credible, and the story will grab readers and not let go until the end of this romp."

—*Manhattan Book Review* (five stars)

"The funniest crime series debut since Stephanie Plum strapped on her bounty-hunting gear, and you'll love every minute of it."

—BookTrib

FINLAY DONOVAN
IS KILLING IT

ELLE COSIMANO

MINOTAUR
BOOKS
NEW YORK

Published in the United States by Minotaur Books, an imprint of
St. Martin's Publishing Group

FINLAY DONOVAN IS KILLING IT. Copyright © 2021 by Elle Cosimano. All rights reserved. Printed in the United States of America. For information, address St. Martin's Publishing Group, 120 Broadway, New York, NY 10271.

www.minotaurbooks.com

Excerpt from *Finlay Donovan Knocks 'Em Dead*
copyright © 2022 by Elle Cosimano

Designed by Omar Chapa

The Library of Congress has cataloged the hardcover edition as follows:

Names: Cosimano, Elle, author.
Title: Finlay Donovan is killing it / Elle Cosimano.
Description: First edition. | New York : Minotaur Books, 2021. |
Identifiers: LCCN 2020037496 | ISBN 9781250241702 (hardcover) |
    ISBN 9781250242204 (ebook)
Subjects: GSAFD: Mystery fiction.
Classification: LCC PS3603.O84 F56 2021 | DDC 813/.6—dc23
LC record available at https://lccn.loc.gov/2020037496

ISBN 978-1-250-83044-9 (trade paperback)

Our books may be purchased in bulk for promotional, educational, or business use. Please contact your local bookseller or the Macmillan Corporate and Premium Sales Department at 1-800-221-7945, extension 5442, or by email at MacmillanSpecialMarkets@macmillan.com.

First Minotaur Books Trade Paperback Edition: 2022

10 9 8 7 6 5 4

For Ashley and Megan,
because I'd bury a body with either of you

CHAPTER 1

It's a widely known fact that most moms are ready to kill someone by eight thirty A.M. on any given morning. On the particular morning of Tuesday, October eighth, I was ready by seven forty-five. If you've never had to wrestle a two-year-old slathered in maple syrup into a diaper while your four-year-old decides to give herself a haircut in time for preschool, all while trying to track down the whereabouts of your missing nanny as you sop up coffee grounds from an overflowing pot because in your sleep-deprived fog you forgot to put in the filter, let me spell it out for you.

I was ready to kill someone. I didn't really care who.

I was late.

My agent was already on a train from Grand Central to Union Station, where I was supposed to meet her for a brunch reservation at a restaurant I couldn't afford so we could discuss exactly how overdue I was on my deadline for a book I had started three times and probably would never finish because . . . Jesus, look around me. Reasons.

My two-story colonial in South Riding was just close enough to the city to make ten o'clock sound reasonable when I'd scheduled it. It was also just far enough outside the city to convince otherwise sane people to buy life-size inflatable dolls so they could slither into the HOV lane without getting a ticket, or without being subjected to a drive-by shooting by any of the rest of us who had not yet sold our souls to buy inflatable dolls of our own.

Don't get me wrong. I'd liked South Riding, before the divorce. Back before I'd known my husband was sleeping with our real estate agent, who also sat on the board of the homeowners association. Somehow, I'm guessing that's not what the saleslady had in mind when she'd described our suburban mecca as having a "small-town" feel. The brochure had featured photos of happy families hugging each other on quaint front porches. It had used words like *idyllic* and *peaceful* to describe the neighborhood, because in the glossy pages of a real estate magazine, no one can see through the windows to the exhausted stabby mommy, or the naked sticky toddler, or the hair and blood and coffee on the floor.

"Mommy, fix it!" Delia stood in the kitchen rubbing her fingers over the patchy wet stubble where she'd scratched herself with the scissors. A thin bead of blood trailed over her forehead and I smeared it up with an old burp rag before it could drip in her eye.

"I can't fix it, sweetie. We'll take you to the hairdresser after school." I pressed the cloth to the bald spot until the bleeding stopped. Then, with my cell phone tucked between my shoulder and my ear, I crawled under the table and scraped together the fallen strands of her hair, counting unanswered rings.

"I can't go to school like this. Everyone will laugh at me!" Delia cried big snotty tears as Zachary rubbed toaster waffles in his hair and gawked at her from his high chair. "Daddy would know how to fix it."

My head smacked the underside of the table, and my two-year-old erupted in a fit of wails. I got stiffly to my feet, brandishing a fistful of my daughter's wispy locks. The rest of the trimmed bits were stuck in the syrup on the knee of my pants. Biting back a swear my two-year-old was certain to repeat for weeks in the grocery cart if I voiced it aloud, I tossed the hairy poultry shears into the sink.

Sometime around the forty-seventh ring, the call went to voice mail.

"Hi, Veronica? It's Finlay. I hope everything's okay," I said sweetly, in case she'd been crushed to death in a car accident or burned alive in a house fire overnight. You never want to be the asshole that leaves a message promising to kill someone for being late, only to find out they've already been murdered. "I was expecting you at seven thirty so I could get to my meeting downtown. I guess you forgot?" My cheerful lilt at the end of the sentence suggested this was okay. That we were okay. But this was not okay. *I* was not okay. "If you get this message, give me a call back. Please," I added before hanging up. Because my children were watching, and we always use our pleases and, "Thank you." I disconnected, dialed my ex, and jammed the phone back under my ear as I washed all hope for salvaging the day from my hands.

"Is Vero coming?" Delia asked, picking at her handiwork and frowning at her sticky red fingers.

"I don't know." Vero would probably pull Delia into her lap and style the whole mess into some trendy comb-over. Or conceal it under an intricate French braid. I was pretty sure any similar attempt on my part would only make matters worse.

"Can you call Aunt Amy?"

"You don't have an Aunt Amy."

"Yes, I do. She was Theresa's sister in college. She can fix my hair. She studied cometology."

"You mean *cos*metology. And no, just because she was Theresa's sorority sister does not make her your Aunt Amy."

"Are you calling Daddy?"

"Yes."

"*He* knows how to fix things."

I pasted on a strained smile. Steven knew how to break things, too. Like dreams and wedding vows. But I didn't say that. Instead, I gritted my teeth, because child psychologists say it's not healthy to bash your ex in front of your children. And common sense says you shouldn't do it while you're waiting for him to pick up his cell phone so you can ask him to babysit them.

"He uses duck glue," Delia insisted, following me around the kitchen as I scraped the breakfast scraps into the trash and dumped the plates in the sink along with my sanity.

"You mean duct tape. We can't fix your hair with duct tape, sweetie."

"Daddy could."

"Hold on, Delia." I shushed her when my ex finally picked up. "Steven?" He sounded hassled before he even said good morning. On second thought, I don't think good morning was actually what he said. "I need a favor. Vero didn't show up this morning, and I'm already late for a meeting with Sylvia downtown. I need to drop Zach with you for a few hours." My son flashed me a syrupy grin from his high chair as I used the damp rag to mop the sticky spot from my slacks. They were the only decent pants I owned. I work in my pajamas. "Also, he might need a bath."

"Yeah," Steven said slowly. "About Vero . . ."

I stopped patting and dropped the burp rag in the open diaper bag at my feet. I knew that tone. It was the same one he'd used when he broke the news that he and Theresa had gotten engaged. It was also the same tone he'd used last month when he told me his landscaping business had taken off because of Theresa's real estate contacts and he was flush with cash, and oh, by the way, he'd talked to a lawyer about filing for joint custody. "I was meaning to call you yesterday, but Theresa and I had tickets to the game and the day just got away from me."

"No." I gripped the counter. *No, no, no.*

"You work from home, Finn. You don't need a full-time sitter for Zach—"

"Don't do this, Steven." I pinched the blooming headache between my eyes while Delia tugged on my pant leg and whined about duct tape.

"So I let her go," he said.

Bastard.

"I can't afford to keep bailing you out—"

"Bailing me out? I'm the mother of your children! It's called child support."

"You're late on your van payment—"

"Only until I get my advance for the book."

"Finn." Every time he said my name it sounded like an expletive.

"Steven."

"It might be time to consider getting a real job."

"Like hydro-seeding the neighborhood?" Yeah, I went there. "This *is* my real job, Steven."

"Writing trashy books is not a real job."

"They're romantic suspense novels! And I've already been paid half up front. I'm under contract! I can't just walk away from a contract. I'll have to give it back." Then, because I was feeling particularly stabby, I added, "Unless you want to bail me out of that, too?"

He grumbled to himself as I knelt to sop up the puddle of grounds on the floor. I could picture him at their spotless kitchen table in her immaculate designer town house over a mug of French-pressed coffee, pulling out what was left of his hair.

"Three months." His patience sounded as thin as the hair on the crown of his head, but I kept that to myself because I needed a babysitter more than the satisfaction of whittling away at his fragile male ego. "You're three months late on the mortgage, Finn."

"You mean the rent. The rent I pay *you*. Cut me a break, Steven."

"And the HOA is going to put a lien on the house if you don't pay the special assessment bill they sent you in June."

"And how would you know that?" I asked, even though I already knew the answer. He was banging our real estate agent, and his best friend was our loan officer. *That's* how he knew.

"I think the kids should come live with me and Theresa. Permanently."

I nearly dropped the phone. Abandoning the wad of paper towels, I stormed from the kitchen and lowered my voice to a harsh whisper. "Absolutely not! There is no way I'm sending my kids to live with that woman."

"You're hardly earning enough in royalties to pay for groceries."

"Maybe I'd have time to finish a book if you hadn't just laid off my babysitter!"

"You're thirty-two years old, Finn—"

"I am not." I was thirty-one. Steven was just bitter because I was three years younger than he was.

"You can't spend your whole life shut up in that house, making up stories. We have real-life bills and real-life problems you need to deal with."

"Jerk," I muttered through a thin breath. Because the truth hurt. And Steven was the biggest, most painful truth of them all.

"Look," he said, "I'm trying not to be a jerk about this. I asked Guy to hold off until the end of the year, to give you time to find something." Guy. His frat-brother-turned-divorce-lawyer. The same Guy who'd done too many keg stands and puked in the back seat of my car back in college was now the attorney who golfed with the judge on Saturdays and had cost me my weekends with my kids. On top of it, Guy had conned the judge into taking half of my advance for my last book and giving it to Theresa, as recompense for the damage I'd done to her car.

Okay, fine.

I concede that getting drunk and stuffing a wad of Delia's Play-Doh in the exhaust pipe of Theresa's BMW may not have been the best way to handle the news when he'd told me they were getting engaged, but letting her walk away with half my advance *and* my husband felt like salt in the wound.

From the empty dining room, I watched Delia twirl what was left of her hair around a sticky red finger. Zach whined, fidgeting in his high chair. If I couldn't earn a paycheck in the next three months, Guy would find a way to take my kids and give them to Theresa, too.

"I'm late. I can't discuss this with you right now. Can I bring Zach to you or not?" *I will not cry. I will not—*

"Yeah," he said wearily. Steven didn't know the meaning of weary. *He* had coffee and got eight uninterrupted hours of sleep every night. "Finn, I'm sorr—"

I disconnected. It wasn't as satisfying as a knee to his groin, and yes, it was probably childish and clichéd, but a small part of me felt better after hanging up on him. The very small part (if there was any) that wasn't covered in syrup and late for my meeting.

Whatever. I was still not okay. Nothing was okay.

I felt another tug on my slacks. Delia looked up at me, tears brewing in her eyes, her hair sticking up in blood-matted spikes.

I blew out a heavy sigh. "Duct tape. I know."

Musty autumn air rushed in when I opened the service door to the garage. I flicked on the light, but the cavernous space was still dim and depressing, empty except for the oil stain left behind by Steven's F-150 on the concrete and my dust-coated Dodge Caravan. Someone had drawn a phallus in the grime on the back window, and Delia hadn't let me clean it because she'd said it looked like a flower, and it all felt like a metaphor for my life right now. A workbench lined the back wall of the garage, topped by a giant pegboard for tools. Only there weren't any tools. Just my ten-dollar big-box-store generic pink planting trowel—one of a handful of things Steven hadn't taken when he'd cleaned out the garage. Everything else belonged to his landscaping business, he'd said. I dug around in the scraps left behind on the workbench—loose screws, a broken hammer, a near-empty bottle of upholstery cleaner—and found a roll of silver duct tape. It was as sticky and hairy as my children and I carried it inside.

Delia's teary doe eyes were gone. She looked at the roll of tape with all the assurance of a girl who had yet to be let down by the most important man in her life.

"Are you sure about this?" I asked, holding a fistful of her tawny strands.

She nodded. I grabbed a knit hat off the coatrack in the foyer and turned back to the kitchen. Zach was watching us, a piece of waffle stuck to his head, pushing and pulling his sticky fingers together and apart with a wide-eyed expression that bordered on mystical. I'm pretty sure he was taking a dump.

Great. Steven could change him.

My scissors were buried under a pile of dirty breakfast dishes, so I drew a knife from the block on the counter instead. The tape peeled away from the roll with a loud shriek, and I held the strands of clipped hair against the side of Delia's head while wrapping the tape around her like a hideous silver crown until the hair was (mostly) secured in place. The knife was dull, barely sharp enough to hack the tape from the roll.

Jesus.

I forced a smile as I pulled the knit cap over her head, just low enough to conceal the evidence. Delia grinned up at me, her tiny fingers raking the mop of Frankenstein-like strands from her eyes.

"Happy?" I asked, trying not to cringe and draw attention to the chunk of hair that had fallen loose and was now resting on her shoulder.

She nodded.

I stuffed the knife and tape in my shoulder bag along with my cell phone and plucked Zach from his high chair, holding him high enough to get a whiff of his droopy drawers. Satisfied, I slung him on my hip and slammed the door behind us.

I was okay, I told myself as I slapped the remote door opener on the wall of the garage. The motor lit up, a horrible grinding noise drowning out the children's chatter as it hauled the door open, flooding the garage with autumn-gray sunlight. I loaded us all into the minivan, setting Zach's sagging drawers gingerly in his car seat. It wasn't as satisfying as a kick to my ex's groin, but today, a sticky two-year-old in a shitty diaper felt like the best I could do.

"Where's Zach going?" Delia asked as I started the van and eased out of the garage.

"Zach's going to Daddy's house. You're going to school. And Mommy . . ." I pressed the remote button on my visor and waited for the door to close. Nothing happened.

I set the brake, ducking down to see into the garage. The light on the motor was off. So were the front stoop lights, and the light in Delia's bedroom window she always forgot to turn off. I pulled my phone from the diaper bag and checked the date.

Shit. The electric bill was thirty days past due.

I thunked my head against the steering wheel and rested it there. I'd have to ask Steven to pay it for me. He'd have to call the power company and beg them to turn it back on—again. I'd have to ask him to come over and manually close my garage. And Guy would probably hear all about it by the time I got home.

"Where are you going, Mommy?" Delia asked.

I lifted my head and stared at the stupid pink shovel on the pegboard. At the darkened window of the office I hadn't stepped foot in for weeks. At the weeds creeping up the front walk and the stack of bills the mail carrier had tossed on the front step when they'd overflowed the mailbox. I put the van in reverse, catching my kids' snotty, syrupy, cherubic faces in the rearview mirror as I backed slowly down the driveway, my heart aching at the possibility of losing them to Steven and Theresa. "Mommy's going to figure out how to make some money."

CHAPTER 2

It was thirty-six minutes after ten when I finally made it to the Panera in Vienna, too late for breakfast but too early for the lunch rush, and I still couldn't find a parking space. When I'd called Sylvia and explained I'd be too late to make our reservation at her fancy brunch restaurant pick, she'd asked for the name of a place that was close to a Metro station, opened early, and wouldn't require one. Feeling guilty and frazzled while navigating a traffic jam on the toll road, Panera was the first place to fly out of my mouth, and Sylvia had disconnected before I could take it back.

The lot at Panera was full, brimming with shiny Audis and Beemers and Mercedes. Who were these people, and why did they not have office jobs? For that matter, why didn't I?

I swung my minivan into the adjoining lot of the dry cleaner and picked a few last strands of Delia's hair from my pants before finally giving up. Slipping on a huge pair of sunglasses that obscured most of my face, I tied my silk wig-scarf around my head, fluffed the long blond waves cascading from the bottom, and smeared burgundy lipstick beyond the natural lines of my mouth. I sighed at my reflection in the rearview mirror. This was the same version of me inside the cover of my books, but also, it wasn't. In my headshots, I seemed mysterious and glamorous, like a romance novelist who wanted to preserve her secret identity from hordes of rabid fans. But in the drab lighting of my run-down minivan, with hairy syrup stains on my pants and diaper cream under my nails, and with a loose strand of my own brown hair poking stubbornly out of the bottom of the scarf, I just looked like I was trying too hard to be someone I'm not.

Let's face it, I wasn't wearing my wig-scarf to impress my agent—Sylvia already knew who I was. And who I wasn't. Today, I just wore it to keep me from being kicked out of this particular Panera. If I could make it through lunch without being recognized as the disaster who'd been banned from this establishment eight months ago, that would be enough.

I threw my knockoff designer diaper bag over my shoulder, took a deep breath, and got out of the van, praying Mindy the Manager had quit or been fired since the last time I'd been here, when Theresa had requested to talk out our differences over lunch.

I stepped into the restaurant, peering through the long blond locks of the wig I'd left hanging over my eyes. Sylvia was already in line, scrutinizing the menu on the wall behind the registers as if it was written in some strange foreign tongue. I stood beside her for a full minute and a half, then said her name before she finally gave me a double take. "Finlay? Is that you?" she asked.

I slipped behind her, shushing her as I peeked over her shoulder at the employees behind the counter. When I didn't see Mindy the Manager among them, or any familiar cashiers, I tucked the loose strands behind my ear. "Sorry I couldn't meet you downtown," I said. "My morning sort of exploded."

"I can see that." Sylvia had gone from scrutinizing the menu to scrutinizing me. She drew her glasses lower over the bridge of her nose with a long red fingernail. "Why are you wearing that?"

"Long story." My relationship with Panera was complicated. I liked their soup. Panera didn't like that I'd poured it over another customer's head. In my defense, Theresa had started it when she'd attempted to justify her reasons for sleeping with my husband.

"You have something on your pants," Sylvia said, grimacing at a hairy patch of syrup.

I pressed my lips tight. Tried to smile. Sylvia was everything you'd imagine New Yorkers to be if you watched too much television. Probably because she was from Jersey. Her office was in Manhattan. Her shoes were from Milan. Her makeup looked like it had flown in on a DeLorean circa 1980, and her clothes might have been skinned from a large jungle cat.

"I can help you over here," an attendant called from behind an open register. Sylvia stepped to the counter, interrogated the young man about the gluten-free options, and then proceeded to order a tuna baguette and a bowl of French onion.

When it was my turn, I found the cheapest thing on the menu—a cup of the day's soup. Sylvia held out her credit card and said, "It's on me," so I added a ham and brie sandwich and a slice of cheesecake to go.

We carried our trays to the dining room to find a table. As we walked, I filled Sylvia in on the gory details of my morning. She'd had children once, a long time ago, so she wasn't entirely without sympathy, but she wasn't exactly moved by the trials of my single motherhood shit-show.

All the booths were full, so we aimed for the last empty table for two in the middle of the bustling dining room. On one side of us, a college student wearing headphones stared at the screen of her MacBook. On the other side, a middle-aged woman picked at her bowl of macaroni and cheese alone. Sylvia squeezed between the tables and settled herself into a hardback chair, looking exasperated. I dropped my wallet in my diaper bag and set it down in the small gap on the floor beside me. The woman next to me glanced at it, then blinked up at me. I smiled blandly, sucking on my iced tea until she finally turned back to her lunch again.

Sylvia made a face at her sandwich. "Tell me again why we picked this place?"

"Because head wounds take forever to clean up. Sorry I was late."

"Where are we with your deadline?" she asked around a mouthful of tuna. "Please tell me I took the train all the way down here for good news."

"Not exactly."

She glared at me as she chewed. "Tell me you at least have a plan in place."

I slumped over my tray and picked at my food. "Sort of."

"They paid you half up front for this job. Tell me you're close."

I leaned across the table, pitching my voice low, thankful the college student beside me was wearing headphones. "My last few murders were so formulaic. I'm becoming too predictable. I feel like I'm falling into a rut, Syl."

"So change up your approach." She waved her spoon in the air, like conjuring a novel was no big deal. "The contract doesn't specify how the whole thing plays out, as long as you get it done by next month. You can do that, right?"

I stuffed in a bite of sandwich to keep from having to answer that. If I really pushed it, I could finish a rough draft in eight weeks. Six tops.

"How hard can it be? You've done it before."

"Yes, but this one's going to be messy." I tested a mouthful of soup. It tasted like cardboard. Like everything else had tasted since my divorce. "I could kill for some hot sauce," I muttered, checking the table beside me. Salt, pepper, sugar, and napkins. No hot sauce. But the woman hardly noticed. She was staring at my open bag on the floor. I tucked my wallet farther inside and folded the handles down, concealing the contents from view. When she continued to stare, I threw her a frosty look.

"I don't understand what's so hard. You've got a beautiful, sweet, sympathetic woman who needs to be rescued from a really bad guy. The bad guy gets handled, our sympathetic woman reveals the depths of her gratitude, everyone lives happily ever after, and you get a big fat check."

I tore the end off my baguette. "About the check—"

"Absolutely not." Sylvia waved her spoon at me. "I can't go back to them and ask for another advance."

"I know. But there's a lot of research involved in this one," I said in a low voice. "We're talking seedy nightclubs, instruments of torture, secret code words . . . This is completely outside my area of expertise. I'm usually very neat. You know, conservative. Nothing too far out there. But this . . ." I severed the end of my cheesecake. "This one's different, Syl. If I pull this off, I could become the next big name in the business."

"Whatever you do, make it quick. Let's bury this one and move on to the next."

I shook my head. "I don't want to rush this. I need this to be a big hit. These two- and three-thousand-dollar advances aren't worth the time or the effort. Whatever deal comes next needs to kick-start my career, or I'm out," I declared around a mouthful of cheesecake. "If this one goes well, I'm not taking a penny less than fifteen thousand for the next one."

"Fine. Knock 'em dead with this one, and we'll talk about the next one." Sylvia's phone vibrated on the table. She narrowed her eyes at the number on the screen. "Excuse me. I have to take this," she said, wriggling out from between the tables. As I twisted to let Sylvia pass, the woman at the table beside me caught my eye. Fork poised over her bowl of cold mac and cheese, she stared at me for an awkwardly long moment that made me wonder if she'd recognized me despite all the makeup and the wig-scarf. Or maybe it was the wig-scarf she recognized. No one had ever asked me for an autograph before. If she asked me to sign her napkin, I'd probably choke. I wasn't sure if I was relieved or disappointed when her gaze fell away and she reached for her purse.

I turned back to my sandwich, checking my phone for missed messages between bites. One from Steven, wondering how much longer I'd be. Two more from credit card companies reminding me I was past due. And an email from my editor, asking how the new book was coming. I had the odd feeling I was being watched, but the woman beside me was bent over a pen and a slip of paper.

After a few minutes, Sylvia's heels clicked back into the dining room. My heart sank when she didn't bother to sit down.

"I'm sorry, my dear. I have to go," she said, reaching for her messenger bag. "I need to grab the train back to the city. I've got a major offer coming in for another client, and it's got a drop-dead date in forty-eight hours. I've got to move fast before the deal's off the table." She slung the bag over her shoulder. "I wish we had more time to chat."

"No, it's fine," I assured her. I was not okay. This was not okay. "It was totally my fault."

"Yes, it was," she agreed, slipping on her designer sunglasses and leaving me with her dishes. "Now get to work on that hit, and let me know when it's done."

I stood up and pasted on a smile as we exchanged awkward cheek-to-cheek kisses that made us seem like friends who didn't actually want to touch each other. Her cell phone was pressed to her ear before she was out the door.

I sank back down in my chair. The woman who'd been seated beside me was gone and I glanced down, relieved to find my diaper bag and wallet still resting on the floor. I cleared Sylvia's tray, sorting her dishes and utensils into the bins by the waste receptacle. When I returned to my table, a scrap of folded paper was tucked under my plate. I looked around for the woman who'd been scribbling beside me but saw no sign of her. I unfolded the note.

$50,000 CASH

HARRIS MICKLER

49 NORTH LIVINGSTON ST

ARLINGTON

And a phone number.

I crumpled up the note and held it over the bin. But the dollar sign—and all the zeroes that followed—piqued my curiosity. Who was Harris Mickler? Why did he have so much cash? And why had the woman sitting beside me left the paper on my tray when she could have just as easily disposed of it herself?

I tucked the strange note in my pocket and gathered my bag. The midday sun glared off the windshields of the sea of cars outside,

and I groped blindly in my bag for my keys, struggling to remember
where I'd parked. I still hadn't found them by the time I reached
the dry cleaner, and I stood beside my locked van, swearing into the
abyss of my bag. A few of Delia's stray hairs tickled my wrist as my
fingers snagged on the sticky roll of duct tape I'd used to fix her hair.
Something bit me as I shoved it aside. With a yelp, I whipped my
hand from the bag.

A thin line of blood beaded along my fingers. Carefully, I plucked
aside the blood-stained burp rag I'd used to clean my daughter's
forehead that morning. Below it, I found the dull kitchen knife I'd
thrown in with it, along with the keys to my van.

I pressed the burp rag to the shallow cut and turned the AC
on high while I waited for the bleeding to stop. The air outside was
cool, autumn-crisp, but the van was boiling in the noon sun and my
hair was already damp with sweat under the itchy scarf. I peeled it
off, dropping it into the diaper bag along with the dark sunglasses.
A heavily made-up woman with a tight mom-bun stared back at me
from the rearview mirror. I swiped off the deep burgundy lipstick on
the burp rag, feeling like an impostor. Who was I kidding? There was
no way I'd finish this book in a month. Every day I spent pretending
to make a living as a writer only put me one day closer to losing my
kids. I should have called Sylvia right then and there and told her as
much.

I dragged my phone from my pocket. The strange note slipped
out with it. I pried it open.

Fifty thousand dollars.

I looked back at my cell. Then again at the note, curiosity making me linger on the phone number written at the bottom.

I could always say I'd misdialed and hang up, right? The phone
beeped as I keyed in the number. A woman answered on the first ring.

"Hello?" Her quiet voice wavered.

I opened my mouth, but nothing intelligent came out. "Hello?"

"You found my note."

I wasn't sure what to say, so I erred on the side of vague. "Did I?"

She expelled a shaky breath through the phone. "I've never done anything like this before. I don't even know if I'm doing it right."

"Doing what?"

She giggled, a panicked, almost hysterical laugh that died in a sniffle. Our connection was so clear, it was like she was sitting right in front of me. I searched through the windshields of the adjacent cars, expecting to see her staring back.

My finger hovered over the red button on the screen. "Are you okay?" I asked, against my better judgment. "Do you need help or something?"

"No, I'm not okay." She blew her nose into the receiver and our connection became garbled, as if she were talking into a wad of tissues. "My husband . . . He's . . . not a nice man. He's doing strange things. Terrible things. If it was just the once, maybe I would understand, but there have been others. So many others."

"Other whats? I don't understand what any of this has to do with me." *I should hang up,* I thought to myself. This was all getting really weird.

"I can't tell him I know. That would be . . . very, very bad. I need you to help me." She drew a deep breath through the phone, as if maybe her finger was poised over the red button, too. After a heavy pause, she said, "I want you to do it."

"Do what?" I asked, struggling to keep up.

"Whatever it is you do. Like you said, neat. I just want him gone. I have fifty thousand cash. I was going to use it to leave him. But it will be better this way."

"What way?"

"He'll be at a networking event at The Lush tonight. I don't want to know how it will happen. Or where. Just call this number when it's done."

The connection went dead.

I shook my head, still lost in the bizarre turn of the conversation. I glanced down at the bloody burp rag in my lap. At the knife in my open diaper bag and the duct tape threaded with Delia's hair. I thought back to the woman's pale face as she listened to our conversation between covert glances at my bag on the floor.

The bad guy gets handled, our sympathetic woman reveals the depths of her gratitude, everyone lives happily ever after, and you get a big fat check.

Oh, god.

I'm not taking a penny less than fifteen thousand . . . Let's bury this one and move on to the next.

Fifty thousand dollars. She thought I'd said *fifty* thousand dollars.

Oh, no. *No, no, no!*

I stuffed everything back in the diaper bag. The paper. What was I supposed to do with the paper? Throw it away? Burn it? Run back into Panera, tear it into pieces, and flush it down the toilet? The faster I got rid of it, the better. I crumpled it and rolled down my window, holding it in my fist over the burning pavement.

Fifty thousand dollars.

I rolled up the window, stuffing the note back in my pocket as I put the van in gear. My heart thumped wildly as I eased out of the parking lot, careful to use my turn signals and check my speed. What if I was pulled over and searched and a police officer found it? My Google search history alone was probably enough to put me on a government watch list. I wrote suspense novels about murders like this. I'd searched every possible way to kill someone. With every conceivable kind of weapon. I'd researched every possible way to dispose of a body.

This was ridiculous. I was foolish to worry about a stupid piece of paper. I couldn't be a suspect for a crime that hadn't happened yet. And there was *no way* I was even *considering* this. If his wife wanted him dead, she could find someone else to do it. And I could get on with my—

Oh . . .

My hands gripped the wheel. This woman had sounded serious. Fifty thousand dollars was serious, right? What would happen if she *did* find someone else to do it? Could I become a suspect? I might.

Unless . . .

I checked my rearview mirror as I merged into traffic. What if no one found a body? What if no one knew for sure this Harris Mickler person was dead? There wouldn't necessarily be a suspect at all, right?

I could practically hear Steven's voice in my head, telling me I was being ridiculous, that I was imagining the worst and making up stories. It was the argument he always fell back on, the one he'd unloaded on me when I first suspected he'd slept with Theresa behind my back.

Only this time, I hated that he was right.

I smacked the steering wheel, cursing myself as I hugged the far-right lane of the toll road. Why was I even thinking about this? I had real-life problems to deal with: looming deadlines without babysitters or advances, overdue car payments, relentless calls from bill collectors . . . And this whole situation with Harris Mickler, this was sick. This was twisted.

This was fifty thousand dollars.

A horn blared behind me, and I jumped in my seat, speeding up a little to stay with the flow of traffic. I should pitch the note out the window, I told myself, and forget this ever happened.

I tapped the wheel. Switched on the radio. Switched it off again. Checked my speed as I glided past the toll booths through the E-ZPass lane, unable to stop replaying the conversation in my mind.

My husband . . . He's . . . not a nice man.

Was he "forgets our anniversary" not nice, I wondered? Or was he "sleeping around" not nice? Because banging your real estate agent isn't a reason to want your husband dead. It might be a legitimate reason to want his balls maimed in an accident involving a Weedwacker, or to wish him a horrific venereal disease whose symptoms include the words "burning discharge." But killing a man for cheating on his wife would be wrong. Wouldn't it?

If it was just the once, maybe I would understand, but there have been others. So many others.

Exactly how many were we talking? Five? Ten? Fifty thousand?

And why would telling him she knew about the others be *very, very bad*?

I turned into my driveway, grinding to a stop beside the stack of unpaid bills on the front stoop, praying that Steven had paid my electric bill as I clicked the button on the remote. A relieved breath rushed out of me when the garage door groaned open. I eased the van inside and shut the door behind me, staring at the empty pegboard as I turned off the engine. The garage was dark and quiet, and I sat for a while, thinking. About my kids. About my bills. About Steven and Theresa.

About all the real-life problems fifty thousand dollars could fix.

I fished the crumpled note from my pocket and peeled it open, wondering how bad a husband Harris Mickler really was.

CHAPTER 3

The clock on the microwave was flashing when I opened the door to the kitchen. I knew I had Steven to thank for it; he would never let our children stay in a home without power. Still, it was hard to feel grateful for hot water and lights when it was Steven's fault our home had fallen apart to begin with. I was pretty sure this was all part of his attorney's plan, conceding to give me as little as possible every month so Steven could swoop in and save the day, restoring the illusion of his moral worth while throwing shade on mine.

The longer it went on, the more I wondered if he was right. I spent the next several hours thinking about Harris Mickler. In my more virtuous moments, I imagined him as a Hugh Jackman look-alike—too charming and attractive to possibly fend off the countless women who must be throwing themselves at him, the poor victim of a jealous wife who would probably benefit from his life insurance policy. During moments I was far less proud of, I imagined him as Joe Pesci on Viagra and strongly considered the fact that, at his height, I could probably lift his lifeless body into the back of my van.

These thoughts were usually accompanied by fantasies of full shopping carts in big-box stores. Fantasies where I let myself calculate how many economy-size packs of Huggies, Lean Cuisines, and baby wipes fifty thousand dollars could buy.

I pressed my forehead to the door of my home office, disgusted with myself. If I needed money, I should just write the damn book my agent and editor were waiting for.

With a sigh, I squeezed the plastic childproof cover and turned the knob. The added security measure was probably unnecessary; I hadn't opened my office door in so long, I'm pretty sure my kids didn't even know this room was here. The air inside was musty and stale. A layer of dust coated my desk and dulled the frame of the college diploma hanging above it—a four-year Bachelor of Arts in English from George Mason University that qualified me to do absolutely nothing.

I toggled on the power to my computer and waited, listening to the high-pitched whine as the screen came to life. It had been Steven's computer in college, and then our home computer up until the divorce. Now, it was so old it would probably take all the child-free time I had left in the day just to boot the damn thing up.

The hard drive hummed, the hourglass flipping over and over on a discouragingly blank screen. Where would I even start? How was I supposed to write someone else's heart-pounding romance when I'd completely failed at my own? It was already close to noon, and Steven was expecting me to pick up Zach in a few hours. Probably so he and Theresa could spend the rest of the day boning each other between a fancy late lunch and happy hour. If I worked every night after the kids went to sleep for the next six weeks, I might be able to finish a really horrible first draft. But why bother? Just so I could blow the remaining pennies of my advance on overdue bills? Judging by the size of the stack on my front stoop, the money would be gone in less than a week.

My home screen flickered to life. A search bar popped up. I typed the word *how*. As in, how do I write this damn book and fix my life?

The rest of the box auto-populated, fueled by a search history full of violent and salacious questions all beginning the same way: How long did it take dead bodies to decompose in a shallow grave in the winter in Virginia? How much damage would the bullet of a Colt 45 inflict on a large adult male with abnormally developed pecs? And how might a person eliminate the identifying features of his corpse?

I should have closed the search engine and opened a Word document instead. I had more than one good reason to get moving on this book. But I also had fifty thousand reasons to be curious about Harris Mickler.

Really, when it came down to it, what was one more search? Just a name to put a face to. Was there really any harm in a quick click through a few public records, just to get a feel for who Harris Mickler really was?

I eased back into my chair, feeling strange as I settled into its familiar dips and curves. Just as I lifted my hands to the keyboard, my phone vibrated on the desk beside it. A profile pic of my ex-husband flashed on the screen, and I swiped right just to make the image disappear. "Hey, Steven."

"Is your power back on?"

"Yes. Thank you for handling it," I said through a forced smile, hoping he could hear it. Zach squealed like an angry pig in the background. Steven grunted.

"Don't thank me. Theresa took care of it. She has a client who works in billing at NOVEC. She pulled a few strings to reinstate your account. Then she and Amy went over to your place on their way to lunch and closed the garage. Speaking of that, Theresa said the service door to the kitchen was unlocked. You really ought to be more careful about that, since you and the kids are there alone so much."

I bit my tongue before I could say something ungrateful and bitter. "I'll take it under advisement. About this Amy person, who is she?" I seemed to have missed the memo.

"You know, Theresa's best friend. Delia's really smitten with Aunt Amy. She babysits the kids for a few hours on Saturdays so Theresa and I can have a break."

A break? From his forty-eight hours with our children?

"Delia has an Aunt Georgia. She doesn't need an Aunt Amy."

"Great," Steven deadpanned. "Let's call Georgia and ask *her* to babysit."

I gritted my teeth.

"Ouch! No, no, Zach! Come back here . . . Christ," Steven muttered, a little winded. "Listen, Finn, I need you to come get Zach. Theresa had an appointment after lunch to show a house, so I took him to the farm with me. I've got a client coming in less than an hour for a meeting, and Zach is all over the place."

"Of course he is." I squeezed my eyes shut, envisioning the chaos playing out on the other end of the line. Steven's sod farm was just a ginormous backyard without a fence. Acres of open space to run, and plenty of tractors and backhoes to climb. It was a toddler's paradise, and unless you medaled in track and field, it was also a parent's worst nightmare.

"Finn?" Between Zach's shrieks, I could practically hear Steven's sanity cracking. His farm was close to the West Virginia state line. It would take me at least forty minutes to get there. And I'd have to pick Delia up at preschool on the way.

"Fine." I rummaged through my wallet and found the twenty dollars I hadn't spent on lunch that morning. Enough for gas. "I'm coming. Give me a few minutes to use the bathroom and grab Delia."

"An hour, Finn. Please." He sounded desperate. And a little pissed off. He'd had only one of our children for less than three hours, and he thought he could handle full custody of both? I considered taking my time, showing up late, just to see how much hair he had left when I finally arrived. But then Zach started crying in the background, the kind of wails Steven had always been too impatient to learn to quiet. I got up from the desk, a layer of dust revealing itself where my hands had briefly skimmed its surface.

This was my life. A two-thousand-dollar contract for months of work, no sleep, and ten minutes in the bathroom alone.

"Tell Zach I'm on my way." I hung up the phone, switched off the computer, and tried not to wonder about Harris Mickler anymore.

CHAPTER 4

Steven had bought his sod farm less than a month after we'd divorced. I'd taken the kids to see it once. I didn't know much about the place, other than the fact that it covered three hundred acres, it produced various kinds of grass he then sold to homebuilders and real estate developers, and he'd been making a small fortune from it since. Mostly, I pictured him and Theresa frolicking naked in emerald fields of cash and fescue, which was probably why I'd never bothered going back.

I had a vague recollection of where it was. My GPS led me the rest of the way, to a huge billboard marking the entrance to a gravel road. ROLLING GREEN SOD AND TREE FARM, it read. The long dirt driveway was flanked on both sides by fields of baby Christmas trees, the next big cash crop Steven would undoubtedly use as Exhibit A in his custody case against me. Not only could he afford to keep my children clothed and fed, he could give them the perfect Norman Rockwell Christmas to boot.

Sitting tall in her booster to see out the window, Delia directed me to park in front of a small construction trailer at the rear of the tree lot. I freed Delia from her car seat and followed her to the sales office, knocking once before poking my head inside the trailer door. Delia scooted around my legs and rushed toward the desk, beaming up at the pretty young blonde seated behind it. The receptionist couldn't have been much older than nineteen or twenty, with a sweet smile and perky boobs. Just like Steven liked them. The poor thing. Theresa probably had no idea, and I almost felt sorry for her, too.

"Hi, Delia," the girl cooed, rubbing my daughter's head. Delia's cap shifted a little, exposing the edge of the duct tape holding her hair in place. The girl wrinkled her nose at it, flashing me a conspiratorial grin as if she had discerned the backstory Delia's hat was struggling to hide.

Oh, honey, I thought to myself, *you have no idea.*

"You must be Finlay?" the girl asked, standing to shake my hand. "I'm Bree. Mr. Donovan is expecting you."

How sweet. She called him Mr. Donovan in the office. I wrinkled my nose and smiled back. "Thanks, Bree. I'm just here to pick up Zach."

"They're in the Zoysia. Just stay on the gravel about a quarter mile, until you pass the tractors on your left. He'll be in the field right behind them."

"Thank you," I said, genuinely sad for her when I thought of all the heartbreak ahead of her—all the phalluses just waiting to be drawn in the dust on the windshield of her future. I wanted to tell her to run. To save herself while she still could. But I had been about the same age when I'd fallen for Steven, and if anyone had told me he'd turn out to be a philandering creep, I never would have believed them.

I took Delia's hand and led her back to the car.

"Can I ride up front with you?" she asked when I opened the back door.

"No, sweetie. You need to be in your booster."

"But Daddy lets me."

"Daddy's setting a bad example. It's not very responsible of him. What if a policeman saw and gave him a ticket?"

Delia rolled her eyes. "This isn't a *real* road, Mommy. Daddy says it's private."

"What if we were in an accident?"

"But nobody ever drives here!" she whined. "Only Daddy's pickup truck. Sometimes, he even lets me ride in the very back." She confessed this bit with an impish smile. I returned it, making a mental note to share that information with my attorney—if he'd bother to take my call. I was pretty sure his invoice was in the pile with all the other outstanding bills on my front step.

I strapped Delia into her car seat and we bobbed down the gravel road, kicking up dust behind us as we cut through Steven's farm. I hated to admit that it was a beautiful piece of land. Wide open and flat with unobstructed views of the rolling Appalachian foothills to the west, the fields neatly sectioned in squares of varying shades of green. I found Steven's pickup truck easily among them. The red paint popped against the bright shamrock backdrop, and I could just make out the arch of Steven's back as he chased Zach behind the cab. Zach zipped around it, emerging on the other side, his heavy diaper nearly dragging along the ground.

Well played, Steven. Well played.

Steven scooped him up at the sight of my van and rushed him toward me, eager to get us all out of his way before his clients arrived. If I knew Steven, he'd have his pretty assistant hold them back at the office until our van was gone. He was a master at shell games, hiding his interests and using distractions to move them smoothly out of sight, preserving his impeccable image. Though I doubted even Steven could hide the toddler-size stains Zach had left on his logo-emblazoned dress shirt.

He dumped our son unceremoniously in my arms, much like I had done to him earlier that morning. Zach's pacifier—the one that clipped to the front of his overalls—was nowhere to be found as he screamed bloody murder in my ear. "Thanks for coming all the way out here," Steven said over Zach's shrieks. "I wish I had time to say hi to Delia, but my client's going to be here any minute." He waved over my shoulder, then swore under his breath. I turned to see Delia already out of her buckles and climbing out of the van. She ran toward us, leaping into Steven's arms. He planted a kiss on top of her cap and set her down beside me, his gaze drifting anxiously down the road.

"Must be a big one," I said, struggling to get Zach to settle.

"The developer for that new planned community in Warrenton I was telling you about," Steven said absently. "Twenty-five hundred units over the next ten years." He held up a finger to one of his crew members, letting us both know he only had a minute to wait.

I bounced Zach on my hip. He rested his head on my shoulder and his wails faded to pathetic moans. "Great, well, I don't want to keep you. Where's Zach's blanket?"

Steven cringed. "I left it at the house this morning. Along with his paci." Which was clearly why he had wanted me to rush out here so fast. I stopped bouncing to gape at him. Zach arched in my arms and started wailing again. "Here." Flustered, Steven fished around in his pocket and unhooked a house key from his key ring. "You can stop by my place and get it. Just leave the key under the mat, and for god's sake don't tell Theresa I let you in." He took me by the arm and began shuffling us toward the van.

I planted my feet and set Zach on the ground. The crying

abruptly stopped, and he gleefully took off running. Steven failed to catch him as Zach waddled full tilt for the field.

I cupped a hand over my eyes, shielding out the afternoon sun as I watched Zach toddle off. "It was a long drive out here and I'm low on gas. All I've got with me is a twenty. Do you mind?" I held out a hand. If he wanted us to go that badly, the least he could do was cover the trip.

Jaw clenched, Steven reluctantly pulled his attention from Zach. "Twenty is plenty to get you home. It's not that far." He smiled tightly. Probably so he wouldn't look like a total asshole in front of Delia.

I reached down and put a hand on our daughter's head, plucking off her cap. A few chunks of loose hair came away with it. Steven's face fell. His eyes darted back to the gravel road behind us as he peeled a twenty from the wad in his pocket and shoved it in my hand. Delia snatched her hat back, repeatedly failing to pull it over her head. I ran to fetch Zach before he could climb the bright yellow tractor that had captured his attention.

"Thanks for watching Zach this morning," I said when he was finally writhing and whining in my arms. "Guess we'll be going."

Dust kicked up behind two approaching cars. The glistening Mercedes came to a stop behind the phallus on the rear window of my minivan, and I'm pretty sure Steven had never looked so relieved as he did the moment I buckled the kids into their car seats and shut the doors.

"It'll be faster if you go out the back way," he said, opening my door for me in a gesture that probably looked chivalrous from a distance. "Follow the gravel road to the end. It connects with the rural route behind the farm. Make a right, then another right, and follow the signs back to the highway." Steven waved good-bye and rushed off to greet his clients, whose cars were now blocking the road we came in on.

I started the engine and rolled down the windows. A cool breeze blew over the acres upon acres of new grass, rippling them like the surface of a huge green sea. As we drove through it, I couldn't help but admire what Steven had built here. Planting, growing, harvesting. Seeing something he'd started and stuck with, all the way through. Tractors turned over the rich dark earth on either side of me, spreading fresh seed into the trenches behind them. Others cut long, crisp strands of dense sod that looked like they could resurface a golf course. And still others pried up long stretches of turf, rolling them into tubes and stacking them onto flatbeds.

Three hundred acres. I couldn't even finish three hundred pages. Couldn't keep one little girl's hair cut as neatly as Steven kept up all these fields.

I left exactly the way Steven wanted me to, out the back where no one would see me, past the fallow field at the end of his farm, the last few acres of dirt he hadn't yet gotten around to covering over with something new.

CHAPTER 5

I wedged Steven's key in the lock with one hand while Zach whimpered on my hip. Delia trailed in after me, slipped off her sneakers, and headed straight for her room. Theresa's house was a no-shoes zone. The wide plank wood floors and pristine white carpets smelled strongly of lemon Lysol, as if Theresa had drenched the entire house in it after my kids had left that morning.

I kept my sneakers on, trailing in some of the sod farm with me as I climbed the stairs to the children's rooms. Zach's was sterile and bland—white carpets, white blinds, and stark pricey furniture with sharp angles and clean lines. Zach's blanket, covered with brightly colored stains and faded puppies, was draped over the changing table beside his chewed-up paci. Zach jammed it into his mouth. He tucked the pilled flannel under his chin, his head resting against my shoulder as he made contented soft sucking sounds. I called for Delia as I descended the stairs but, as usual, she was reluctant to come. This house was still new to her, novel and different with frilly new princess bedding and shiny new Barbie playthings. She never played with Barbies at home. And she didn't much care for princesses. But this was her daddy's world, and she was perfectly content to play dress-up in it.

I stood in Steven's foyer, amid the countless posed portraits of Steven and Theresa that ran from the landing all the way to the front door. Their bedroom was probably covered in them, too. Every inch of his place was a reminder of why he was here and who he was attached to, lest he forget, like he did before with me when Theresa came along.

When Steven and I had lived together, less than a handful of framed photos of the two of us had dotted the walls—a candid from our college formal taken by friends we hadn't talked to since the divorce, our engagement photo with my parents, and one of us stuffing cake in each other's faces at our wedding were the only ones I could recall. Maybe that was where I'd gone wrong. Maybe I hadn't memorialized us enough. Maybe I'd failed to remind him of what we had, or what he stood to lose. Or maybe none of that would have made a difference at all. He wasn't exactly Old Faithful; just because Bree-from-the-sod-farm wasn't caught in the frame of any of Theresa's pictures didn't mean she wasn't in the background somewhere.

My shirt was wet under Zach's round cheeks. His nose was running, and I resisted the temptation to slide a finger under it and wipe a booger under one of the glass-covered portraits, right under Theresa's nose. But that would be petty. A booger wouldn't go unnoticed in Theresa's perfect world for long, and, with any luck, neither would Bree.

Calling Delia's name again, I pulled a tissue from a box in the kitchen. Theresa's laptop sat open on the breakfast bar beside it, the Windows logo bouncing from one end of the screen to the other while it slept. Curiosity got the better of me, and I tapped the space bar.

The laptop came to life without prompting me for a password, revealing the home screen—a search engine. A cursor blinked in the empty search field.

I peeped around the corner into the hall. Delia's conversation with her Barbies trailed down the stairs from her room. Zach wriggled as I shifted him to my other shoulder, his eyes drifting closed again as he sucked softly on his pacifier.

With my free hand, I henpecked Harris Mickler's name.

Social media accounts and photos flooded the screen. Facebook, LinkedIn, Instagram, Twitter. I clicked open his Facebook profile. An attractive forty-something man smiled back at me. Harris Mickler, age forty-two, married to Patricia Mickler, and vice president of customer relations for some up-and-coming financial services firm.

Patricia . . . It felt strange to put such an innocuous name to the face of the woman who'd offered me fifty thousand dollars to kill her husband. Sifting through his online albums, I managed to find only one picture of them together—a single token anniversary photo taken five years ago. The wide-eyed surprise captured by the flash of the camera was the same expression she'd worn when I'd caught her staring at me in Panera.

Delia's make-believe princess voice tinkled quietly upstairs. Zach's paci fell limp between his lips as he slept. I clicked on Patricia's profile. I don't know what I'd hoped to find—a duck-face selfie attention-seeker? One of those annoying social media friends who vaguebooks between posting online quizzes and political memes?— but Patricia was none of those things. Her posts were spare and thoughtful, and she rarely included photos of herself. According to her profile, she was an investment banker, which you'd think would make her an entitled, rich asshole. Instead, as far as I could tell, she was equally unpretentious with her money. She volunteered frequently at her local animal shelter, made donations to crowdsourced fundraisers for friends who were down on their luck, and seemed most comfortable in faded denim and sweatshirts. The only ostentatious thing about her was her wedding ring, crusted in diamonds and boasting a grossly large center stone. It seemed disproportionately extravagant, given the little I knew of Patricia. And yet, it featured prominently in every photo of her.

Curious, I zoomed in on one. Patricia cuddled a shelter cat in her arms, the ring on full display. Everything else about her was casual and plain: unadorned jeans, well-worn sneakers, a shelter T-shirt covered by a simple blue hoodie . . . I tipped my head, angling to look more closely. A black band peeked out from the sleeve of her sweatshirt, looping around her hand and circling her lower thumb—a wrist brace. I clicked backward through her photos, pausing on one taken three months earlier—a bandage on her forehead. Then another before that—a splint on her finger.

I can't tell him I know. That would be . . . very, very bad.

I clicked back through her photos again, searching for bruises in the dark rings under her eyes, for a telltale knot in the aquiline shape of her nose, or the bulge of a cast under a baggy sweatshirt, liking Harris Mickler less and less with every blemish on Patricia's body that may or may not have been a scar. I clicked back to his Facebook profile, even though I knew I shouldn't. He was a member of dozens of social networking groups, as far east as Annapolis and as far south as Richmond.

And just like Patricia had said, he was confirmed to attend an event tonight at a trendy bar in Reston. The Lush was only a few miles from here . . .

I tried to brush off the errant thought, but it stuck. I could go.

Just to see. I could have a cocktail and watch him from a discreet corner of the bar. Just out of concern for Patricia.

I closed the browser and cleared the search history. This was ridiculous. I didn't even have anything to wear.

From upstairs came the soft chime of Delia's voice as she played. I laid Zach on the sofa with his blanket and his paci and crept back up the steps, pausing in front of Steven's bedroom. Theresa had been inside my house just that morning. She'd told Steven my door was unlocked, a fact she would only have known by testing it. At least *I* had been given a key.

Steven's bedroom door was cracked, and I nudged it open with a finger, surprised by the chaos on the other side. I'd expected to find the bed linens pressed and throw pillows artfully arranged. Had braced myself for silk flowers on the vanities and candles around the bathtub. But Theresa and Steven's bedroom was a disaster. Their bed was a temple of unmade sheets. Bras and socks had been strewn everywhere, and the only thing adorning the tub was a pile of mildewing towels. A single framed photo of the two of them hung crooked on the wall. All this time, since I'd first caught them cheating, I'd feared the private spaces they shared would look far tidier than my own. But as I kicked a pair of Steven's boxer shorts aside and stood in front of their open closet, their life behind closed doors didn't feel much different from the way mine and Steven's had, and suddenly it made sense to me why Theresa didn't want me inside her home.

I crept to her side of the closet. Shirts, dresses, and skirts hung in no particular order—just enough space between them to keep her clothes from wrinkling so no one would suspect she was secretly a slob. Sliding the hangers over one by one, I paused at a little black dress. She had at least five of them, by my count. Slipping it from the rod, I draped it over myself in front of the mirror. With a tuck and a few pins, I'd look good in this. She probably wouldn't even notice it was gone.

I gnawed my lip, considering all the things she'd ever secretly taken from me. All the things she was *still* trying to take from me. Before I could change my mind, I rolled the dress into a ball and tucked it under my arm, leaving her bedroom door cracked exactly as I'd found it.

I called Delia's name, insistent this time. Her heavy sigh reminded me more and more of her father, and her tiny feet tromped sluggishly down the stairs behind me.

"Can't we stay longer, Mommy?" she whined.

"It's time to go home." I stuffed her arms into the sleeves of her coat. She stomped her foot as I wrangled her into her shoes.

"*This* is going to be my home. Daddy said so." The words cut like a knife through my heart. I bit back a wince as I scooped up Zachary with his blanket and paci and grabbed Delia's hand, careful to take every last trace of my children with me. And as I locked my ex's house tightly behind me, I couldn't help wondering what kind of custody lawyer fifty thousand dollars could buy.

CHAPTER 6

I stuck the kids in front of the TV with a bowl of Goldfish crackers and dialed Vero's number as soon as I got home, afraid that if I thought about it too much longer I might lose my nerve.

I waited for the beep. "Hi, Vero? It's Finlay. Look, I know Steven told you we wouldn't be needing you to watch the kids anymore. That wasn't my choice, by the way. Clearly, he didn't ask me before he decided to . . . you know . . . let you go," I said through a grimace. I had no business asking her for anything. I took a deep breath and asked anyway. "But something's come up tonight, and I could really use a sitter. Seven o'clock would be great if you're free. I won't be out long." But if I was going to pay for a sitter anyway and get all dressed up, I might as well give myself the evening off. "Eleven at the latest," I added. "I know it's last minute, but I can pay double your usual rate." From Steven's PayPal account. The password still worked. I'd been saving it for an emergency, but after the day I'd had, I was pretty sure my need for a drink qualified. "If you can't"—or won't—"I totally understand. I can probably take the kids to my sister's. But if you get this message in the next few minutes, give me a call and let me know. Please?"

I set the phone down and watched the screen dim. Then I picked it up, checking it as I paced the kitchen and chewed on my thumbnail. Theresa's little black dress hung from the knob on the pantry door. With a plunging neckline, a fitted waist, and a seductive slit up one thigh, it looked like something the heroine in one of my stories would wear. I bet it looked amazing on Theresa. I hadn't seen a single pair of mom-sweats or practical underwear in those messy piles on her floor.

I swiped on the phone and dialed my sister's number.

"Hey, Finn."

"Hey, George. Are you working tonight?"

The heavy pause was telling. My sister's a terrible liar. She's honest. Too honest for her own good. Which is probably what makes her such a good cop. "Why?" she asked cautiously.

"I need to bring the kids to your place." My sister wasn't good with kids. She was good with criminals. Georgia had been single since she came out of the womb, and, according to her, she preferred it that way. She'd rather spend her nights busting down doors and issuing arrest warrants than watching *Sesame Street* and *Dora the Explorer*. For that matter, wouldn't anyone? "Just for a few hours," I pleaded. "I'll feed them first and Zach will probably conk out for the night before we even get to you. They'll sleep most of the time, I promise."

A news broadcast played in the background. "Sorry, Finn. I can't. Haven't you seen the news? The local arm of the Russian mafia scored another win in court this morning. I'm supposed to

meet up with a few of the guys from OCN tonight to talk about it."
OCN. Organized Crime and Narcotics. Georgia worked in Violent
Crimes.

"You don't work Narcotics."

"No, but I keep them company when they cry in their beers."

The channel changed in the background. A theme song played,
reruns of some evening cop drama Georgia watched just so she
could bitch about all the details of her job the writers got wrong.
"Come on, Georgia. This is important."

"Can't you call Vero?"

"Steven laid her off this morning and she won't even answer
my calls. I don't have anyone else. And I really need to do this." Do
what? What the hell was I doing? Jesus, was I actually doing this?
Yes, goddamnit. I was actually doing this. "It's research for a project
I'm working on, and I can't take the kids with me."

"What about your friends? Can't they help?"

"They're not close enough." I dug my fingers into my temple, thinking of the handful of people I probably could call, but
wouldn't. Steven had never liked my friends. Maybe because they
had never liked him. And over the years, consciously or not, I'd let
them all drift. I'd chosen Steven over all of them. And in the divorce,
Steven's friends had chosen him.

She muted the TV in the background and swore quietly. "Isn't
there a babysitter in the neighborhood who can watch them?"

Right. Like Aunt Amy? "My babysitter just hired an attorney
to file for custody of my children, and he laid off my nanny! So no,
Georgia, I don't have anyone else to watch them."

She heaved a sigh that could blow the doors off a meth lab.
"Fine. But just for a few hours. If you're not back by ten, I'm putting
out an APB and organizing a manhunt."

With a rushed thanks, I disconnected before she could change her mind. I popped a tray of chicken nuggets in the oven, bathed and fed the kids, and put a fresh diaper on Zach before rushing upstairs to get ready for the night. As I blew the dust from an old beaded black handbag and stuffed my wig-scarf and makeup inside, I wondered what Harris Mickler was like behind closed doors. What kinds of secrets did he and Patricia hide in their closet, and were Harris's faults really worth fifty thousand to get rid of?

CHAPTER 7

I'd been to my share of bars. College bars, dive bars, upscale bars with Steven when he was wining and dining clients, cop bars with Georgia, gay bars (also with Georgia), and seedy strip bars in the not-so-nice parts of town in the name of research for a book you've probably never heard of. But no matter how many bars I'd stepped foot in before, it was always unsettling to walk into one alone. I hated that feeling of every eye in the place turning to check out who just came in.

Or worse, when none of them bothered to turn at all.

The Lush was packed with suits and ties and little black dresses, and no one seemed to notice or care when one more squeezed in. I checked to make sure my wig-scarf was securely in place, drawing my oversized sunglasses down the bridge of my nose to let my eyes adjust to the dim light inside. The brass-and-cherry island bar was dressed in colorful bottles and backlit etched glass, studded with unreasonably attractive young bartenders who probably spent their days circulating headshots and skimming the internet for casting

calls in DC. I wove through the place, nudging my way around high
tables and tight knots of conversation, finally managing to grab the
last empty stool at the far end of the bar. I reached to sling the strap
of my diaper bag over the back of my chair before remembering I'd
left it at Georgia's with the kids. Instead, I set my handbag down
on the counter in front of me, feeling uncomfortably light without
all my usual baggage, as if I'd forgotten something important at
home. Aside from my ID, all I had with me was a tube of burgundy
lipstick, Steven's twenty, my phone, and the crumpled slip of paper
from Harris Mickler's wife.

I searched the faces of the men at the tables. Then the women.
They all reminded me vaguely of Steven and Theresa, but I was
pretty sure I didn't know any of them. I peeled my glasses off and
tucked them in my handbag. I thought about ordering a beer, but
this place didn't exactly give off Budweiser vibes. Instead, I ordered
a vodka tonic, casually scanning the bar for Harris Mickler as I
sipped it. Medium height, medium build, pepper-brown hair a little
salty at the temples. His eyes, small for his face, thinned to two deep
creases when he smiled. I didn't see anyone who resembled him anywhere, so when the bartender passed, I raised a finger, catching his
attention. He leaned across the bar, his hands flat against it, tipping
his ear to hear me better over the hum and chatter.

"Where do the corporate types usually hang out?" I asked him.

He glanced at the bare ring finger of my left hand. With a knowing smile, he jutted his chin toward a loud group of men and women
laughing around a handful of raised tables. "Real-estate types usually
huddle over there." Then he tipped his head to the group beside them.
"Banking and mortgage types don't stray far." He hooked a thumb
over his shoulder toward a lively group at the other end of the bar.
"Entrepreneurs, pyramid schemes, home-based businesses," he said

with an annoyed quirk of his brow that suggested he'd picked this side of the bar for a reason. "The top-shelf corporate suits usually reserve the booths in the back." He plucked a glass from under the counter, letting his eyes slide over me. "You don't look like the top-shelf type."

I stabbed my lime with my stirrer and sucked down the last of my drink. "And you don't look old enough to serve me."

"Ouch!" he said through a laugh. He bit his lip and eyed me with renewed interest. "I only meant you don't seem clichéd and up-tight."

I swirled the ice in my glass. "Mmmm . . . clichéd. Is that an SAT word?"

Our fingers brushed as he took my empty glass. "LSAT, actu-ally." He paused, gauging my reaction before swapping the glass for a new one. I hadn't even noticed he'd been making me another. "What's your name?"

I sucked on a lime wedge while I considered how to answer that. What the hell. Why not? "Theresa," I said, holding out a hand.

"I'm Julian." His handshake was good. Not a testosterone-driven assertion of dominance. Not a weak suggestion that he underestimated mine.

"What are you planning to study, Julian?"

"I'm in law school," he corrected me. If I'd hurt his feelings, he didn't let on. "Third year of criminal law at GMU."

I raised a cynical brow. "Aren't state prosecutors also clichéd and uptight?"

He slung a bar rag over his shoulder. "I don't have such lofty aspirations. I figure the world could use a few good public defenders. How about you? What do you do?"

I nursed my drink, letting the ice clink against my teeth while I thought about what to say. I'd made it a point never to tell strangers what I did for a living. The conversations always turned weird. And memorable. I looked down at Theresa's dress and picked a lint fuzz off the fabric. "Real estate."

"Sounds boring."

I choked out a laugh. "Terribly."

"Don't take this the wrong way," he said a little cautiously, "but you don't seem like the real-estate type either."

"Really?" He was cocky, but endearing, and maybe it was the second vodka tonic, but his smile was growing on me. "What's my type then?"

Julian studied me as he polished a glass. "Cold beer and takeout pizza. Barefoot, jeans, and a loose-fitting faded T."

I felt the blood race to my cheeks, surprised by how on the mark he was, and by the fact that I didn't mind his candor. Or the way he was looking at me. I drained the last of my vodka tonic as I considered the differences between Theresa and me, wondering if Steven had ever been into takeout pizza, or if his tastes had always run top-shelf and I'd just been too ignorant to see it.

"Too bad you're not interested in family law. The world could use a few honest divorce lawyers, too." I laid the twenty on the counter and slid down from my stool. I had to pee, and the restrooms were probably at the back of the bar, near the booths Julian had mentioned. I could check them out on my way. Just for curiosity's sake.

"Hey," Julian said, cupping a hand over mine before I turned away. "My shift ends in an hour. If you want to wait around, we could grab something to eat after."

A honey-colored curl hung low over his eye, and his smile felt perfectly uneven. I won't lie and say I didn't grant myself a few seconds to think about it. "Thanks." I slid the twenty across the bar toward him. I needed to get home to my kids before my sister sent every patrol car in the city out to track me down. And the last thing I needed was for them to find me rolling in pepperoni in the back of my minivan with a cougar-hunting coed. "I'm not really dressed for pizza."

He sank his teeth into his lower lip, suppressing a grin.

I thanked him and pointed to the back of the bar, letting him know that, as tempting as it was, my plans for the night hadn't changed. And then I set off to find the ladies' room. And maybe Harris Mickler.

The booths behind the bar were private, with black leather seats and high wooden backs and warm, dim lighting, making me look like the world's biggest creep for trying to see into each one as I hobbled by in a pair of heels I hadn't worn in years. A blister had formed where the tight strap dug into the joint below my right toe, and the two vodka tonics I'd just sucked down on an empty stomach weren't making navigation any easier. I felt myself listing slightly as I slunk down the narrow aisle between the booths toward the sign for the restrooms. A phone chimed as I approached the last one.

"Would you excuse me," a man said. "I have to take this call." The man slid out without looking up from his phone, nearly knocking me over as he stalked toward the bar. "This is Harris," he said in a low voice into his phone as he brushed past me.

Harris. I rested a hand on the back of the nearest booth for balance as I turned to catch another glimpse. The couple sitting beside me looked at me curiously, so I bent over my heel and made a show of adjusting my strap while a woman eased out of Harris Mickler's booth. Her high heels clicked down the hall and disappeared into the ladies' room. I lingered for a moment, attempting to listen to Harris's conversation a few feet away, but it was over quickly and he pocketed his phone. Flagging the nearest bartender, he ordered two glasses of champagne and returned to his seat. I rushed for the bathroom, surprised to find my heart racing as I slipped into an empty stall.

What was I doing? This was ridiculous. *I* was ridiculous. So Harris Mickler was stepping out on his wife. So what? Plenty of men had done it before. Including my own husband. As much as I hated him for it, I could never imagine killing him. Not even for fifty thousand dollars. Yet here I was, spying on a man I'd never even met.

I relieved my bladder as quickly as I could, washed my hands, and opened my purse to reapply my lipstick, pausing at the sight of Patricia Mickler's note crumpled in the bottom of my handbag. I should flush it right now. I should shred it and wash it down the sink.

The lock on the stall behind me snapped open and I quickly shut my purse.

Harris Mickler's date bent over her smartphone, her long blond hair hanging like a curtain around her face, over the shoulders of her dove-gray suit. I smeared on a fresh coat of lipstick, watching her in the mirror as she dialed and pressed the phone to her ear. A stunning diamond ring glittered on the fourth finger of her left hand, flanked by a diamond-encrusted wedding band.

"Hey, babe," the woman cooed into her phone as I tucked my lipstick back into my purse.

Maybe she was one of Harris's colleagues from work, I told myself. Maybe they'd just closed a huge deal and had come to celebrate.

"I'm sorry, sweetheart," she said. "I have a client meeting. It's running later than I thought. There are leftovers in the fridge, and Katie's allergy medicine is on the counter. Do you mind putting the kids to bed for me?"

Okay, so Harris was definitely cheating. With a married woman.

Big deal. He may have deserved a raging case of gonorrhea, and if he was beating his wife he definitely deserved to be in jail, but nothing I'd seen so far suggested Harris Mickler deserved to die. I adjusted my wig-scarf in the mirror and checked the time on my phone. It was early. I could still charge a few cartons of Chinese takeout to Steven's account, bring dinner home for Georgia, and forget this ever—

Harris Mickler's date leaned against the counter and raised her voice. "It's an important client, Marty! What do you want me to do?"

I slipped out of the bathroom and the door drifted closed, muting their heated argument. I hurried down the corridor back into the bar just as Harris Mickler's waiter set two bubbling champagne flutes before him. I caught the flash of Harris's crisp white shirt-sleeve as he tucked a folded bill into the waiter's hand. When the waiter turned, something slid from Harris's palm into one of the glasses. The white pill glowed against the golden bubbles, fizzing as it wafted to the bottom of the flute.

Head down, I walked fast past Harris's booth and slipped into an empty space at the bar. The angle was too sharp to see Harris Mickler's face, but near enough to see his arm as he swirled the glass. I hardly noticed the bartender step in front of me to take my order. I was out of cash anyway, and I craned my head to see over his shoulder as Harris switched the position of the champagne flutes.

The bartender leaned into my field of vision. Julian smiled when our eyes caught. I tried to catch discreet glimpses of the restroom door down the hall. The woman would be coming back any second. What should I do? Tell Julian? Ask him to swoop in on their table? Track down the woman in the bathroom and tell her what I had seen Harris do? Any of those would make me a witness. I'd have to wait around for the police to come and take a statement. They'd ask me who I was and what I was doing here. I'd have to explain why I was wearing a wig and a stolen dress and calling myself Theresa. I'd have to explain why I was the subject of a police manhunt, because I had failed to pick my children up from my sister's house.

Georgia, I thought.

Georgia was a cop. If Georgia had been there, what would she do? Every scenario that came to mind involved a service weapon or handcuffs, or some knowledge of jujitsu. I had none of the above.

"Change of plans?" Julian asked with a curious tilt of his head.

"Maybe," slipped out before I could take it back.

His grin widened a little. "Want a drink while you wait?"

This was the part of the story where the heroine had to think on her feet. What would the heroine of my story do? Definitely not call the police while she had a promissory note for a hit job hidden in her purse.

"Bloody Mary?" I asked.

He raised a brow at my beverage choice but didn't argue. I watched the bathroom door while he poured tomato and vodka over ice and dropped a plume of celery in the glass.

"Thanks," I said, plucking it from his hand before it hit the counter. "I'll be right back." I picked my way quickly back toward the dark hall to the restrooms and flung open the door, relieved to find Harris's date leaning in front of the mirror, touching up her rouge.

I took a deep breath and prayed the woman didn't have a

concealed carry permit. Then I pretended to stumble, flinging the contents of my glass and drenching the back of her suit in tomato juice.

Her spine went rigid as the icy liquid soaked through the pale gray skirt.

"Oh, oh no! I am so, so sorry!" I set my empty glass in the sink and snatched a wad of paper towels from the dispenser.

She swatted away my clumsy attempts to wipe the mess, twisting with a look of disgust to see the damage in the mirror. "It's all over me!"

It could be a lot worse.

She swiped at her back, unable to reach the worst of the stain behind her. "Club soda," I said, backing toward the door. "We need *lots* of club soda. You stay here. Don't move. I know exactly what to do." I pried the door open just wide enough to sneak through.

Harris's head snapped up as I exited the bathroom. His smile fell away when I stopped in front of his booth. My heart hammered. It was now or never.

"Harris? Harris Mickler? Is that you?"

He blanched, casting anxious glances at the tables around us. "Uh, no. I'm not—" His eyes flicked back to the bathroom door. "I'm sorry," he said, his expression caught between confusion and annoyance. "Do I know you?"

"Harris!" I said, swatting his arm. "We met at that party . . . you know, that Christmas thing a few years ago." Smooth, Finlay. Real smooth. I'd have kicked myself if I didn't think I'd fall over doing it. "Well, get up and give me a hug, you big, dumb idiot!" I grabbed his hand, practically dragging him out of the booth and throwing my arms around him as if we'd known each other since high school.

He stood stiff, hands limp at his sides as I hugged him with one arm. The other reached around him for the nearest champagne flute, but it was too far away to grasp. Harris gently pushed me back by the shoulders, mumbling that I must be mistaken. I held him tighter and leaned into him, determined to reach it.

Still too far.

"Hey!" he exclaimed as his back connected with the table. "What are you—?"

I slid my hand over his ass. He shut up, his squinty eyes widening with surprise as I gave it a squeeze. Oh, god. What was I doing?

"Right," he said with a sudden curiosity as the fingers of my other hand closed around the champagne flute. "Of course, I remember." Something hard began to press into my stomach, and I was pretty sure it wasn't his belt buckle. What a creep. Quickly, I slid the flute across the table until their positions were reversed. Then I dropped down into the empty side of the booth, eager to put a barrier between us as I reached for the closest drink.

"Mind if I join you?"

Harris maneuvered himself uncomfortably into the bench and eased himself down, his eyes glued anxiously to the bathroom door behind us. "Um ... I don't know if—" I tipped the flute to my lips and drank half of it down in one swill. It wasn't strong enough to wash away the ickiness of what I'd just done, but the shocked expression on Harris's face took the edge off.

I dangled the glass from my fingers. "You weren't waiting for anyone, were you?" I sat up, clasping a hand to my chest. "Oh, no! I hope it wasn't that poor woman in the bathroom. She was on the phone arguing with someone. It must have been her husband. She was really upset. I saw her leave through the back door."

Harris's face fell. He scowled as he reached for his glass and drained it, staring absently in the direction of the emergency exit at the end of the restroom corridor.

Oh, crap, I thought to myself as his Adam's apple bobbed with his final swallow. How long did these things take to work? I set my flute down. My lipstick marked a distinct red shape on the side of the glass, and my fingerprints dotted the stem. If he passed out here and a hospital did a toxicology screen, this would look very, very bad for me.

"Hey, Harris," I said, casting anxious glances into the booths around us. I leaned over the table and whispered, "What do you say we get out of here? Go somewhere more . . . private." I jerked my chin toward the door he'd been staring at, relieved when a perverse smile spread over his face. I had parked behind the Dumpsters out back, as far from the front doors and windows as I could. His address was written on Patricia's note in my purse. If we could get him to my van, I could take him home to sleep it off. Then I could burn the note and forget the whole thing had ever happened.

Harris flagged down the waiter with a raised finger. "Check, please."

He worked his tie loose as we waited, a sheen of perspiration shining along his hairline and a frown pulling at his cheeks. "So remind me, how do we know each other?"

"Oh, uh . . ." I dug back through my memories of his social media profile, but my mind was frozen with fear. I couldn't remember the name of a single group he'd belonged to. "We were in that . . . you know . . . we did that special thing," I said, with a dismissive wave of my hand, "with that Northern Virginia . . . finance group." I lowered my voice to a conspiratorial whisper, hoping he'd fill in the blanks. "The one whose name I can't—"

"You work for Feliks?" He darted anxious glances around the room.

"Yes!" I said, clapping my hands together. "That's exactly how we know each other. I work for Feliks," I repeated absently, eyes glued to the door to the ladies' room, hoping like hell Harris's date didn't come out.

"Oh," he said, rubbing his breastbone as if he had heartburn. He looked a little queasy. "What exactly is it you do for Feliks?"

My knee bobbed under the table. "Oh, you know, this and that." Harris shook cobwebs from his head, his gaze growing glassy and unfocused. I kicked him under the table. "Stay awake, Harris," I said cheerily. I craned my neck, searching for the waiter. How long did it take to bring a damn check?

"That was some pretty strong champagne," he said, his head loose on his neck. "I'm feeling . . . a little funny." His speech had slowed, the edges smearing together into a drunken slur. He blinked, his eyelids growing heavy. "What's your name again?"

"Theresa."

"Right, Theresa," he said as the waiter finally appeared, balancing a tray of drinks as he slid the black leather bill folder onto the table and quickly disappeared again. Harris's chin sank lower, and I was grateful the waiter hadn't stopped to chat.

"Let's go, Harris." I stood up, checking to make sure no one was watching as I pulled him to his feet. The Lush was packed, too many bodies crammed together for anyone to notice, and Julian was busy pouring drinks behind the bar. Harris leaned against me as I grabbed his wallet from his back pocket, fished out a hundred-dollar bill, and left it on the table to cover the tab. Wrapping his arm around my shoulder, I steered him clumsily through the back hallway toward the illuminated EXIT sign, flinging the door open wide enough for both of us to pass through.

By the time we reached the parking lot, Harris was noticeably heavier. My heels wavered under me as his head slumped toward my shoulder. Heaving him higher, I aimed us toward the dumpster, making a slow, wavering line toward the shadow of my van behind it. The employee lot was dark and quiet, and I propped Harris against the side panel, holding him in place with my body to keep him from falling over while I fished my car keys from my bag. His hands roved over me, sloppy and restless. One of them groped around under my dress, and I recoiled when his wet tongue slipped inside my ear.

"Oh, Harris." I leaned away from it, my tone laced heavily with sarcasm as he pawed me. "You're a naughty one, aren't you?" I fumbled with my key fob and the sliding door rolled open, nearly knocking Harris to the ground. I held him steady as he plopped down on the floor in front of Zach's car seat, apple juice and Goldfish cracker goo sticking to the backside of his expensive suit as I pushed him backward with promises of the good time waiting for him if he climbed inside and laid down on the floor like a good boy. He growled in my ear as I nudged him in, slurring about all the things he'd do to me if I crawled inside with him, most of which made me cringe and arguably would have justified accepting Patricia's offer. Then, finally, he slumped into a deep sleep.

I stuffed Harris's feet inside the van and shut the sliding door behind them. Dogs barked somewhere close, and I peered around the dumpster into the bright parking lot on the other side, praying no one had seen what I'd done. A couple walked arm in arm into the bar. A group of women huddled smoking out front but didn't look my way. The dogs' barks faded into the background.

I dug in my bag for my cell phone as I raced around to the driver's-side door. I should call Patricia first. Make sure she was home. Then I'd explain the conversation she overheard in Panera and set this whole misunderstanding straight.

"Theresa!" I stiffened as a cool voice cut across the parking lot.

I spun to see Julian crossing the lot toward me, wearing an easy smile and spinning his car keys around his finger. The top two buttons of his dress shirt were unfastened, his sleeves rolled to his elbows as if he'd just signed off for the night.

"I was hoping you hadn't left." He leaned against the side of my van, and I silently thanked god for the darkness. And Dodge, for tinted rear windows in minivans.

"I am so . . . so sorry," I stammered, pressing my fingers to my forehead and struggling through a rushed apology. "I totally wasn't intending to ghost on you. And I didn't mean to leave without paying for that last drink. I just—"

"Whoa, whoa, whoa," he said gently, easing upright and taking a half step back, his hands raised. "You don't need to apologize. You don't owe me anything."

"But the Bloody Mary—"

"Was more than covered by your tip," he said, keeping a comfortable distance between us. "I just wanted to make sure you're okay to drive home. I can call you a cab," he added, making it clear this wasn't a come-on, "if you need a lift."

"Thanks. I'm okay." I pressed my lips shut to keep myself from babbling and saying too much. I was far from okay. There was an unconscious pervert stuffed in the back of my minivan and an IOU in my purse from the woman who wanted me to kill him. And I was going to be late to pick up my kids from my sister's house, which meant she was going to start looking for me. I thumbed my cell phone awake, surprised Georgia wasn't already blowing it up.

"Can I see your phone?" Julian asked. I handed it over to him. There was something so disarming about him. About the softness of his voice and the earnest concern in his eyes. He opened my contacts and programmed his number. "Just in case you need it," he said, returning it to me and tucking his hands in his pockets. "Or . . . you know . . . in case you change your mind about going out with me sometime."

He backed away from my van, his narrow waist silhouetted by the streetlight behind him. He cut a nice shape against the darkening sky, and a not-so-small part of me wished I had stayed to hang out with him at the bar earlier, even if I was too old for him.

"I have kids," I called across the parking lot. "Two of them."

His smile caught the lamplight. "I've got nothing against minivans."

I fought back a surprised laugh as I watched him go. What the hell was happening, and how was this my life? I climbed into the driver's seat and stared at his number. If I made it through the night without being arrested by the highway patrol—or worse, by my sister—maybe I'd call him sometime.

With a heavy sigh, I pulled the crumpled note from my purse and dialed Patricia's number. Listening to the ring through my Bluetooth, I pulled into traffic heading in the vague direction of the Micklers' home. Finally, Patricia answered.

"Is it done?"

"Are you home?"

A pause. "Yes."

"Are you alone?"

"Yes."

"Thank god." I reached into the center console for a pack of gum. I smelled like a distillery. "Your husband tried to drug some woman at a bar. I . . . He accidentally drugged himself instead. I have him and I'm bringing him home," I said, feeling oddly connected to this woman I hardly knew. And far too familiar with her husband. I merged into the far-right lane, staying under the posted speed limit.

"No! You can't bring him here!" Her objections rose to a fevered pitch. "You have to get rid of him. I'm not paying you unless you get rid of him like you said . . . neat!"

"I never said I would do anything. You overheard a conversation you didn't understand." An Audi cut me off as it darted to make the ramp to the toll road. I leaned into the horn, adrenaline pumping as I checked my rearview mirror for flashing lights, relieved to find none. "Look, just because he's an asshole and a creep doesn't mean he deserves to—"

"Do you have his phone?" Patricia asked.

Her question pulled me up short. "Maybe. I don't know." I knew Harris had his wallet. Last I'd seen his phone, he was tucking it into the breast pocket of his jacket. "I think so. Why?"

"Find it. His password is *milkman*. Go to his photos. Then call me when it's done."

"I don't want to see his—"

The line disconnected. I smacked the steering wheel, uttering a swear. What was I supposed to do now? Clearly, Patricia wasn't going to open the door if I showed up at her home. With my luck, a neighbor would see me dump him in his yard and report my license tag number.

Crap. This night kept getting better and better.

I pulled off the toll road into a corporate center parking lot and put the van in park. Lifting my armrest, I climbed into the back of the van, trying not to impale Harris Mickler with my heels. *The state would like to present Exhibit A for the prosecution, the defendant's right Louis Vuitton knockoff, also known as the murder weapon, Your Honor.* I choked out a laugh, wondering how Julian would defend me from that as I squeezed into the space between my children's car seats and fished around in Harris's jacket pocket for his phone. The screen was locked. I cringed as I typed in his password.

My finger hovered over the icon for his photos. Knowing what I knew of Harris Mickler, what awaited in that app at best would not be pleasant, and at worst could be potentially scarring. Or at least vomit-inducing. Against my better judgment, I tapped it anyway. A handful of files with the usual titles: Facebook, Instagram, Twitter, Screenshots, Camera . . . Private.

Peeking through one eye, I tapped the last one, surprised when it wasn't a collection of really gross porn. Instead, I found a collection of numbered folders. Thirteen of them. All labeled with names: SARAH, LORNA, JENNIFER, AIMEE, MARA, JEANETTE . . .

I opened the first folder and scrolled through the contents, slowly at first, pulling the screen closer to make sense of the images as Harris snored shallowly beside me. As far as I could tell, it was a series of candid shots of a woman, captured from odd angles, as if they'd been surreptitiously taken. A blond woman in line at a coffee shop. The same woman getting into her car. Another shot of her pushing a grocery cart through a parking lot, this one revealing a clear shot of her face. I recognized her. She was the same woman I'd just doused with tomato juice in the bar.

Harris Mickler was a stalker.

If it was just the once, maybe I would understand, but there have been others. So many others.

I closed that folder and opened the next one. My breath caught in my throat.

These photos started just like the others, with dozens of surreptitious pictures. But the photos in these other twelve files gave way to more disturbing ones: posed images of Harris with these women, seemingly on a date, same as he had been tonight. Then those same women in various staged poses—naked, eyes closed, expressions slack as he touched and kissed and violated them, their glittering custom wedding bands always carefully captured in the frame.

I swallowed back bile, scrolling through countless images of these other twelve women he'd stalked and then dated over the last thirty-six months, all of them slightly similar in appearance and build, sickened by the realization he'd probably drugged and raped them all. The final image in each woman's folder was a horrifyingly intimate photo with a message pasted in text over top.

Do exactly as I said, and be discreet, or I'll show these pictures to your husband and tell him what you've done.

I felt sick as the puzzle pieces slammed into place. He was blackmailing them. Blackmailing them to ensure their silence. Harris was preying on married women with children. Women with successful, rich husbands who had the means, social standing, and resources to completely ruin their lives. He had purposefully taken misleading photos, suggesting he'd been dating his victims, that the sex was consensual. When in fact, Harris was a twisted, sick predator who apparently preferred his victims passed out in the back of his car.

I sagged against the bench seat and stared at Harris's phone. Then at Patricia's note. Patricia was right. I didn't know where I was taking him, but there was no way I was returning this monster to Patricia Mickler's home.

CHAPTER 8

It was nearly ten o'clock when I jerked to a stop in my driveway.

And I still hadn't figured out what to do with Harris Mickler.

I sat in the van, engine idling, knuckles white on the steering wheel as the garage door lifted on its track. The headlights reflected off the pegboard as I pulled inside, casting eerie shadows over the interior of my garage.

This was not okay.

The unconscious kraken on the floor of my minivan was not okay.

I should call Georgia and tell her everything. She would know what to do. And she probably wouldn't let anyone put me in jail because then she'd be stuck watching my kids indefinitely.

I got out of the van, my body dimming the headlights as I navigated the tight space between the bumper and Steven's workbench, the humming engine warming my legs as I brushed past. The night had grown cold, and the exhaust from my van billowed in thick white clouds down the driveway toward Mrs. Haggerty's house. Her kitchen windows were dark across the street, and I sent up a silent prayer of thanks that the neighborhood busybody had already gone to sleep.

I threw open the door to the kitchen. The room smelled like the wet waffle scraps on the piled dishes in the sink, and the cordless phone was still sticky with syrup, on the table exactly where I'd left it. I hit redial and pressed it to my ear, counting rings as I slid down the back side of the door in the dark, too afraid to turn on the light.

"Finn?" Zach wailed in the background. I pinched my forehead. My children's cries were a language I'd learned to understand through years of trial and error and sleepless nights.

"Couldn't get him to sleep, huh?"

"What am I doing wrong?" she asked, a little breathless. Georgia was cool in a hostage crisis, but a toddler meltdown was obviously more than she felt qualified to handle.

"Nothing. He's just overtired," I said, pressing the heels of my hands into my eyes. Funny how the sound of your child screaming could silence everything else in your mind.

"Then why won't he sleep?"

"Because he's two. Listen carefully to my instructions," I said in my best hostage-negotiator voice in the hopes that it would calm my sister and keep her focused. "Do you have his blanket?"

Her shuffling was drowned out by his howls. "Yes, I have his blanket."

"Wrap it over him and hold him against you. Then put his paci in his mouth. Press it in place with a finger while you pat his back."

"I'm not an octopus."

"Or you can let him scream until I get there."

"How long until you get here?"

"That depends."

"On what?"

I rested my forehead on my knees. "How long will a grown man stay unconscious after taking a roofie?"

Georgia's pause was punctuated by Zach's pathetic whines. "You lost me."

"Research. I'm working on a book."

"I thought you said you had something important to do tonight."

"This is important." Why did everyone think my job wasn't important? "I'm stuck on a plot point."

"Roofies?" she mumbled. "Depends on the size of the man and the strength of the drug. Maybe a couple hours. Maybe a whole night." The phone rustled as Georgia wrestled Zach into his blanket, his cries stifled by the pacifier she'd popped in his mouth. More rustling. Zach sniffling. "Okay, I think it might be working."

"So if you were the heroine of a story, and you drugged a really terrible man who'd done really horrible things—?"

"Like what kind of things?"

"Illegal things."

"Are we talking misdemeanor things or felony things?"

"Definitely felony things. And let's say he was passed out in the trunk of your car. What would you do with him?"

"Could you prove he had committed felonious crimes?"

"Does it matter?"

"Of course it matters," she said, as if the answer should be obvious. "If your heroine has evidence, she ought to dump him at the police station and turn that evidence over to a detective. Let the authorities handle it."

I lifted my head, blinking in the dark of the kitchen. Harris's cell phone pictures. I had physical evidence that he had surreptitiously photographed and blackmailed who knows how many women. And

I'd witnessed him try to drug one of those women, which supported the likely fact that he had drugged the others as well, which was evidence of assault. I could turn him over to the police and give them Harris's phone. Hell, I could take him to Georgia's house and leave him and his cell phone with her. I didn't have to tell her about Patricia's note. I'd just tell her I was out at a bar, realized he was trying to drug someone, and switched his drink. "Would I . . . Would my character get in trouble for drugging him?"

"Depends on the circumstances. Premeditated? Illicit drugs? Probably."

"Are we talking a lot of trouble, or a little trouble?"

"Does it matter? It's a romance novel."

"Yes, it matters! I want it to be accurate."

Georgia heaved a sigh. "Well, I guess if she turned herself in, a prosecutor might go easy on her and cut her a deal."

I sat up. That was it. I could turn myself in to Georgia. Given the choice between arresting me or letting me go, she would definitely let me go. The alternative was being stuck with my kids until someone posted bail for me, and she wouldn't keep them a minute longer than absolutely necessary.

"So are you coming to get Zach and Delia now that we've solved your fictional problem?"

Zach was asleep. I could hear his snotty-nosed soft baby breaths over the quiet hum of the van in the garage and the distant barks of a neighbor's dogs down the street.

"Yeah," I said. "I'm wrapping things up now. I'll be over soon."

Georgia disconnected. I set the phone on the floor. It was still sticky, furry with strands of Delia's hair. Somehow, the day had gone from bad to worse. I was no further along on my book, and no closer to being able to pay my own bills. And once the police report was filed, Steven and Theresa's attorney would have one more reason to paint me as an unfit parent. It wouldn't matter that a monster like Harris was in jail and off the street. I'd been out at a bar in a wig and a stolen dress, drinking the money my husband had given me for gas. I had drugged a man, and then abducted him in the back of the family minivan.

Or . . .

I could make Harris Mickler disappear, pray Patricia Mickler wasn't lying about the money, and hope I was lucky enough not to get caught.

I pushed myself to my feet and brushed waffle crumbs off my backside. Then I carried my heels and my wig-scarf upstairs to change into a pair of clean underwear and comfortable clothes, just in case I ended up getting arrested after all. I took my time brushing the taste of the bar from my teeth, washing Harris's spit from my ear, and wiping the makeup from my face. When I was done, I stood in front of my bathroom mirror and took a deep breath, preparing myself for what I was about to do. I was going to turn Harris Mickler—and my statement—over to my sister.

Because, let's face it, I'm not exactly the luckiest person I know.

CHAPTER 9

My feet were heavy as I descended the steps to the kitchen. I stood in front of the door to the garage, my forehead pressed against it as I convinced myself (again) that this was the right thing to do. Resigned, I opened the door. The air on the other side was thin and hot, and the fumes hit me like a punch to the throat. I choked into my sleeve, swatting away exhaust. The hum of the minivan seemed deafening in the closed space, and I rushed to throw open the door to the backyard before turning the ignition off.

Silence fell over the garage. The breeze that blew in from the yard was cold and crisp, and I leaned against the van's hood, berating myself for leaving the damn thing running as the fumes began to filter out. Slightly light-headed, and maybe a little buzzed from the champagne and vodka tonics I'd drunk on an empty stomach in the bar, it seemed like a good idea to wait a few minutes for my head to clear and the garage to air out. Though if I were being honest with myself, I was only putting off the inevitable. I didn't want to turn Harris Mickler over to my sister any more than I wanted to kill

him. In fact, I didn't want anything to do with Patricia or Harris
Mickler ever—

Oh . . . Oh, no.

I lurched upright as the last of the fog drained from my head.

I'd left Harris Mickler in the van.

I ran to the passenger side and threw open the sliding door, unsure if I should be relieved or horrified that Harris was right where
I'd left him.

"Harris?" I shook him by the feet. "Harris, are you okay?"

I climbed over Zach's seat and knelt beside him, slapping the
side of his face. When nothing happened, I slapped him harder. His
cheek was a little warm, but then again so was I, and I was pretty
sure *my* heart had stopped beating about thirty seconds ago. I called
his name, uncertain of what I would do if he actually responded.
I didn't know what was worse: being trapped in the back of a van
with a dead serial rapist I had abducted, or being trapped in the
back of a van with a very angry, awake serial rapist I had abducted.

I pressed two fingers to the side of his neck and felt . . . nothing,
which meant I was either doing it wrong, or—

Oh no, oh no, oh no . . .

I laid an ear against his chest. Nothing moved. I reached over
the front seat for my purse, digging frantically inside for my com-
pact and flipping open the mirror, holding it suspended under Harris's nose. The glass didn't fog, and I fell back on my heels.

Harris Mickler was definitely not okay.

"Oh, shit." My thoughts sharpened with my sudden sobriety.
"What would Georgia do? What would Georgia do?" Georgia would
arrest me. Or shoot me. That's what Georgia would do. A hysterical
laugh bubbled out of me. Shock. I was in shock. That was the only
explanation for it. "It was an accident. Negligent homicide's a lesser

charge. No big deal, right?" I babbled, my breaths coming faster. "Only it won't exactly look negligent when they find out I drugged you and drove you to my house, then left you in the garage with the engine running." Or when they found the hit order from his wife in my purse.

"No. No, no, no! You cannot be dead!" I hollered at his lifeless body in my most commanding mommy voice. Because it was not physically possible for my day to get any worse. Wedging myself in the space between my children's car seats, I leaned awkwardly over Harris's body. More than slightly revolted, I pinched his nose with one hand and pulled his chin down with the other. His slack mouth parted. It smelled like boozy garlic olives and cheese dip and I fought the urge to hurl. Eyes shut, I pressed my mouth to Harris's quickly cooling lips, exhaling three quick breaths into his mouth. But it was no good. There wasn't enough room. I couldn't find the right angle and all the air escaped out the sides. It felt more like I was making out with a dead guy rather than trying to revive one, not unlike the last few times Steven and I did it before the divorce. Apparently, I couldn't save anything then either.

I clambered out of the van, grabbed his shiny leather loafers, dug in the heels of my sneakers, and pulled. His body was like lead, his expensive suit clinging to the short fibers of the carpet on the floor of the van and snapping with static sparks.

"Come on, Harris, you sadistic fuck!" Leveraging my weight, it took me three hard tugs to move him. His butt hovered just over the running board and I threw my whole body into it as I pulled again. His rump slid forward, followed by the rest of him, his skull smacking the side of the van with a loud crack as he slumped out. I winced when it finally thudded against the concrete.

I let go of Harris's feet. The soles of his dress shoes thumped against the floor. I dropped to my knees beside him, swearing to myself as I lowered my mouth to his. Suddenly, from behind me I heard—

"Oh, shit! Sorry, Ms. Donovan, I didn't know you were home. I just came to get my . . ."

My head snapped up at Vero's startled gasp.

My children's nanny stood in the kitchen doorway holding a cardboard box. I swiped my lips furiously against my forearm. Her false lashes widened on Harris as I stumbled to my feet. "Vero? What are you doing here?"

"What are *you* doing here?" she asked, stealing narrow-eyed glances at the dead man behind my back.

"You first." I planted my hands on my hips, standing as tall as I could make myself to shield Harris from view.

"Why?"

"Because it's my house." Sort of. Actually, it was Steven's since he'd refinanced me out of it, making him my landlord. But that hardly seemed important at the moment. "How did you get in?"

"Through the front door. With my key. You said you were going out, so I came to get my stuff." Vero hoisted the cardboard box higher on her hip, her crop top riding up her midriff as she peered around me. "Who's that?"

"Who?"

She jutted her chin at Harris's feet.

"Oh, him?" I scratched my neck, perspiration making the skin itch as I angled myself to stand in her way. "He's just . . . someone I met earlier . . . in a bar."

She leaned sideways to see around me. Her jaw fell open as she crept down a step closer. Her voice climbed an octave and broke. "Is he dead?"

"No!" My nervous smile made the muscles in my face do weird things, and I pressed my hand to my cheek, feeling the blood rush to it. "Don't be ridiculous. Why would you think that?"

"Because he looks dead!"

I risked a glance down at Harris. His lips were purple and his skin was a strange shade of grayish blue. *Oh, god.*

She sidestepped away from me, toward the wall. "You know what? Never mind. I'm just going to go." She tapped the button to open the garage door. The motor kicked on, whirring above our heads, but the door didn't budge.

"Wait! I can explain."

"Nothing to explain," she insisted, smacking the button again, harder this time, her eyes darting between me and the garage door. "I didn't see anything. I don't know anything. I don't care about the dead guy," she said over the hum of the motor.

"Please," I said. She jabbed her thumb at the button, cursing the garage door when it didn't move. "Vero." I lowered my voice, struggling to keep it steady. "I know how this must look, but it's not what you think. This man is not a nice person. He did some very bad things."

"I'm guessing he's not the only one." Vero backed toward the kitchen, muttering under her breath as the motor fell quiet, looking frantically around her, probably for a weapon. "You know what? You're both crazy. You and your husband."

"Ex!" I snapped. "Ex-husband!"

"Fine! Your ex-husband. Whatever. You're both nuts!" She held the cardboard box out between us like some kind of a shield. A familiar stainless-steel handle protruded from the loose flaps on top.

"Hey!" I pointed at my favorite nonstick pan. "That's mine! What are you doing with that?" I reached for the handle, but Vero grabbed it, letting the rest of the box fall to the floor. She crouched, wielding the frying pan like a bludgeon.

"Worker's comp," she said, her stance daring me to come near her.

"You think you're entitled to cookware because my ex-husband laid you off?" She took a swing at me and I leapt backward, nearly falling over Harris's body.

"Your husband didn't lay me off! I quit!"

"Quit?" I reached behind me for the workbench, my fingers skimming the surface for a screwdriver or a hammer. Anything I could use to defend myself against my favorite All-Clad pan. My grip closed around the small pink gardening trowel and I held it out in front of me, crab walking around the perimeter of the garage away from her. "I thought you liked my kids!"

"I love your kids!"

"If you love my kids then why would you quit?"

"Because when I went to your ex's house to collect my check, he told me he'd only keep paying me if I slept with him!"

My hand went limp. The garden shovel dropped to the floor with a hollow thud.

I laughed, silently at first, then out loud through my painfully tight throat, just to keep myself from crying. "Oh . . . Oh, that is so Steven." I sank down on the rough wooden step to the kitchen. "You know what? Keep the damn pan." She'd put up with enough. She deserved that much. I buried my face in my hands, revolted by the smell of vodka and Harris Mickler's mouth on my own breath. "You're right. We're both nuts," I muttered, swatting at a tear.

Vero eyed me sideways. She crouched a safe distance away, carefully placing the last of her spilled contents back inside her cardboard box as if she was afraid to make any sudden movements. She stood up slowly, the box tucked under her arm. I didn't care how much of it was mine. What did it matter? I was going to lose everything anyway.

"It was stupid to think I could do this," I said as she tiptoed to the garage door. She heaved it open a few inches with one arm, the box still propped under the other.

Great. The garage door was broken. Just one more thing Steven knew how to fix, and I didn't. And now I'd have to pay some handyman to repair it.

I shook my head, mentally stacking one more bill on the pile outside on the stoop. "If Steven hadn't insisted on being such an asshole, I never would have thought about it," I said to myself. "I never would have gone to that bar and brought this creep home. But can you blame me? Anyone in my shoes would have considered it for fifty thousand dollars."

Vero's hand froze. The door hung open, level with her knee. "What did you say?"

I choked out a dark, desperate laugh. She already thought I was nuts. There was a dead guy on the floor of my garage and now I was talking to myself. "I said you're right. My ex is an asshole. I'm sorry for what he did to you."

The door fell closed, the clatter reverberating off the walls of the garage. I lifted my head, expecting her to be gone, but Vero was still there, holding her box to her chest.

"How bad?" Her eyes darted curiously to Harris's body. Her ponytail bounced as she jutted her chin at him. "You said he did some bad things. How bad are we talking?"

"Really bad."

"Fifty thousand dollars bad?"

Vero's fingers closed tighter around the frying pan as I rose slowly to my feet. I crossed the garage to the van and fished under the seat for Harris's cell phone. Angling it toward her, I swiped open his photo album and held it out for her to see.

"What's this?" She set down the box, clutching the pan as she took the phone from me. I told her everything . . . about my meeting with my agent and the conversation Patricia Mickler had overheard. About the note Patricia had left me and what I had witnessed at the bar. Her expression warped with equal parts horror and disgust as she swiped from one image to the next.

"I never meant for this to happen," I explained. "I only followed him because I was curious about why his wife would want him dead. I tried to tell her she had the wrong person, but then I saw him put that drug in that woman's glass, and the next thing I knew—"

"You killed him."

I winced. "Not intentionally."

She passed me Harris's phone. "What are you going to do?"

"I was going to turn him over to my sister, but then . . ." I glanced down at Harris. I'd made the decision to turn him over to Georgia while he was still breathing. Before I knew he was dead. "If I explain to the police that it was an accident, it won't be so bad, right? It's not like I murdered him. Manslaughter's a lesser charge."

"I don't know, Finlay." Vero set down her pan. "After the Play-Doh incident, this looks pretty bad." She was right. The charges Theresa had filed against me were a matter of record. I had never intended to hurt her—only to damage her car—but to the police, it might look like I had used my car to poison Harris on purpose. Especially after I'd stalked him, drugged him, and brought him home.

I sniffed, exhaling a shaky breath as I considered what I was about to do. "Delia and Zach are already at Georgia's place. If I turn myself in and the police arrest me, will you help her with the kids?"

Vero nodded, her full lips turning down at the edges.

"I guess I should tell Patricia that he's . . ." We both looked over at Harris's ashen face. If I told the police everything, Patricia would be implicated for conspiracy to commit murder. She would serve time in prison right alongside me. The least I could do was give her fair warning. With shaking hands, I pulled out my phone and dialed Patricia's number.

"Is it done?" she asked with a desperation I finally understood. Harris was a horrible man. I couldn't blame her for wanting him dead.

"Yes, but I think there's been a misunderstanding. I'm not—"

"Did you get rid of his body?"

"No. That's why I called. I can't—"

"You have to," she insisted.

"I'm turning myself in to the police."

"You can't do that!"

"You don't understand. This wasn't supposed to—"

"You have children, don't you?"

My breath caught. Something in her tone had shifted, hardened. A deep crease of worry formed between Vero's brows as she watched my face fall. She leaned closer, listening. "Why would you ask me that?"

"That was a diaper bag you were carrying in Panera. There were baby wipes inside. I saw them. If you love your children, you will dispose of my husband's body."

"Or what?" Vero and I locked eyes.

"Or the police will be the least of your worries." The words shook. "My husband was involved with some very dangerous people. And if they find out what we've done, they'll come for both of us. They will find us, and they will kill us. It won't matter if we're behind bars. They have eyes and ears all over this town. They have friends in very high places. You and your children will never be safe. They can't know. No one can know. Do you understand me?"

"What kind of people?" I asked.

"Believe me, you're safer if you don't know." I did believe her. I believed the wobble in her voice that said she was every bit as afraid of these people as she had been of her husband. Maybe more. "Get rid of Harris tonight. I don't care where. Just make sure no one ever finds him. That's the only way we'll both be safe. Don't contact me again until it's done."

The call disconnected.

Numb, I lowered the phone from my ear.

"Do you think she meant all that . . . about people coming after you?" Vero asked, her eyes wide.

"I don't know," I said in a small voice. But I wasn't sure I wanted to take any chances. Not with my kids. Or my life.

We were both quiet for a long time.

"Assuming you don't get caught, she's still going to pay you, right?"

"I guess."

Vero paced the garage. She tapped her nails on her crossed arms, thinking. "And you know about this stuff? I mean, you write books about it, right?"

"Yes, but—"

"So you know how to get rid of a body." Vero stopped pacing. She raised a thinly plucked brow when I didn't answer. I knew how to get rid of a fictional body, but the one on my garage floor was very, very real.

"I think so."

The tension slid from her shoulders, as if she'd resigned herself to some decision. "In that case, fifty percent." My mouth hung open as she folded her arms over her chest. "I help you get rid of the body, and we split everything. Fifty-fifty."

What was happening? Was my children's babysitter seriously offering to help me get away with murder? This was definitely not okay.

With an impatient roll of her eyes, she said, "Fine. I won't take a penny less than forty percent. But I want my job back. Plus forty percent of any referrals."

"Referrals?" I sputtered. "What do you mean referrals?"

"We don't have all night." She planted her hands on her hips, tapping her nails on her waist when I didn't answer. "Are we doing this together or not?"

Together.

This was not okay. *We* were not okay. But *together* sounded a whole lot better than doing this alone.

She extended her hand. My fingers trembled as I shook it. Hers did, too. Vero bent to put my pan back in her cardboard box. She pulled a fifth of bourbon out by the neck, twisted the cap, and took a sip, wincing as she held the bottle out to me.

"That's mine, you know," I said, snatching it from her hand as we both slid down the side of the van.

"Only sixty percent of it," she said.

I threw her a sharp look as I took a swig.

"I should probably just move in with you," she said. I choked, spraying bourbon down the front of my shirt. "Don't worry. I'll take the smaller bedroom."

I took another gulp. It burned all the way down. When I opened my eyes, Harris Mickler was still there, one hundred percent dead, Vero was still sitting beside me on the floor next to a box of stolen household gadgets that, by my best estimates, were now only sixty percent mine, and I was pretty sure we'd spend the next forty percent of our lives in prison if we couldn't find a way to pull this off.

CHAPTER 10

In fiction, it always came down to the shower curtain. A hotshot cop would tear a crime scene apart, searching for evidence, and immediately spot the glaring absence of a shower curtain. Because people *use* shower curtains. They *need* shower curtains. And if you're involved in a homicide investigation and don't have a shower curtain, you might as well call 911 and slap the cuffs on yourself.

Which was why I was wrapping Harris Mickler's body in my best silk table linens.

They'd been a wedding present from my Great Aunt Florence eight years ago when I'd married Steven, and I had never once used them. And since I'd sold my dining room furniture six months ago on Craigslist to make my van payment, if some hotshot cop *did* come to search my house, I was pretty sure he wouldn't even notice they were gone.

Vero and I spread the maroon fabric on the garage floor at Harris's feet. Then Vero took his hands and I took his ankles. Together, we hoisted him a few inches off the ground and swung him down in the middle of the sheet.

I dropped his legs, rearranging the linens at an angle to cover him, kind of like arranging a sandwich on a sheet of cellophane. Then, with exhaustive effort and a lot of grunting, Vero and I rolled Harris Mickler into a giant corpse burrito.

"His feet are sticking out," I panted as we finished the last roll.

"Better than his head." Wisps of Vero's hair had escaped her ponytail, and sweat bloomed on her chest. She was almost ten years younger than I was, and in far better shape. My muscles screamed as I bent over my knees.

"Why are you doing this?" I asked between labored breaths. She was young, single, smart. Once she finished her degree, she'd have her whole life ahead of her.

"I need the money."

"What for?"

"Student loans."

I put my hands on my hips, chest still heaving as I gaped at her. "Let me get this straight. You're helping me dispose of a *body* to pay for school?"

"Clearly, you're too old to remember how much a bachelor's degree costs," she said bitterly.

"I'm not too *old*. I just . . . never had to worry about it."

"Yeah, well, I'll be paying interest until I'm fifty."

"Assuming we don't get arrested first." We both stared at the messy enchilada on the floor.

There was no way we were unrolling him—it had been hard enough to roll him up the first time—but he'd be far too unwieldy with his feet dangling out. Rummaging through the contents of Steven's old workbench, I found a lone bungee cord in a bucket of rusted nails. The hook on one end was missing, which was probably the only reason he hadn't taken it when he'd left. I wrapped the elastic around Harris's ankles and tied it in a knot, leaving the single remaining hook wobbling off the end.

"I have to pick up the kids at my sister's house," I said, afraid to check the time on my phone.

Vero gestured to Harris. "What do we do with him?"

I couldn't put him back in the van with my kids. But I couldn't leave him lying in the middle of the garage where they might see him when they got home.

"We'll put him in your car."

"My car?" Vero's eyes flew open wide, her ponytail swinging with her recoil. "Why my car?"

"Because you have a trunk. Everyone knows dead bodies go in the trunk. Don't look at me like that. What do you want me to do? Strap him in Delia's booster seat? His shoes are sticking out!"

Vero muttered a string of expletives in Spanish as she pulled her keys from her pocket. We snuck out the side door, where I waited in the rhododendron bushes, watching for faces in the neighbors' windows as Vero crept to the street and backed her Honda tightly to the door of the garage. We turned off the porch lights and the lights inside the garage, and by the dim glow of the streetlamp at the foot of my driveway, together we heaved open the broken garage door and attempted to hoist Harris Mickler into her trunk.

"I think he's gotten heavier," Vero said after our third breathless try. My hands were raw and red with the effort. Damp flyaways had come loose from my mom-bun and were plastered by sweat to the side of my head. "How did you get him in the van by yourself?" she asked.

"I lured him with promises of sex," I panted. Vero quirked an eyebrow, unconvinced. Clearly, amateur-killer-in-sweaty-yoga-pants was not my best look. I rolled my eyes and said through a huff, "He was under the influence of drugs, okay?"

Vero snorted.

She was right though. There had to be an easier way to do this.

"Grab Delia's skateboard," I said. More likely, it was the bourbon talking when I pointed to the hot pink plastic deck propped against the far wall.

Vero wheeled it alongside Harris. "Did you get this idea from one of your books?"

"Not exactly." I was pretty sure it came from an episode of *Sid the Science Kid*. At this point, I didn't care as long as it worked.

On the count of three, we hefted Harris onto the board and rolled him to the open trunk of Vero's car. Using the bumper for leverage and Harris's head as a counterweight, inch by inch, with a lot of cursing and grunting, we managed to stuff him inside. When it was done, I leaned against the rear quarter panel of the Honda, dripping sweat and feeling a strange sense of accomplishment.

Vero grabbed the small pink trowel from the workbench and tossed it on top of him.

"What's that for?" I asked as she slammed the trunk closed.

"What else do we have to bury him with?" She shrugged and got in the car.

CHAPTER 11

According to our parents, the first question out of Georgia's mouth the day I was born was, "When can we send her back?" Georgia had never asked for a baby sister, and in her defense, she'd only been four years old at the time. But this remained the defining question of our relationship until the day Georgia left home for the police academy. As kids, I had always been the bad guy—the one person in the house Georgia could point a finger at whenever anything went wrong. But once Georgia became a cop, it was as if she'd suddenly run out of fingers to point at me. The bad guys were everywhere else, and by comparison, I guess I wasn't so bad.

Only it didn't feel that way as I stood in the doorway of my big sister's apartment, smelling like vodka and sweat and Harris Mickler's saliva, fully aware that his body was probably slowly decomposing in the trunk of Vero's car. Hopefully, Georgia would be so relieved to see me, she wouldn't notice anything odd.

Zach was splayed on her shoulder when she answered the door. She wrangled my limp toddler into her arms, pausing as I leaned in to take him from her. She wrinkled her nose. "I thought you said you were working."

Damn cop senses. Georgia's nose might as well be a Breathalyzer. "I was."

I reached for Zach. She held him just out of reach. "Why do you smell like booze?"

Because bourbon might be the only thing holding me together right now. "Writer's block. I needed something to loosen up my brain."

"Are you okay to drive?"

"I didn't." I hitched a thumb over my shoulder at my partner in crime.

Georgia rose up on her toes, glancing over the balcony. Below it, Vero's butt stuck out the back of her Accord as she wrestled the kids' car seats into place. "I thought you said Steven let her go."

"He did." I scratched my still-sweaty neck, finding it hard to look her in the eyes. "She came over to the house to pick up her things, and we ended up . . ." *Destroying my table linens, dividing what's left of my assets, and stuffing a dead guy in her trunk.* ". . . working something out."

As if summoned, Vero appeared behind me. "I'm going to move in and watch the kids in exchange for room and board," she said, reaching for Zach.

And forty percent of my soul.

Georgia sagged as if a huge weight had been lifted off of her as she hefted Zach into Vero's arms and she whisked him off to the car. Georgia rubbed her shoulder, inclining her head toward the sofa behind her. Delia lay curled under a blanket, her fine blond hair rising in a staticky halo around a silver crown of duct tape, her brow furrowed in her sleep. The TV was on low, its pale glow flickering over Delia's soft cheeks. I was glad she wasn't awake to hear it as the anchorman recounted the details of three grisly homicides only a few miles away. I glanced up at the headline: *Man suspected of ties to mafia acquitted of all charges.*

I gestured to the TV. "I'm sorry you missed your night out with the boys from OCN."

Georgia loosed an exhausted sigh as she watched two men descend the courthouse steps and disappear into a sleek black limo on the screen. "There'll be plenty more nights like it," she said, shaking her head. "Nothing sticks to these guys. The Russian mafia could murder half the city and still find someone to bribe. That asshole will never spend a day behind bars as long as Zhirov's around to bail him out."

I hadn't watched the news in as many weeks as I could remember, and I had no idea what Georgia was talking about, but I nodded sympathetically as I slid the diaper bag over one shoulder and scooped Delia onto the other.

"Thanks for watching them for me," I whispered, feeling the weight of Georgia's eyes on me all the way to the door. The day, the adrenaline, and the hangover were all catching up to me, dragging at my heels.

"Finn." My name was a quiet command. Slowly, I turned around, terrified I'd given something away. "I've been worried about you," Georgia said. She handed me Delia's cap and scratched her chest, grimacing as if something inside it made her uncomfortable. She stared at her feet, at the diaper bag, everywhere but right at me when she said, "I'm glad you're not alone."

I swallowed the painful lump in my throat, suddenly unsure which was worse: the secrets I was hiding from my sister, or the body I was hiding in Vero's trunk. Georgia was always alone here. And as much as she'd insisted that was exactly how she wanted it, sometimes—times like this—I wondered how she could stand it.

I folded Delia's cap into my pocket and held her body a little tighter. The duct tape in her hair stuck to my jaw. For a moment, I considered telling Georgia everything. About what had happened in Panera. About what had happened in my van, in my garage.

Georgia reached for the TV remote on the table.

"Georgia . . . ?" I started in a thin voice, clutching Delia to my chest. When my sister looked up at me, it was hard to hold her stare. My gaze skipped away, to the replaying scene on the TV behind her. All I could think of was Patricia's warning. About dangerous people with friends in high places. About how my children would never be safe if anyone knew what I'd done. If Georgia and her police friends couldn't keep dangerous people off the street, maybe Patricia had a reason to be afraid. Maybe Vero was right, and I didn't have any choice but to see this through and keep it to myself.

"Thanks," I murmured.

I turned for the door, feeling those cop-bright eyes on my back all the way to Vero's car.

"Where to now?" Vero asked as I shut the door. She made a face at Delia's duct tape crown in her rearview mirror. The kids slept like the dead in the back seat, as still as Harris Mickler had been when we'd shut him in the trunk with the little pink trowel.

"I don't know." I hadn't had time to think about what we'd do with the body. Maybe because part of me figured we'd never make it this far. I gnawed my thumbnail, my mind spinning over every gory bit of research I'd ever done about body disposal. If we tossed him into a river, with my luck he'd wash up. And a fire would attract far

too much attention; the last thing I needed was an arson investigation on top of a murder charge. "I guess we should find a place to
bury him."

"Any ideas?" She pulled slowly out of my sister's apartment com-
plex, careful to use her turn signal as she eased out onto the road.

I choked back a laugh. Part of me wished Steven was here. I'd
never been good at hiding things. I could never keep secrets the
way he could. He'd always been the one in charge of hiding the
Christmas presents from the kids and the Easter eggs in the yard.
In hindsight, the hardest ones to spot were the most obvious, loosely
covered in foliage or patio cushions right under the kids' noses. It
was the same way he'd hidden his affair with Theresa for months.
He hadn't taken her on extravagant trips or squirreled away money
in strange bank accounts. He'd screwed our real estate agent during
his lunch breaks in her home office right down the street and buried
the scent of her perfume under his own cologne. He'd handled all
the household bills, so I'd never see the expenses and connect the
short distance between the dots. Like the fling he was probably now
having with Bree, Steven kept his secrets close, hiding his indiscre-
tions in mundane places no one would bother to . . .

"Oh." I felt the breath slip out of me. Felt Vero's eyes dart to my
face as an idea took hold. "Go to Steven's house," I said.

"Why the hell would we go to Steven's house?"

"Because we need a shovel." A really big shovel. And if anyone
had the tools to bury a secret as big as Harris Mickler, it was definitely my ex-husband.

CHAPTER 12

It was well after midnight by the time we snuck the shovel from Theresa's shed and made the long drive to Steven's sod farm. The dark, unmarked rear entrance to the property wasn't nearly as inviting as it had been in the daylight. Vero killed the headlights and we sat in the car, listening to the children's soft breaths in the back seat, waiting for our eyes to adjust. Blue moonlight draped over the grass. It billowed for acres all around us, except for a single square plot in the rearmost field where the earth had been freshly turned, waiting to be planted.

Vero and I got out of the car and walked to the edge of the field. The muddy clumps of churned-up dirt glowed gray under the moon. The night was warm for October, quiet except for the rush of fallen leaves tumbling along the line of tall cedars behind us. There wasn't a headlight or porch light anywhere for miles. I could picture Steven and Bree out here, screwing in the back of his pickup after hours. It was the kind of place secrets could go undiscovered for years as new grass grew up all around them.

I drove the tip of Steven's shovel into the ground, relieved to find it soft, pliable. Mercifully, Steven and Theresa hadn't been home when Vero and I parked a few car lengths from her driveway and I'd crept along the thin tree line behind their town house to raid the toolshed in the backyard. I'd slunk off with a heavy shovel boasting a broad steel blade, along with a pair of gardening gloves.

"We'll take turns," I told Vero. "I'll dig first. You keep watch." With any luck, Steven would seed this field before anyone knew Harris Mickler was gone.

My throat went dry as I stared down at the shovel. If this had all been a novel, this moment would be a turning point. A point of no return. If we left right now and went back to Georgia's house, we could still claim negligent homicide. I could tell her everything that had happened in that bar. How I'd accidentally killed Harris Mickler when I'd left my van running in the garage. I could turn in all the evidence on his phone and try to do the right thing, even if it meant going to prison and losing my kids for a while.

I glanced back at the car where they were sleeping. Once this hole was dug, there was no going back. Stealing a shovel, burying a body, claiming the money Patricia Mickler promised—it all pointed to a premeditated crime. A felonious, horrible, unspeakable crime. And as my foot hovered over the lip of the shovel, I wasn't sure I was any less a monster than Harris Mickler.

"C'mon, Finlay!" Vero's sharp hiss jolted me. I leaned into the shovel and hauled out the first full scoop of dirt as she paced, her breath bursting out in short hot clouds that looked like ghosts against the night sky. "How far down do we need to go?" she asked, bouncing on her heels, her eyes darting between me and the kids and the rural road through the line of cedars behind us.

I'd hoped for six feet—deep enough to keep the farm machinery

from accidentally tilling up his corpse, but my back was already on
fire, I had a cramp in my side, and I hadn't even cleared the first foot.
At this point, I'd settle for four.

Impatient, Vero grabbed the pink trowel and jumped into the
field with me, scooping up the small mounds of dirt that cascaded
over the sides of my shovel.

"Next time we do this—"

"There isn't going to be a next time," I panted, glaring at Vero
sideways as I dug faster, anxious to be done with it and get home.
"This was an accident. That's all."

"Maybe the world could do with more accidents," she said under her breath. "If I had as much money as Patricia Mickler, I probably would have hired you, too."

I paused, letting the shovel rest against the ground. I'd assumed
Vero had so readily signed up for this because of the money. I hadn't
stopped to consider the money wasn't worth the risk for either of us.
That maybe she had her own reasons for digging herself into this
hole with me. She threw me a sharp, urgent look and shoveled faster
with her trowel. My own hands were already stiff and sweaty inside
my gloves, and the skin was raw with searing, fresh blisters. I kept
digging anyway.

"Who would you have gotten rid of?" I asked between scoops.

Vero only shrugged. "I'm just saying, there's no shortage of
assholes out there. And in this town, there's no shortage of money
either. I say we corner the market while it's hot."

I dumped a pile of dirt beside the hole, the edge already level
with my knees. "Easy for you to say," I said between labored breaths.
"*You* have the *small* shovel."

"Exactly why we need one of those." She pointed her tiny pink trowel at the hulking outline of the front-end loader Zach had been so eager to climb only hours ago.

I held out the big shovel, swapping it for the pink trowel, hoping after fifteen minutes of heaving dirt she might feel differently about the likelihood of a "next time." Or maybe because I was worried I might start feeling differently about that front-end loader if I had to shovel any more. I checked the time on my phone. An hour had already passed. At this rate, we wouldn't be home until dawn.

"We don't even know how to drive one," I reasoned.

She jammed the shovel into the ground, her sneaker braced against the blade, grunting as she heaved out a scoop. "There's nothing you can't learn on YouTube," she said between ragged breaths. "My cousin Ramón learned how to hot-wire a car. How hard could it be?"

Her cousin sounded like *he* should be the one out here digging the hole. "We are not adding grand larceny of farming equipment to our growing list of felonies."

"Think about it." She leaned against her shovel, her face coated in grime. "We could have had this entire hole dug in five minutes with one of those things. I learned about this in economics class. It's the time value of money. If we're going to be professionals, we need to start *acting* like professionals."

"And *professional* contract killers bury bodies with front-end loaders?"

"I'm just saying, we should be working smart. Not hard."

"Killing people for money is not smart!"

Vero clapped the dirt from her gloves and hauled herself out of the waist-deep hole. She traded me the shovel for the little pink trowel and pointed it at me. "We'll see how you feel when you've got your fifty thousand dollars."

She popped the trunk of her car. I climbed out of the hole and peered over her shoulder, sighing at the human-shaped lump wearing my table linens.

"Come on," she said, grabbing the bungee cord around his ankles. "Let's bury this pervert and get out of here."

Together, we heaved Harris Mickler out of the trunk, balancing his weight against the lip before dumping him to the ground and unrolling him. Vero bundled the linens and stuffed them back in the trunk. I took Harris's phone, car keys, and wallet from his pockets and passed them into her waiting hands.

"Shouldn't we burn off his fingerprints and yank out his teeth or something?" she asked.

I threw her a sharp look, even though she was probably right. If anyone did find Harris Mickler's remains, even without his wallet and phone, it wouldn't be hard to identify him.

I grimaced as I took Harris under the arms. His hands were already cold, his fingers and neck slightly rigid, his arms and legs grossly limp. "Digit removal and dentistry are where I draw the line," I said through a grunt as we dragged him to the edge of the hole.

"I wonder if we could charge extra for that."

"I'm going to pretend you didn't say that."

Vero and I gave Harris Mickler one last look.

"Are we doing the right thing?" I asked.

In answer, she reached in her pocket and offered me Harris's phone. I didn't take it, unable to stomach the thought of opening those photos again. Vero slipped the phone back in her pocket. Then we rolled Harris Mickler onto his side beside the grave we'd dug, and on the count of three, we dumped him in.

CHAPTER 13

I'd first met Veronica Ruiz eight months ago, while the kids and I were in line at the bank. It had been a busy Friday afternoon, payday for people with regular jobs, and while getting a regular check made most people happy, apparently the man in line behind me was an exception to that rule. He'd grumbled to himself about the noise. Zach had been teething, his raw, chapped face distorted with angry tears because I wouldn't let him down to run wild through the lobby. He'd thrashed in my arms, refusing to quiet. We'd made it almost all the way to the front of the line when Delia decided she had to pee and couldn't hold it any longer. Left with no other options, I'd abandoned my place in line and ushered my children to the restroom. By the time we came out, the line had grown a cramped and winding tail, extending all the way to the vestibule.

I'd been ready to give up and walk out when a teller waved me to the front of the line from behind her Plexiglas divider. She'd gestured at the cranky man who'd been standing behind me, signaling him to wait as I approached the counter. Zach stopped crying, flashing

Vero a shy smile from under my neck. Meanwhile, the cranky man had started a ruckus, spewing insults at Vero as she slid a red lollipop through the slot in the glass for Delia. Vero cashed the check Steven had written me, her sharp dark eyes trailing the man as he'd stormed from the line in search of a manager. She'd counted out my crisp bills with a snap of each one and waved good-bye to Delia and Zach. As I'd turned to hold open the vestibule door for Delia, I saw the manager approach Vero's register. His harsh admonishments had filtered through the garbled speakers in the glass, and I'd hovered in the open door, listening, riddled with guilt as Vero put up her CLOSED sign, gathered her things, and left through an exit around back.

Taking Delia's hand and hoisting Zach higher on my hip, I'd rounded the building and found Vero kneeling in her high heels, slashing a small hole in her boss's tire.

"You seem to like kids," I'd said as she stood and wiped the grime from her hands. "I could really use a sitter." I'd held out a wad of cash, nearly half of the check I'd just cashed, partly out of guilt and partly desperation. Vero had raised an eyebrow as she considered the money, then my children, and that had been that.

Vero and I sagged in our seats, the closed garage door looming in front of us, both of us too exhausted to muster the effort it would take to open it. Vero's hands were raw and red, stiff around the steering wheel. My own were coated in a layer of filth, my cuticles ringed in dark crescents of soil. I extricated myself painfully from Vero's car and hobbled to the keypad beside the door. Fighting to uncurl the fingers of my right hand from the ghost of the handle of the shovel, I punched in the four-digit code before remembering the opener was broken. I rested my forehead against the keypad as the motor whirred on the other side of the motionless door.

Then, my back groaning and the blisters on my palms screaming in protest, I heaved the garage door up its track so Vero could pull her car into the empty space beside my van. Mrs. Haggerty's kitchen windows were dark across the street, but I knew better than to assume the old woman wasn't watching. My arms shook as I held the door above my head. Still, I was tempted to flip her off with one hand, just to see if anything moved behind her curtains.

Mrs. Haggerty had been the one who'd first discovered Steven and Theresa's affair when Steven had made the mistake of bringing Theresa to our house while I'd taken the kids to visit my parents. The old woman had cornered me against the mailbox as soon as I'd returned home, asking me if I knew about the attractive blond woman my husband had been entertaining while I was gone. I know they say "don't shoot the messenger," but I'm pretty sure whoever came up with that line of horseshit didn't live across the street from someone like Mrs. Haggerty.

Exhaust bloomed hot around my ankles as Vero's Honda inched past me into the garage. As soon as the car was safely inside, I let go of the door.

The full weight of it came slamming down, the clang of metal on concrete loud enough to rattle the walls. If Mrs. Haggerty hadn't been watching us from her kitchen before, I was certain she was watching us now.

Vero got out of the car and threw me a sharp look as Zach and Delia stirred in their seats. We leaned back against the side of the car, waiting through the fragile silence as the children settled back to sleep. When their breaths became long and even, Vero hauled

Delia into her arms, frowning at the uneven spikes of tacky, clipped hair sticking up around my daughter's face. I hugged Zach to me, nudging the car door shut with my hip.

A pale, watery dawn was just beginning to seep around the edges of the curtains of their rooms as we tucked them into their beds. If we were lucky, Vero and I might have time for a hot shower and a cup of coffee before they roused for the day, and I groaned, remembering the mess of spilled grounds I'd left on the kitchen counter just yesterday.

Without a word, Vero and I stripped down to our underwear in front of the washing machine. We loaded in our clothes, dumping the table linens and gardening gloves and our shoes on top, pouring in two capfuls of color-safe bleach, and finishing it off with a mountain of powdered soap. Vero set the machine running before disappearing into the spare bedroom. She locked herself inside with a soft click.

I padded to the kitchen, determined to clean up at least one mess I'd made before trying to sleep. Careful not to draw unwanted attention from Mrs. Haggerty's house, I left the lights off, searching for the spilled grounds by the dusky morning light filtering through the kitchen curtains, but the mess was gone. The floor and counters were already wiped clean, the dirty dishes that had filled the sink already rinsed and put in the machine. Vero must have tidied up last night as she was packing my frying pan into her cardboard box. Right before she'd found me trying to resuscitate a corpse.

Maybe Vero was right.

Maybe Harris Mickler did deserve what had happened to him. Maybe his wife would show up tomorrow with an envelope full of money and we would actually get away with murder. But as I scraped the loose grounds from the inside of the coffeepot and dumped them into the overflowing trash can under the sink, I wasn't feeling optimistic. I'd killed a man. Whether or not I had done it intentionally hardly seemed to matter anymore. I'd buried him, which made me guilty of something, even if I wasn't entirely sure what that something was. Or what it would become if I took Mrs. Mickler's money.

I woke to the clank of silverware against cereal bowls in the kitchen. The chatter of cartoon voices from the TV was almost loud enough to drown out the low thrum of the vacuum downstairs. Bright sun seared through the blinds of my bedroom. I checked the time on my phone and buried my face in my pillow. It was damp and cold where my still-wet hair had soaked through it when I'd climbed into bed after a long, hot shower, less than four hours ago.

My muscles were stiff, reluctant to wake as I dragged on a pair of sweats and twisted my loose hair into a bun before shuffling downstairs to the kitchen. The dishwasher hummed quietly in the background. The stack of bills from the front stoop had been brought inside, sorted into leaning piles, and organized on a folding table in the empty dining room.

Delia blinked up at me from her chair, her spoon poised over her cereal bowl. A dribble of milk trailed down her chin as she chewed. I blinked back, only partly certain the girl staring back at me was my daughter. Her hair had been shorn close to the scalp, cleaned of the sticky adhesive. The scratch where she'd sliced herself with the scissors was just visible between the errant gelled spikes that remained. A pair of reflective Aviator sunglasses rode on her nose, dwarfing her freshly scrubbed face. And her clothes—a pair of artfully shredded jeans and a torn hot pink T-shirt layered over gray long-john sleeves—had been sprinkled with bleach to complete the ensemble.

I raised an eyebrow. She raised one back as she stuffed another dripping spoonful of cereal into her mouth. Her tiny hands were wrapped in a pair of striped fingerless gloves that had definitely had fingers when I'd bought them last week, and had been far less fashionable yesterday.

Vero's sunglasses slipped down the bridge of Delia's nose as she chewed. "It's a mood," she said with a careless shrug, as if answering the question on my face. "That's what Aunt Vero says."

I clamped my lips against the retort building behind them.

The vacuum cleaner stopped. Vero came into the kitchen wearing one of my sleep shirts and a pair of my yoga pants. I didn't want to think about what she was—or wasn't—wearing underneath them, and I sorely hoped my underwear was cataloged under the sixty percent of personal belongings I would never have to share with her. Her long hair swayed from her loose ponytail as she set my cell phone down on the counter. Her hands were clean, the nails scrubbed, trimmed, and filed short, sporting a layer of fresh pink polish that matched the color peeking through Delia's gloves.

"Aunt Vero, huh?"

Vero smirked. "If Theresa can have an Aunt Amy, you can have an Aunt Vero."

Zach laughed in his high chair, his own hair gelled into matching spikes long enough to curl over themselves. My poultry shears were nowhere to be seen, and no one was bleeding or throwing a tantrum. Too tired to argue, I lumbered sleepily to the table.

"Go get dressed," she said, setting a cup of coffee in front of me and giving me a cursory once-over. I took a greedy sip. "And do something with your hair. You're meeting Mrs. M at Panera in an hour. Try to look the part."

I choked, spitting coffee down the front of my shirt. "What did you do?" It sloshed over the sides of the mug as I rushed to pick up my phone. I scrolled, my face falling, numb as I read the two-word message from Vero to Mrs. Mickler.

It's done.

Mrs. Mickler had replied almost immediately. *Panera 11:00.*

"Jesus, Vero," I whisper-hissed, hoping the children wouldn't notice. When I glanced over, they were engrossed in whatever cartoon Vero had playing on the TV in the next room. "No, I am not meeting with her!"

She planted her hands on the table in front of me. "You *are* meeting with her. How else are we going to get paid? I did not get these calluses for nothing."

I grabbed Vero by the sleeve and dragged her into the dining room, pitching my voice low. "I am not taking that woman's money. If I do, that makes us guilty of murder for hire."

"As opposed to what?" she hissed back. "Just murder? The only difference between them is fifty thousand dollars. Fifty. Thousand. And I vote we take the money."

"Oh, you vote? Well, last I checked, I still held a majority. Which means my vote counts more!"

"Think about it, Finlay. We need that money." She gestured with a sharp finger behind her. Stacks of bills were piled on the folding table, sorted in order of importance. House payments first, then van, then HOA, insurance, and electric bills, followed by a stack of miscellaneous overdue invoices to credit card companies for accounts I'd maxed out months ago. "We finished the job and we might as well get paid for it. Just give her Harris's wallet and phone and take the money. That's all."

I looked at the mountain of envelopes on the table. Maybe Vero was right. Not paying my bills wasn't going to make me a better person or absolve me of what I'd already done.

Vero's shoulders unwound, as if she sensed I was giving in. "I put Steven's shovel in the back of the van. The sooner we get rid of it, the better. You can drop it by Theresa's shed on the way to meet Mrs. Mickler. Then take the van to the car wash and vacuum the shit out of it on the way home. I've watched every episode of *Bones*. If Brennan and Booth can get a conviction with a single speck of pollen, then those boneheads your sister works with could probably arrest you for a freaking hair from Mickler's pants." I grimaced as she held out the van keys.

"I'll clean the car and return the shovel, but I'm *not* meeting Patricia. How am I supposed to look her in the eyes?"

Vero snatched up an envelope from the dining room table and held it in front of me. The scales of justice were emblazoned on the top left corner in dark red ink—another unopened letter from Steven's attorney. "You can either look Patricia in the eyes and take her money. Or you can look in the eyes of your husband's lawyer as he takes your children from you." She held the van keys and the unopened custody letter side by side. One of them felt decidedly more wrong than the other. I took the keys. Then I sucked down my coffee, kissed my children on their heads, and stomped upstairs to get ready to take Patricia Mickler's money.

CHAPTER 14

The wig-scarf itched like hell. I was clearly being punished. God or karma or Harris Mickler's ghost was determined to make me miserable. I wedged a finger inside it and scratched, hoping a brown strand didn't come loose as I searched the packed dining room of Panera through the dark lenses of my sunglasses. My gaze settled on the tables we'd occupied the first time Patricia and I had laid eyes on each other. I heaved a relieved sigh when I didn't see her sitting there. Now I could honestly tell Vero I'd come and I'd tried, and Patricia Mickler hadn't shown up. Then I could go home and eat a bucket of Ben & Jerry's and cry. I just wanted to put this whole nightmare behind me and pretend it never happened. Regardless of how creepy Harris Mickler was, or the terrible things I knew he'd done, I'd killed him. Killed him and buried his body where I hoped no one would ever find it. And it seemed wrong to collect a reward for that.

I pushed my dark glasses up the bridge of my nose, ready to leave, when I caught a flicker of movement in the corner of my eye. Mrs. Mickler hunched in a booth in the corner, her purse tightly clenched in one hand, her other still raised as if she'd been waving me over. It withered as our eyes met. She cast an anxious glance around the dining room as I tucked a blond lock behind my ear and walked briskly toward her.

Her face was as pale as I remembered, with that same wide-eyed look she'd worn when I'd caught her staring at the bloody rag and duct tape in my diaper bag, her expression vacillating between horror and fascination as I slid into her booth.

I clutched my own purse tightly under my elbow. Harris's wallet and car keys and cell phone were in it, Exhibit A, just in case Mrs. Mickler insisted on seeing proof. But in truth, all I wanted was to be rid of them. All I wanted was to get out of here and spend fifty thousand dollars' worth of quarters on the industrial vacuum at the car wash—to suck every cell and fiber that had ever belonged to Harris Mickler from my life.

"It's really done?" she asked with a furtive glance at the neighboring tables.

I nodded.

Patricia's hands shook as she withdrew an envelope from her purse and pushed it across the table. Her eyes were ringed in purple shadows, as if she hadn't slept. I imagined she wanted this whole ordeal over with as much as I did. Still, I hesitated to reach for the envelope.

"You can count it. It's all there," she insisted, pushing it toward me another inch.

"I believe you." The envelope was fat, stuffed so thick the flap hardly closed. I whisked it off the table into my lap and reached into my purse for Harris's wallet, keys, and phone. Patricia took the key ring, her trembling fingers fumbling over it as she separated one tiny key from the others.

"I'll wait until tonight to report him missing," she said, palming the key. "That should give you time to wrap up any loose ends." She pushed the rest of the ring back across the table, along with Harris's wallet and phone. She swallowed hard, unable to look at them, as if she wanted to be rid of every part of him, too.

"You want *me* to get rid of them?" I asked.

"Isn't that what I'm paying you for?"

The nerve of the woman. If Delia had opened a mouth like that I would have sent her to her room for being sassy and confiscated her toys. Patricia withered, clearly mistaking my mom face for something else . . . some callous expression worn by contract killers and hit men. Maybe they're similar. I wouldn't know. Her nervous smile made her lips quiver as if she might start crying.

I bit my tongue as I slid her husband's personal effects back into my purse along with the money.

"I hope you don't mind," she said, clearing her throat. "A friend of mine . . . more of an acquaintance, really. We have Pilates together at the club on Tuesdays and Saturdays," she admitted with a guilt-ridden wince, as if stretching was the crime. "She's having some . . . *issues* . . . with her husband. I told her I might know someone who could help." The folded slip of paper she pushed across the table left me with an ominous sense of déjà vu. My mouth fell open, my tongue fumbling over all the arguments scrambling to get out. Until I read the numbers beside the dollar sign.

All seventy-five thousand of them.

I stared at the name—Andrei Borovkov. The address was some fancy high-rise condominium in McLean. I folded the note and slid it back across the table.

"Look," I started, "you've got the wrong idea about all of this. I don't . . ."

The rest of my argument fell away. Patricia's seat was empty.

I pivoted in the booth, searching for her by the trash bins. By the hall to the restrooms. By the dessert counter. But she was already gone. Through the window, I saw her duck into a car. The brown Subaru wagon tore out of the lot like it was on fire, the bumper stickers obscuring the back window as she darted between oncoming cars.

I stared at the slip of paper. The name on it felt familiar for reasons I couldn't begin to guess. Or maybe it was just this moment, this all-too-familiar feeling of dread that I'd crossed a line I couldn't come back from just by holding it. I tucked the note in my purse with the money and the contents of Harris Mickler's pockets, wondering what the hell to do next.

CHAPTER 15

I left Panera and drove straight to The Lush. The bar wouldn't open for another hour, and the parking lot was empty of all but a handful of cars, making Harris Mickler's easy to find. A Mercedes logo was emblazoned on his fancy key fob, and the ring attached to it had only held three keys: one most likely to his office and one most likely to his house. The smaller key that had dangled between them—probably the key to a gym locker or to a secure cabinet or file drawer—Patricia had kept. I didn't care. I wanted them gone. The last thing I needed was for some detective to track me down and find them inside my house.

My van idled between the only two Mercedes in the lot. I pressed a button on the key fob and caught the flash of taillights in my rearview mirror. Lining up our driver's-side doors, I backed my van into the space beside Harris's car. Then I used one of Zach's burp rags to wipe everything down: his phone, his keys, his wallet . . . Curious, I pried open the billfold, my eyes widening at the crisp bills nested inside. I could take them, I thought. Make it look like a robbery. But then why would a common street thug leave a wallet full of credit cards and an expensive cell phone in Harris's car?

No, better to leave it neat.

If there was no sign of foul play, maybe the police wouldn't investigate his disappearance too deeply. Maybe they'd assume he'd left the bar, ditched his life, and run off to Tahiti or Milan with some mystery woman he'd just met.

Still wearing my wig-scarf, I slunk out of the van with my sunglasses on, the long strands of the blond wig hanging loose to conceal my face as I fidgeted with Harris's key fob. His car alarm blared. The taillights flashed and the horn honked in time with my heart. I frantically pressed buttons until the commotion stopped.

Peering around the parking lot, I used my sleeve to open Harris's car door. Then I wiped down the key fob and dropped his possessions on the driver's seat inside. I'd never been arrested and booked before, so I knew a fingerprint couldn't be used to find me. But it could definitely be used to convict me if I ever became a suspect.

I locked his car from the inside, my heart still pumping double time as I climbed back in my van and turned the key in the ignition.

"Oh, no," I whispered, depressing the brake and turning the key again as the engine made a stubborn clicking sound. "No, no, no, no!" I'd have to call a tow truck. Which meant there'd be a record of my vehicle being towed from this lot, from the parking space right beside Harris Mickler's car.

This was not happening.

I jerked the hood release, stumbling out of the van in my rush to pop it open. I don't know why I bothered. I had no idea what I was looking at as I stared at the mass of metal, tubes, and wires under the hood. I knew how to fix diaper rash, skinned knees, and dinners that came in a box. Auto maintenance—or any maintenance, for that matter—had always been Steven's department.

"Theresa?" I spun toward the voice behind me, my back pressed against the heat of the van's grill, my heart beating so fast I thought it might fly right out of my chest. I pressed a hand to it, willing it to slow as I sagged against the bumper. It was just Julian.

Julian, the bartender who saw me here last night.

Julian, the law student who could probably smell my guilt from across the parking lot.

Shit.

"Sorry." His gaze fell to the panicked flush I felt creeping up my neck. "Didn't mean to sneak up on you like that. Everything okay?" He frowned over my shoulder at the open hood.

"Fine! Everything's fine," I blurted. My mind reeled. Had he heard the alarm? Had he seen me leave Harris's wallet and phone? "Probably just a dead battery. What are you doing here?" I cringed at my own stupidity for asking.

"Early shift." He slung a crisp collared work shirt over the shoulder of his snug-fitting cotton T. Body wash and shampoo smells wafted from him as he raked his damp curls away from his eyes. He gestured to the engine. "Want me to take a look?"

God, yes.

Hell, no.

"Sure." I cleared my throat and hooked a thumb over my shoulder. "The keys are in the van."

The corners of his eyes creased with his smile. I hadn't noticed their color in the bar last night. In the bright sunlight, his irises seemed torn between subtle shades of green and gold, and I was pretty sure I'd be content staring at them until they made up their mind. He leaned into the van and turned the key. I pressed the heels of my hands into my eyes as the engine made that terrible clicking sound.

"Definitely the battery," Julian said, stepping out from behind the driver's-side door. "I've got a set of jumper cables in my Jeep. Hang on. I'll pull it around."

There was an easy bounce in his step as he jogged to a maroon Jeep with a soft top. Weaving it through the lot, he pulled it in front of my hood until our bumpers were just a few feet apart. He emerged with a set of black and red jumper cables, and I tried not to stare at his backside as he popped his hood and leaned over the engine to connect them.

Probably as hard as I'd tried not to kill Harris Mickler and take his wife's money.

"Was it giving you trouble before?" he asked.

"Um, no. It was fine," I told him as he hooked the other end of the cables to the battery in my van. That wasn't entirely true. The van had been giving me trouble for weeks, and I'd ignored the occasional odd noises and dimming lights, hoping they'd eventually disappear, just like the money in my bank account. I guess things could have been worse. This could have happened last night while Harris was passed out in the back.

"It's probably your alternator. We'll let it charge for a few minutes and get you back on the road, but you should swing by a mechanic on your way home and have it checked out." Julian was closer now. Or maybe I was. Close enough to notice his face was smooth and he smelled faintly of shaving gel. And something intoxicatingly cool under that. "So what are you doing here anyway?" he asked with a lift of his brow. "The bar doesn't open for a while yet."

It was the fumes, I told myself. Or maybe the heat coming off the engine making the air feel thin. It was definitely not the way he smelled. Or the way his hair fell over his eyes when he tipped his head. Or the way they glinted in the sun.

"I . . . lost something in the parking lot last night." Like my common sense. Or at least my good judgment. "But I found it," I lied.

"Oh," he said with a wounded smile. "I was hoping you'd changed your mind."

I blinked away an image of Julian in the back seat of my minivan. I'd had one too many men in the back of my van this week already, and look where that had gotten me. The only thing I planned to do in this van was vacuum it. Or set fire to it. "Maybe next time?"

"I'd like that." The silence dragged out, unrelenting and awkward. He lowered his gaze, hiding a self-effacing smile. I tucked a lock of fake hair behind my ear as he checked his watch. He nodded once. "Go ahead and fire it up. It's probably been long enough."

I reached into the driver's-side door and tried the key. The engine turned over, and I exhaled pure relief as Julian disconnected the cables. He dropped his hood, slapping his hands together, his fingertips colored by grease and grime. Remembering the crisp white shirt he'd brought with him for work, I grabbed a pack of wet wipes and a dry burp cloth from my van, checking to make sure it didn't smell like sour milk and that there wasn't any blood or hair on it before I handed it to him.

"Thanks," he said, wiping the pads of his fingers.

"Baker!" Julian turned toward the bar. A balding man with a broad belly held the door open and tapped his watch. I ducked my head, the loose blond strands falling over my face as I moved behind Julian, letting his body obscure me from the man's view. Julian acknowledged the man with a nod.

"That's my boss. I've got to go. You sure you don't want to stick around for a while?"

"I can't," I said quickly, gesturing behind me to the humming engine. "I have to get home. To my kids. And . . . you know . . . real estate stuff."

"Right." His mouth quirked up on one side. It was a great smile—genuine and warm. The kind of smile that made it hard for me to lie.

"But thanks for jumping me." His sunlit eyebrows disappeared under his curls, and heat poured across my cheeks. "That . . . Wow, that did not come out the way I intended it to. I'm sorry. It's just been a really, *really* weird day."

"It's okay. I know what you mean." He bit his lip to keep a laugh from escaping. I wanted to crawl under the concrete as he handed me back Zach's burp rag. "Still have my number?"

I nodded.

"Then I hope I'll be seeing you around, Theresa." He backed toward his Jeep, his eyes trailing over me in a way that felt totally innocent yet still managed to melt the skin from my bones. I climbed into the van and thumbed through my phone, checking to make sure his number was there as he swung his Jeep back into its parking space.

My fingers hovered over the keys as he sauntered into The Lush with his dress shirt slung over his shoulder. If I texted him, he'd have my number. And I was sure that would be a very, *very* bad idea. Harris was in the ground, and I'd just accepted fifty thousand dollars for murdering him. I should've been putting as much distance as possible between me and the place Harris and I were last seen together.

And yet . . .

Still okay with a minivan? I typed fast and hit send before I could change my mind. Clearly, I had not yet found my good judgment in this parking lot.

I dropped my head against the steering wheel, the seconds drawing out painfully long while I waited for his reply. What if I'd misread him? What if he was just being polite? What if the burp rag killed the moment?

My phone buzzed in my lap. I sat up and covered my eyes, barely brave enough to read his text through the gap between my fingers.

Pick me up anytime. You know where to find me.

I glanced up at the tinted windows of The Lush. I could just make out Julian's white dress shirt on the other side, the subtle wave of his hand through the glass. I lifted my fingers from the steering wheel, wondering if he could see me wave back. Wondering if he saw through me—everything about me—the way he'd seen straight through me last night.

CHAPTER 16

Exhaustion washed over me as I stood in the garage thirty minutes later, staring at the space where we'd wrapped Harris Mickler's body just yesterday. The concrete floor was wet and smelled faintly of bleach, the bay door left open to the afternoon sunshine to dry it. Vero must have hosed it out while I was gone. The little pink trowel had been washed and dried, returned to its usual place on the pegboard. Harris Mickler's personal possessions had been wiped clean and locked in his car at The Lush. Steven's shovel was back in his shed. And I'd just burned through twenty dollars in quarters vacuuming every trace of Harris Mickler from my minivan. I'd done everything I could think of to cover our tracks, but I couldn't shake the feeling I was missing something.

Guilt. This gnawing, nagging feeling that kept pulling me back to the garage had to be guilt. And it would probably follow me around for the rest of my life.

A flutter caught my attention across the street, the subtle shift of Mrs. Haggerty's kitchen curtain falling shut. I strode to the garage door, stretching up on my tiptoes to drag it down with both hands. It slammed closed, rattling the garage.

Stupid. I'd been so stupid. I sank down on the short wooden step to the kitchen as my eyes adjusted to the dark, all the *what-ifs* of last night crashing down around me, as heavy and jarring as that damn garage door.

What if I had never called Patricia Mickler? . . . What if I'd never borrowed Theresa's dress and gone to that stupid bar? . . . What if I'd never stuffed Harris in my van? . . . What if I'd never driven him here, to my own freaking home? . . . What if I hadn't left the engine running after I closed my gara—

My back stiffened, one chilled muscle at a time. As I lifted my head, my focus jumped from the van to the garage door. The details of the night before were still fuzzy in my mind, blurred by champagne and panic, as if someone had taken an eraser to the edges, but I remembered . . . I remembered pulling into the driveway. Remembered clicking the remote on the visor and waiting for the door to grind open. The bright cone of the van's headlights had illuminated the pegboard and that little pink trowel, and I distinctly remembered getting out of the van and squeezing between the workbench and the bumper, eyes narrowed against the glare as I'd raced into the house. The kitchen had been dark. Quiet except for the hum of the engine through the wall as I'd slid down it and made that call to my sister . . . Those details in my memory were all vivid and clear.

It's what I *didn't* remember that stuck in my throat now.

I didn't remember tapping the button on the wall as I entered the kitchen. Or the mechanical grinding sound of the garage door lowering to the floor . . .

I hadn't shut the garage.

I had left the van running. But I hadn't shut the garage.

I stood up fast, flipping the light switch on the wall. The single bulb in the center of the ceiling washed the concrete floor in dim yellow light. I stood under it, staring up at the motor that mechanized the door. My eyes climbed the dangling red emergency cord, pausing on the pulley that raised and lowered the door. The pulley was disengaged from the belt. That explained why the motor had run when Vero pushed the button on the wall, but the door wouldn't budge—the door wasn't connected to it.

But that didn't make sense.

The opener had been working when I got home from the bar. I'd pressed the remote on my visor, the door had opened itself, and I'd pulled into the garage. Yet, just twenty minutes later, when I'd come out of the house, Harris was dead and the garage door was disengaged from the motor. It was shut—though I was certain I hadn't shut it.

But how?

I stared up at the red cord dangling above my head.

Pulling the emergency release cord was the only way to disengage the belt and free the door from the motor—the only way to *manually* open or close the door. Which meant someone must have pulled the cord and shut the door while I was inside the house. While the van was running. Which meant . . .

I didn't do it.

I wasn't the one who'd killed Harris Mickler.

Vero leaned back, one leg propped against the wall of the garage, watching me out of the corner of her eye as if I'd lost my mind.

"You actually think someone pulled that red cord and closed the garage door while you were *inside* the house."

"Yes."

"Why?"

There was only one possible explanation for it. "Someone else must have wanted Harris Mickler dead. Whoever it was must have seen us leave the bar and followed me home. When I went inside and left the van running, I left a perfect window of opportunity to kill him." It was the kind of crime I might have written about. The kind no one would buy because it was so . . . neat.

Vero plucked Patricia's envelope from my hand. I'd been squeezing it so tightly, I'd forgotten it was there. "Are you sure this isn't just your guilt talking?"

"I may be guilty of a lot of things, Vero, but I did not close that garage door."

She withdrew a stack of cash and held it to her face, her eyes closing as she fanned the edges and inhaled deeply. "Do we still get to keep the money?"

I reached behind me for the roll of duct tape on the workbench and threw it at her.

"Okay, fine," she said, using Patricia Mickler's envelope as a shield in case I decided to throw anything else. "Let's assume for a minute you didn't close the garage door and someone else did. Why pull the cord? Why not just push the button on the wall and run?"

I gnawed my thumbnail, sifting back through the events of the night. It would have taken awhile for the carbon monoxide to fill the garage. Which meant the killer must have closed the door right after I went inside. I'd been sitting on the floor of the kitchen, my back against the wall directly beside the garage as I'd talked to Georgia. We'd talked so long, I'd forgotten I'd left the van running. Then I'd gone upstairs to wash up and change. My bedroom was right above the garage. "No." I shook my head. "No, they couldn't have used the wall button, or even a remote. The motor's too loud. I would have heard it. Whoever pulled that cord wanted to be silent."

My eyes lifted to the red handle. Something still didn't add up. The emergency release cord was anything but quiet. I'd used it one winter during a power outage, when the garage door was stuck open and the snow was blowing in. As soon as I'd pulled the cord, the door came crashing down, bouncing against the concrete with a bone-jarring smash, just as it had when I'd dropped it a few minutes ago to startle Mrs. Haggerty. Steven had heard the noise from our bedroom and had come running to see what had happened. He'd lectured me for a week about how I could have destroyed the frame. How I could have hurt myself or one of the kids. How I should never pull the release cord when the garage door is open. Not unless . . .

"What's that look? I know that look," Vero said as I grabbed the rusted step stool from the corner. "That's the same look you got before you stuffed the Play-Doh in Theresa's tailpipe."

"Open the door," I said as I positioned the stool under the red emergency cord.

"It's heavy! You open it."

"I can't. I'm getting on the stool."

Vero uttered a few choice words about where I could stick said stool as she hauled the garage door open with both hands. She shivered as a cold autumn wind sliced under the opening and rustled her hair. Cursing me under her breath, she slung the garage door high above her head on its track until it was fully opened, resting parallel with the ceiling. I climbed up the rungs and reconnected the belt to the pulley, the way Steven had shown me. Then I pulled the cord.

Vero shrieked as the door slid freely down the tracks, picking up speed as it dropped. She lunged, catching it before it hit the ground. "Are you nuts?" she hissed. "The last thing we need is Mrs. Haggerty hearing all this and poking her nosy ass all up in our business!" Vero eased the door to the ground with a quiet thud, a sound so small I might not have heard it inside the house.

"There were two of them," I said, climbing down from the stool. Vero wrinkled her nose at me. "It's the only way someone could have shut this garage without making any noise. One person pulled the cord. Someone else caught the door and controlled the drop."

"So let me get this straight," Vero said. "You mean to tell me someone else . . . no, *two* someone elses . . . killed Harris while you were on the phone with your sister?"

"Making it look like an accident."

"Or setting you up to take the fall." Vero picked up the envelope and slid it into the waistband of her yoga pants—*my* yoga pants—as if she were afraid I might suddenly decide to give it back. She yelped as I yanked it free, but there was nothing to be done about it now. I had already claimed the money. Regardless of who'd shut Harris inside the garage, I was the one who'd accepted payment for the hit job. And if anyone ever found Harris's body, we were the ones who'd go down for it.

When the kids went down for their afternoon naps, I retreated to my office and closed the door. Patricia's envelope rested on top of my desk. It was noticeably lighter since Vero had counted out her forty percent of the cash, but that didn't make it any easier to look at, and I tucked it inside my desk drawer.

The money from Patricia was no different from my book advance, just one more unearned payment for a job I hadn't done. Just one more thing to feel guilty about. As many problems as Patricia's money could solve, it had come tied to even bigger ones. Scarier ones. The kinds of problems that meant losing my kids. The kinds of problems that meant spending the rest of my life behind bars. And the only way I'd ever have a leg to stand on if Harris's disappearance came back to bite me was to know for certain what had really happened in my garage. To be able to prove, beyond the shadow of a doubt, that I hadn't been the one to murder him.

I flipped on the old PC, waiting as it coughed and sputtered to life. I opened a blank Word document and titled it, typing the first words that came to mind, the one thing Sylvia and my editor were expecting of me—THE HIT by Finlay Donovan. The screen was blindingly white. The cursor stared back at me with an indifferent, slow blink as my calloused fingers hovered over the keys. It had been months since I'd been able to climb out of my own mire of self-defeating thoughts. Since Steven left, I hadn't been able to cobble more than a few words together on a page. Every plotline seemed hopeless, every romance fell flat, and every story I dreamed up felt like a complete waste of time.

When I'd missed my first deadline after Steven moved out, Sylvia had called to lecture me. I'd told her I had writer's block, but she'd insisted I push through it. Sometimes, she'd said, you can't see the whole story until it's laid out on the page, and the only way to figure out what happens next is to write your way through it, one scene after the next, until it's done. Sylvia was all about tough love and finding your own answers. Mostly, Sylvia was all about earning a paycheck. Maybe I should've been, too.

I touched the keyboard, trying to figure out exactly where to start my contracted novel, but I couldn't stop thinking about Harris's story. Probably because, through my own stupidity, I'd managed to put myself in the middle of it. If the police managed to trace Harris from The Lush to my garage, I'd become their prime suspect. And Vero and I would go to prison unless we could prove the murder had been committed by someone else.

I knew the opening scene. Harris Mickler had been murdered right under my nose. All I had to do was uncover the backstory to figure out the rest of the plot. I just had to put myself in the heads of the characters—to figure out who they were, what they wanted, and what they stood to lose. It all boiled down to means, motive, and opportunity. How hard could it be to solve my own crime?

I started typing, beginning with the note Patricia had slipped on my tray during lunch, recalling as many details as I could: the call I placed from my van, my trip to The Lush, sneaking Harris to the parking lot, then finding him dead in my garage. As I wrote, I lost myself in the story, letting my memory fill in the gaps. The names—Harris's, Patricia's, Julian's, mine, even the name of the bar—I changed, letting the rest of the events of the night spill unfiltered onto the screen.

The keys clicked with increasing speed. Paragraphs became pages, and I typed until the sun pulled its tired pink fingers from the slats between the blinds. Until the clatter of dishes quieted in the kitchen, and the kids fussed in their beds before finally drifting off to sleep. I wrote through the long hours of silence that followed, until the light from my screen was the only light in the house.

CHAPTER 17

The house was quiet, the kids already down for their afternoon naps when I woke the next day. Vero had fallen asleep on the couch, her blistered hands curled around the throw pillow under her head and her face slack with exhaustion. I didn't see any sense in waking her when I left. A local news channel was playing softly on the TV in the background. She'd probably been up all night watching the head-lines, listening for the police, waiting for them to show up at our front door. The only way either of us would ever sleep peacefully again was if we knew who had really killed Harris Mickler.

I'd written through the night but was no closer to understand-ing the chain of events that had led up to that moment when I'd found Harris dead in my garage. Who, aside from Patricia and me, had a reason to want to kill him? Everything I knew about Harris had come from his social media profiles and his cell phone. Surely every woman in those horrible photos had had a motive to want to end Harris's life, but I'd locked it in his car at The Lush, and I couldn't risk going back for it now. Patricia was the only person who could help me solve Harris's murder. That is, if she'd bother to answer any of my calls.

Desperate, I tracked down the number for the firm where Patricia was employed. The receptionist apologized, explaining Patricia had called in sick that morning, and she would be taking leave for the remainder of the week. I didn't know much more about Patricia than I knew about Harris, but thanks to the note she'd left on my tray in Panera, I knew her home address.

North Livingston Street was already dressed for Halloween, cottony cobwebbing strung from the limbs of the trees and bright pumpkins dotting the front porches. I eased to the curb a block away from number forty-nine. The Micklers' house was a modest 1960s split level, landscaped to blend in with its unassuming surrounds. Like most of the others in this zip code, the simple brick shell had probably been remodeled inside, with granite counters and ornate trim and sunken jetted bathtubs to suit the lofty price and high-end tastes of this corner of North Arlington.

The plantation shutters through the windows I could see were all drawn shut, and the driveway was empty of cars. As far as I could tell, no cops were poised to pounce outside.

I dialed Patricia's number for the third time since I'd left my house, tossing my phone in my drink holder with a muttered swear when an automated voice told me her mailbox was full. I got out of my van, aiming for nonchalant as I strolled casually up the sidewalk toward the Micklers' house. Most of the neighbors were probably at work, which was precisely where Patricia Mickler should have been.

She'd been foolish to call in sick the day after she'd paid someone to kill her husband. Or maybe she was just playing up the role of the worried wife. I hoped, wherever she was, she hadn't skipped town. If she ran, the police would be sure to find her, and if they questioned her about her husband's disappearance . . . Well, I didn't want to think about what she might confess in exchange for reduced prison time.

Satisfied I wasn't being watched, I crossed the street to Patricia's house. The front stoop was neat: no stacks of mail, no knickknacks or Halloween decorations. I rang the bell. Its faint chime was just audible through the foyer window. No thump of approaching feet. No barking dogs. I waited a minute before rapping hard on the door. The house remained quiet. I peered through the window. The lights were off inside.

Where would she have gone?

I turned to go, pausing by the mailbox mounted beside the Micklers' door. My hand hovered over the lid. I was pretty sure tampering with someone's mail was a criminal offense, but if Harris's mail was anything like mine, it contained plenty of things I didn't want people to know about me.

I glanced over my shoulder, then both ways down the street, before cracking it open. The stack inside was thin. Slender enough to fit inside my coat without drawing notice. Before I could talk myself out of it, I tucked the mail into my open jacket and hurried to my van. Locking myself inside, I hurriedly thumbed through the envelopes.

A handful of bills, some coupons, a few advertisements . . . All the mail had been jointly addressed to Mr. & Mrs. Harris Mickler. Except a single monthly bank statement, addressed to an LLC— Milkman Associates.

Milkman, like the password to his cell phone.

I slipped my car key inside the flap and sliced it open, scanning the statement. This was clearly not an account he shared with Patricia. There were no withdrawals for groceries or utility bills or mall stores. No hair salons or doctor appointments or routine expenses related to their house. My stomach went sour as I read the charges. Payments to upscale bars and high-end restaurants, a flower shop in Vienna, and the glitzy Charleston-Alexander jeweler in town. There were several recurring charges to the Ritz-Carlton Hotel, halfway between Harris's house and The Lush. This must have been Harris's operating account—the one he used to wine and dine his victims before he drugged and blackmailed them into silence.

I flipped the page and found a list of twelve deposits, all for the same amount—two thousand dollars—all bank-to-bank wire transfers on the first day of the month. Harris must have been doing some financial consulting on the side. And, apparently, his consulting business was doing well. By the looks of it, he had twelve regular clients on retainer, making payments every month. In the last week of September, Harris's balance on the account had been a little more than a half million dollars. But the total in the account by the end of that month, when the statement closed, was . . . zero?

I flipped back to the withdrawals. Harris had withdrawn the full balance of his account the week before he was killed. A week before Patricia had attempted to hire me.

Or had he . . . ?

I was going to use it to leave him. But it will be better this way.

Suddenly, it made sense how Patricia had come up with fifty thousand in cash so easily. She must have withdrawn it from her husband's account, planning to use it to run away, hoping he'd never come after her. But then she'd met me and figured she had enough cash to ensure he never would. The missing money would fit the narrative she had probably planned to tell the police—that he'd cashed out his assets and run off with another woman. Meanwhile, Patricia had all the money she'd need to start a new life someplace else.

Only two questions remained: Who killed Harris? And where had Patricia Mickler gone?

As I tucked Harris's bank statement in my pocket and prepared to return the rest of the envelopes to the Micklers' mailbox, a sleek black Lincoln Town Car rolled slowly past my van. I ducked low in my seat as it stopped in front of the Micklers' driveway.

A man swung open the passenger-side door. The long legs of his tailored suit took crisp, precise strides to Patricia's front door. He rang the doorbell, running a hand over his dark, meticulously styled hair as he waited for someone to answer. The driver stayed back in the car, concealed behind its tinted windows.

The man rang the bell once more, following it up with two sharp knocks I could hear in my van. When no one answered, he moved to the garage, his tall frame allowing him to peer easily inside the high, narrow windows. He turned back to his car with a tight shake of his head.

The driver's door flung open. A pair of broad shoulders and sturdy, thick legs wedged their way out. With heavy, lumbering strides, the driver stalked around the side of the house, a silver blade slipping from his sleeve into his meaty hand as he disappeared behind it.

The man in the suit laced his fingers behind him, casually pacing the driveway, his eyes roving the street as he waited beside the Town Car. I sank lower in my seat, peering over the top of my steering wheel, hoping he couldn't see me with the low afternoon sun at my back.

A moment later, the driver returned. He brushed his empty hands together, and with a tight nod to his passenger, they ducked back into their fancy black car. Heart racing, I dropped to the floor-board as the Lincoln reversed out of the driveway and swung in my direction. I waited for the purr of its engine to pass before cautiously sitting up.

Were these the people Patricia had warned me about? The ones with eyes and ears all over town?

My husband was involved with some very dangerous people.

Checking my mirror to be sure they were gone, I threw open my door and returned the mail to the box. Every voice in my head was screaming at me to go. To run. But what if Patricia had been home all along? What if she'd been hiding, not from me, but from those men? The driver had been carrying a very large knife, and it hadn't been in his hand when he'd come back. I couldn't just leave without making sure Patricia was okay.

I crept to the garage, leveraging myself on the edge of a raised planter beside the driveway to peek in the window. A brown Subaru wagon was parked inside, the same one she'd disappeared in when she'd left me in Panera, its rear window layered in stickers—JMU, Animals Are Friends Not Food, Adopt Don't Shop, and Shed Happens. Stick figures of a man and a woman and two stick-figure dogs trailed across the glass.

Patricia was home.

I ran through the side yard and rounded the Micklers' house, stopping short in the middle of her back porch. Sunlight glimmered off the long blade of the knife embedded in the trim beside the door. A piece of paper fluttered, held in place by its teeth.

YOU'VE TAKEN SOMETHING THAT BELONGS TO ME.

YOU HAVE 24 HOURS BEFORE MY PATIENCE RUNS

OUT.—Z

I touched the bank statement in my pocket. Had all those small, incremental monthly deposits been retainer payments from clients? Or had Harris been embezzling money from his clients' accounts?

... if they find out what we've done, they'll come for both of us.

I had assumed Patricia had meant these dangerous people would find us if they knew what we had done to Harris. But what if that wasn't what she was suggesting at all? What if she was referring to what she and *Harris* had done? What if the money in his account had belonged to these men and she'd stolen it—not from her husband, but from them? Could these men be the ones who had killed Harris?

I blew out a shaky breath. At least the men hadn't gone inside.

I banged on the back door, cupping my hand to peer in the window. The kitchen was dark, the sink empty of dishes and the counters tidy. I dragged my sleeve over my hand and tried the doorknob, but it was locked. So was the window beside it. I looked around for a pet door I might open and shout through, surprised she didn't have one. I knocked again, but if she was home, she clearly had no intention of answering. After what I'd just seen, I couldn't say I blamed her. If I were Patricia, I would have hidden under my bed and called the ...

Oh, no.

I let go of the knob, ears alert for the sound of sirens, nearly tripping off the porch stairs in my rush to get back to my van. Patricia would be fine, I told myself as I shut myself inside. By the end of the night, forty-eight hours would have passed since Harris's disappearance, and the police would be crawling all over this place. The scary man in the suit and his very scary driver wouldn't be foolish enough to come back. And if I were smart, neither would I.

CHAPTER 18

I was being prodded by instruments of torture. I prayed to every god, in every corner of the globe, my prayers consisting mostly of four-letter words, to please, please, for the love of all that was holy, make it stop.

Peeling open one eye, I waited for the room to come into focus. Delia sat on the edge of my bed, her spiky hair silhouetted against the light streaming into my bedroom from the hallway. She rocked me fervently back and forth, her tiny hand pressing into my right kidney until my bladder threatened to burst. Zach leaned over me with his milky breath, his pudgy finger poking my cheek.

I covered my face with a pillow.

Delia plucked it away from my head. "Wake up, Mommy. Vero says it's time for dinner."

"Dinner?" I pushed up on an elbow. What day was it? What time was it? The last thing I remembered was putting my computer to sleep, closing the door to my office, and lumbering to my bedroom like a zombie.

Zach giggled when his wet pacifier found my ear. I shuddered at the memory of Harris's tongue as I sat up, the events of the previous three days slowly coming back to me. "How long have I been sleeping?"

"All. Day. Long." Delia rolled her eyes so hard I could see their whites in the dark.

"I know. I get it. It's a mood." I sat up and stretched, the muscles in my back and shoulders howling. I was sure it was karma. The pain I was suffering for burying Harris Mickler was directly proportional to my own stupidity.

Maybe Vero had been right about the front-end loader.

I switched on the bedside table lamp, wincing as the light threw my life into stark relief. My captors took my hands and dragged me from my room. The hallway smelled like garlic butter, oregano, and simmering tomatoes, and my stomach growled as I hoisted Zach onto my hip and carried him downstairs.

Something was different. Or maybe everything was different. I looked around the kitchen as I strapped Zach into his high chair. At the clean stretches of countertop where random piles of clutter used to gather. At the vacuum tracks in the living room carpet and the baskets of clean, folded laundry. At the open notebooks and calculator and accounting textbooks where the missing piles of collection notices in the dining room had been yesterday.

A sinking feeling swept over me. "Where are the bills?" I asked Vero.

"I handled them," she said, serving out bowls of spaghetti and garlic bread.

"What do you mean, you handled them?"

"I paid them."

"With what?"

She raised an eyebrow as she slid Delia's plate onto the table. I ran upstairs to my office and threw open my desk drawer. Patricia Mickler's envelope was gone.

I rushed back down, nearly slipping on the fresh floor polish at the bottom of the stairs. "Where's the money?" I whispered, darting an anxious glance at the kids. Delia slurped up a long noodle. Zach picked up a handful of pasta and sauce, dropping it onto his tray with a squeal.

Vero sat down in the empty chair beside them. "I started an LLC in your name, opened an account, and used it to pay off your bills." She tore off a mouthful of garlic bread. "You're welcome," she said around her food.

Appetite gone, I sank heavily into my chair. "All of them?"

Vero speared her fork into her spaghetti, as if the answer should have been obvious.

"Don't you think that's going to look a little bit suspicious? How am I supposed to explain that to Steven when he asks me where the money came from?" Delia's eyes lifted from her plate at the sound of her father's name, and I let my argument drop.

"It's a new account. And it's your company. His name isn't on it." Vero shrugged as she poured herself a glass of wine. "By the time he realizes the bills have been paid, your book will be done."

"What book?"

"The one you've been working on at night." She took a long sip. "It's good, by the way."

"What do you mean, it's good? How could you possibly know it's good?"

"And who's Julian Baker?" She waggled an eyebrow.

"Were you snooping on my computer?"

"You left your browser open on his Instagram page." She smirked at me over the rim of her glass. "He's hot."

"Who's hot?" Delia asked.

"No one." I glared at Vero as I shook a mountain of parmesan onto my plate and slammed down the can. The muted TV flickered in the living room, set to the local news station. Vero's eyes darted to the ticker as she ate. "He's just a friend," I muttered into my plate.

"A little young, isn't he?" Vero asked.

I stabbed at my pasta. "I'm thirty-one. It's not like I've got one foot in the grave."

"Last I saw, you had two."

I kicked her under the table.

"How about Andrei Borovkov? What's his story?"

I stopped chewing. I hadn't mentioned anything to Vero about Patricia's rich friend or the seventy-five-thousand-dollar promissory note I'd tucked in my desk drawer. "How do you know about that?"

Vero dropped her garlic bread, her wide eyes focused on the TV behind me. Her chair screeched as she lunged to the counter for the remote and turned up the sound. My stomach took a nosedive when I turned and saw the familiar faces on the screen.

According to police, an Arlington husband and wife have gone missing in two separate incidents, causing investigators to consider the likelihood of foul play. Patricia Mickler contacted her local sheriff's office at approximately seven o'clock Wednesday night to report her husband, Harris Mickler, missing, saying she hadn't heard from him since he'd left work the night before. But when police arrived at her home to take her statement, Mrs. Mickler didn't answer the door. Police say they grew concerned after they made several attempts to reach her by phone, and more than one unanswered visit to

*her home. Tonight, police are launching an investigation into
the couple's whereabouts.*

The camera cut away to the Micklers' street, where neighbors
all seemed to be saying the same thing. No, they hadn't noticed anything strange. No, the Micklers were perfectly ordinary, a quiet couple, no children or pets. They both worked long hours at respectable
jobs and had never caused any trouble.

Vero was still gripping my arm when the news anchor cut to a
commercial break.

"Mommy, can I be excused?" Delia pushed her half-eaten bowl
away, a deep wrinkle in her nose.

"Yeah, sweetie," I said in a hollow voice. "Go wash your hands.
You can play in your room."

As soon as Delia was up the stairs, Vero turned to me. "What
do we do?"

This was not a plot twist I had planned on. "We are not going
to panic," I insisted. Who was I kidding? We were definitely panicking.

"Where the hell is she?"

"Patricia? She probably got scared and left town."

"It makes her look guilty!" Zach's sauce-covered face snapped up
at her outburst. His eyes ping-ponged between us and Vero lowered
her voice. "If the police find her, she could confess everything." She
swiped my cell phone from the counter and held it out to me. "Call
her and tell her she's making a mistake. She needs to come back."

"I've called her a dozen times. She wouldn't answer my calls, so
I went to her house—"

"Are you crazy?"

"No one saw me." At least, I hoped not. I swallowed hard, re-membering the knife protruding from Patricia's back door. "But . . . while I was there, two men showed up."

"What men?"

"I don't know. But I think they might have been the men Patri-cia warned me about. They left a note. I think they might have been Harris's clients. I think he was stealing from them. When I opened his mail, I found a bank statement—"

"You opened his mail? Your fingerprints are probably all over the envelope!"

I reached inside my pocket and put the bank statement on the table. "It's fine. I took it with me."

Vero choked. She snatched it off the table and opened it, her eyes narrowing as they skimmed the statement. "Twelve deposits, all on the first of the month, for the same amount. You think he was embezzling from his clients?"

I nodded. "It gets worse. Turn the page." Vero flipped to the balance sheet, her mouth forming an *oh* around the big fat zero at the bottom. "The note said Patricia had twenty-four hours to return what she'd taken."

"You think these men were the ones who killed Harris?"

"They definitely had a motive. They want their money back. And we have fifty thousand of it."

Vero hugged my phone as she paced the kitchen. "Patricia paid us in cash. If these men did follow you home from the bar, they could just assume you were on a date and he'd had too much to drink. They'd have no way of knowing Patricia hired you. With a half million dollars, she could run anywhere. If they don't find Pa-tricia, they won't find out about us, right?"

"Right."

Zach fussed in his high chair. I wiped pasta sauce from his face, plucked him from his seat, and set him down to toddle after his sister.

Vero fell into her chair. She pushed her plate to the middle of the table, looking at it as if she might be sick. "What if the police find Patricia before we do?"

"The only thing she knows about me is my number. She doesn't know my name or where I live. I doubt she could even identify me in a lineup." I'd been wearing a wig and high heels and plenty of makeup. Hopefully it was enough. "Besides, I have *you* for an alibi," I said, dropping into the chair beside her.

"I thought I was an accomplice."

"Not if they can't prove it. As far as anyone else is concerned, I was here at home with you the night Harris Mickler went missing. I called my sister from the house phone in the kitchen. And Georgia saw us together when we picked up the kids. All we have to do is get rid of any evidence that could lead the police back to us."

Vero looked down at my phone. She dropped it on the table in front of me as if it were crawling with lice.

"Relax. It's a prepaid cell. Verizon shut off my account last month when I was late on my bill. I bought this one at the pharmacy."

"Can't the police find a record of the payment?"

"My credit cards were all maxed out. I paid in cash." I rested my elbows on the table, digging the heels of my hands into my eyes. "There's nothing tying the phone to me."

"Don't you watch *Law and Order*? They can trace those things!"

"Only to the nearest tower it pings."

"How close is that?"

"I don't know . . . a few miles maybe?"

"Too close for me." Vero rose from her seat. My head snapped up as she threw my phone down on the cutting board. She grabbed a meat tenderizer from the utensil drawer and raised the metal mallet behind her head.

"Wait!" I snatched my phone before she could smash it. Turning my back on her, I thumbed through my contacts. Vero stood on her tiptoes, peeking over my shoulder as I copied Julian's number onto a sticky pad.

"Just a friend, huh?"

"He's a lawyer," I said, tucking the sticky note in my pocket. "His number might come in handy."

"He's too young to be a lawyer."

"He's a public defender," I quipped. "Or at least, he will be. Someday. When he graduates."

"Nu-uh." Vero nixed that idea with big exaggerated sweeps of her head. "If we get caught, we're not hiring some Abercrombie underwear model to keep us out of prison. I want an old white dude with cuff links and a Rolex. Like your ex's attorney."

"My ex's attorney is not *old*. He's only three years older than me. And he charges two hundred dollars per hour."

"If we kill Andrei Borovkov, we could afford that."

I gave her a withering look.

"Where'd you meet him anyway?"

"Borovkov?"

"No," she said, yanking away my phone. "Julian Baker."

She drummed her nails against the counter, waiting for an answer.

"He was bartending," I confessed, "the night I kidnapped Harris from The Lush."

"*He's* the bartender? The one from your story? Have you lost your mind!" she hissed, gesticulating wildly. "You can't keep his phone number. What if he turns you in?"

"He doesn't even know who I am! I was wearing a blond wig and I gave him a fake name. He thinks I'm a real estate agent named Theresa."

The kitchen fell silent. Vero's mouth fell open and she blinked at me. A laugh started deep in her throat, building into a cackle until it exploded out of her. I started laughing, too. "You didn't."

"I did."

She shook her head as she crossed the kitchen and filled both of our wineglasses. She handed me mine, watching me with a level of amusement she usually reserved for my children as she sipped. "You like him, don't you?"

I leaned against the counter beside her, mostly so I wouldn't have to look her in the eyes. I took a long swig, pretty sure the answer was obvious.

Vero drained her glass. She set it down and put an arm around my shoulder. "You know you can't call him, right? If he figures out who you are, he could blow your alibi to pieces. You said it yourself. We have to get rid of anything that could tie us back to the Micklers." I knew she was right. And yet, I couldn't make myself get rid of his number. "You think we should kill him, just to be sure?"

"No!" I turned to gape at her. "We *didn't* kill anyone! And we're not *going* to kill anyone! Not Andrei Borovkov. And definitely not Julian. This is it. End of story."

Vero laughed, her cheeks flushed from the wine. "Relax, I was only kidding!"

I popped open the phone and threw the SIM card in the garbage disposal. Water poured from the tap, and Vero's laughter died as I flipped the wall switch. We both started at the sudden grind of metal on metal. The sound trailed down my spine, dragging a shiver from me as our last tie to Patricia Mickler rattled down the drain.

CHAPTER 19

I'd learned two very important lessons having a sister for a cop. One, you can find almost anyone on the internet. And two, you're more likely to get caught committing crimes in your own home than in plain sight.

Which was why I was committing mine in my local public library.

The kids were with Steven for the weekend, and Vero was home studying for her midterm accounting exams. I hadn't exactly been lying when I'd told her I was going to the library to do research for the book. How else was I going to know what happened in the next chapter of the mystery surrounding the Micklers if I couldn't figure out where Patricia went?

I claimed a seat at the last workstation in the back of the room and opened a browser. Then I typed in Patricia's name, scouring social media sites and white pages for any information I could find about her: neighborhoods where she used to live, people she was close with, places she frequented . . . In less than an hour I was yawning, and not one step closer to finding her. Patricia Mickler's life made mine look glamorous by comparison. With the exception of her office, the animal shelter where she volunteered, and the weekly Pilates class she'd mentioned, it seemed she rarely left the house. Apparently, she had even fewer friends than I did.

Patricia's online profile featured more animals than people, the only exception being a photo of some shelter volunteers, taken at an adoption event the month prior. Patricia, clearly the oldest of the group, cuddled a white-faced mutt with a patch of black fur covering one eye. The caption said the dog's name was Pirate, and Aaron—the young, curly-haired volunteer beside her—held the dog's littermate, Molly.

I clicked over to her friends list, searching for the faces of the volunteers in the photo, but didn't find any matches. Patricia didn't appear to connect with them beyond the time she spent at the shelter. I guess I shouldn't have been surprised; the other volunteers were all young, probably in college, and Patricia, betrayed by the smile lines and shadows around her eyes, stuck out from the fresh-faced group like a sore thumb. Maybe this was the reason she chose to compartmentalize that part of her life. Still, she looked younger in the photo than the weary, defeated woman I'd met in the Panera. Happier and more at ease somehow. As if this place were her home, and these animals were her family.

According to public records, Patricia had been an only child and her parents were deceased. From her social media pages, I knew she and Harris had met in college at the McDonough School of Business at Georgetown, which meant she'd lived within a four-mile radius of the DC beltway her entire life. I couldn't see her cashing out and leaving town to start over someplace else alone. She seemed far too timid for a bold move like that. Maybe she was just confused and scared, holed up in a hotel room, too terrified to face what she'd done. Or too afraid of the men Harris had been tangled up with.

Wherever she was, if she didn't come out of hiding soon, the police were going to find her. And they were going to ask her questions. And those questions would inevitably lead them to me. She'd paid me for a job. And I'd told her I had done it. As far as the police were concerned, it would seem like an open-and-shut case. My only hope was to find her first and explain to her what had happened. That I hadn't been the one to kill her husband. Maybe, together, we could find a way to prove those other two men were guilty.

I pushed back my chair and extended my sore legs. Almost four days had passed since we'd buried Harris, but every muscle I'd used to dig his grave still felt like it was punishing me. My back groaned as I reached above my head. There had to be someone Patricia trusted enough to confide in. Someone who might know where to find her.

My arms froze midstretch.

Pilates.

The note Patricia had slid across the table had come from a woman she knew from her weekly Pilates class—Andrei Borovkov's wife. Patricia had said they were only acquaintances, but that had clearly been a lie. If Patricia felt close enough to this woman to refer her to a contract killer, it was possible she trusted Mrs. Borovkov with other sensitive information about her life . . . like where she'd planned to go after paying me to murder her husband.

I slid my chair back toward the computer, preparing for the usual barrage of social media hits as I searched for Andrei Borovkov's wife. But the first hit—and almost every hit after—was the headline of a news article about a recent triple homicide.

I remembered Georgia talking about that crime scene weeks

ago; three local businessmen had been found with their throats slashed in a warehouse in Herndon. According to the headlines on my screen, the case had resulted in a mistrial.

Every article I scrolled through featured the same photo—two men ducking into a limo at the bottom of the courthouse steps. One was formidable-looking, with a bald head and hooded eyes. The other was polished and well-dressed, probably his attorney. It was taken from the same video clip I'd seen on the TV in Georgia's apartment.

I zoomed in on the image, leaning closer to see.

My stomach dropped.

These were the same men who'd been driving the Lincoln Town Car. The same men who'd jammed the knife in Patricia's back door.

That's why Andrei's name had felt so familiar when I'd read it on his wife's note. Because I'd heard it before. On the news. It had been playing in the background at Georgia's house when I'd picked up my kids the night we'd buried Harris.

Andrei Borovkov wasn't just any problem husband. He was the murder suspect OCN had failed to convict. The one Georgia's friends had been so upset about. He'd been acquitted that morning, the same day Harris Mickler was killed.

According to the article, Irina Borovkov's husband worked as a bodyguard for a wealthy businessman named Feliks Zhirov—a man with known ties to the Russian mob.

I slapped a hand over my mouth to stifle a gasp.

You work for Feliks?

That's what Harris had asked me in the bar, when I'd casually suggested we belonged to the same vague financial group. He'd looked sick when he said it, and I'd assumed it was because of the drugs. Patricia didn't just know Irina Borovkov from Pilates. Their husbands were in business together—*mafia* business.

Harris had been stealing from the mob.

I cleared the search from the screen with shaking hands, afraid someone might see it. Then I cleared my entire search history, unsteady when I shot to my feet. Andrei Borovkov wasn't just a bodyguard. Bodyguards protected people. They didn't get arrested for slashing up businessmen in warehouses. They didn't leave death threats on people's back doors when they thought someone had stolen their boss's money.

I'd been hired to kill an enforcer for the Russian mob.

Suddenly, I wasn't sure which was scarier—the possibility that I'd be caught by the police for a murder I didn't commit, or the likelihood I'd be murdered by Andrei Borovkov once he learned what his wife had done.

I slammed the door to the kitchen and fell back against it, my breath racing out of me. The lights in the house were off, and Vero's car was gone from the garage. I bolted the door and kicked off my shoes, taking the stairs to my office two at a time. I shut myself inside, my fingers clumsy and trembling as I locked the door behind me.

The kids were safe at Steven's house, I reminded myself. And Andrei Borovkov's wife had no idea who I was. As long as I didn't call the number in Irina's note, Mrs. Borovkov's very scary husband would never know who his wife had hired, or how to find me.

A pink flash caught my eye. One of Vero's sticky notes fluttered, taped to my computer screen: HOT DATE. DON'T WAIT UP. I'LL BE HOME IN TIME FOR DELIA'S PARTY.

Crap. Delia's birthday party was at eleven A.M. tomorrow. In all the chaos, I'd almost forgotten. A loose-leaf sheet of notebook paper lay across my keyboard, titled "My Birthday Wish List" in Delia's oversize careful letters. Only one wish made the list . . . a puppy.

Under it, I found another certified letter from Steven's attorney. I didn't have to open it to know what was inside.

I plucked the sticky note from the monitor. By lunchtime tomorrow, my house would be teeming with kids screaming for pizza and cake. I was nowhere near ready for Delia's birthday. I hadn't even bought her a gift yet.

Maybe Steven was right. Maybe I was unfit to mother my own children. Steven had never been the model parent, but the plot of my own life had gone off the rails since he'd left, and I was no closer to knowing what to do about it. The only thing I knew for sure was that I wasn't going to sleep until I was certain no one was looking for me. Somehow, I had to avoid the police and steer clear of Andrei Borovkov.

I crept to the window, eyes peeled for strange cars outside. I caught the flash of Mrs. Haggerty's kitchen curtains falling closed, and I quickly drew mine shut. I turned, surprised to find my socks had left impressions in the fresh vacuum tracks in the carpet. I touched my fingers together, but they were clean; the slats in the blinds were suspiciously free of dust. I sniffed the room, inhaling the sour smell I'd assumed was my own sweat-laden panic, but it was only the white vinegar Vero used to cut grime when she tidied up.

Something loosened inside me as I trailed a finger over the squeaky-clean surface of my desk. It was a relief, having someone around to balance the load. A comfort to have someone to handle the bills and help me clean up my messes, rather than rubbing my face in them. The house felt too quiet without Vero and the children. Too empty with all of them gone for the night.

I opened the top drawer of my desk, ready to burn Irina Borovkov's note. But it was gone, too. Vero must have put it in the disposal in her panic last night. The only loose paper in the drawer was the one with

Julian's number on it. I took it out and held it, remembering Vero's warning. She told me it would be stupid to call him, but then again, she hadn't tossed his number in the sink.

Julian would know if the police had come snooping around the bar, looking for Harris's car. And he might have noticed if a black Lincoln Town Car had followed me out of the parking lot that night.

Before I could change my mind, I dialed his number into the new prepaid phone I'd bought at the pharmacy earlier that morning. The call connected on its fourth ring, and my heart did an anxious flip.

"Hello?" The answering voice was deep, rough with sleep. I considered hanging up. "Whoever you are, I'm already awake. You might as well start talking." Definitely Julian. And definitely not happy. The clock on my computer said it was already past noon, but if he'd worked last night, he probably hadn't gone to bed before three. "If you don't say something, I'm hanging up."

"It's Theresa." The name rushed out on a held breath.

"Hey," he said after a beat of silence. There was a rustling in the background. An image of him in a pair of clingy pajama pants and very little else parked itself front and center in my mind, completely unbidden. "Did you change your number? You came up as 'unavailable' on my phone."

No, I am definitely available. It's stupid, how available I am. "Yeah," I said, shaking that thought from my mind. "There was an unfortunate incident involving a garbage disposal."

"Sorry to hear it." The words seemed to curl around a sleepy smile. "I'm glad you were able to salvage my number."

God, I probably sounded desperate. "I'm sorry. I completely forgot you work nights. I shouldn't have called so early, but . . ." But what? I hadn't considered what I would actually say if he answered. I couldn't come out and ask him if anyone had come to the bar asking questions about Harris, or if anyone had followed me out of the lot that night. Not without piquing his curiosity. And if I was really being honest with myself, I wasn't even sure that was the only reason I'd called.

I shut my eyes and leaned my head against the wall. "The truth is, I've had a really, really crappy week, and I just needed to talk. Has anyone ever told you you're really approachable?" His laughter chipped away at some of the tension in my shoulders. I sagged, feeling ridiculous for bothering him. "You know what, that probably sounds crazy, and I should probably just hang up now—"

"No," he said, "it's not crazy." A lazy Saturday morning softness returned to his voice. "I was actually kind of hoping you would call." In the silence that followed, I pictured him lying on his back, one arm folded behind his head, his honey-blond curls falling over his eyes. "I was worried about you."

"You were?" I sat up straight, determined to ignore the flutter in my stomach.

"Yeah, I was wondering if you made it home okay. Did you get your alternator checked?"

I blew out a sigh as I remembered the battery. "Not yet," I confessed. "But I will. Thanks for your help the other day."

"I was just glad for the chance to see you again."

A reluctant smile pulled at my cheeks. "I'm sorry I couldn't stay longer."

"I was hoping you'd stop by the bar last night, but it's probably for the best that you didn't. The place was nuts. We wouldn't have had much time to talk."

"Oh?" The hair on the back of my neck prickled at the sudden shift in his tone. "Nuts how?"

"There's some police investigation going on. A detective came by. He kept pulling the waitstaff off the floor to ask questions. I was in the weeds all night."

"What happened?"

"Some guy's wife reported him missing. He was at the networking event on Tuesday night and no one's heard from him since."

"Really?" I swallowed. "Did the detective . . . talk to you?"

"He was mostly interested in talking to the waitstaff who worked the floor, but the waiter who served the guy was off last night, and the rest of us were too busy to remember much." A relieved breath rushed out of me. It caught in my throat when he said, "One of the busboys remembered seeing him leave the bar with a blond woman in a black dress."

I drew my knees to my chest, hugging them tight. "Oh?"

"I told the cop I could count at least two dozen blond women in black dresses at The Lush on any given night. But the only one that stood out in my mind was you."

"Me?" I asked around the knot in my throat. "Why me?"

"Aside from the fact that you're beautiful and easy to talk to?"

A nervous laugh broke free. "Did you . . . What did you tell him about me?"

"Only that I bumped into you in the parking lot as you were leaving. And that, try as I might to persuade you otherwise, I saw you get into your car alone." My head thunked against my knee. Good. This was good. Julian wasn't a witness. He was an alibi.

An alibi who thought I was beautiful. And easy to talk to. And possibly wanted to date me.

I'm sure Vero would agree it would be smart to keep the lines of communication open, right?

"So, you thought I stood out?" I asked, picking at a loose thread in my sock.

"Without question."

"Did anyone else in the bar . . . you know . . . stand out to you?"

"No one else ordered a Bloody Mary at nine o'clock at night, if that's what you mean." His laugh was soft, disarming, unwinding something inside me until a laugh bubbled out of me, too.

"You didn't . . . by any chance . . . happen to notice if anyone followed me when I left . . . did you?"

"No." Julian's silence was tinged with concern. "Why? Did something happen?"

"No, no, it's fine," I said quickly. Of course he hadn't noticed. He'd probably already gone, while I'd lingered in the parking lot those few extra moments to call Patricia. And now he probably thought I was paranoid and clingy. I raked my hair from my face, surprised he couldn't hear the rush of blood to my cheeks through the phone.

"Seriously, Theresa." I loved the way he said my name, low and close, like we were in the same room. And I hated that the name he was whispering wasn't mine. "Bloody Mary aside, I haven't been able to stop thinking about you. So, to get back to your original question, yeah, I'm really glad you called. And if you want to know the truth, I'm still a little worried about you."

I bit my lip, wishing I could take back so many things. Wishing I could start the week all over.

"You want to tell me all about your crappy week? I'm a bartender, which makes me highly qualified to listen."

"No," I said through a weary smile, wishing I could. "I'm better now. Thanks." I was surprised by how true it felt. All I needed to do was plan a birthday party and not kill anyone else. Simple, right?

"I'm here if you change your mind. And I'd still like to take you out sometime."

Sometime . . . when I wasn't hiding from the police and the mafia. When I wasn't pretending to be someone else.

"Maybe I could call you again," I said, "when things aren't so complicated."

"Anytime." Something in his voice made me think he really meant it. And I wondered if they still gave you one phone call from jail.

CHAPTER 20

My cell phone rang as I stuffed the last of the goodie bags. My mother's name flashed on the screen, and I considered not picking up. Zach was running circles through the kitchen, his diaper hanging low, a ribbon of orange streamer hanging from the crack of his butt like a tail. Delia and her friends chased after him, ordering him to "sit" and "stay."

"Hi, Mom. It's kind of a bad time." I wedged the phone between my ear and my shoulder while I poured bags of pretzels and Gold-fish crackers into serving bowls. My house was already crawling with kids. I just hoped Vero made it home with the pizzas soon.

"I won't keep you. Your father and I are having cocktails on the Promenade Deck at five. I've always wanted to say that." She tittered. My parents were celebrating their fortieth anniversary on a cruise ship somewhere in the Mediterranean. "Let me talk to the birthday girl."

I grabbed Delia by the back of the shirt as she scurried by. The doorbell rang. I pressed the phone to my chest and counted heads.

All the girls Delia had invited were already here. I'd been expecting Steven nearly an hour ago, but he never bothered to announce himself; he usually just barged in.

The doorbell rang again. My feet were rooted in place. What if it was the police? What if they came to arrest me during my daughter's birthday party? Or worse, what if it was Andrei and Feliks?

"Aren't you going to answer the door, Mommy?" Delia asked.

I thrust my cell in her hands. "Here, talk to Grandma. She called to wish you happy birthday."

Wiping Goldfish cracker crumbs on my jeans, I crept to the door and peered around the curtain just as the boy on the other side stood on his tiptoes and reached for the bell a third time. Relief washed over me. I threw open the door and flung a hand over the buzzer, my nerves fried. "Hi, Toby. What are you doing here?" Toby's dad was a friend of Steven's, but Toby and Delia weren't close. He hadn't been on the guest list, which had consisted entirely of girls.

Toby shrugged. A gift bag dangled from one hand, and he swiped at his snotty nose with the other. He gestured down the street toward his father's house. "My dad heard Delia was having a party. He dropped me off. He had somewhere to go." Toby walked under my arm into the foyer. "He said I could eat lunch here." Toby spent weekends with his dad. And his dad spent most of those weekends stealing time with his new girlfriend, pawning Toby off on his neighbors and friends. I didn't have the heart to turn him away.

"The pizza and cake will be here soon. But there are crackers and pretzels in the kitchen if you're hungry."

"I'm gluten-intolerant," he said, dropping Delia's present on the floor and helping himself to the bag of party favors I'd been stuffing.

"Of course you are." I felt a headache coming on. I turned to shut the door and slammed face-first into a brightly colored box. I backed up to make room as Steven carried it into the house, his face obscured by the huge pink bow on top. Theresa followed him, her heels clacking on the hardwood, her outfit decidedly dressy for a five-year-old's birthday party. "What's this?" I asked Steven.

"It's Delia's present," he said, loud enough to draw her attention as he set it on the floor beside Toby's gift bag. Delia whirled, thrusting my phone at me as she sprinted across the kitchen into his arms. I uttered a quick good-bye to my mother and disconnected. Steven brushed back Delia's spikes, kissing her forehead before setting her down. My headache sharpened when Delia ran to hug Theresa next.

"Thanks for coming," I said, determined to take the higher road, even though he was almost an hour late. It could be worse. He could have chosen not to come at all.

"Wouldn't miss it," he said. Theresa looped her arm around Steven's. She smiled tightly at the balloons and streamers, her disapproving gaze landing everywhere but my face.

"And thanks for letting us have her party here." My gratitude stuck in my throat. Having the party here had been Theresa's idea. The kids technically belonged to Steven on the weekends, but she didn't dare risk having a horde of feral five-year-olds trash her tidy house, and Steven had balked at the rental fees to have it someplace else. I pasted on a pleasant smile. "Is Aunt Amy coming? Delia was hoping she'd be here."

"No," Theresa said without looking at me. "Amy was busy."

"We can't stay," Steven said. "We're having lunch with a developer in Leesburg. We'll swing by on our way home to pick up Delia and Zach. I just wanted to bring her present. I thought maybe she could open it now before we go."

Before I could open my mouth to argue, Steven had wrangled Delia and her friends, assembling an audience in front of the gaudy box that took up the breadth of my foyer. Theresa and I stood awkwardly beside each other in the small envelope of space that was left. She made a show of checking her messages on her phone, her fat diamond engagement ring on full display as she scrolled. We'd exchanged hardly more than a few words since the Panera incident. Unless you counted our testimony in court about the Play-Doh incident a few months ago.

"Delia sees right through you," I said. "She's five, not stupid."

Theresa raised an eyebrow. "I guess her powers of perception didn't come from her mother."

"Nice."

"If the shoe fits." She glanced down at my sneakers as if she'd never be caught dead wearing the same ones.

"You can't buy Delia's loyalty."

"Maybe not," she said, examining her nails, "but I can buy her a decent haircut."

Theresa hadn't looked at me once since she'd walked into my house. Maybe it was guilt, but I doubted it. She'd looked me dead in the eyes the day Steven told me he was moving out, hungry to record the precise moment of my emotional demise. She'd practically gloated the day he put that ring on her finger. Shame wasn't a color that existed in Theresa's wardrobe. So what was she hiding now? "Why are you doing this? You don't even like children."

"Because having the children with us will make Steven happy." Her red lips pressed into a tight, thin line. So that was it. Steven wasn't happy. And that bothered her, enough to sacrifice her pristine white carpets and her bustling social life. This was the dark mess in her closet, the secret she was hiding from their families and friends.

"Taking my kids won't fix your relationship. But why stop with my husband, right?" Theresa shifted on her designer heels. She checked the time on her phone, pretending she hadn't heard me. "You know, I was willing to let Steven go without a fight, but not my children."

"Why don't you have your attorney call mine. Oh, wait," she said, thoughtfully tapping a nail to her chin. "I forgot. You don't have one."

The blow hit low. Vero was right. I needed a lawyer who could compete with Guy. An old lawyer. A rich lawyer. I needed a fifty-thousand-dollar lawyer. "I won't make this easy for you."

"You already have." She whirled on me, her fiery green eyes narrowing on mine. "I don't like this arrangement any more than you do, Finlay. Who do you think is going to end up mothering your children when you're not able to do it anymore? If you loved your kids as much as you say you do, maybe you'd be nicer to me."

My mouth fell open. Delia squealed as she managed to untangle the bow from the box and tear her gift from the paper. She gasped, the puppy on her wish list all but forgotten. The Barbie Dreamhouse was three stories high, just like Theresa's town house. "We'll take it to your room at Theresa's," Steven told her, hefting the box. "You can play with it tonight when you get home."

Delia chased him to the door, clambering for one last look at it. The small plush dog I'd bought and gift wrapped for her suddenly seemed pathetic, a token of something she wanted that I couldn't afford. Theresa was right. I had made this easy for them. And if I went to prison, Steven and Theresa were the only parents my children would have left.

I jumped as a car door slammed in the garage. Delia raced to the kitchen to meet Vero, who'd be walking in any moment with the pizzas. Steven hurried out the front door, ushering Theresa in front of him, anxious to be gone. "Make sure the kids are packed and ready by five. I'll be back for them after the party," he called over his shoulder. The front door closed just as Vero came in through the kitchen, a mountain of pizza boxes stacked in her arms.

That night, after Steven had picked up the kids, I sat on my front stoop, the cold from the concrete seeping through my socks as I stared after the shrinking taillights of his truck. The kids would only be gone one night. They'd be home again tomorrow, and they were only a few blocks away, but I hated how easily he swooped in, took what he wanted, and left. I hated how unfair it was, and how nobody else seemed to notice or care.

That had always been Steven's MO. He'd always been smooth, quick to cover his tracks. Like today, when he'd slipped into Delia's birthday party an hour late, accomplished exactly what he wanted, and slipped right out again before Vero ever laid eyes on him, without Delia even noticing he'd left. His sense of timing was impeccable, his shell game unerring. He'd been screwing Theresa for weeks behind my back. If Mrs. Haggerty hadn't seen him and spilled the beans, I might never have known what they had been—

I lifted my chin from my hands. Across the street, Mrs. Haggerty's curtain flashed closed. I got up and crossed the road, heading straight for her door. If anyone had seen two strangers sneaking around in my garage the night Harris Mickler died—if anyone could stand up for me as a witness and prove I was telling the truth—it would be the neighborhood busybody. I banged on the NEIGHBORHOOD WATCH sticker on the glass.

"Mrs. Haggerty?" I called through it. "I need to speak with you!" I pressed my ear to the door, certain she was listening on the other side. I banged again, harder this time. "Mrs. Haggerty! Will you please open the door? It's important." Her TV was on. A muted laugh track of some evening sitcom played in the background. "Fine," I muttered, finally giving up.

This was all Steven's fault. After she'd blown the whistle on his affair with Theresa, he'd called her an old hag and told her to mind her own damn business. I hadn't been much kinder once I'd heard how far and wide the rumors of his affair had spread. She'd refused to speak to either of us since.

I shuffled back across the street in my socks, my feet numb by the time I reached my front door. I closed myself inside, leaning back against it, waiting for the feeling to return to my toes as I thought about Mrs. Haggerty.

Between the time I had arrived home with Harris and the time Vero had let herself in through the front door, someone had snuck into my garage without Vero or me noticing. Mrs. Haggerty was the president of the neighborhood watch. If she had seen anything suspicious, she would have called the police to report it before we'd even stuffed Harris in the trunk. But the police never came, so I could safely assume she hadn't seen much.

So how did the killers get past Mrs. Haggerty without her noticing?

Vero and I had surprised each other that night because she'd come in through a different door. And Steven had missed Vero entirely at the party for the same reason. What if the killers had parked down the street and snuck through the neighbors' backyards, approaching my garage from the back?

The more I thought about it, the less it all made sense. Andrei and Feliks didn't seem like the types who'd sneak around. Andrei Borovkov had slashed up three men and left them bleeding out on a warehouse floor. He hadn't gone to the effort to clean up and didn't seem concerned about concealing his crime. Why bother? Georgia said nothing would stick to them anyway. Clearly, they'd had no problem bribing their way to a mistrial. So why frame a suburban mother of two for a bloodless, quiet crime? If they'd wanted Harris dead, why not slash his throat and leave him on the floor of my garage?

No, this MO felt cowardly. The killers never had to touch the body. Never had to shed blood. They didn't even have to be present at the moment when Harris's life left him. This didn't feel like the work of two shameless violent criminals. I was willing to bet the killers had never done anything like this before. The timing of the whole thing felt opportunistic. Or impulsive.

But clearly, *something* had been planned. They'd staked him out at the bar, then stalked us to my house. They'd waited until he was unconscious and vulnerable to strike, just like . . .

Just like Harris had with each of his victims.

My back stiffened against the door. Maybe the MO wasn't impulsive.

What if it was deeply personal?

I ran upstairs to my office, past Vero's closed door, where she was cramming for her midterm finals. I opened my desk drawer and unfolded Harris's bank statement.

There had been twelve deposits on the first of the month.

And there had been thirteen numbered files on Harris's cell phone—twelve containing photos of his previous victims, plus the one I'd doused with tomato juice in the bathroom.

Do exactly as I said, and be discreet, or I'll show these photos to your husband and tell him what you've done.

Twelve deposits, two thousand dollars each, on the first of every month.

What if the deposits hadn't been embezzled from Feliks Zhirov? What if they'd been hush payments? What if he'd been extorting them for money?

I skimmed the payments again, certain I was right. Two thousand dollars was a small sum for a high earner in these close-in suburbs of DC, an amount that might easily go unnoticed if a man's wife quietly wired it from her personal spending account. Harris had been making a small fortune off of his victims—an amount that was probably growing every month, with every new woman he exploited—threatening them with photos, convincing them he would tell their spouses they'd been unfaithful if they didn't comply with his demands. And why wouldn't they? The photos painted a very different picture than the reality of what had been done to them. And they probably had no memory of their night with Harris to support their own account of what happened after the drugs had knocked them out.

Every single one of those women had a deeply personal motive for wanting Harris dead. And the MO felt like a perfect fit. But which one had actually done it?

Harris's phone was probably already in the hands of a police detective by now. Without it, there'd be no easy way for me to trace the deposits back to individual accounts, but there might be a way to figure out who these women were and narrow down the list.

I grabbed a piece of paper from the printer, jotting down as many of those twelve first names as I could remember. Then I opened my browser and searched for Harris's social networking group. Clicking on the membership page, I pulled up a roster. More than seven hundred thumbnail images filled the screen.

It was going to be a very long night.

CHAPTER 21

My mother had assured me when Steven and I first married that some dishes were impossible to screw up. Theoretically, no one should need a recipe to throw together a decent chicken soup or a simple meat loaf, but certain things about motherhood had always eluded me and cooking had been one of them. Apparently, marriage had been the other.

The pan in the oven was bubbling, browning at the edges. I cracked the oven door and gave it a cautious sniff. I'd found the casserole recipe online—which was more than I could say about my search for Harris's victims—and the fact that I already had all the ingredients in my kitchen had felt like a small victory.

My search last night hadn't gone as well as I'd hoped. With only first names and physical descriptions to go on, I'd spent hours combing individual profiles, narrowing possibilities. Some, I'd felt certain I'd managed to identify. And after a bit of hunting and pecking through other social media pages, I was able to weed them out as possible culprits. Some had moved. One was in the hospital.

Some had posted photos of other family activities or events they'd attended that night. But a handful of names still eluded me. More than a few had deleted their networking profiles from the Facebook group altogether, which had made them impossible to find.

I set the table, put a load of clothes in the wash, made the beds, and scooped a mountain of toys off the living room floor. I'd given Vero the day off for her midterm exams and had spent the day scrubbing cake frosting stains out of the carpet, researching the names of Harris's possible victims, and catching up on chores.

A car door slammed in the garage. I looked up from the dishwasher as Vero blew into the kitchen, dropped her purse on the counter, and kicked off a pair of black stilettos. I stacked a few clean dishes on my arm and set them on the table, taking in her sharp tailored suit and crisp white collar, her sleek French twist, and her bloodred lipstick. These were not Monday-afternoon-community-college clothes. These were not even Monday-hot-lunch-date clothes. These were high-dollar-accounting-firm-job-interview clothes. And a small part of me worried about where Vero had been all afternoon.

We hadn't really talked since the day before Delia's party. I hadn't even had a chance to ask her about her date. I'd recapped my conversation with Theresa as we'd cleaned up after the party. Then we'd eaten cold pizza for dinner, Vero had studied for her exam, and I had shut myself in my office to write.

"How was your midterm?" I asked, hoping she wasn't about to give me her notice and tell me she'd found a better job. One that came with health insurance and paid sick days and didn't involve diapers. Or corpses.

She shrugged, peeling off her sunglasses as she wrinkled her nose. "What's that smell?" She cracked open the oven and peered inside.

"Tuna casserole."

She fanned at the billow of smoke that poured out. "Is it supposed to be black?"

Vero leapt aside as I flung open the oven door and ran to open the windows before the smoke alarms blared to life. I was standing on a kitchen chair, waving a dish towel at the detector on the ceiling, when Vero reached in her purse and slapped a brick of cash on the counter. "I'm not eating that. We're ordering takeout."

I dropped the towel, nearly falling off the chair as I gaped at the thick stack of hundred-dollar bills. I scrambled down to shut the windows and snap the curtains closed. "What is that?" I asked, jabbing a finger at the money.

"That," Vero said, "is thirty-seven thousand and five hundred dollars minus forty percent. You can buy me dinner to thank me."

"For what?"

"For meeting with Irina Borovkov and collecting half of our money up front." Every ounce of breath left my lungs. My knees buckled, and I slid down onto the chair I'd been standing on. "Finn? Finlay, what's wrong?" Vero kicked the leg of my seat, and I swung my gaze up to meet hers.

"Do you have *any* idea who that woman's husband is?" My voice was eerily quiet, disproportionately small compared to the depth of my panic.

Vero turned her back on me with a dismissive wave. She opened the refrigerator. "Sure. Irina told me all about him. The guy sounds like bad news. I'm pretty sure we can do this with a clean conscience." Irina, Vero had called her, as if they were already old friends.

"Vero," I said in a tightly controlled voice. "Andrei Borovkov is an enforcer for the Russian mob. He murders people for a living.

He cuts people's throats. Like those three men they found in that warehouse in Herndon over the summer."

"Like I said. Bad news. I'm sure there will be plenty of people who . . ." Vero closed the refrigerator. She turned to face me, knuckles white around her Coke. "Wait. Run that by me again. I might have misheard that last part."

I buried my head in my hands. "We were supposed to be severing ties, getting rid of every scrap of evidence! Do you have any idea what this means?"

I jumped out of my skin as Vero popped the top on her Coke can. She set the can down hard on the table, snatched up the money, and waved it at me. "It means you can afford a decent divorce lawyer and hold on to your kids. That's what this means!"

I stared at her, dumbstruck. Last night, I'd told Vero every word Theresa had said, about how they were buying Delia's affection and I had no money left for an attorney. About how Theresa was going to take my children from me, even though she didn't want them. All that time, I'd been fussing about Steven and his damn Dreamhouse when I should have been telling Vero what I'd learned about Andrei Borovkov.

"We are not taking this money!" I said, shoving it back at her. We'd paid all my debts. I was finally right-side up. As long as I didn't do anything stupid, I stood a better chance at holding on to Delia and Zach. "You're going to call that woman right now and you're going to tell her it was all a misunderstanding. Then you're going to give her the money back."

"I can't do that."

"Why not?"

"Because I spent some of it."

"How much?"

"Forty percent."

My tongue stuck to the roof of my mouth as I did the math in my head. "You spent fifteen *thousand* dollars in one afternoon?" She nodded, looking contrite as she hunched over her Coke. "On what?"

Vero sat up, her voice rising as she pointed a finger at me. "*You* were the one who said we should get rid of every speck of evidence! So I did."

"What does that mean?"

"It means there was a corpse in the trunk of my Honda! I've watched every episode of *CSI,* and you know there's no way to cover that up." Vero cast me a guilty look through the thick coat of mascara on her lashes. "So I sold my car to my cousin Ramón for parts."

"And . . . ?"

"And I bought a new one."

I got up and threw open the garage door, blinded by gleaming graphite curves and sleek silver pipes the second I turned on the light. The Charger looked wildly obscene parked beside my mini-van. A dealership sales sticker was still taped to the back window, obscuring my view of the two child safety seats buckled behind it. "What is that?"

Vero wrung her hands. "A 6.2-liter V8 . . . with a really big trunk?"

I slammed the door.

Vero headed for the liquor cabinet. "I think we're going to need something stronger."

I opened my mouth to swear at her in at least five languages I hadn't learned yet when the house phone rang. Vero and I both went still. We stared at it as it rang again. No one ever called the house phone except telemarketers or groups soliciting donations. Groups like our local order of police.

Vero took a slow step back from it. "Who do you think it is?"

Part of me hoped it was Andrei Borovkov, just so I could tell Vero I told you so. I steeled myself as I reached for the phone. "Hello?"

"Finlay, where the hell have you been? I've been trying to reach you for three days! Why haven't you been answering your cell phone?" My shoulders sagged at the sound of Sylvia's voice.

"I know, I'm sorry," I said, sliding into a chair and massaging a temple. I couldn't deal with a lecture from my agent right now. She'd emailed me on Friday afternoon for an update on my manuscript, and I'd closed the email without bothering to reply. "My cell phone died. I have a new one. I'm sorry, Syl, it's been a crazy couple of days. I'll email you the number."

"Your editor wants to know where you are with the book. I tried putting her off to give you more time, but she's demanding to see what you have so far."

"What? No!" I sputtered. "I can't send anything." All I had was Harris's story. Even with the names changed, it teetered far too close to the truth. It'd be too risky to send it. "It's a mess. I haven't even proofread it. It's nowhere near ready."

"I'll tell you what's a mess! You are in breach of your contract. Do you understand what that means? They can cancel your next book and call back your advance. You have to send me something. Anything. How much do you have?"

"Not enough."

"Finlay." Jesus, she sounded like my mother.

"Okay, okay. I've got a few chapters I can send you." She was going to hate it anyway. But at least she could tell my editor I'd tried. "It's not the project we talked about, but it's all I have."

"How much?"

"I don't know. Maybe twenty thousand words?"

"Get it to me now."

"I'll send it to you tonight."

"No, Finlay. *Now.* I'm not hanging up this phone until I see it in my in-box."

I tucked the cordless under my chin and carried it upstairs. All I wanted was to get Sylvia off the phone so I could figure out what to do about Andrei Borovkov, the cash in my kitchen, and the fifteen thousand dollars of mob money that was now parked in my garage.

Without bothering to fill in the subject line, I sent the file to Sylvia. "There, are you happy now?"

Sylvia's nails clicked against her keyboard as she grumbled, "I'd be *happy* if you weren't three months behind on your deadline. I'd be *happy* if I hadn't spent the last two days leaving you unreturned voice mails. I'd be *happy* if Gordon Ramsay showed up in my apartment and insisted on making me dinner tonight. But this," she said through a deflated sigh, "will have to do. Give me your new cell."

I pulled the prepaid phone from my pocket and rattled off the number.

"I'll give this a read and see if I can use it to buy you more time. Meanwhile, get your butt in that chair and start typing or you can kiss your advance good-bye."

"Thanks, Sy—" There was an abrupt click as she disconnected.

I leaned on the desk, my hands planted on either side of the keyboard, my head hanging over it. I was going to be dropped by my agent. And then by my publisher. What I had sent to Sylvia was hardly intelligible. I wasn't even sure it was a coherent story. Thankfully, Harris's and Patricia's disappearances hadn't made national news. My agent and editor lived in New York. Still, I prayed like hell I had remembered to change all the names before sending it out.

Who was I kidding? My writing was terrible. Sylvia probably wouldn't make it through chapter two before she kicked it back to me and told me to start over.

I drew in a slow breath. The entire house smelled like burned tuna and cheese and my stomach growled. Feeling hollow, I trudged back downstairs and found Vero sitting at the kitchen table, her head braced on her hands, a shot glass beside the open bottle of bourbon we'd started drinking the night we buried Harris. I wasn't sure how much we'd have left by the end of the night.

She filled the shot glass and pushed it toward me. It burned going down. My eyes watered as I stared at the stack of money. At least if my editor dropped me, I'd have a way to pay back the advance I owed my publisher.

Three weeks . . . I had three weeks to finish a book and find a way out of this.

I peeled a fifty off the stack.

"Subs or Chinese?" I asked Vero. "Even killers have to eat, right?"

CHAPTER 22

The animal shelter parking lot was packed on Tuesday after school, so I grabbed the last available spot along the road, making sure to leave plenty of room between the front of my van and the car parked in front of me in case the van decided not to start and I had to call for a tow. Julian was right. I needed to get it looked at, but if I took it to a mechanic, they were going to find a laundry list of problems—the alignment was off, it was overdue for a tune-up (or two), the brake pads were shot, the transmission was rocky, I was late for a state-mandated emissions test, and I could probably use a few new tires. For now, I was throwing up a prayer and a swear every time I turned the key. It was cheaper.

"We could have taken your car," I grumbled at Vero.

"Nu-uh. My car is a pet-free zone." Vero hefted Zach from his car seat, I grabbed Delia's hand, and we crossed the street to the shelter.

"We're only looking. We're not bringing one home."

"Why not?" Delia huffed. "Daddy said we could have a dog when we go live with him."

"Did he?" I muttered. Considering the shade of Theresa's immaculate carpets, I guessed she hadn't been around when Steven had dangled that little carrot in front of our daughter. "Then why don't we make Daddy a list of the ones you like the best?"

A clamor of barks and whines assaulted us as we neared the high perimeter fence. Zach covered his ears and burrowed into Vero's shoulder. I let go of Delia to swing open the heavy door. The reception area wasn't much quieter. The plexiglass viewing window hardly muted the torrent of barking on the other side of the desk. A woman sat in front of her computer playing solitaire, and I peeked past her, through the window into the kennels, searching for familiar faces from Patricia's photos.

"Hello?" The attendant dragged her attention from the screen. "My children and I are interested in adopting a dog," I said. "We were wondering if we could look around."

"Sure. But don't let the children put their hands inside the enclosures. The hinges are self-closing and they might get pinched. If you see a dog you like, let me know, and I'll have a staff member set up a visitation room for you."

She pressed a button under her desk. The sound of the buzzer made me shudder. All the plexiglass and bars felt a little too much like the ones where Georgia worked. All I wanted was to find a clue to Patricia's whereabouts—to find her before the police or the mafia managed to—so I could figure out who killed Harris, find proof of my innocence, and go home.

Dogs stood on their hind legs against the sides of their kennels to bark at us as we shuffled the kids into the deafening room. I could hardly hear Delia's squeals of delight as she hopped from door to door inspecting each dog. She paused, kneeling in front of one of the enclosures.

The dog huddling in the back corner of the cage was small with shaggy tangles and eyes as aching and desperate as my daughter's.

"Would you like to pet him?" asked a voice behind us.

"Can I, Mommy?" she asked with a pleading look as the young volunteer knelt beside her. He fished a set of keys from his pocket. He was gangly and tall, with unruly curls and watery blue eyes. I recognized him immediately from the team photo on Patricia's Facebook page. HELLO. MY NAME IS AARON was printed on his name tag.

"Sure," I said, "if Aaron says it's all right." Vero and I locked eyes over his head. She must have recognized him from Patricia's Facebook photos, too.

Delia clapped as he thumbed through his ring of keys and unlocked the crate. The dog whimpered, curling deeper into his enclosure as Aaron slipped the leather belt from the loops around his waist. Careful not to startle the dog, he wedged it into the hinge, propping the kennel door open. Then he reached inside his pocket and put a dog treat in Delia's hand. He sat on the floor, patting the space beside him. She sat quietly, following Aaron's lead, holding the treat out in front of her.

"This one's special," he said, his voice little more than a whisper over the howls and yelps from the other cages. "His name's Sam. He's a little shy, so we have to be really gentle with him and help him feel safe. Can you do that?"

Delia nodded.

The dog's nostrils fluttered out from the shadow of his kennel. He dipped his head, inching forward, his ears pulled flat and his tail tucked between his legs. Aaron whispered to Delia, encouraging her to be patient. That the dog would come to her when he knew it was safe.

Delia sucked in a shallow breath when the dog finally poked his head from the crate, his nose extended toward the treat. Slowly, he approached her, taking it gently in his mouth. Distracted by the chewy morsel, he didn't object when Aaron lifted him and settled him in Delia's arms.

Zach started to fuss, reaching for the cages. Vero bounced him on her hip, giving me a pointed look as she carried him away, jutting her chin toward Aaron as she wandered from view.

"What happened to Sam?" I asked, noting the small cast on the dog's hind leg.

"Sam was a rescue." Aaron smiled as he watched Delia stroke Sam's back. "I found him about a few weeks ago, caught up in his own chains. Sam's sweet. He's just a little anxious. Nothing a loving home won't fix. Rescues make great companions." He reached for the clipboard hanging beside him on the wall. "Speaking of which, we ask all of our adopting families to fill out an application." He passed me the clipboard and a pen.

While Delia played with Sam, I stared awkwardly at the questionnaire. The last thing I wanted was a record of my visit here, but it might seem suspicious if I refused. Aaron smiled politely, trying not to be obvious as he checked the time on his phone.

I started filling out the form, putting Theresa's and Steven's names and address in the blanks. It seemed fitting, since getting a dog had been Steven's idea, and he'd promised Delia it could live with them.

Delia giggled at my feet as Sam showered her with kisses, eager for another treat. She cooed in the dog's ear, fussing over his injuries.

No wonder Patricia spent so much time here. It probably made her feel good to care for these animals who had been abandoned or unloved or saved from horrible owners. It probably felt safe to be around people like Aaron, who were gentle and kind, after being chained to a man like Harris for half her life. If this shelter was her safe place, and these people she worked with were the closest thing she had to a family, wouldn't she have confided in someone here?

I handed the form back to Aaron. "Last time we visited, I spoke with a woman named Patricia about a particular dog—it had a black spot around its eye and mottled fur, about this big," I said, gesturing with my arms as I described the dog I'd seen her holding in the photo.

"You mean Pirate?"

"Yes! That was his name. I don't see him here. Do you have a number where I can reach her to ask about him?"

"No, I wish I did," he said, his face falling. "We've all tried calling her. Patricia didn't come in last week, and no one's heard from her since. As for Pirate, he and his sister, Molly, were adopted together a few weeks ago. I'm sorry."

"Oh, that's a shame," I said, scrambling for a new angle. "I'd really like to get in touch with her. Patricia said she had a great Pilates instructor, but I lost the name of the club she belonged to."

Aaron shrugged, his cheeks going pink as he skimmed my application. "Sorry, I wouldn't know. Pilates isn't really my thing. And she never mentioned anything about a club."

"Was she friends with anyone else who might know where I can find her?"

He looked askance at me. "I don't think so. The police have already asked everyone else."

"The police?" I asked, feigning surprise. "Why would the police be looking for her?"

He frowned. "It was on the news. Patricia and her husband are missing. No one knows where she is."

"Oh, I'm sorry to hear that." It wasn't hard to look upset by the news. If she hadn't talked to anyone here, this was just one more dead end. "Do the police have any leads?"

"They didn't say. A detective searched her locker. He asked a lot of questions. I told him she'd been anxious and a little jumpy the last few shifts, but she never mentioned anything about going anywhere. Mostly, they wanted to know about her husband. A few of us . . ." His weak jaw clenched. He cast an anxious glance around us and lowered his voice. "A few of us think she might not have had the best relationship with him. He sounded like a real dick." Someone called Aaron's name. He rose up on his toes, searching over my head. He lifted a finger to them, indicating he'd be right there.

"I should probably put Sam away," Aaron said, his frown lingering as he bent to extricate the dog from Delia's hands and return Sam to his crate. "Did you want to see any other dogs while you're here?"

"Sure," I said, catching Vero's eye across the room. "We'll look around a little more if you don't mind." Vero walked briskly toward us, accidentally bumping into Aaron as he threaded his belt through the loops of his pants. They exchanged hurried apologies. As soon as he turned the corner I asked, "What did you find?"

"There's an employee lounge in the back," she said quietly. "The door's unlocked. I poked my head in, but there are a few volunteers hanging out in there."

"What did you see?"

"Every employee has a locker with their name on it."

"Did Patricia have one?"

Vero nodded. "It's worth a try." Maybe there was something in Patricia's locker that would give us a clue to where she was. But how would we open it without being seen?

"We can't exactly waltz in and snoop around."

"Leave that to me." Vero waved Aaron's key ring in front of me.

"Where did you get those?"

"Slipped them off his belt loop just now. He didn't feel a thing." She dumped Zach in my arms. "Meet me in front of the lounge."

"When?"

"You'll know." She slunk off into the rows of cages. I followed Delia from kennel to kennel, eyes peeled for Vero's sign, unsure exactly what I was looking for.

A sudden high-pitched yowl erupted, followed by the slam of a crate door. A cacophony of shrill barks ripped through the shelter as two cats tore down the center aisle, tails flared and backs arched. Another slam. Four dogs barreled in their wake, teeth bared and jaws snapping in pursuit. Children wailed and parents shrieked as the animals flew past. Zach burrowed into my shoulder. Delia didn't object when I reached for her hand and hurried her down the aisle toward the lounge as the last of the volunteers rushed out to wrangle the loose animals.

Vero waved me along faster, scooping Zach from my arms. "Hurry, the room's empty, but I don't know for how long." She checked to make sure no one was looking, then shoved me inside, the sounds of shrieking cats and howling dogs muffling as the door fell closed. I made a beeline for the row of lockers, searching the names until I found Patricia's. If there had been a lock, it was gone now. Which meant Aaron was right, the police had already searched it.

The metal door clanged open, rustling the yellow police tape stretched across the opening. The inside of her locker door was covered with animal photos—mostly of Pirate and Molly. A business card was stuck in the corner: Detective Nicholas Anthony, Fairfax County Police Department. He was probably the detective assigned to Patricia Mickler's case.

Careful not to disturb the police tape, I rummaged through the contents of her locker, pulling back a sweatshirt from its hanger. The navy fabric was layered in black and white dog hair, obscuring the Tysons Fitness Club logo on the front. The shelf above it contained a rolling sticky brush, a receipt for dog food, and one for a couple of coffees from Starbucks. Unless the police had discovered something I hadn't, there was nothing here to suggest where Patricia had gone.

I shut the locker, scanning the lounge for anything Vero or I might have missed. Brightly colored thumbtacks dotted the bulletin board by the door. Team photos and work schedules. Patricia was on the Tuesday/Thursday team along with Aaron and a handful of others. She sat close beside him in the photo, wearing the same gym sweatshirt I'd seen in her locker, with Pirate and Molly perched on their laps. I leaned closer to the photo, my gaze narrowing on her hand. Her ring finger was naked, her diamond-encrusted wedding band noticeably absent.

A commotion rose from the kennels. I cracked open the door and peered out. A few yards away, Vero was distracting two volunteers in shelter uniforms. Her eyebrows rose, her expression urgent as I slipped out of the lounge.

"Mrs. Hall? Mrs. Hall?" A voice called over the barking dogs.

"Theresa!" Louder this time. I turned. Aaron was rushing down the aisle toward me, looking flustered, and I realized with a start he was talking to me. "You haven't by any chance seen a set of keys, have you? I must have dropped them in all the commotion."

I shook my head, my hands reaching instinctively to a phantom itch in my hair. I never should have written Theresa's name and address on that form. The police had already been here, I reassured myself. They'd already searched Patricia's locker and questioned everyone. And yet, I couldn't shake the feeling I'd made a terrible mistake coming here. "Sorry, I haven't found any keys."

My skin prickled with regret as an orange tabby darted between us, and Aaron took off after it.

CHAPTER 23

I shot bolt upright in bed, eyes wide and blinking, roused from sleep by a sudden loud buzz. This was it. They were coming to arrest me. I started, clutching my blankets to my chest as my cell phone vibrated across the nightstand. Sylvia's number glowed in the dark. I fell back against my pillow, waiting for my heart to slow. Not the police. Just my agent.

I reached blindly for my phone and checked the time, unsure if it was quarter to six in the morning or at night. I'd stayed awake for most of the last three nights, working through the list of Harris's victims, determined to figure out who'd killed him, and I'd still only managed to narrow the list from seventeen possible suspects to nine. Exhausted and no closer to solving the crime, I'd quit and fallen into bed an hour before dawn.

"Hello?" I grumbled into the phone.

"I hope you sound tired because you've been writing all day." Night then. I rubbed my eyes. "Are you sitting down?"

"Not exactly."

"I read your manuscript." I threw an arm over my face and braced for the worst. "I sent it to your editor last night. She's prepared to make you an offer."

I sat up slowly, my mind groping for a scrap of sense. "An offer? But I'm already under contract for the book."

"Not anymore."

I clapped a hand over my eyes. This was worse than I'd thought. The offer was probably a re-payment plan. Not only had I lost my contract, but I'd have to return the advance. And Sylvia's commission. And then she would probably drop me as a client. I didn't even want to think about what Steven would say when he found out. "Sylvia, I'm sorry. Isn't there anything we can—"

"I told her I was buying you out of your contract."

I shook my head, certain I'd misheard. "You did what?"

"I told her I knew this book was going to be a huge breakout hit, and they weren't paying you enough for it. I told her I would personally pay back your advance, and I wanted your rights back."

I flipped on the lamp in case I was still sleeping. My watering eyes narrowed against the light. "What did she say?"

"She read your draft. And she agrees with me. She thinks you're on to something big with this one."

"She does?"

"It's a fabulous setup—the timid wife hiring someone to kill her horrible husband, the plucky heroine and the hot young lawyer . . . They have great chemistry on the page, by the way. I mean, it's sizzling, Finn. Your best work yet. I'm dying to see who the killer is."

A dark chuckle slipped past my lips. "Me, too."

"Your editor's offering a preempt if you promise not to take it anywhere else. She'll increase your offer to two books, raise your advance, and give you an extension to finish the draft."

"Raise my advance? To how much?"

"Seventy-five thousand per book." I'm pretty sure my jaw was somewhere in my lap. My editor was going to pay me one hundred and fifty thousand dollars. For the story of Harris Mickler's murder. In which I'd described every detail of the crime. Which was currently under investigation, and which I was secretly a party to. "Finn? Are you there?"

"I'm here," I croaked. "Can I have a few days to think about it?"

"Believe me, Finn." Sylvia's voice was honeyed butter. "I know exactly how you feel. The same thought crossed my mind."

I choked back a slightly hysterical laugh. "I seriously doubt that."

"I get it. I do. And you're right. The pitch is strong enough that we could probably buy out the contract, take the manuscript to a few other big-name editors, and maybe it would go to auction. But this is a bird in the hand, Finlay. And with your crappy sales record, we probably shouldn't get too cocky. I say we take the money and give them what they want."

"I don't know, Syl—"

"Excellent, I'm glad we're in agreement."

"It's not that simple! I can't just—" Through the phone, I heard the swooshing sound of her computer sending an email. A moment later, a notification beeped on my phone.

"I'm sending you the revised terms, and I negotiated a few extras for you. Your editor thinks you should go out under a new pen name. We're thinking Fiona Donahue has a nice ring to it. I told her you were thrilled. She's already sent it to her people, and we should have the revised contract and the balance of your advance in a few weeks. You've got thirty days to get her a draft, so get to work. I'll call you in a few days to check in."

Sylvia disconnected. Numb, I fell back against the pillows.

Suddenly, I was rolling in money. More money than I ever could have imagined. Enough for a full-time sitter and a pricey attorney. Enough to fix my car, and, most important, save my kids. Enough to get Steven and Theresa off my back.

I didn't know which was worse. That I was actually proud of myself for the first time in my life, or that every single penny I'd earned could put me in prison for the rest of it.

I was still hungover the next morning when Steven came to pick up the kids. Vero had insisted on celebrating the sale of the book over a bottle of champagne after Delia and Zach had gone to sleep, and there hadn't been a drop left when we'd finished. She'd been so excited (and drunk) she hadn't even minded when I told her I was going to contact Irina Borovkov and arrange to give back the advance. The champagne fog was the only explanation for the fact that I didn't hear Steven slide his key into the lock and let himself in. By the time I made it downstairs, he was already stuffing Delia and Zach into their coats. I intercepted them, stealing quick hugs that made my insides ache.

"The doorbell works, you know." I glared at Steven over the heads of our children.

"It's cold outside and I didn't feel like waiting." He opened the door for Delia and Zach, nudging them through it. "Go out and wait in Daddy's truck with Theresa and Aunt Amy. I'll be there in a minute." We both clamped down our arguments as they waddled out in their puffy coats.

"It's my house, Steven," I said as soon as the door closed behind them. "You can't just barge in anytime you feel like it."

"Sure I can. My name's on the deed."

Vero appeared in the opening to the kitchen behind him. She reached around him, snatched the keys from his hand, and promptly began unwinding my house key from the ring. Steven's mouth fell open as she popped it off with a flourish. She carried it to the powder room, opened the door, and dropped it in the Diaper Genie with a satisfied smirk. His face turned a hideous shade of red as she turned the crank, making a poop sausage of his only copy of my key.

"What the hell is she doing here?" he hissed at me as she wiped her hands together and closed the lid. "I told you I'm not paying for your babysitter."

"I happen to be Ms. Donovan's accountant and business manager," Vero interrupted, cocking a hip. "And your rent is already in the mail."

"Not all of it," Steven said smugly.

"All of it," Vero fired back. "And let's get something straight, Landlordy McLandlord. Just because your name is on the deed, it doesn't give you the right to bust in here anytime you feel like it. Maybe you should read your rental agreement, specifically paragraph four, clause b, which explicitly states you have to notify your tenant of your intent to enter the property. Next time you come waltzing in here unannounced, you might accidentally walk in on something you wished you hadn't seen."

"Like what?"

Please don't say a corpse. Please don't say a corpse.

"Like Finlay's hot new underwear model boyfriend."

Steven's eyes flew wide. I pinched Vero in the elbow.

"He's not an underwear model," I said.

"He just looks like one—"

"And he's not my—"

"He's really an attorney," she finished. I felt a headache coming

on. Or maybe that was the hangover. "I suggest next time you ad-
here to the terms of your lease, or I might have to hire him to provide Ms. Donovan with his full range of services." Vero let her eyes
trail down Steven's body, unimpressed. "And if you have a problem
with that, you can stick it up your arrogant, cheating—"

I pressed my fingers into my temple. "Vero is living with us, Steven." Steven's attention snapped to me, his face a mask of disbelief.
Before he could open his mouth to speak, I said, "*I'm* paying her."

"*You're* paying her?"

"Let's just say neither one of us was happy with your terms."

Silence fell like a hammer. Vero batted her eyelashes at him
with a closed-lipped triumphant smile. A vein bulged in Steven's
forehead.

"Paying her with what?" he asked, looking at us like we'd both
lost our minds. "You have no money, Finn. You're months behind
on all of your bills. There's no way you can afford that."

"Ms. Donovan has *plenty* of money," Vero quipped. "And matters of her financial solvency, beyond the rent she no longer owes
you, are none of your concern."

"What is she talking about?"

I glared at Vero. She scrutinized her manicure, picking at the
polish as she pretended not to notice. Steven had me penned in. I
had to tell him something, or he'd take his burning questions about
my assets straight to Guy. "I sold a book."

"Two books," Vero corrected me. A lump formed in my throat
at the pride I saw in her fierce dark eyes. No one had ever treated my
job as . . . well . . . a job. No one had ever defended it, been proud of
it, boasted about it. It had always been me, alone behind my desk.

"So what'd that get you? Three thousand dollars?" Steven's lip
curled, the implication dripping so thickly with sarcasm I could

have lubed my van with it. "What about the maxed-out credit cards? And the van payments? And her . . ." he said, hooking a thumb to Vero. "She must be costing you—"

"Ms. Donovan's revenue is *also* none of your business," Vero said, getting up in his face.

"Bullshit!" Steven glared down at her as he pointed at me. "There is no possible way she made enough money from those crappy books to pay down all that debt." The blow hit me square in the chest. It knocked me back with the same suffocating shame I'd felt every time I opened an advance check in front of him. He'd placate me with a pat on the back, making backhanded remarks about how we might have enough to pay for a few boxes of diapers, or, if we were lucky, maybe some groceries. He gesticulated behind him to the front porch, where all the unopened mail had been stacked. "Those bills have been piling up for months. She owes me a lot more than . . ." His face fell. His forehead creased and his arm sagged, his eyes swinging through the house like searchlights. "Where are the bills?" He shouldered his way past us into the kitchen and rifled through the thin stack of leaflets and coupons on the counter with Vero tight on his heels. I could hear them bickering as I bounded up the stairs to my office.

I was done being belittled and made to feel like what I did wasn't important. That I couldn't take care of myself or our children. I was done being made to feel like I didn't belong on the top shelf with people like Steven and Theresa. I opened my email, shoved a piece of paper in the printer, and silently cursed Steven as it started humming. When it finished, I snatched the paper off the tray and stormed downstairs, where Vero and Steven were nose to nose, ready to claw each other's faces off.

I reached between them, slamming the paper down on the table.

Vero eased back and folded her arms, the painted edge of her smile so sharp it was practically cutting as she raised her eyebrow at Steven, daring him to look at it.

"What's this?" he asked, reluctant to pick it up.

"My offer letter. You want to know what my crappy books are worth? See for yourself."

Steven swiped the paper off the table. His blue eyes skimmed it like a laser, and I felt a flutter of satisfaction when they burned a hole through the dollar sign somewhere in the middle.

"What's that number?" he asked.

"That's the amount of my advance."

His mouth moved, but his tongue was slow to follow. It might have been the first time I'd ever seen him speechless. He handed it back to me as he cleared his throat. "It's about time they paid you a reasonable wage. But it's still not enough to—"

"Keep reading," Vero said, shoving it back in his face. "It's a two-book deal. She makes double that, plus extra when she sells media, film options, and translation rights. That's all *before* she collects her *royalties*. Do you want to do the math, or would you like me to help you with that?"

Steven dropped the offer on the table. He glared at Vero and shouldered past her for the door. He didn't look at me. Maybe because he couldn't. He hadn't been able to see me as anything other than a failure in years. It was as if he had forgotten how to see me as anything else.

"I'll be back on Sunday with the kids," he mumbled.

"Ring the doorbell next time," Vero called after him.

He flipped her off without bothering to look back, and his dismissal of her pissed me off more than all the rest of it.

"Steven." The command in my own tone surprised me. His feet

paused just before the door. "You and Theresa might want to reconsider your custody suit. According to my accountant, we have the resources to fight it."

The stubble on Steven's jaw worked. He threw open the front door and slammed it behind him.

Vero put a hand on my shoulder as I watched Steven go. I heard the steps creak under her as she headed up to her room. "Why did you do it?" I asked.

She paused. "Do what?"

"That night. With Harris. You could have left me in the garage. Why did you bury him with me?"

Vero shrugged. "I liked your odds." At my puzzled look, she said, "I did the math when you first hired me. I needed to know what I'd sacrificed that bank job for. As far as I can figure, your chances of landing an agent were about ten thousand to one. And your odds of landing a book deal were even worse. Somehow, you'd managed to pull off both. Getting away with murder had to be easier than that, right?" She started back up the stairs, then paused again, turning to look at me over her shoulder. "My mom was a single mother. She was resourceful and gutsy . . . like you. If I had to pick a partner to stake my future earnings on—and maybe my freedom," she added with a wry smile, "I figured it was a safe bet to put my money on you." She retreated up the stairs to her room, and for the first time in a long time, I knew when I sat down in front of a blank screen later that night, I wouldn't be facing it alone.

CHAPTER 24

"What do we do with it?" I asked on Sunday afternoon as I held the bag up to my eye.

"He's not an *it*. He has a name," Delia said. I bit back all the arguments swimming up my throat. If we named it, it was more than a fish. It was a pet. And my track record for keeping things alive these last few weeks wasn't exactly stellar. "His name is Christopher."

"Christopher? Seriously?"

With a scowl, she reached to snatch away the bag, and I held it out of reach. "Daddy liked it."

"Christopher is a lovely name," I conceded. "I was just thinking he looks exactly like a Christopher. Christopher's parents must be very proud."

Vero smirked at me from the hallway, one shoulder leaning against the doorframe of Delia's room, her body language daring me not to kill it.

I unwound the rubber band and poured Christopher into the glass punch bowl—a forgotten wedding-day relic from Steven's

grandmother that I'd dug out of a box in the garage. Delia put
her face close to the glass, her forehead creased with worry as she
watched Christopher wobble and list to one side, his bulging eyes
wide and his mouth gulping. Great, it wouldn't be the first creature
I'd starved for oxygen within minutes of bringing it home. At least
this one would be easier to bury.

With a bright orange shimmy of scales, Christopher rallied. Zach
squealed as the fish zipped around in circles inside the glass bowl.

The doorbell rang downstairs. "I'll get it," I told Vero. "Steven
must have forgotten something." She rolled her eyes. "Hey, at least
he used the doorbell this time."

"Some animals can be trained." She followed me down the
stairs. My feet dug into the bottom step when I caught a glimpse
of the car in the driveway through the window. A plain, navy-blue
Chevy sedan, with several antennas on the trunk lid and a dome
light on the dashboard, was parked in front of my house.

Not Steven.

Vero slammed into my back, nearly knocking me down the last
step. She swore, falling silent as she followed my line of sight to the
figure standing with his back to the front door. Tall, dark hair, broad
shoulders. He even stood like a cop, feet spread to shoulder width apart
and his hands planted on his hips. He looked up and down the street
before turning slowly toward the door. As he did, his sidearm peeked
from the holster inside his jacket and a badge glinted at his belt.

"Shit, shit, shit." Vero moved around my frozen body and tiptoed into the kitchen, peering through the slit in the curtains. "Oh
shit, oh shit, oh shit," she whispered. "What do we do?"

The house closed in around me until all I could see was the cop
on the other side of the window. My options narrowed with it, and
I was seized by a sudden clarity. "We're going to answer the door," I

said with a forced calm, "and we're not going to say anything without an attorney. If he's here to arrest me, you're going to stay here
with Delia and Zach. Then you're going to call my sister and tell her
to meet me at booking and bail me out."

Vero paled. Nodded.

I moved to the door and commanded my hands to stop shaking
as I twisted the knob.

The door cracked open. The plainclothes officer on the other
side smiled.

"Jesus, he's hot," Vero said over my shoulder.

I threw an elbow into her ribs. Cleared my throat. "Can I help
you, Officer?"

A deep dimple cut into his five o'clock shadow. He extended a
hand, forcing me to open the door wider to shake it.

"My name's Detective Nick Anthony and I'm with the Fairfax County police. I'm looking for Finlay Donovan." My knees
threatened to buckle, and I held fast to the door. The officer's brow
creased. "If it's a bad time, I could come back." His voice had the
rough edges of someone who spent his days barking orders, but his
dark eyes were soft under thick, long lashes, and my name had come
out more like a question than an order.

"I'm Finlay," I said cautiously, looking behind him for his partner. If he was here to arrest me on suspicion of murder, he probably
hadn't come alone.

His hesitant smile warmed, stretching to the sun-deepened
creases around his eyes. "I'm a friend of your sister's. I'm working a
case you might be interested in, and Georgia thought it might be a
good idea if I talk to you."

"Me? Why me?" I asked, my body half-hidden by the door as
Vero listened behind it.

The detective scratched the back of his head, his smile becoming almost sheepish. "I hit a wall, and she thought you might be able to help me." He glanced over his shoulder at Mrs. Haggerty's window. "Mind if I come in?"

He wasn't flashing a warrant or reading me my Miranda rights. It didn't seem like he was here to arrest me. I held open the door, hoping it wasn't a mistake. "Sure. Okay."

Vero raised an eyebrow, appraising his long legs as they stepped into the foyer. I jerked my chin toward the stairs, but she shook her head. Detective Anthony stopped short when he saw her. "I'm sorry. I didn't realize you had company. I probably should have called first." He hitched a thumb at the door. "I can come back later—"

"No," Vero and I said at the same time. If he walked out now, I'd spend the rest of the day panicking over why he'd come here in the first place. Better to get this over with and rip it off like a Band-Aid.

"This is Vero, my nanny—"

"Accountant," Vero interjected, shaking his hand.

"Vero lives with us. And she was just going upstairs." I threw her a pointed look. "We can talk in here," I said, steering Detective Anthony into the kitchen. "Can I get you something to drink? Coffee, soda, or anything?"

"Soda would be great." He slid off his windbreaker as I opened the fridge. I watched him over the refrigerator door. A brown leather holster crisscrossed his back, and the black grip of his gun seemed to point at me as he took a seat at my table.

My throat bobbed with my hard swallow. "So . . . Detective Anthony—"

"Please, call me Nick."

"Nick." If he was here to arrest me, he wouldn't be so informal, right? And he probably wouldn't be smiling. Or maybe he would. My sister said some cops were assholes that way. "You know Georgia?" Ice rattled in the glass as I set his Coke on the table in front of him.

"Yeah, we were in the Academy together years ago." He didn't look much older than my sister. The thick stubble coating his jaw was free of gray, and dark hair peppered the corded muscles of his forearms below the rolled sleeves of his Henley. "We go out for beers once in a while. So you're the writer. She's told me a lot about you. You and the kids."

I casually pulled my chair a few inches farther away before I sat down, keeping some distance between us. "Really?"

"Don't worry. It's all good."

I choked on a nervous laugh. He laughed, too. But I felt his keen eyes taking in every detail of me, and it made me squirm a little. "So . . . you're working a case?"

Color rushed into his cheeks, that single deep dimple making another unexpected appearance. "Yeah, right. The case. I feel a little odd about this," he said almost shyly, "but Georgia insisted you wouldn't mind. She thought maybe we could help each other."

My suspicion shifted direction. Maybe this had nothing to do with Harris or Patricia. It wouldn't be the first time Georgia had tried to set me up with one of her friends from work. I glanced at his left hand as he reached for his soda. No wedding ring. No suspicious tan line where one should have been. I narrowed my eyes at him. "Help each other how?"

"It's a missing persons case. You might have seen it on the news. The couple who went missing from Arlington—Harris and Patricia Mickler?"

My mouth went dry. The floor creaked at the top of the stairs in the hall where Vero must have been listening. "I think I may have seen something about it."

"I don't have any leads on the wife yet, but we know the husband disappeared from a bar in McLean twelve days ago. We found his car in the parking lot, along with his wallet and phone. Apparently, he met a woman for drinks, but she had some kind of an emergency and ended up in the bathroom for a while. A waiter remembered seeing him leave with someone else. We believe we've been able to identify her."

Ice trailed down my spine. "You have?"

He nodded. "She was a member of a social media group that Harris was part of. He was at the bar for some kind of networking event. The woman never RSVP'd or confirmed her attendance on-line, but the name of the woman at the bar matches the one on the social media group profile, and she fits the description given to us by the waitstaff."

A shaky sigh of relief slipped out of me. They had a suspect. And it wasn't me. "So what does any of this have to do with me?"

"That's where things get a little weird." He set down his drink, trailing a line of condensation with his thumb. "I'm not saying she's a suspect. But she's definitely a person of interest in the case." His dark eyes lifted to mine. "We think Harris Mickler may have left the bar with your ex-husband's fiancée, Theresa Hall."

I knocked over my glass, soda spreading over the surface of the table. The detective and I jumped up at the same time, both of us reaching for the napkins in the holder. I grabbed a wad of them, muttering apologies, my hands shaking as I mopped up the mess.

What had I done?

I braced myself against the table. Nick reached to steady me as I sank into my chair.

I'd told Julian my name was Theresa. I'd told him I was in real estate. I'd been wearing a blond wig and Theresa's black dress. I hadn't even looked to see if I recognized anyone else on the networking event page when I'd vetted Harris. There had been seven hundred members in that group. Even this week, I'd only been searching the roster for names that matched the ones I'd seen on Harris's phone.

"Are you sure?" I asked. "I mean, that isn't much to go on."

"If that was all I had to go on, no. But Harris's cell phone pinged a tower later that night, within a three-mile radius of her house."

No. Not from Theresa's house. From here. Harris's phone pinged from my garage. Right down the street from Steven and Theresa's town house.

"Have you talked to her?" I heard myself ask.

"I caught up to her at her office this morning. She vehemently denied that she was at the bar that night. A bartender there remembered serving a woman meeting her description. He gave us her first name and said she was a real estate agent, but he never asked for her ID, so we can't confirm it's actually her. All the evidence we have is circumstantial at this point, but it's piling pretty high, and Theresa has no verifiable alibi for the night Harris disappeared."

"What do you mean?" Theresa wasn't at the bar that night. I'd combed every inch of that place looking for Harris. If she'd been there, I would have seen her.

"Wherever she was, she doesn't want to tell me. She's insisting she was home alone. And your husb—" Nick corrected himself. "Steven says he was out entertaining clients. He can't confirm she was home that evening."

"That doesn't mean she wasn't." I couldn't believe I was actually defending her. But the woman was about to become my children's stepmother and she was dangerously close to being charged with a felony.

He gave an emphatic shake of his head. "I'm telling you, Finlay. I've been doing this a long time, and I'm pretty good at reading people. Theresa was definitely hiding something. She was so nervous she was practically tripping over herself."

"You're a cop," I said, gesturing to his gun. "Cops make people nervous. And even if she had been at the bar, what possible reason would she have for kidnapping Harris?"

"That's where I'm stuck." Nick scrubbed a hand over his stubble. There was a weary edge to his voice when he said, "We found some photos on Mickler's phone. He'd taken pictures of himself with dozens of women, some of them of an . . . intimate nature, and we suspect some of them may not have been taken with the women's consent." I schooled my face into a neutral expression, careful not to let on that I already knew. But Theresa hadn't been in any of those photos. I'd made myself look at every single one, terrified I'd see someone I knew. "About a year ago, a woman called the tip line at the FCPD. She claimed she'd been drugged and sexually assaulted after meeting Harris for drinks."

"Who was she?" I asked, trying not to sound anxious. "Did she give her name?"

"The tip line's anonymous. The operator tried to talk the woman into coming in and filing a report, but the woman said Harris threatened to tell her husband they were seeing each other. She said he would ruin her marriage if she ever came forward. Given all the pics on the guy's phone, it's likely he's a serial offender. Who knows how many women might be out there, wanting to get even with a guy like that? I'd thought maybe Theresa was one of them, but she wasn't in any of the photos on his cell, and with the exception of the networking group they were members of, I can't find any other common thread connecting her to Harris. If I can't come up with a motive, the investigation's dead in the water."

"I still don't understand what any of this has to do with me."

He raked the dark waves of his hair from his eyes, rubbing them as if he hadn't slept in a week. "I probably shouldn't have said anything. And I wouldn't have. Except I was unloading all this on Georgia over a few beers last night. I had no idea she even knew Theresa. Then she mentioned your custody case. She said there was no love lost between you and Theresa, and she thought maybe if I asked you, you might know something."

A cold sliver of unease poked at the edge of my mind. "What are you asking me to do?"

He reached in his pocket and slid his business card over the table toward me. "I know Theresa's hiding something. If you can help me figure out what it is, maybe I can gather enough evidence to bring her in. And if I'm right, and she was actually involved with Mickler, then it seems to me like that might help you, too."

"Help me how?"

"If Theresa's arrested on suspicion of murder, your ex-husband's attorney would probably advise him to let go of the custody fight."

"Murder? I thought you said Harris was missing," I said cautiously.

Nick laced his hands together, leaving the card untouched on the table between us. "He's been gone more than a week. So has his wife. There's been no ransom call, and no activity on their accounts. Like I said, I've been doing this for a long time." He let the implication hang in the silence that followed.

I picked up Nick's business card, trailing a finger over the pointed edges. It would be far too easy to frame Theresa for my own crime and let her take the fall for it. Maybe Theresa did deserve to lose her future husband and family. After all, she'd had no qualms about stealing mine. But no matter how I felt about her, she was going to be Steven's wife—my children's stepmother. She might have done a lot of terrible things, but kidnapping Harris wasn't one of them.

I'd been the one to put Theresa in the spotlight, even if I hadn't intended to. I'd used her name and worn her clothes. I'd crossed a lot of lines these last two weeks, but if I let Nick arrest her for my mistakes, what kind of monster did that make me?

This. This had to be the line I wasn't willing to cross. I couldn't bring Harris back from the dead, but maybe I could keep someone else from paying the price.

I held Nick's card to my chest. "I'll do some digging and see what I can find."

CHAPTER 25

"This was a terrible idea." Between the flashing lights and screaming kids and blaring video games, I was one Whac-A-Mole away from a migraine. I had made the mistake of letting my sister choose the destination for our monthly lunch date. I'm guessing this animatronic house of horrors appealed to her because it didn't require her to keep Zach entertained for an hour while he was strapped like a sanitarium patient to a high chair. At least here, we could let him loose to run.

"Driver's choice," Georgia reminded me, brushing a grease stain from her shirt with a wad of paper napkins.

"Easy for you to say," I said absently, checking the time on my phone. Still no messages from Vero. That couldn't be good. "You've got the keys to the getaway vehicle."

When the van hadn't started that morning, I'd given Vero my keys and asked her to call her cousin Ramón to have it towed to his shop. On the way home, she was supposed to stop by the bank and take out a loan for the fifteen thousand dollars we were now short to pay back Andrei Borovkov's wife—or sell the car. She'd opted for the loan. Vero was supposed to then arrange to meet Mrs. Borovkov, gracefully back us out of the deal, and return the advance Irina had paid us. I, for one, would feel much better once the woman's blood money was out of my house.

"The kids are having fun. And you said you wanted pizza." The sirens and lights didn't seem to bother Georgia at all. She folded a greasy slice into her mouth while I tried to keep one eye on Delia and Zach in the climbing structure that wound above our heads. "How's the book research coming along?"

"Is that why you sent Nick to my house? So I'd have somebody else to bug with all my weird questions?"

"I sent him to your house," she said around a mouthful of pizza, "because Steven's fiancée is a person of interest in a high-profile missing persons investigation, and I don't like the idea of my niece and nephew spending too much time over there until we figure out how Theresa's involved."

"So you sent Nick to keep an eye on me?"

She washed that down with a mouthful of soda. "Let's just say Nick volunteered."

I slumped back in my bench. "Great, so now I have a babysitter."

"He's not a babysitter. He's a detective. And a damn good one," she said, pointing her straw at me. "And since you both have a vested interest in making sure Theresa's not a felon, I figured you could help each other out."

"Is that all?"

"Consider it a favor to me, if it'll make you feel better."

"Since when do I owe you any favors?"

"Since I babysat two weeks ago." I opened my mouth to argue but closed it at Georgia's withering look.

"Nick's partner's going to be stuck in the hospital for a while.

The big C," she added solemnly. "Nick's lonely. He could use the company." My sister had always been a terrible liar.

"So this is a setup."

She shrugged. "He's a nice guy, Finn. He's single, he's honest, and he's gainfully employed." She licked pizza grease off her fingers. "Cops get good health care and retirement, you know."

"I don't need a babysitter *or* a husband. I'm doing just fine." Georgia wore her skepticism like a favorite shirt. I jutted my chin at her. "What about you? When are you going to find yourself a wife? It's been like a decade since you went out on a date, and you don't hear me giving you grief about it."

"Don't be hyperbolic. It hasn't been a decade." I raised an eyebrow as she shoveled the last of her pizza in her mouth, tapping a finger against my crossed arms as she chewed. She pushed herself back in her bench and wiped her hands. "It's been eighteen months, if you must know. And I don't need a wife. I have my own retirement and health care. You, on the other hand—"

"Seriously, Georgia. I'm fine."

"How fine?"

"I got a book deal." Georgia made a face. She bumped her fist against her chest, releasing a soft belch. "Nice. Keep doing that in public and it'll be a decade before you know it."

Georgia rolled her eyes. "I thought you already had a book deal." I'd had plenty of book deals before, and after Sylvia took her commission and Uncle Sam took his cut, there'd hardly been enough left to buy dinner and a decent pedicure.

"I got a better one."

She took a long, disinterested sip of her soda. "Yeah? How much?"

"A hundred fifty thousand for two books."

Georgia's mouth fell open. A dribble of grease slipped down her chin. "Shut the fuck up."

"I'm serious. I've got less than thirty days to get a draft to Sylvia, and I don't have time to entertain your friend on his wild goose chase."

Georgia smacked the table. "Holy shit, Finn! You did it!" I shrank in my seat as the mom in an adjoining booth turned to scowl at us. "I can't believe it. That night you asked me to watch the kids, I figured you just wanted a night to yourself. I didn't think you were actually working or anything."

"Thanks for your vote of confidence."

She crumpled her napkin and tossed it at me. "I mean it, Finn. I'm seriously proud of you." She was. I could see it in the shine in her eyes. The last time Georgia had looked at me that way was the day Zach was born. And Delia before that. It was the same way my parents had looked at Georgia when she'd graduated from the police academy, and with every promotion she'd earned since. My throat burned with bittersweet pride, and I hid it behind a long sip of soda. I had finally written a worthwhile story and it would probably land me behind bars. "Have you called Mom and Dad to tell them the news yet?"

I shook my head, fidgeting with my straw. "You know how they feel about it." It was fine to have a hobby when I was married, my mother had said. But after Steven had left, they were both very clear that writing books was an irresponsible career choice. They'd been pushing me to get a government job ever since.

Georgia leaned over the table and lowered her voice. "Now that you've got some serious money coming in, maybe you can get Steven and Theresa off your back about the custody stuff. With any luck, you and Nick will figure out where she was that night. Maybe that'll put an end to it."

I choked back a mirthless laugh. Oh, it would definitely put an end to it. If Nick followed the bread crumbs and found Harris's body, I'd be lucky to see my kids ever again.

I shook my head. "Theresa may have done a lot of shitty things, but I honestly don't think this is one of them. Innocent until proven guilty, right?"

Georgia sucked a tooth. "If she wasn't at the bar that night, she's got nothing to hide."

Nothing to hide. Except the shovel in her shed, the search history on her laptop, and the body buried in her fiancé's sod farm. Theresa was treading thin ice, and she didn't even know it. All she needed to prove her innocence was a solid alibi for the night Harris disappeared. Which meant all I had to do to keep her out of prison was figure out where she'd been that night.

The navy-blue sedan parked in my driveway was suspiciously non-descript. Similar to Detective Anthony's, with fewer antennae and a little more rust. A ripple of anxiety shot through me.

"You expecting someone?" Georgia asked, pulling in behind it after lunch.

"Probably one of Vero's friends. Thanks for the ride. I'll call you later."

I fished the kids out of the back seat and punched in the code for the garage door. Vero's Charger was there, but my van was gone.

Vero sat at the kitchen table eating the last of the Oreo cookies from the bag. Zach took off like a bullet to the playroom, peeling out of his coat as he ran. I picked Delia's off the floor and slung it over a chair, waiting until they were safely out of the room before asking, "Where's the van?"

She glanced at me over her glass of milk. "Ramón's waiting on some parts. He gave you a loaner until they come in."

My pent-up anxiety slipped out on a long, tired breath. "That was nice of him. So what's the bad news?" I sat across from her as she pushed a receipt across the table.

"It needs a lot of work."

I skimmed the invoice. The only surprising thing on it was the bottom line. "Ouch."

She sucked down the last dregs of her milk and set down her glass with a dispirited sigh, as if she wished she'd dunked her cookies in something stronger. "The good news is that we won't have any problem paying him." Vero got up and fished a fat zip-lock bag from the freezer. She dropped it on the table with an icy thunk.

The hair on my arms stood on end. "What's that?" The contents of the bag were rectangular and green, and I was pretty sure it wasn't frozen spinach.

"I met with Irina. I tried to explain. I told her that we made a mistake—that we didn't realize who her husband was. I told her the job was too dangerous and we were returning the advance. She thought it was a ploy to renegotiate and get more money out of her since we figured out who Andrei works for and how much he's worth. So she doubled the amount of the offer and refused to take no for an answer."

I sank into a chair, the room wobbling. "No. No, no, no, no, no!" I pressed my fingers into my temples and shook my head. Vero's voice rose over the screams in the back of my mind, that this could not actually be happening.

"I tried, I swear, Finlay! I practically shoved the money in her hand, but she wouldn't take it. She says she doesn't care how you do it, but she wants it done. Soon."

I lowered my voice so the children wouldn't hear. "Andrei Borovkov is a cold-blooded *professional* murderer! Have you googled him? He was arrested last year for burning a man alive! Six months ago, he was charged with dismembering some guy in a parking lot and shooting all the witnesses, execution-style. And let's not forget the three men found with their throats slashed in a warehouse in July!"

"He wasn't convicted of any of them," she said defensively. "Maybe he's not as dangerous as he sounds."

"He got off because someone mishandled evidence, Vero! Because Feliks Zhirov has cops in his pocket! How the hell am I supposed to kill an enforcer for the mob?"

"I asked Irina the same thing. She said you'll come up with something. You just need the right motivation." Vero's complexion turned a little green, her dry lips speckled with Oreo crumbs.

"And what's that?" I snapped. "More money?"

"Not exactly."

She stared numbly at the empty package of Oreos, and a cold dread settled in the pit of my stomach. "What kind of motivation?"

"We take care of her husband in the next two weeks, or . . ." Vero's throat bobbed with her hard swallow.

"Or what?"

Her eyes shimmered with fear as they lifted to mine. "Or Irina will tell her husband we stole the money. And then she'll send him to find us."

CHAPTER 26

There was only one thing to do about Irina Borovkov, and that was to talk with her face-to-face like adults. No more middlemen. No more disguises. No more envelopes full of cash. I would simply explain that Patricia had been mistaken when she'd hired me, that I was not who she thought I was. Then I would explain that I hadn't killed Harris Mickler—that someone else had broken into my garage and done the actual killing part—and therefore, I was not qualified (or willing) to assassinate her problem husband.

And then?

Then I would do the most adult thing of all. I would throw the backpack full of cash at her and run before she had a chance to stop me. Possession was nine-tenths of the law. I wasn't sure whose law, or if the mafia even cared about the law. But math was math, no matter who was holding the calculator. If I didn't have Irina Borovkov's money, she'd have no leverage against me for robbing her and she wouldn't send her scary husband to slit my throat.

The parking lot of the Tysons Fitness Club was packed with

cars, all shiny and imported, with monthly payments that probably amounted to more than the mortgage on my house. I parked
Ramón's loaner between an Audi and a Porsche, careful not to ding
anyone's door as I eased myself out. The rusted sedan stuck out like a
sore thumb. Apparently, I did, too. My knuckles were white around
the strap of Delia's Disney Princess backpack as I walked to the front
desk. This had to be the right club. The name and logo matched the
one on the sweatshirt in Patricia's locker at the shelter, but this place
didn't feel like it fit Patricia Mickler at all. The inside of the fitness
club was swanky as hell, with a juice bar in the lobby, a courtyard
with a fountain, and long, bright corridors lit by tinted glass ceil-
ings. I couldn't picture Patricia walking down those halls wearing
a plastic smile and a tennis skirt, but based on Vero's description of
Andrei's wife, I could definitely picture Irina Borovkov here.

The woman waiting in line behind me made a sound like a
snort. I glanced over my shoulder and caught her staring at my backpack. Then at my hair and my sneakers. I hoisted Delia's pack higher
on my shoulder, ignoring the titters and stares of the women who
passed the desk. If they knew how much money was in that Disney
Princess bag, or what I'd done to get it, they wouldn't be smirking
so hard.

"May I help you?" The perky young receptionist wore a lot of
makeup and a logo-emblazoned polo. A fingerprint reader glowed
red on the counter.

"I hope so," I said, eying the scanner warily. "I'm interested in
taking a Pilates class. Your instructor was recommended to me by a
friend—Irina Borovkov? I called earlier and the receptionist mentioned there was a class starting at ten. I'd like to try it out and see
if I like it before joining." I'd watched a Pilates video that morning,

and Vero was right. You really could learn anything on YouTube. I could totally pull this off. "Do you know if Irina is here?"

"Reenie? Sure, she just got here. But she's taking a Spin class today. It starts in ten minutes. Would you like me to page her for you?" She reached for her desk phone.

I rushed to stop her before she could pick it up. "No, no, it's fine!" The element of surprise was probably the more sensible approach here. After all, what would I ask the woman to say? *Attention, Mrs. Borovkov. The contract killer you hired is in the lobby to see you.* I plastered on a smile. "I'll just catch up to her in class, thanks."

"Will you be needing shoes?"

I glanced down at my sneakers. Shook my head.

"Great, I just need you to fill out these health and safety waivers for me. When you're done, I'll need a quick scan of your finger. Then the women's locker room is down the hall to your right, and the trainers on the floor can show you where to find the class."

"Thank you." I took the clipboard, scribbling a fake name and address in the blanks as she greeted the next person in line. While her back was turned, I ditched the clipboard on the counter and hurried to the locker rooms before she could ask for my fingerprint.

I kept my head down, only glancing up to peek into the workout rooms, eyes peeled for the sleek, dark hair and surgically sculpted face that matched Vero's description of Irina.

A crowd of women gathered in a long hallway flanked by brightly lit racquetball courts. One by one, they filtered into a training room. I caught a flash of raven hair among them and hurried to catch up. Irina's money bounced against my back as I wedged myself into the line for the Spinning room.

I merged into the flow of traffic, careful not to step on anyone's feet. They were all wearing the same black shoes, like bowling slippers with Velcro and cleats. My white sneakers stood out starkly in contrast, as out of place as Delia's backpack.

I followed the herd into a dark, square room where rows of stationary bikes were illuminated by purple lightbulbs that dangled from the trendy exposed ductwork in the ceiling. The women around me each claimed a bike. They climbed on, adjusting their seats and snapping their water bottles into holders, talking animatedly as they stretched in their stirrups.

The instructor perched on a bike in the center of the room, testing the volume of the microphone that dangled from the headset around her ears. I caught the flash of Irina's onyx hair as she leaned to buckle her shoes into the pedals. Her ponytail glowed violet under the black lights as the room dimmed, and I rushed to the open bike beside her as the music started.

"Is this one taken?" A techno beat blared through the speakers on the wall behind me. I raised my voice over the music and asked again.

Irina glanced up at me. She shook her head and smiled placidly, her brows rising when she caught sight of my bright white shoes. She didn't look at my face again, showing no sign of recognition. This was good. A dark room, lots of people, loud music. She wouldn't get a good look at me, and we probably wouldn't be overheard.

I planted my feet in the stirrups, my neon-white shoes beginning to move in lazy circles as I pedaled. Watching Irina out of the corner of my eye, I mimicked her movements. This wasn't so hard, I thought to myself as the instructor called out a series of commands to the group.

The class rose in unison, pushing up in their stirrups like a wave, then down again as the lights switched with the beat of the music from purple to green to blue. I tried to find a rhythm, rising and falling with them, but I was always a half beat off. The faces of the riders around me were focused, concentrating. It was now or never.

"Irina?" I said her name as loud as I dared, just loud enough to be heard above the music.

Her head turned by a fraction, the only indication she'd heard me.

"You met my friend," I said between breaths as I pedaled. "You gave her some money and asked me to do a job for you. But I think there's been a mistake. I'd like to talk to you."

Her eyes drifted to my arms, my legs, then my shoes as they struggled to stay connected to the pedals. She'd hardly broken a sweat. "There's no mistake," she said. Her voice was as dark and severe as her eyes, the clipped words heavily accented. "The money's yours," she said, jutting her sharp chin at me, her pin-straight bangs falling in jagged layers around her face. "You get the rest when the job's done. There's nothing to talk about."

The instructor called out to the group, "You ready to pick up the pace, ladies?" Cheers erupted as the tempo quickened. I tried to keep up, rising out of sync with the wave, my butt smacking onto the seat as my pedals lurched out from under me. The stirrup bit painfully into my heel before I managed to catch the pedal again. I was pretty sure I wasn't getting paid enough to be here.

"But see . . . that's the problem," I panted. "I'm not who you think I am. I'm not qualified to do the type of work you hired me for."

"That's not what Patricia said. She said you were competent. Neat."

"She was wrong."

"I don't think so. Patricia knows my husband's line of work. She would not have recommended you if she wasn't confident you were suited to the job."

"But it wasn't me!" I let go of the handlebar with one hand, pressing it to my chest. The gesture cost me my balance and I slipped again. I wedged my foot back into the stirrup. "I wasn't the one who . . ." I looked around, lowering my voice as much as I could over the persistent thump of the bass. "I wasn't the one who finished that job." Sweat dripped down my neck, and my thighs were beginning to burn. "Can we go somewhere private where I can explain? I have something of yours. I'd like to give it back." As I pedaled, I cut my eyes to the Disney backpack on the floor between us.

"There's nothing to explain," she said, dipping low, then back up again, in perfect time with the other riders. "Patricia's husband is handled, yes?"

"No," I said between searing breaths. "I mean, yes. But . . ." I looked around anxiously, but the women around us were entirely focused on the instructor, pushing up and dropping low, pedaling like crazy people. The music was so loud, I could barely think.

"Increase tension!" the trainer called out.

Irina adjusted a knob between her knees and crouched over her handlebars, her butt perched high over her seat.

I pumped my legs, determined to keep up. My pedals were flying like living, hungry beasts. I moved faster, afraid if I stopped they'd chew the backs of my feet off.

"You are my only option," she said, her forehead beginning to glisten. "My husband knows everyone else in your line of work. You," she said, smirking as sweat drenched my collar. "You he does not know. It will be easy. He won't be expecting it from someone with your . . ." My shoes slipped precariously on the pedals and I nearly came flying off the bike. Her grin widened. "Your modest skills."

Great. Just great. In her mind, not only was I qualified, but I was perfect for the job.

"More tension!"

No, damnit. No more tension!

"Aren't you afraid someone might find out?"

"Who? Feliks?" she asked, taking me off guard. She waved dismissively, never once breaking rhythm. "Feliks does not involve himself in domestic affairs. If Andrei is careless enough to allow himself to be subdued by a pretty face, I'm sure Feliks would agree that Andrei deserved whatever happened to him. Andrei has been reckless. He's become a liability. Andrei is only lucky Feliks hasn't done it himself."

"Push it out, people!" the instructor bellowed. "Really push it!" Was the woman kidding? I hadn't pushed this hard since I was in labor with Zach.

The group grunted with a collective burst of speed, like something out of a nightmare. I couldn't feel my legs, and yet every inch of me was in pain. Irina leaned into her bike with a savage grin as the room took on the colors and tone of a disco. Lights flashed, sirens blared, the bass thumped. My heart was slamming out of my chest.

"I respect you for telling me no," she said over the music. "I understand your position."

"You do?"

"And I respect you for insisting on more."

"I wasn't . . . I didn't . . ."

"That's right! Give me a little more, ladies!" the instructor roared.

"No," I wheezed, "I don't want any more."

Irina smiled, endorphins loosening the stern lines of her face. She actually looked like she was enjoying this. The woman was a masochist. "It is a hard thing to be a woman in a man's world," she said over the music. "We are conditioned to believe we are not worthy. But this is why I believe in you. You will do this job for me. And I will pay you what Feliks would pay any man to do the same work. Women must stick together. It is the same reason Patricia gave me your number. Because this is something she understood."

"Aren't you the least bit worried about her?" I panted.

"Why should I be worried?"

"The police are searching for her. What if they find her?"

"What makes you think there's anything left of her to find?"

My legs stopped moving, my shoes carried by the momentum of the spinning pedals as her words spun around in my head. "What do you mean?"

Irina's eyes were cold and cutting as she looked at me sideways, her chin held high, above any judgment or remorse. "Patricia Mickler no longer exists. I made certain of it."

I couldn't catch my breath to speak. I looked around me, wondering if anyone else had heard what Irina Borovkov had just confessed. But all the eyes in the room were straight ahead, on the instructor. All but Irina's. Her faintly amused and crooked smile was angled sideways, toward me. A bead of sweat trailed down her temple. Somehow, she looked cool in spite of it, as if her heart rate was completely unaffected by any of this.

"It is better for everyone this way," she said. "Better for you, too. Patricia has always been skittish, easily intimidated. If the police pushed too hard, she might have said something foolish. And that would have been very bad for both of us."

My mouth hung open, my legs numb as I struggled to keep up. Patricia Mickler was dead. Irina had had her killed just to keep her from talking. To conceal a crime I hadn't even committed yet. I thought they were friends. What happened to women sticking together?

The music hit a fevered pitch, the thundering bass stealing every breath and every sound. My lungs burned. My mouth was so dry I was unable to form words. I told myself I would follow Irina to the locker room after class. That I would give her the backpack full of money and tell her I never wanted to see her again. Whatever had happened between her and Patricia had nothing to do with me. I cried out in relief when the music stopped and the women in front of us dismounted their bikes. Irina turned to me as she patted her face with her towel.

"You will be in touch when it is done." She swung a leg over her stationary bike, threw her towel over her shoulder, and headed for the door before I could catch my breath to speak.

"No, wait!" I called after her. I brought my foot over the side of the bike, tripping over Delia's backpack. My legs buckled out from under me, and I collapsed in a sweaty, clumsy heap on the floor. The cyclist in front of me turned, extending her hand to help me to my feet. I lost sight of Irina as she slipped into the hall. My knees were weak as I rushed to the exit, the backpack heavy against my cold, drenched shirt. By the time I shuffled out of the room, Irina was gone.

I trudged to the water fountain, eyes closed as I gulped mouthfuls of coppery cool water past the lump in my throat. Cupping some in my hand, I splashed my sweat-drenched face, wishing I would wake up and find this entire conversation had been a bad dream. The woman who'd hired me to kill Harris Mickler was dead—the one person who could both implicate and exonerate me—and I wasn't sure how to feel about it. The only thing I was certain of was that

Irina Borovkov was every bit as dangerous as her husband, and I still had her money. I wasn't sure what would happen to me if I didn't finish the job. Or, for that matter, what she would do to me after I *did*.

Every bone in my body groaned as I straightened and turned around, face-first into the person waiting behind me for the fountain.

The man gripped a racquet in one hand and held the hem of his shirt over his face with the other as he mopped sweat from his brow. A tight, tanned abdomen glistened beneath it. My throat closed around any coherent thought as his shirt fell back in place and Julian Baker raked back his curls. His cheeks were flushed with exertion, his honey-blond hair tinged dark with sweat.

I lowered my head, letting the hair that had come loose from my ponytail fall over my face. GMU was only a few miles away. And like an idiot, I hadn't even considered the possibility that I might run into him here. Or what might happen if I did.

I shifted sideways away from the fountain as he moved to let me by. We accidentally stepped on each other's feet.

"Sorry," I muttered as he steadied me.

"No, don't apologize, it was my fault. I wasn't paying attention." His hand was gentle on my upper arm. I averted my gaze as he tipped his head, trying to make eye contact. Turning tail and running would be suspicious . . . and rude. But if he figured out who I was—if he could place me here, in the same class with Irina Borovkov—then his next conversation with Detective Anthony could be (as Irina would say) very, very bad for both of us. Maybe he hadn't noticed which room I'd come out of. If I walked away right now, maybe he wouldn't recognize me.

"Spinning, huh? Killer class," he said between ragged breaths, gesturing loosely toward the room I'd just come out of with the tip of his racquet.

"You're not kidding." I turned away, my face angled down and sideways as I rushed toward the locker rooms.

"Wait," he called after me, jogging to catch up. "Do I know you?"

"I don't think so." I wasn't wearing a stitch of makeup. I was hot and blotchy and probably beet-red, my limp brown hair and the sleepless bags under my eyes on full, hopeless display.

"Are you sure?" he asked, following a few steps behind me.

I paused, torn between stealing one last look at him and running away. His smile was soft and his face was kind, and he was sweaty enough for me to see the outline of every muscle through his clothes. "Pretty sure I'd remember you."

"It's just . . . You look kind of familiar." His voice was close behind me as I reached for the locker room door. Close enough that I could smell the clean sweat coming off his skin, his breath still a little heavy with exertion.

I should not turn around. I should *definitely* not turn around. Vero was right. Communicating with Julian was dangerous and foolish. Especially now that Nick had been to The Lush asking questions. Julian was the one person who could positively identify me if he figured out who I really was. And yet, part of me wanted to turn around and confide everything to him.

I peered around the curtain of my hair, just enough to see his eyes narrow as they struggled to put the pieces of me together.

"I should go." I clutched my backpack to my chest as I pushed through the door into the locker room. "I'm probably late for . . . something."

I ducked inside and leaned back against the door. But when I looked around the locker room, Irina was already long gone.

CHAPTER 27

"I can't believe Patricia Mickler is dead." Vero hunched low in the driver's seat of the Charger, watching the door to Theresa's real estate office from the far side of the parking lot where we'd strategically positioned her car. Zach babbled to himself behind us, munching on Goldfish crackers while he watched cartoons on Vero's phone. "I can't figure out if that's a good thing or a bad thing."

"How could that possibly be a good thing?"

"Because now if they find her, she can't rat you out."

"No, but Irina can." And if I didn't kill her husband, I was sure she'd have no problem rolling me under whatever bus she'd used to squash Patricia.

"Do you think she got her husband to kill Patricia?"

I shuddered at the memory of the knife in her back door. "Probably." Irina had managed to put me in an impossible situation, forcing me to deal with Andrei before she gave Andrei a reason to deal with me. But I didn't have time to think about that now. First,

I had to ferret out Theresa's alibi, so that in the likely event of my untimely demise, my children had someone to live with.

I squirmed in my seat as I checked the time, regretting the second cup of coffee I'd had at breakfast. Delia was only in preschool until lunch, and nothing exciting had happened since we got here an hour ago.

"I have to pee," I said.

"You can't pee. We're on a stakeout."

"This is not a stakeout."

"Yes, it is. And *this* is a stakeout vehicle."

"My bladder doesn't care."

"If you pee in my new car, I will kill you on principle." Easy for her to say. She was twenty-two and had never had children. She could probably hold it until menopause.

"We don't even know what we're looking for," I grumbled.

"You heard the hot detective. We're looking for anything suspicious."

"Wouldn't it make more sense just to ask Theresa where she was that night?"

Vero gave me a heavy dose of side-eye. "When has Theresa Hall ever been honest with you? You seriously think she's gonna come out and tell you what she was doing on some random Tuesday night when she didn't bother telling you she was doing your husband all last year?"

I sank lower in my seat. My ass had fallen asleep thirty minutes ago. "Theresa's here and Steven's at the farm. Why don't we just go to their house and poke around?"

"One," Vero said, holding up a finger, "because that's breaking and entering, and we don't get paid for that. And two, because if she was up to something shady while Steven was at work that night, she wouldn't have left any evidence at home where he could find it. Even Theresa's not that dumb. Anything incriminating would be on her laptop or her phone, and she's probably got those—"

"That's her," I said, sinking lower as Theresa's long legs and high heels became visible through the glass doors to the vestibule. The double doors swung open. A man in an expensive-looking suit strode out behind her. "Holy shit. That's Feliks Zhirov."

The familiar black Town Car pulled to the curb in front of them. Andrei emerged from the driver's seat to open Feliks's door. Theresa extended her hand to Feliks, a purely professional gesture, but Feliks used it to draw her close, whispering in her ear before pressing a kiss to her cheek. She blushed, darting an anxious glance behind her to the windows of the building.

"I'm getting a little more than a professional vibe here," Vero said.

Feliks gave Theresa a long, appraising look as he slid into the back seat of his car. As soon as the Town Car pulled away from the curb, Theresa made a beeline for her BMW.

"What do you think this means?" Vero asked.

"I don't know." The only thing I knew for sure was that I didn't want Detective Nick Anthony figuring it out before I did. I reached into the back seat for the diaper bag and rummaged inside for the wig-scarf, tying it around my head before snatching Vero's mirrored sunglasses off her nose. "Stay here. I'll be right back."

"Where the hell are you going?" Vero hissed as I slid the sunglasses on my face and got out.

"To find out what Theresa's doing with Feliks Zhirov." And where the hell she was the night I was at The Lush. I crossed the parking lot and slipped through the vestibule before I could change my mind. The receptionist looked up as I approached the desk.

"Can I help you?" she asked.

I pushed the glasses down the bridge of my nose just far enough to look down at her over the frames. "I'm Mr. Zhirov's personal assistant. He just met with Ms. Hall and he forgot something very important in her office. He asked me to fetch it." I put my glasses back in place.

The woman reached for the phone. "She just left. Let me call her cell and catch her—"

"No!" I said too quickly. I took a second to compose myself. "That's not necessary, and Mr. Zhirov does not have time to wait. I can get it myself."

I started toward the glass doors at the end of the hall, throwing my hips with a purpose that dared her to stop me. "Which is her office?" I called over my shoulder as I pulled them open.

"Last on the left," the woman sputtered. "Are you sure I can't—"

The glass door swished closed behind me. Head down, I walked past rows of cubicles, pausing when I reached the corner office at the back. I turned the knob, praying it wasn't locked. The door cracked open. Through it, I could make out four desks—a shared office. Three of the desks stood empty. Only one agent was working, her back toward me and a phone pressed to her ear. I slipped inside, careful not to make any noise.

Theresa's desk wasn't hard to find. It was as spotless as her town house, the surface adorned with framed engagement photos. No day planner or desk calendar. Just a computer and some file drawers. I glanced over my shoulder, checking to make sure the woman's back was still turned as I wiggled the mouse. The screen prompted me for a password.

Shit. I had no idea what Theresa's password might be, and I didn't have time to guess. The only thing I knew for certain about Theresa was that she never kept her dirty laundry out in the open where people could see it. I slid open her desk drawer. Half-opened packs of gum, chewed-up pens, loose paper clips, some change, and crumpled sticky notes . . . I rummaged under them, finding a thin stack of folders and a yellow legal pad. The pages of the notepad were filled with barely legible notes. I thumbed through the files, grabbing the one with Zhirov's name on the tab and putting the others back. I flipped quickly through the contents—real estate listings, maps, and handwritten notes. All the listings inside had been printed two weeks ago—the same day Harris Mickler went missing.

I pressed the file and notepad to my chest and shut the drawer. If I could find proof Theresa had been showing properties the night Harris went missing, I could tell Nick she was with a client and get him off her back.

I was just about to turn and leave when a photo on her desk made me pause. I don't know why it drew my attention. Maybe because it was the only picture that wasn't of Steven. Or maybe because the girl in the photo seemed vaguely familiar in a distant and hazy sort of way. Her arm was slung around Theresa's shoulders, both of them young and tan and blond, wearing sorority sweatshirts with Greek letters across the front. The inscription on the frame read BFFS 4EVR.

This had to have been the Aunt Amy I'd heard so much about— the woman who'd taught my daughter to apply eye makeup and spent Saturdays with my kids, the woman who would probably help raise them if I ended up in prison—and I'd never even met her before.

"Oh, hey, Theresa. Did you forget something?" I stiffened, so lost in the photo, I hadn't heard the agent behind me hang up her phone. My wig-scarf itched and I resisted the urge to turn around.

"Yes," I coughed into my hand.

"Did you find what you needed?"

For Theresa's sake, I sure as hell hoped so.

I held up Feliks Zhirov's file, using it to obscure my face, praying the answers I needed were inside it as I rushed past her out the door.

Vero and I sat on the floor of my office while the children napped, Feliks's files and Theresa's notes spread across the carpet between us. All I needed was an alibi to get Nick off her back, some clue about where Theresa might have been that Tuesday night, and more important, why she didn't want anyone to know about it. With a notorious client like Feliks Zhirov, maybe she was only trying to maintain a low profile. But that didn't fit the Theresa I knew. Theresa was all about social cachet and prestige. If there was a chance to flaunt a high-profile client like Feliks by sticking her head out of the roof of his slick black limousine and shouting it to the moon, she wouldn't miss a chance to do it. Whatever her relationship with Feliks Zhirov, I definitely didn't want the Fairfax County PD to know about it—at least not yet. Sniffing down that lead would bring them far too close to Andrei. Which would inevitably bring them close to Vero and me.

"I bet they're sleeping together and she doesn't want Steven to know," Vero suggested.

"Maybe. Or maybe she wasn't with Feliks that Tuesday at all. Maybe she was with someone else."

"Then why not just come out and tell the police what she was doing? No, she's definitely banging the Russian. You saw the way he looked at her. That kiss had *I'm picturing you naked* written all over it."

I sifted through the contents of Feliks's file: a signed agency agreement appointing Theresa to represent him in the purchase or lease of property, a bullet-point list of search criteria, a handful of addresses that had already been scratched out . . . Judging by the stack of listings and lot diagrams, he was shopping for land. The maps featured large rural parcels. The property lines had been highlighted in yellow with notes scribbled in the margins: too close to main roads, too many trees, too few trees, poor drainage, too many easements, too much slope . . . He'd rejected them all.

"I'm guessing they weren't touring rolling country hills at nine o'clock on a Tuesday night." I dropped the maps and rubbed my eyes. Maybe Vero was right.

"I'm telling you, they were probably screwing in the back of his fancy car."

I wasn't sure what was worse. That her deduction was plausible or what that meant for Steven. It's not like I felt sorry for him. He was clearly entertaining himself with Bree at the sod farm. The more I learned about the hidden messes in their relationship, the more I was convinced Steven and Theresa deserved each other. And the less jealous I felt about what they had.

My thoughts ran to the photo of Theresa and her friend Amy. I wondered if that photo had been like the others she'd framed in her foyer at home—showcasing what she wanted everyone to see . . . if she and Amy were really best friends at all.

Vero bent over the yellow notepad, sifting for clues. She'd taken care of my kids like they were her own. She'd stood up to Steven and paid my bills. She'd read my manuscript because she liked it. She'd helped me bury a body, for Chrissake, and I didn't have a single photo of us together. Maybe because I didn't need to. Because we'd already proven whatever we needed to prove to each other.

"I kind of feel sorry for them," I said.

"Who?"

"Steven and Theresa."

Vero expelled a dry laugh. "You shouldn't waste the energy. I have no idea what he sees in that woman anyway. I mean, aside from the obvious."

I glanced down at my baggy T-shirt, at the aged yellow baby for-
mula stains and the small tear in the hem. If I stripped it all down
and stood in front of a mirror, I'd still be looking at a mom. The
purple sleep-deprived shadows under my eyes told no lies. Neither
did the holes in my practical cotton underwear or the thin silver
stretch marks each of my children had left behind.

The first two times Julian asked me out, I'd been dressed like
Theresa. I wondered if he would have been so interested at the gym
yesterday if he'd known who I really was.

"What's wrong?" Vero asked, pinching the toe of my sock.

"Why is it that guys fall for women like Theresa?" Why did
men look at her the way Feliks had—like he was picturing her
naked?

"Believe me. They wouldn't if they could see past the successful
blond bombshell to the disaster underneath." That was exactly what
I was afraid of. With a dispirited sigh, I tossed Feliks's file on the
floor. Vero scooped it up and handed me the yellow notepad. "Here,
switch with me. Maybe we missed something."

I skimmed the yellow sheets. The pages were full of chicken-
scratch notes: lot numbers, addresses, hair appointments, grocery
lists . . . I paused at a change in handwriting. Steven's bulky block letters were immediately familiar.

T—

MEETING A CLIENT AT THE FARM. ZACH'S WITH ME.
FINN HAD AN EMERGENCY. NEED YOU TO RUN OVER TO
HER PLACE AND CLOSE UP THE GARAGE. POWER'S OUT.
OPENER'S STUCK. TAKE AIMEE WITH YOU. YOU'LL NEED
SOMEONE TO GRAB THE DOOR WHEN IT DROPS.
THANKS. I OWE YOU ONE.

He'd written this the morning I'd met with Sylvia. The morning I'd lost power at the house and the garage door wouldn't close.

. . . she and Amy went over to your place on their way to lunch and closed the garage.

Not Amy. *Aimee.*

"His pictures . . ." I whispered.

Vero looked up from the notes she was studying. "Whose pictures?"

I leapt to my feet and dropped into my desk chair.

"What is it?" Vero asked, watching me like I'd lost my mind as I powered on my computer.

"Aimee was the name on one of the files in Harris's phone. I'm sure of it."

I opened a browser and found Harris Mickler's networking group. Clicking on the membership page, I scrolled through its roster, past Theresa's thumbnail, pausing at a screen name—Aimee R. The thumbnail was a blank placeholder. I clicked on it, but her profile was empty. Aside from her screen name, her details had been wiped clean.

The links to her other social media pages all led to dead ends, her accounts all deleted or closed. Aimee R was a ghost.

This had to be her. The spelling of Aimee's name was unusual, and she fit the profile of Harris's victims. And it would make sense that she and Theresa would have been in the same social networking group. They did everything together.

"This is her. I'm sure of it," I said. "The date of her last post to the networking group was a little over a year ago. That would have been around the same time Nick said a woman had called the police to register an anonymous complaint." A scene was slowly unfolding in my head. "Two people killed Harris. What if Nick's hunch about Theresa is right? What if Theresa and Aimee were waiting for Harris outside The Lush?"

"You think they were stalking him?"

"They would have known he was going to be there. They might have seen me walk him out to my van." In the dark, they might have assumed I was the one who was staggering. Under Harris's weight, we were both unsteady on our feet. "Maybe they got the wrong idea and thought I was his next victim. Theresa could have recognized my van and followed us here. Maybe she hadn't intended to kill him. Maybe she only intended to stop him. But then I ran inside the house and left them a perfect opportunity." I showed Vero the note from Steven. Her dark eyes narrowed as she read it. "They already knew how to close the door without using the motor. They'd done it together before."

Vero's face paled. "No wonder Theresa didn't want to tell Nick where she was that night. You really think Theresa and Aimee could have murdered Harris Mickler?"

"I don't know. But Nick said all he needed to bring her in was a motive." Theresa had a big one. And I had given her the means and opportunity to act on it.

But if I told Nick his suspicions were right . . . If I told him about Aimee and gave him just enough information to find her and make the connection himself, regardless of whether or not Aimee and Theresa were guilty, that trail of bread crumbs would lead Nick straight back to my garage. Suddenly, the possibility that Nick might find out about Feliks didn't seem quite as terrible.

I grabbed Nick's business card from my purse.

"What are you doing?" Vero's voice was tinged with panic. "You can't tell Nick about this!"

"I'm not," I said as I typed. "I'm giving Theresa an alibi."

Vero leaned over my shoulder, reading the carefully worded text I'd just sent to Nick: *I think Theresa is having an affair.*

CHAPTER 28

My fingers itched as I walked past my office. I'd felt stuck after I'd written the scene in the garage. I'd had no idea what was supposed to happen next until this new revelation about Theresa's involvement had opened a door to the next chapter of the story. This plot line made sense. All the pieces seemed to fit. And I had less than a month to finish this book without implicating myself in the process.

Even if I changed their names, Theresa and Aimee couldn't be the murderers in my story. It would be foolish to skirt so close to the truth. No, the story had to lead somewhere else. Somewhere less believable. The killer had to be some larger-than-life character, some archetypical villain people could believe I had made up because they'd already seen him play out on a TV or a movie screen. And the only other person I could picture playing the part was the real-life villain I planned to feed to Detective Anthony.

Feliks Zhirov was virtually untouchable. According to Georgia, he'd never spent a day in jail even though he was guilty as sin. If Feliks smelled an investigation—even one he wasn't directly involved in—I was pretty sure he'd bring the case crashing to a dead end. He was my safest option. And maybe the only person capable of keeping me and Theresa out of jail.

I sat down at my desk and opened the draft of my story, skimming the scenes I had written so far: A seasoned contract killer takes a job to kill a problem husband. She vets the target, stalks him in a bar, drugs him, and takes him to the dump site in an abandoned underground garage.

I dropped my head against the desk, kicking myself for sending this draft to my agent without thinking it through. The details were all steering far too close to home. But maybe I could get away with tweaking it a little.

I dove back into the manuscript, picking apart what I had written so far, making subtle changes to the characters and setup: The problem husband is an accountant working for a high-profile mob boss. He also happens to be super wealthy with a sizable life insurance policy that will go to his wife. Sometime between the first drink and the drugged one, my heroine realizes the wife never transferred payment into her offshore account as agreed upon. Too late to change direction, my heroine loads her mark into a utility van and drives him to the underground garage to let him sleep it off. The assassin steps outside to call the wife, to tell her the job is off for nonpayment. Meanwhile, someone else slips in behind her and uses a silencer to put a bullet between the husband's eyes. Determined to seek a vigilante-style justice and solve the mystery of who murdered her mark, she investigates his death, pairing up with an unsuspecting hotshot detective to stay one step ahead of the police and tracking down the runaway wife in the process.

Yes, I thought, cracking my knuckles over the keyboard. Yes, this felt like it could work! There was nothing in this story about hot young bartenders who studied law, or real estate agents who stole other people's husbands. There were no subplots involving lewd photos or extorted hush payments. No mentions of custody battles or starving authors doing questionable things to pay their bills.

Hours passed. My fingers ached and my mind felt weary. Smells started wafting from the kitchen—baking bread and steamed vegetables and the buttery, rosemary-coated skin of a roasting chicken. Night fell outside my window to the clank and clatter of silverware downstairs, the slide of the high chair from the table, and the hand-vac as Vero tidied up after dinner. No one knocked on my door. Three fresh chapters later, I jumped at the bright ring of my cell phone.

Steven's number flashed on the screen, and I contemplated not answering.

"Hello," I said, rubbing my eyes as I registered the time. The kids were probably already in bed. I hadn't even kissed them good night.

"Hey, Finn. 'S it a bad time to call?" A slur smoothed over the worn edges around my name. I wondered how many drinks it must have taken for it not to sound like a curse coming out of his mouth.

"Why?"

"Just needed to talk." He sounded tired, and maybe a little defeated, and I hated myself for the soft spot in my chest that still managed to ache at moments like this, even after all he'd done.

"You okay?" I turned off my monitor and sat in the dark, listening to liquid bubbling down the neck of a bottle and his hard swallow on the other end of the line.

He coughed. Said in a rough voice, "I don't know. Maybe. Not really."

The fact that he'd called me instead of his fiancée told me a lot, and at the same time, opened the door to so many more questions.

A year ago, we were together, all four of us under one roof. Why'd he have to go and screw everything up?

"What's wrong?"

"It's Theresa," he said. "I'm worried I made a mistake." I held my tongue, biting my lip to keep from saying the harsh things I wanted to say. "I was stupid to trust her. She's hiding something. I don't know exactly what it is, but . . ."

"But what?" I asked cautiously, afraid of scaring him away. "Why do you think she's hiding something?"

He hesitated. Took another swig and swore under his breath. "I found cash in her underwear drawer. A lot of cash, Finn. And some cop called the house the other day looking for her. When I asked her about it, she got all defensive and refused to talk."

"Maybe there was nothing to talk about."

"I don't know, Finn. She's got this new big-shot client. She's with him all the time. She says he's only looking for property, but I've seen the guy and he's . . ." Steven's voice trailed.

"Attractive?"

"Sleazy's more like it," he grumbled. "I looked him up, Finn. He's into some shady shit. What if he gave her all that cash? What if she's planning . . . ?" Steven fell quiet.

"To leave you for someone else?" In the silence, a siren wailed, and I heard it in stereo, loud outside my window and more faintly through his cell phone. "Where are you right now?" I pushed my chair from the desk and crossed the room, peeling back the blinds to find Steven's truck parked outside. He waved sheepishly through the window. "Hold on," I told him. "I'm coming out."

I bundled on a coat and slipped on my tennis shoes. I didn't bother to check my hair or change out of my yoga pants. Steven and I were beyond all that. Arms folded against the cold, I crossed brittle grass to his truck. He reached over the front seat to open the door for me, and I climbed inside the cab. The air was close and warm, thick with the tang of whisky on his breath and the earthy smell of his farm that still clung to his clothes.

He looked awful, and for the first time in a long time, I didn't take any joy in that. An empty pint bottle lay on the bench between us. His jacket hung open over his untucked flannel, and his hair stuck up as if he'd been dragging his fingers through it.

A curtain shifted in Mrs. Haggerty's kitchen window. She'd be on the telephone first thing tomorrow, making sure all the neighbors knew Steven was here, having a clandestine meeting in his truck with his ex-wife. "You want to go somewhere else?"

Steven followed my line of sight to Mrs. Haggerty's house. His shoulders shook with a somber laugh as he turned the key in the ignition and made a clumsy three-point turn, his huge tires chewing tracks in her front lawn.

Steven's hand was loose on the wheel. I wondered if I should offer to drive, but a moment later he pulled over in front of the small community park at the end of our street. He killed the engine and got out, and I followed his slow, unsteady steps to a set of swings illuminated by a dull halo of moonlight.

The chains groaned as he eased into one. I settled into the swing beside him, shivering as the cold seeped from the hard plastic seat through my clothes. We sat, listening to the low hum of traffic on the nearby highway, watching the flashing lights of the planes overhead.

"This reminds me of the night Delia was born," he said, staring up at the night-bright sky. I gave him a long side-eye. Our memories of that night were very different. All I remembered was the pain and the long hours of labor, leaving frantic messages for him between contractions as the time between them grew shorter. All I remembered was Georgia's face. The smell of coffee on her breath, her hand clutching mine as she shouted at me in her police officer voice to keep pushing, and the fat lip she gave my husband in the hospital parking lot when he finally showed up, hungover and terrified. He'd been there all night, drinking in this park, afraid of becoming a father and screwing it up. "I'm scared, Finn."

"Of what?"

"I'm scared Theresa's involved with him."

I raised an eyebrow, twisting in my seat to look him squarely in the face. The chains spun around each other, keeping tension on the swing. If I took my feet off the ground, they'd turn me away from him and pull me straight again, and I found something oddly reassuring about that. "Aren't you involved with someone, too?" I asked.

He glanced up at me, surprised. "That obvious?"

"Let's just say I know the signs."

He shook his head, staring at the sod and mud on his boots. "It's not just that. I know I'd probably deserve it if all she was doing was sleeping around. But I'm worried that she's in over her head with this guy. He's bad news, Finn. I'm afraid she's going to do something stupid and get herself in trouble. Something that could cost me my business or my kids. The business I could come back from, but I already lost our kids once, and I don't think I could . . ." A muscle bobbed in his throat and his eyes shone, reflecting the streetlamp on the sidewalk. "I'm sorry," he said in a choked voice. "For everything."

"I know." I reached out, my hand held open in the space between us. It hung there for a moment before I felt Steven's cold, calloused fingers in mine. I squeezed them. Not because I forgave him for doing what he'd done. But because this was a fear I understood. Because I shared it. Because of all the things I had to be afraid of right now, this was the one that terrified me most, too.

Steven's eyelids were heavy. With a gentle tug of my hand, he pulled my swing closer, until I could smell the liquor and fear and hopelessness on his breath. His head tipped, just enough to be an invitation. Just close enough for our foreheads to touch. It would be so easy to lean into him. It was all so familiar, something I could fall into without thinking. I lifted my feet, my fingers sliding from his as the swing pulled me back to its center.

"Are you really dating an underwear model?" he asked through a sleepy, drunken grin.

A smile tugged at my lips. "My attorney would probably advise me not to answer that."

Steven nodded. He kicked softly at the circle of dirt under his swing, making me wonder if he was jealous. Which made me wonder if that mattered to me.

I stood up, pulling Steven from his swing, making sure he was steady on his feet before letting him go. "Come on," I said, taking his keys from his pocket. "I'll drive you home."

CHAPTER 29

Steven's key was a warm, satisfying weight in my pocket as I walked home from his town house. When I'd driven him home, I'd slipped his house key off his key ring. It had seemed only fair since he'd kept a copy of mine for a year. He'd wake up tomorrow morning and realize it was gone. He'd tell Theresa some bullshit story about how he lost it, and then he'd nag me about it until I gave in and eventually gave it back. Even if it was only temporary, the sense of control it gave me felt good, and the walk home in the fresh air gave me time to think.

My shoes were soft on the sidewalk, fallen leaves crackling as the breeze tossed them over the light frost on the grass. I froze halfway across my yard, staring at the dark shape lying supine on my porch.

"So tell me," Nick said, leaning back on his elbows on my front steps, his long legs stretched out in front of him. "What'd you dig up?"

I took a cautious step closer, only releasing my held breath when

I caught the flicker of his smile. It billowed out in a white cloud as I sat down beside him.

"You scared me to death," I said, clutching my chest. "I didn't see your car."

He gestured along the street, where the retired cruiser melted into the dark. "Sorry I couldn't get here earlier. I was tied up. What'd you find out?"

Keep it simple, I reminded myself. *As close to the truth as you can. Just enough to keep him busy.* "I think Theresa's having an affair with one of her clients," I said. "I think that's who she was with that Tuesday night, and she doesn't want Steven to find out."

"If Steven doesn't know, how did you hear about it?"

"Vero and I staked her out."

Nick's lip curled with a wry smile, his laughter coarse and teasing. "A stakeout, huh? Did your sister teach you that?"

"I've been on a few ride-alongs," I said defensively. "I'm not a total amateur."

His teeth flashed white in the dark. "Okay, Detective. What did you see?"

I ignored the playful twinkle in his eye. "She came out of her office with an attractive man. Well-dressed. Late thirties. Nice figure. Dark hair."

"And why do you assume they're having an affair?"

"Their good-bye was a little less than professional."

"How so?"

"He kissed her cheek, whispered in her ear, and, according to Vero, he was picturing her naked."

His eyes fell over me with a cop's scrutiny. "And what exactly does that look like?"

"I wouldn't know." Blood rushed to my cheeks. I was grateful he couldn't see them in the dark.

"So you don't know for a fact that she's having an affair with this client. Or that he's a client at all. Or that she was definitely with him the night Harris disappeared."

"No, not exactly. But I talked to Steven tonight. He said she's been spending a lot of time with this guy. He's worried they're sleeping together."

This earned a less skeptical nod. "Do you know the client's name?"

"No." The longer Nick chased his tail trying to figure it out, the better.

"What makes you so sure she wasn't at the networking event?"

"I checked out that networking group online—the one you said she was involved in. That group is full of real estate agents and mortgage brokers. She probably knows half the people who were in the bar that night. If she'd been there, someone would have remembered seeing her." I watched his face for a reaction, certain I was right. Theresa was definitely not at The Lush that night. At least, she hadn't been *inside*. Nick was sharp. He'd said it himself, he'd been doing this for a long time. He would have interviewed the people on the RSVP list first. And if she had been there, her colleagues would have confirmed it.

A few days ago, Detective Anthony had been certain Theresa was guilty. Today, his confidence seemed shaky at best. All I had to do was wear it down and throw him off her scent.

Nick sat up slowly, bracing his elbows on his knees. "I went back and talked to the bartender at The Lush tonight."

"Yeah?" I cleared the surprise from my throat. "What did he say?"

"I showed him a photo of Theresa Hall. He said he didn't think it was the same woman he'd talked to, but . . ." He shook his head, frowning at the lawn over steepled fingers.

"But what?"

"Before I showed him the photo, I told him why we were looking for her—that she was more than just a witness, but a person of interest in the case. He was cocky. Told me I was barking up the wrong tree, like it was no big deal."

"So?"

"So he's a law student, straight A's and honors at GMU. Last summer, he interned with a staff attorney at the public defender's office. He knew exactly what we were after. He just kept repeating the same story, insisting that he'd seen her leave the bar alone. But then I showed him Theresa's photo, and something changed. He clammed up. Said he didn't think it was her. But if it wasn't the same woman in the photo, why was he so upset about it?"

My stomach turned. Of course Julian was upset. Because I'd lied to him. At the gym, he'd looked at me as if he wasn't quite sure who I was. As if he wasn't sure he knew me. He'd had no idea how on the mark he was. Vero was right. Even if I was foolish enough to call him to apologize, I'd be lucky if he'd ever speak to me again.

I pressed the heels of my hands into my eyes. "You can't seriously believe Theresa was involved in this."

"Until I have a reason to rule her out, yeah. I do."

I jammed my hands in my pockets, scraping my knuckles on the pointed teeth of Steven's key. There had to be a way to throw Nick off Theresa's scent. And mine.

"You all right?" he asked.

"Fine," I said through a sigh, "just tired. It's been a long night. Steven showed up about an hour ago, drunk out of his mind."

Nick's posture grew rigid. An abrasive edge sharpened his voice. "You want me to put in for a restraining order? If he's giving you a hard time, I can—"

"No, it's nothing like that. He just wanted to talk." Steven had never been an angry drunk. If anything, it just brought his guard down and made him a little more honest. "I let him complain about Theresa for a while and then I drove him home."

Nick's laugh was a low rumble in his chest. "If you ask me, the guy sounds like an idiot."

"Why, because he gets drunk and falls back on old habits?"

"Because he let you go."

I hunched into my coat. "I guess he had his reasons."

"That's no excuse." Nick pressed his lips shut tight, as if he'd like to say more but wouldn't.

"Have you ever been married?" I had a hard time believing Nick had always been single.

"Came close once."

"What happened?"

He blew out a long frost-laden breath. "She changed her mind. I guess she didn't want to be saddled with a cop for the rest of her life."

"Well, clearly she missed out." He tipped his head, his crooked smile inviting me to elaborate. "According to Georgia, we should all marry cops for the health insurance." His sudden burst of laughter creased the skin around his eyes. The silence in its wake felt loaded, heavy. I looked down at my feet.

"Hey," he said, bending low to catch my eye. "Don't worry about the custody hearing. By the end of this investigation, I'll have enough dirt on Theresa to give any judge a reason to put on the brakes. And Georgia told me about your book deal. With paychecks like that, your ex won't have a leg to stand on."

My polite smile crumbled. "Georgia told you about that?" The last thing I needed was for Nick to ask me what the book was about.

"She paraded the news around the whole damn department. She's pretty proud of you."

My throat closed around a mountain of guilt. If Georgia had any idea where my source material came from, she wouldn't be bragging about me. I rose to my feet. "Speaking of that, I should probably get inside and get back to work." Nick stood up, too, his attention shifting to the narrow gap between Mrs. Haggerty's bedroom curtains.

"You doing anything tomorrow?" he asked as I reached for the door.

"I don't think so."

"Feel up to a little field trip?" His eyes gleamed in the dark.

"What kind of field trip?" I asked warily.

"Just a little research for your book." This was probably Georgia's idea. She'd probably put him up to this. And right now, I didn't have the heart to disappoint her.

"Sure, I guess."

He slid his hands in his pockets as he backed down the sidewalk to his car. "I'll pick you up at eleven."

I watched him go, wondering if he would be so excited about this field trip if he knew how steeped in my research he already was.

CHAPTER 30

"You do realize this is breaking and entering," Vero said stubbornly.

I wedged my cell phone under my jaw and adjusted my wig-scarf in the rearview mirror. "This is not breaking and entering. I have a key."

"A stolen key," she pointed out.

"It's not stolen," I argued into the phone. I had offered to drive Steven home, and in his inebriated state he had relinquished his keys. I had just neglected to give this particular one back.

"Well, don't get caught. Detective Anthony is picking you up for your field trip in an hour."

Theresa didn't have a Mrs. Haggerty to worry about as far as I could tell. Still, I parked Ramón's loaner a few car lengths farther away than the circumstances called for and pushed my oversize sunglasses higher on my nose. My wig-scarf itched like hell. I resisted the urge to rip it off until I was safely inside Steven and Theresa's house.

I shut myself in, my back against the door, my cell pressed against

my ear, breath held as I listened. The house was quiet; the only sound
was Zach's babbling in the background through the phone.

"I'm in," I whispered. I stuffed my scarf in the pocket of my
sweatshirt and slipped off my sneakers, tucking my keys inside them
and leaving them beside the door.

I crept upstairs to Theresa's bedroom.

"Find what you need and get out of there." My anxiety spiked
with every squeak in the floor, and Vero's nagging wasn't helping
my nerves.

The bedroom door swished open over the dense carpet. The
blinds were drawn, and the room still smelled faintly of Steven's
hangover—stale liquor, sweat, and unwashed breath. His side of the
bed was a restless mess of tangled sheets, and a packet of Excedrin
sat on his nightstand beside a bottle of Mylanta.

"Where are you?" Vero asked.

"Theresa and Steven's bedroom." I slid open Theresa's nightstand drawer and rummaged through the contents. I wasn't sure
exactly what I was looking for. A note, a phone number, or a receipt.
Some clue to Aimee R's identity. Proof that they'd definitely been
together that Tuesday night, preferably nowhere near The Lush.

I closed the drawer and crept down the hall, pausing in front of
Delia's room. The bed was unmade, the pink princess sheets rum-
pled, the dense feather pillow hollowed in the shape of a grown
woman's head. A pair of Theresa's dress heels was tossed on the floor
beside the Dreamhouse. "Looks like Theresa slept in the spare room
last night."

Vero choked on a laugh. "Good old Mrs. Haggerty must have
told the whole neighborhood Steven got drunk and came looking
for you."

"I just hope she didn't mention anything about Nick," I muttered.

Vero sobered. "I hadn't thought of that."

I walked toward the cone of sunlight streaming through the door of Theresa's home office. Her desk was cleared of clutter. A loose connector hung where her laptop should have been plugged in. No antiquated PC. Not a speck of dust. I drew open the top drawer, the random contents threatening to spill over the edge onto the floor. Nothing inside revealed who Aimee was or where they had been the night Harris Mickler was murdered, but knowing the mess was there made me feel better.

I turned to the bookshelves on the opposite wall. "Bingo."

"What is it?"

"Her college yearbooks." I pulled a thick hardbound book from the shelf: GMU Class of 2009. I sank to the floor and opened it to the index, then flipped back to Theresa's sorority photo, skimming the names in the caption. Her sorority sisters were identified in order by row, and there beside Theresa was Aimee.

"Aimee Shapiro," I told Vero.

"Her online profile said her name was Aimee R."

"Aimee must have taken her husband's name when they married."

A door slammed downstairs.

"What was that?" Vero asked.

I sat bolt upright as a set of keys dropped against the table in the foyer. Heels clicked across the hardwood floors.

Theresa.

I disconnected the call and silenced my phone. Then I slipped the yearbook back in place on the shelf and eased to my feet. My socks were silent on the plush carpet, and I was grateful I'd thought to leave my shoes by the . . .

Oh, no.

My shoes.

I pressed myself into the corner beside the bookshelf, certain my heart was pounding loud enough for Mrs. Haggerty to hear it down the road. Maybe Theresa had only forgotten something. Maybe she'd have a quick lunch and leave without noticing my shoes beside the door. Maybe she'd go to the bathroom and I could slip out without her knowing.

Her feet thudded up the stairs.

My gaze shot to the window across the room. I was only one story up. I could probably jump without killing myself . . . if I had my shoes. And if I didn't have to worry about kicking out screens or bleeding all over the rhododendrons under the windows.

I fished my phone from my pocket and texted Vero.

Finn: *Need help. Trapped. Theresa's home.*

Vero: *Try a window.*

Finn: *My shoes and keys are in the foyer.*

Vero: *You suck at this.*

Finn: *I know!*

The phone stayed dark for an interminable amount of time.

Vero: *I've got a plan. Hang tight. Ten minutes.*

I pressed back against the wall, willing myself invisible as Theresa loaded the washer and dryer across the hall and returned to her bedroom to watch TV. Her room was beside the stairs. There was no way to sneak past without being seen.

Her cell phone rang. She muted the television.

"Thank god it's you. What am I supposed to do?" Theresa's voice grew louder, then quieter as she paced up and down the hall. "I can't tell him where I was. He'll completely freak out. And now I've got this detective calling . . ." I held my breath, struggling to hear as her voice faded into her bedroom. "I can't risk Steven finding out. We're in the middle of this damn custody thing with his ex and he says she's hired a lawyer." Theresa blew her nose into a tissue. She sniffled through a pause. "Apparently, she found some money some-where. Something about a book. All I know is that the old crone saw her get into Steven's truck last night, and by the time I got home, he was passed out drunk . . . Can you come by tomorrow? I could really use a—"

The conversation was lost in a deafening clatter. A diesel en-gine rumbled outside Theresa's office window. Hydraulics whined. Chains rattled.

"Hold on, I'm having trouble hearing you." Theresa stormed into the office, using her free hand to push down the plastic slats of the window blinds. I pressed back into the wall, breath held and eyes wide, praying she didn't turn around and see me crouched in the corner beside her bookshelves. "Some asshole's towing my car!" Theresa spun on her heel and rushed past me, her feet flying down the stairs as an engine revved.

I snuck to the window as a white tow truck labeled RAMÓN'S TOWING AND SALVAGE dragged Theresa's BMW down the street. Theresa ran after it, barefoot and shouting, waving her phone. I sprinted downstairs and grabbed my shoes, checking to make sure Theresa wasn't looking back before tearing out of her house. The tow truck had stopped a block away. A man, presumably Ramón, wrote on a clipboard, ignoring Theresa's demands to put the car back where he found it. I dragged on a shoe as I stumbled over her lawn, nearly tripping myself in my rush to get back to the loaner car. As I fought to pull on the second one, I looked up. And froze.

Detective Anthony was parked across the street with his window down, listening as Theresa threatened to kill Ramón twenty ways from Sunday. But it wasn't Theresa Nick was watching.

He crooked a finger at me, beckoning me to his car. His stern expression left no room for argument.

Shoe in hand, I dashed for his car, slung open the door, and collapsed inside.

CHAPTER 31

Nick's sedan was a standard-issue retired police cruiser. Navy blue and obvious as hell. I lowered the visor and ducked, peeking out from below the dashboard as Ramón backed Theresa's car slowly into her driveway while Theresa watched him like a hawk.

"Do I want to know what's happening here?" Nick asked. I shoved my hands in my pockets, making sure my wig-scarf was tucked safely out of sight. As I opened my mouth to defend myself, Nick raised a finger. "Be very careful how you answer that."

"Can we please just go now?" I sank low in my seat, arms folded over my chest as Nick shook his head and put the car in gear. He hadn't recognized the loaner car I'd left parked down the block, and I didn't feel like making a spectacle of myself to get it now.

"What are you doing here? You weren't supposed to pick me up until eleven."

"I got here early. I saw Theresa's car pull up as I was heading to your place. Figured I'd watch the house and see if anyone interesting showed up." A slow grin spread over his face as he turned into my driveway.

"I'm glad you're amused." I stormed out of his car and stuck my key in my front door, but Vero threw it open before I could turn the lock. Her jaw hung open when she saw Nick standing behind me.

"Tell Ramón I owe him one," I said as I brushed past her into the house.

"Detective Anthony, so good to see you." Vero's gaze slipped down the length of him as he followed me in. I threw her a reprimanding glare as I peeled off my sweatshirt and draped it over the railing at the foot of the stairs.

Delia peeked around it at Nick. "Who's that?"

"This is your Aunt Georgia's friend from work," I said, trying and failing to smooth down the staticky pieces of my hair that had come loose under the wig-scarf. I tore out the elastic band and scratched the ghost of the itch from my scalp. "His name is Nick."

She wrinkled her nose. "What's he doing here?"

I sniffed my shirt. "He's helping me with research for my new book."

"Are you going to date him?"

I choked on my tongue. Nick suppressed a smile, daring a sideways glance at me.

"Delia Marie Donovan," I sputtered, "what kind of question is that?"

"Come on." Vero snickered as she took Delia's hand. "Let's let your mom and Detective Nick talk for a bit." She turned over her shoulder as she led the kids up the stairs. "Why don't you all take this conversation somewhere little ears won't hear you?"

"I'm right here, you know," Delia huffed. "And I'm not little. I know what a date is . . ." Her argument trailed into her bedroom as Vero closed the door.

"I'm sorry about that. She's five," I said, as if that was explanation enough. He scratched the back of his neck, loosening the reins on his smile.

"Kid doesn't pull any punches. She'd make a heck of a detective."

I reached to take his coat. "Don't tell my sister that. We've got enough interrogators in the family."

Nick slipped out of his jacket. The leather was supple, the liner warm from his body. The coatrack was behind him, and I maneuvered awkwardly around him, accidentally brushing his shoulder holster as I reached to hang it up. The hall suddenly felt too small. Too close. Nick's face was freshly shaven, and he smelled like mouthwash and musk. Even in jeans and a tight, dark Henley, he looked sharp, his focus on me far from casual.

"I need to clean up a bit," I said, gesturing loosely to the stairs behind me. "You want something to drink while you wait?" Heat flooded my cheeks as he followed me to the kitchen. I grabbed a glass from the drainboard and reached into the freezer for some ice. A ziplock bag full of money peeked out from under a bag of broccoli.

I slammed the freezer closed.

"How about we grab something on the way?" I said in a strained voice. I held up a finger and sidestepped away from the fridge. "I'll be two seconds. Don't . . . go anywhere." I set the glass in the sink and raced to my room to change. After a quick scrub in the sink, I dragged a comb through my hair, threw on a pair of clean jeans, a T, and a fresh hoodie, and skidded back down the stairs.

"Come on," I said, grabbing his coat and my purse from the

rack. "Let's get out of here." I shouted a rushed good-bye to Vero and locked the door behind me, catching the quick flash of Mrs. Haggerty's curtains as I slid into Nick's passenger seat. "Jesus, does the woman have nothing better to do?"

Nick clicked his seat belt and started the car. The radio under the dash squawked to life. "Who? Your neighbor?" He adjusted his rearview mirror, his eyes crinkling at her reflection in her kitchen window.

"The woman's a nuisance." I resisted the urge to flip her off as we rolled out of my driveway.

"Are you kidding? Neighbors like that are a detective's dream. I bet nothing happens on this street that old lady doesn't see." He moved his mirror back in place and rolled down the street.

"She sees plenty," I said bitterly. I stiffened as he eased to a stop near Theresa's house, directly behind Ramón's loaner. "Where are we going?" I asked.

"We're taking your car."

"But that's not my—" Nick was already out of the sedan, my car keys in his hand. He unlocked the driver's-side door and let himself in. I followed, trailing a string of whispered expletives as I dropped into the passenger seat.

"How did you get my keys? And how did you know this was my car?"

"You left your keys on your kitchen counter when you went upstairs. And I was behind you this morning when you parked." He pulled the loaner away from the curb. Theresa's BMW wasn't in the driveway. Still, I relaxed when her house disappeared in my side mirror. "That was a pretty sloppy B and E, by the way. You're lucky you didn't get caught."

I gaped at him. "You knew I was stuck in that house with her, and you did nothing?"

"That would be aiding and abetting."

"I wasn't a criminal," I said stubbornly. "I had a key."

His lip curled with a self-satisfied grin. "I'll admit your getaway was impressive."

"That was Vero's idea. And it was *your* fault I was in her house."

"My fault?" He swung Ramón's car into a fast-food drive-through.

"You told me to dig into her secrets. So I was digging."

He chuckled darkly. "And what'd you find?"

"Nothing. She came home right after I got there." It was unnerving how perceptive he was. How he always seemed to be one step in front of me.

Nick ordered two burgers for himself, then called my order into the intercom. He ate both of his as we drove, which made me feel better that Delia was wrong and at least this wasn't a date. I scarfed down my burger and fries, watching the buildings roll by as Nick turned down a side street and slowed as we passed Theresa's real estate office.

"Where are we going?" I asked, crumpling my wrappers and dumping them in the empty bag. The car braked and swung around, flinging me against the side panel as Nick made an illegal U-turn.

"You wanted to play detective, right? I'm taking you on a real stakeout." He pulled the loaner car to the curb and cut off the engine. The burger turned to cement in my stomach.

"Why are we staking out Theresa if the bartender said that it wasn't her in the bar?"

Nick wiped his greasy fingers on a napkin, his eyes raking the parking lot until he spotted Theresa's car. "Because I think they're both hiding something, and I want to know who she was with that night."

"How are we going to do that?"

He reclined his seat back, crossed his arms, and closed his eyes. "We're going to wait for her boyfriend to show up."

Twenty minutes passed. I was pretty sure Nick spent most of it with his eyes closed, a ball cap draped loosely over them. At least now I understood why he hadn't ordered us anything to drink.

"What am I supposed to be looking for anyway?" The vinyl seat creaked as I tried and failed to get comfortable. If I reclined my seat back as far as Nick had, neither one of us would be able to see.

His voice was groggy when he finally answered. "Just tell me when Feliks's Lincoln shows up."

My spine went rigid. "Feliks?" I plucked the cap off Nick's face. "So all this time you knew who Theresa's client was? At what point were you planning to tell me?"

Nick opened one eye, a lazy grin carving a dimple in his cheek. "You never asked."

"What else have you figured out that you haven't told me?"

He opened his other eye and stretched, his arms reaching for the ceiling behind him. He laced his fingers behind his head, his knees bent slightly on either side of the steering wheel and his jacket hanging open around the gun holstered against his ribs. "I know Theresa's client is a man named Feliks Zhirov. He's very wealthy, very powerful, and very deep in organized crime. And, according to our guys in criminal intelligence, Feliks has Harris Mickler's accounting firm on retainer."

A nervous laugh slipped out. "That's probably a coincidence, right?"

Nick drew on his cap, curling the bill over his eyes. "When it comes to the mob, there are very few coincidences. Unfortunately, the man's made of Teflon. Nothing sticks. He should've been locked up a dozen times, but there isn't a judge in the state with the balls to convict him. Even if we could, he has friends that can make almost anyone disappear . . . new name, new passport, and wipe them off the map as if they'd never existed. He'd skip bail, and we'd never see or hear the name Feliks Zhirov again."

"What does he want with Theresa?"

"That's what I plan to find out." As if reading my face, he sighed and said, "Look, Finlay. I'm not trying to ruin Steven's life, or even Theresa's. If Feliks is involved in Mickler's disappearance, then I'm guessing Theresa's a victim in all this too somehow. I promise, we'll figure it out. And you and your kids will be okay. I plan to keep the three of you as far out of the investigation as possible. Georgia made me swear to it."

"She did?"

He winced. "She did."

Curiosity got the best of me. "What else did she say?"

He looked out his window, a flush creeping over the back of his neck. "She said you had your heart broken pretty bad. And if I do anything to hurt you, first she'll take my badge, and then she'll break my face."

I shook my head, chuckling to myself. "Between my sister and my kid, you must think this is all just one big setup. I swear, none of this was a ploy to get you to ask me out."

"Would it be so terrible if it was?" He turned from the window, his eyes moving over me the same way they had last night on my porch. Only this time, his appraisal of me felt far less professional.

My laughter died. A charged silence settled over us, prickly and hot. Nick was attractive and single. He was friends with my sister, which meant he had already passed the world's most stringent background check. I was pretty sure he wanted to kiss me right now, and I was also pretty sure I'd like it.

A bead of sweat trailed down the small of my back. I reached over the center console for the thermostat just as he reached for the radio. Our hands brushed. When I glanced up, our faces were close, the bill of his hat shadowing our faces. Neither one of us moved, and my heart beat a little faster as Nick laced our fingertips together.

"I have a confession," he said in a low voice that left me a little breathless. "This wasn't all Georgia's idea." I didn't pull away as the vinyl creaked and he leaned closer. My adrenaline spiked and the air felt thin. I couldn't remember the last time I'd been this close to a man other than Steven.

"Is this all right?" he asked, our foreheads touching under his cap. Nudging it loose.

No, this was not all right. What I wanted right now was very, very wrong. Wrong for a million reasons. I nodded, dizzy, the inch of distance he was holding back testing every ounce of my self-control. Our noses brushed as a long black hood rolled past the window behind Nick's head.

I pulled back sharply. "That's him," I said. "That's Feliks's car."

Nick fell back against his headrest with a quiet swear. He closed his eyes, releasing a heavy sigh before raising his seat back.

The Lincoln parked along the curb in front of Theresa's office. Andrei opened Feliks's door and followed him into the building.

"Looks like they'll be here for a while. Stay here for a minute. I'll be right back." Nick got out before I could ask him where he was going. He walked briskly toward the office, pausing when he dropped his keys behind Feliks's sedan. I lost sight of him as he knelt to pick them up. A second later, he stood, slipping something into his pocket as he withdrew his phone. He pressed it to his ear, making a hurried call as he wandered back toward Ramón's car.

"What was that about?" I asked him as he ducked into his seat and shut the door.

"Just checking a hunch," he said, a little distracted.

"Now what do we do?" Every part of me from the neck down hoped we'd pick up where we left off. The other part was pretty sure that would be a very bad idea.

Nick's eyes were glued to the office doors. "Now we wait."

A moment later, Andrei emerged and held open the door. Feliks came out, his palm on the small of Theresa's back and a smile on his face. His hand strayed lower as she dipped inside his car.

"See, I told you they're sleeping together. Now that we know what Theresa was hiding, we can go, right?"

Nick started the engine. He waited a beat before pulling into traffic a few car lengths behind them. He was quiet, his brow furrowed as he followed them west onto the interstate, away from the city. We tailed Feliks's Lincoln for the better part of an hour, forced to hang back when they veered onto an exit ramp and the roads narrowed with the rural terrain. They made four stops in front of large farm tracts with FOR SALE signs posted on their fences. Each time, the Town Car slowed to a crawl, but Feliks never once got out. After the fourth drive-by, the Lincoln returned to the interstate, doubling back to the city the same way we'd come.

"Looked like a pretty normal real estate meeting to me. Seems innocent enough." I hoped Nick would agree and take me home.

"Nothing Feliks Zhirov does is innocent. He's shopping for land."

"So?" The plots they'd visited today were a lot like the ones Theresa had scratched out on her notepad. By the looks of it, he hadn't liked these four options any better than the others.

"So the question is, what does Feliks want the land for?" Nick shadowed the Lincoln's movements, careful to stay a few car lengths behind as it moved toward the exit ramp. "Feliks's outfit runs drugs, weapons, and human traffic. He buys a lot of buildings and warehouses to keep his inventory moving. All the land he scouted today is west of Dulles, within close proximity to the airport and two major interstates, but far enough from the city to stay under the radar. Good for flying merchandise in, and then trucking it out."

My stomach turned at the idea of my children's soon-to-be stepmother sleeping with this man. "He sounds like a real winner."

"Believe me," he said as the Lincoln circled into the real estate parking lot. "I'd love nothing more than to put Feliks Zhirov away for the rest of his life."

"Is that why we're here?"

Nick barked out a laugh. "I'd have a better chance of winning the lottery than landing Feliks Zhirov in prison. We're here because every ounce of Zhirov's business is dirty and dangerous. And if Theresa's working for him in any capacity, then she's already in over her head." We watched Theresa get out of the car alone and disappear inside her office. Nick didn't follow the Lincoln as it pulled out into traffic again.

"Shouldn't we be following him?"

Nick gave a thoughtful shake of his head, his eyes glued to the door of the office. "We'll learn a lot more following Theresa. I find it a little too convenient that she's a person of interest in a murder investigation while she's acting as Feliks's agent."

"You mean a missing persons investigation," I corrected him.

"If it looks like shit and smells like shit, it's probably shit," he deadpanned. "We found Patricia Mickler's Volvo at the bottom of the Occoquan Reservoir last night."

"Are you sure it was hers?" The car I'd seen in Patricia's garage had been a Subaru.

"Her personal effects were inside, and the VIN was a match." I sank back, a queasy feeling stirring in my stomach. Nick shrugged. "Harris and his wife will eventually turn up. Bodies always do."

I rested my head against the cold glass. Harris's body turning up was exactly what I was afraid of.

Nick reached over, gently tugging the string of my hoodie. "Hey, it's gonna be okay. I promise." His hand slid over mine, his thumb tracing slow circles over my knuckle. This was wrong. I couldn't get involved with Nick. It would only complicate things.

"Nick," I said, turning in my seat to face him. "About earlier. I think maybe . . ." My thought trailed as a flash of red caught my eye.

Nick's head started to turn, following the direction of my stare as Aimee came through the vestibule door in a bright red scarf with Theresa at her side. If Nick spotted Aimee and recognized her from Harris's photos, this could all go very, very wrong.

I clamped a hand over my face. "Oh, crap! I think I've got something in my eye."

Nick whirled back to me, ducking closer to see as he gently pried my hand away. "You okay?"

"I don't know." I squeezed one eye shut hard enough to make it water. I struggled to see past Nick's head with the other as Theresa and Aimee dropped into Theresa's car.

"Here, let me look at it." Nick took my face in his hand, delicately drawing down my lower lid with his thumb. My breath caught as he tipped up my chin. Our eyes locked and held. His thumb trailed down, caressing a tear from my cheek.

"Better?" he asked quietly.

"I think so," I breathed.

Nick's eyes closed. He leaned in, closing the narrow gap between us. I might have forgotten about Theresa and Aimee altogether when his mouth grazed mine.

This was nice. This was . . . so much better than good. *Oh, hell.*

His tongue skimmed past my teeth. My fingers slid into his hair, and the seat-belt latch pressed into my hip as our bodies met over the console. He made a hungry sound deep in his throat, his fingers digging into the seams of my jeans before roaming under my sweatshirt and spreading across my back.

Holy mother, it had been a long time since I'd made out in a car. I arched into him, shutting out the voice in my head that said I was going to regret this.

His breath was ragged against my neck. "I want to take you in the back seat right this minute. But if I do, your sister's going to shoot me." He gave me a last lingering kiss that made my toes curl and left me panting. "Now," he said as he nuzzled my ear, "what happened in the parking lot a minute ago that you didn't want me to see?"

I froze, feeling the curve of his smile against my jaw as he slowly pulled away. He didn't look mad. Just surprised. And maybe a little impressed. "If you didn't want me to follow her, you could have just said so." He leaned back in his seat, gauging my chagrin through heavy-lidded eyes. "You may be a helluva storyteller, Finn, but you're a terrible liar."

"How'd you know?"

There was a hint of nostalgia in the thoughtful creases around his eyes. "Because I've been shot and cut and had the snot beat out of me, and I'd take any of those over a corneal abrasion any day."

"Don't exaggerate."

He shook his head at my cynical look. "I'm dead serious. My first week out of the Academy, I blew my first traffic stop when some punk dumped his ashtray in my face. It hurt so bad, I couldn't think straight. I stumbled across two lanes of moving traffic, desperate to get that shit out of my eyes. I was lucky I didn't kill myself. I couldn't see for a week."

I slumped back in my seat, feeling foolish. And irritable. He'd known all along there was nothing in my eye. "If you knew I was lying, why'd you kiss me?"

"I was hoping it'd be worth it."

Blood rushed to my cheeks. It had been more than a year since I'd kissed anyone. More than ten since I'd kissed anyone other than Steven. I'd spent the last year doubting myself, wondering why my husband had left, contemplating the possibility that maybe he hadn't left me for Theresa's hair or body or money or clothes. Maybe he had just left *me*. "Was it?"

Nick's smile was wolfish. "Let's just say I seriously considered letting your sister shoot me." He scrubbed his hands over his face and adjusted his seat back. "I'll take you back to South Riding. I've got to pick up my car and get something to the lab in Manassas before it closes."

I knew from listening to Georgia that "the lab" was the regional forensics lab. When Nick had stooped behind the Lincoln, he'd tucked something into his pocket as he'd reached for his phone.

"You found something?"

"Don't know yet."

Whatever it was, it must have been important. "Want me to come with you?"

His low laugh was husky, his grin slightly dangerous. "Right now, I want a whole lot of things. Which is why I think I'd better take you home."

I rested my head on the glass as he started the car, unsure if I was more curious about what he had hidden in his pocket or what would happen if I went along for the ride.

CHAPTER 32

Vero took one look at my hair and my clothes as I came through the door, folded her arms thoughtfully, and said, "You made out with him, didn't you?"

"I did not," I whispered, darting a look into the family room, hoping Delia hadn't overheard.

"Don't try to deny it." She tapped the side of her neck, jutting her chin toward mine. "The detective left a little evidence at the scene of the crime." She wagged her eyebrows.

"No!" My hand flew to my throat. I hadn't had a hickey since high school. "I swear, I'll kill him—"

Vero doubled over, stifling a cackle. "See, I knew it. You should see your face right now!"

I bundled up my sweatshirt and threw it at her.

"Relax," she said, choking back her laughter, "they're napping." She dragged me by the sleeve to the kitchen, shoved me into a chair at the table, and set a bag of Oreo cookies in front of me. "On a scale of one to ten, how was he?"

I reached for a cookie. Vero yanked the bag away, holding my Oreos hostage. "Spill! I want to know everything."

I snatched it out of her hands. "He's an eleven," I mumbled, stuffing a cookie in my mouth.

She leaned back in her chair and stole one for herself. "I knew it. I've always wanted to make out with a cop. I bet he was all fifty shades of assertive," she said, fanning herself.

"Not exactly." Vero narrowed her eyes at me, as if she was rarely wrong about these kinds of things. "I sort of egged him on."

She smacked my arm, stifling a cackle.

"I didn't have any choice! I had to keep him from spotting Theresa and Aimee together, so I pretended I had something in my eye, and he leaned in to help me, and then one thing led to another—"

Vero's laughter died. Her mouth dropped open around her cookie. "Theresa and Aimee were together? What happened? Did he see them?"

I shook my head. "Aimee showed up at Theresa's office. It looked like they were going out to lunch or something. Nick didn't see them leave. But there's more," I said, peeling another cookie from the package. It had definitely been a two-Oreo morning. "He already knew she's been meeting with Feliks Zhirov."

"Shit," she said. "That didn't take long."

"He's still convinced she was involved in Harris's disappearance, only now he thinks Feliks was behind it. Not only that, but Nick went back to The Lush and talked to Julian. He showed Julian a photo of Theresa, and when Julian insisted it wasn't the same woman he'd talked to, Nick suspected Julian was just covering for her. So now, on top of everything else, Julian knows I lied to him."

Vero winced. "It could be worse. You could have given him your real name. Then you'd really be in trouble." She pushed her glass of milk across the table, letting me drown a corner of my Oreo in it. "You think Nick will find anything that'll lead the investigation back to you?"

I sighed. "I don't think so. There's nothing connecting me to Feliks or his business."

Vero pushed the entire bag of cookies at me. "Nothing but Andrei Borovkov."

That night, I sat in front of my computer watching the cursor blink. I'd revised a solid chunk of my manuscript to keep my secrets safe. I'd written the hot young lawyer out of my story and replaced him with a hotshot cop, and while the heroine and the cop had great chemistry on the page, the lawyer's absence from my story felt wrong for reasons I couldn't seem to shake. I missed the banter between them and his easy smile. I missed the way he seemed to see right through her—through her wig-scarf and her makeup and her borrowed dress—and even though she was a killer with a complicated backstory, he still seemed to like what he saw underneath.

I nudged my phone closer and scrolled to Julian's name, staring at his number. My finger hovered over the delete key. There were so many reasons I should press it. So many reasons I should have edited him out of my life days ago.

Instead, I picked up my phone, slid to the floor beside my desk, and tapped his name on the screen. Hugging my knees, I listened as Julian's phone rang, waiting for the telltale voice-mail beep. When he actually answered, I was too stunned to speak.

The line was silent.

"My name isn't Theresa," I confessed quietly. "And I'm not really in real estate." I listened for any sign he was still there. "I'm not blond. And you were right, about all those other things you said about me at the bar. I didn't belong there. The dress I was wearing wasn't even mine."

I held my breath through a long pause, certain he'd hung up. I was just about to give up and disconnect when he asked, "Was any of it true?" There was no suggestion of blame in his tone. No expectation or demands.

"Some." I buried my head in my hands, surprised by how guilty I felt. "I have two kids. I'm divorced. I'm in the middle of a messy custody fight with my ex." I looked down at the Oreo crumbs on my stretched-out T. "And you more or less nailed my sense of style and dietary preferences."

He sighed. Or maybe it was a heavyhearted laugh. "Who are you?" He sounded genuinely curious.

I leaned my head back against my desk. "I don't think I can tell you. Not yet."

"Why not?"

"I want to." I raked my hair back, my nails dragging over the phantom itch in my scalp. "I just . . . need to clear some things up first."

"Are you in some kind of trouble?"

"I don't want to be," I said, fighting back tears. "I keep trying to do the right thing, and somehow it keeps backfiring." All I had wanted was a chance to hold on to my kids. To prove to Steven that he was wrong about me. But what if he wasn't?

"Did this Mickler guy—the one who went missing," he asked gently, "did he hurt you?"

"No," I said. But I thought about all those names on his phone. "Not me."

"Did you hurt him?" There was no insinuation of guilt. No condemnation or judgment. Maybe there should have been.

"No. But I doubt anyone would believe me."

"Maybe if you tell me what happened, I could help." He sounded so earnest. So honest. I wondered if it would feel like confessing at church, to pour all my ugly truths into the phone to him. I wished I could utter a few Hail Marys and the rest of the world would absolve me the way Julian seemed to want to.

"I can't. This thing I'm tangled up in . . . It's complicated." It was wrong of me to drag him into this. "I'm sorry. I shouldn't have called—"

"Why did you?" he asked before I could hang up.

The question pulled me up short. I picked at the fraying knee of my jeans. "I guess I just wanted you to know that I'm not a terrible person. And I never wanted to mislead you. If things weren't so screwed up right now, I would tell you my name. I'd take you up on that offer to go out for pizza and tell you everything over a beer. But . . ."

"It's complicated," he said softly. "I know."

"Do you believe me?" I closed my eyes and braced for his answer, surprised by the wash of relief I felt when he finally spoke.

"Yeah, I do."

"Why?"

"Ever heard of Hanlon's razor?" I tipped my head back and closed my eyes. The low timbre of his voice was even and calm, a balm on my frazzled nerves. "There's an old saying that goes something like . . . 'Let us not attribute to malice and cruelty what may be referred to less criminal motives.' I make it a point never to assume the worst about people."

"Maybe you should."

"Sometimes people just make mistakes."

We both fell quiet. I wondered if he would feel the same way if he knew the depths of the mistakes we were talking about. If he knew Harris Mickler's body was buried at the bottom of them. "I should probably get rid of this phone and never call you again."

"Is that what you want?"

"No."

"Then keep it." It was the voice of a lawyer giving counsel. There was something reassuring in it, something solid I could hold on to. "I still don't know your name," he reminded me. "This could be anyone's number in my phone. The detective's only interested in some woman named Theresa, and since your name isn't Theresa, there's no reason for me to tell him about you. Is there?"

I swallowed the painful lump in my throat. "No."

"Promise me if you need help, you'll call."

I wished I could tell him this wasn't as simple as a bad alternator. That I was in way over my head, and it was going to take more than a set of jumper cables and a wet wipe to fix the mess I'd made.

"I'll be okay," I said as I disconnected the call. I only wished I believed it.

CHAPTER 33

According to her engagement announcement in the local paper seven years ago, Aimee Shapiro had married a young entrepreneur who owned a chain of car washes. His name was Daniel Reynolds. According to a white pages search, Aimee and Daniel Reynolds now lived in a town house in Potomac Falls, about fourteen miles away. And according to the name tag pinned to the dress suit she'd been wearing when she left home that morning, Aimee Reynolds, aka Aimee R, was on her way to work.

Vero and I tailed her to a parking lot at Fair Oaks Mall, then into the cosmetics department at Macy's. We huddled in the dress racks, watching her organize the displays under the glass counter.

"Go talk to her." Vero nudged me with her elbow.

I pulled Zach from her arms. "I can't be the one to talk to her. She might recognize me from the photos in Steven's house."

Vero rolled her eyes. "Yeah, right. Like Theresa's got your face hanging all over her hall of fame."

Point taken. "If Aimee was there the night I brought Harris

to the house, she might have gotten a look at my face. You have to do it." I watched Aimee surreptitiously as I slid dresses down the metal racks. "Dial my number and leave your phone on in your pocket. I'll listen from here. And put your ear thingy on so you can hear me."

"What am I supposed to say?" she argued as she stuffed the Bluetooth in her ear.

"I don't know." I angled Zach out of reach of a designer silk bustier before he could stuff it in his mouth and use it as a teether. "Make small talk. Find out if she was working here the night Harris disappeared."

Vero held out her hand. "Give me your credit card."

"You can't use my credit card! My name is on it!"

"Then give me some cash. I can't just loiter at the counter and not spend anything."

I fished a few bills from my purse, stuffed them in her hand, and pushed her toward the makeup counter. Propping my phone under my ear, I hoisted Zach on my other hip and pretended to be on a call. Using the tall dress racks as camouflage, I wandered to the edge of the cosmetics department until I was near enough to eavesdrop.

"Can you hear me?" I said into my phone.

"All the damn time," she muttered.

"Can I help you?" Aimee's voice was light, pleasant through my receiver.

"I hope so," Vero said a little too loudly. "I'm looking for a gift for a friend. She doesn't get out much. She's one of those lonely, re-clusive, cat-lady types."

"I don't have a cat," I said grudgingly.

"But there's this guy who might be interested in her. He's a cop. So hot." Vero fanned herself. "I keep telling her she can't go out on a date wearing sweatpants. At the very least, she ought to make an effort. I mean, come on, put on a little makeup, right?"

"Why?" I grumbled. "So I'll look better in my mug shot?"

"Oooh!" Aimee's eyes sparkled. She leaned on her elbows against the glass. "This sounds exciting."

"You have no idea," Vero said.

Aimee spread her hands to reveal the colorful rows of palettes under the counter. "I can help you pick something out for her. Tell me about her best features."

Vero's eyes rolled to the ceiling. "Wow, that's a tough one."

"Watch it," I said.

"Well, she's got sort of wavy, reddish-brown hair. It looks nice when she's trying. Which isn't often."

I snapped a hanger over the rack.

"And hazel-green eyes. They change colors when she's mad and her face turns real red. Most of the time, she's sort of pale like a vampire, because she doesn't leave the house much. But she's got a few freckles here and there, so more like a friendly neighborhood sparkly vamp than one of those creepy coffin-dwelling kinds."

Aimee let loose a full-throated laugh.

"I'm glad she's amused," I muttered.

"Well, let's play up her eyes. They sound pretty." Aimee slid open a glass cabinet and set a tray of samples on the counter.

"Get on with it," I growled, earning a nasty look while Aimee's head was down.

Vero tapped her chin, studying Aimee's face as she arranged the palettes. "Have we met before?"

Aimee looked up. She tipped her head. "I don't think so."

"Are you sure?" Vero asked. "Because I was just here a few weeks ago for a makeover and I'm sure you were the one who sold me some blushers. Let me think . . . It would have been on a Tuesday, in the evening."

"No." She smiled politely. "That wouldn't have been me. I don't work on Tuesday nights. It may have been Julia," she added with a lilt. "People get us confused all the time."

Vero nodded. "Oh, sure! Julia rings a bell. Hey, is that a promotion?" Vero rose on her tiptoes to point out a display on the far side of the counter. As Aimee twisted to see it, Vero turned to me and mouthed, "What do I do?"

I swatted the air. "Don't look at me! Find out where she was that night."

"So," Vero said loudly, pulling Aimee's focus back to the counter, "you're off on Tuesdays? You must go out on Tuesday nights then. I bet you hit all the best spots in town."

"That was subtle," I deadpanned.

Aimee's smile was uncertain. Maybe a little uncomfortable as she returned to her task.

"I've heard great things about a place called The Lush. You know anything about it?"

Aimee's head snapped up as she dropped a tray of eye colors. The clatter of breaking plastic echoed through the store, drawing the attention of a floor manager. Aimee apologized, her cheeks flushing a hot shade of pink as she bent to scrape it up. "No, I'm sorry. I don't go there." Even from where I stood in the clothing racks, I could see her hands shaking as she wiped powder on her pant leg.

"My friend says the bartender's an underwear model. She says they have good drink specials on Tuesday nights. Are you sure you've never been there before?" The color drained from Aimee's face.

"Laying it on a little thick," I warned.

Aimee darted anxious glances around the counter, checking to make sure no one was listening when she said, "Are you a cop?"

Vero's head rocked back. She cocked a hip as they sized each other up.

"No, no, no," I hissed into the phone. "You are not a cop!"

Vero raised an eyebrow. "What if I am?"

"Look," Aimee said in a harsh whisper, "I don't know how you found me, but I had nothing to do with that man's disappearance. I haven't laid eyes on him in more than a year. I saw his name on the news just like everybody else."

"Then I'm sure you won't mind telling me where you were the night he went missing."

Breath held, I waited for her answer.

"I was at my AA meeting at the Episcopal Church on Van Buren. Same place I've been every Tuesday night for the last eleven months. You can check with my sponsor. She's there every week. Meetings start at eight," she said. "Just leave my husband out of it."

"Is that why you're working here?" Vero asked in a low voice. "To keep your husband out of it? Is that how you've been paying Harris off, using your paychecks to keep him from talking to Daniel?"

Aimee's mouth fell slack. Her eyes darted anxiously around her. "I don't know what you're talking about."

"It's okay," Vero said softly. "The police already know about the photos. He won't be able to hurt you again. If there's anything you want to say, you can tell me."

Aimee's eyes glimmered with the threat of tears. She pulled herself up by her spine. "Would you like me to wrap anything up for you?" Her voice fluttered, fragile under the artificial edge she tried and failed to hone.

Vero must have heard it, too. "You know what, I'll take that whole palette." Vero pointed to a set under the glass. Aimee rang it up, smiling tightly as Vero put the bills in her hand. Our eyes caught as Vero took the bag off the counter. I was pretty sure we were thinking the same damn thing.

Aimee had a motive. But she also had an alibi. So if Aimee hadn't helped Theresa kill Harris, who had?

"What does this mean?" Vero asked, throwing the bag of cosmetics in my lap and slamming her car door.

Aimee Reynolds was definitely the same Aimee on Harris's phone. And she was definitely the same woman who'd made the anonymous call to the police, But if she'd been at her AA meeting from eight to nine, there's no way she could have made it to the bar in time to see me leave with Harris.

"It means Aimee wasn't there but Theresa definitely had a motive. And she still doesn't have an alibi." I thought of the cash Steven said he'd found in her underwear drawer. What if she'd killed Harris for far less noble reasons than revenge? What if she'd killed him for money? "What if Nick's hunch is right and Theresa's in over her head with Feliks?"

Vero tipped her head back, rolling it sideways against the headrest to look at me. "You think Theresa's working for Feliks on more than just real estate deals?"

"It's possible." Nick had been right about everything else. "Harris clearly had a type. If Feliks wanted Harris dead, Theresa would have been the perfect lure. Maybe I just beat her to him."

"What are we going to do about Nick? That man is like a dog with a bone. If he keeps after her like this, he's going to end up right under our garage door."

I shook my head, maybe just to convince myself. "As long as there's no body, there's no case." It was possible to convict someone of murder without a body, but I knew from talking to Georgia, those cases were hard to prove. Nick would need solid evidence. He couldn't arrest us on a hunch. "Julian told Nick he was certain the woman in the photo wasn't Theresa. Theresa hasn't blabbed yet and neither have we. And Nick's not likely to get within three feet of Zhirov without Feliks's lawyers putting up a wall. Nick said it himself: nothing sticks to Feliks. Assuming none of us talks, any evidence Nick has is circumstantial at best. At some point, Nick will get tired of chasing dead ends and the case will go cold." I stared out my window at the rows and rows of cars, at the bright collective glare shining off the windshields. People went missing every day. As time went by, cases would pile up. Eventually, I told myself, Harris would get lost in the sea of them.

"Then you'd better make sure there aren't any sod farms in this book of yours."

"It was a cemetery," I muttered against the window, the words almost lost under the steady stream of Zach's babbling in the back seat. Vero looked at me askance. "In the book," I explained, "she buries the guy in a cemetery, in a freshly dug grave. You know, on top of some other guy who'd been buried there earlier."

Vero thought about that. She nodded appreciatively, as if she were tacking it to a corkboard in the back of her mind. "That's good. We should have thought of that before. We'll have to try that when you kill Andrei."

"We are absolutely not killing Andrei."

"Try telling that to Irina Borovkov."

CHAPTER 34

Ramón's shop was dark, with the exception of a single dim light in one of the office windows. On our way home from the mall, I'd gotten a text message from Vero's cousin, letting me know my van was fixed and would be ready for pickup at eight. But when I'd pulled up to the shop, the garage bay doors were already rolled down and the neon sign in the window was off. The dashboard clock of his loaner car said I was right on time, but everything about the place screamed, "Go away, we're closed."

Loose pebbles in the weatherworn asphalt crackled under my sneakers as I got out of the car and nosed around the lot. I found my van parked behind the garage, but the doors were locked and I hadn't brought a spare set of keys. I kicked the tire. Apparently, I'd driven all this way for nothing.

I groped in my purse, muttering a swear. I must have left my cell phone in my diaper bag when we'd gotten home from the mall that afternoon. Which meant my phone was at home with Vero. With a heavy sigh, I banged on the bay door. Maybe Ramón was still inside somewhere.

The knock was tinny and hollow. I shouted Ramón's name. When no one answered, I tried the side door to the office, surprised to find it open.

The bells on the door jangled, the sound echoing eerily off the smoke-stained walls and the mildew-stained ceiling. A water cooler gurgled in the shadowy corner of the waiting room. The place smelled like exhaust and ashtrays and the moldering hot rod magazines scattered over the plastic chairs.

"Ramón?" I called out. The door clanged shut behind me. "Ramón? It's Finlay Donovan. I'm here to pick up my—"

Snick.

I froze as a firm pressure, cold and sharp, pressed into the soft skin below my jaw.

My purse hit the floor with a thud. It was the only sound in the room.

Slowly, I raised my hands. I didn't dare move as a heavy boot kicked my purse out of the way. The contents spilled out of the open zipper, my blond wig splaying, loose change rolling, a tube of red lipstick skittering across the floor.

I aimed a glance at my wallet where it fell, careful not to lower my chin. The man's boot was huge, with wide steel toes and thick grooved soles. His clothes smelled like cigarettes, and his breath smelled strongly of garlic.

I swallowed carefully against the blade. "My wallet's on the floor. My keys are in my pocket. The car's out front. Take it and go."

He had the deep, husky laugh of a smoker. I yelped as he grabbed me by the hair and shoved me down the dark hall ahead of him.

Heart in my throat, I let him push me through a doorway, into the belly of the shadowy garage. He pulled me up short, barking gruff words I didn't understand. A smooth, cool voice responded in a guttural language that sounded decidedly Russian, and the man behind me let go of my hair with a grunt.

"Sit down, Ms. Donovan." The disembodied words ghosted from the far side of the room. The man's English was inflected with a subtle accent, and the frosty edge of his tone sent a shiver down my spine. I blinked, my eyes slowly adjusting to the darkness. The white collar of the man's dress shirt became visible in the dim light filtering through the high, narrow windows from the streetlamp outside. He stepped closer, his silhouette assuming the shape of a crisply tailored suit.

A metal folding chair creaked as he jerked it open in the middle of the garage.

When I didn't move, the man behind me yanked me toward it by the hair. With giant, meaty, calloused hands, he set me roughly down into it.

"You know who I am, Ms. Donovan," the man in the suit said. It was not a question.

I glanced over my shoulder at the ogre wielding the knife. Clearly, he hadn't received the memo about the dress code. He wore a tight black T-shirt and dark denim jeans over a stocky, muscular frame. My eyes traveled upward, to a smoothly shaven head over heavy, expressive eyebrows, and a nose that looked like it had been broken a few times. Up close, Andrei Borovkov was every bit as terrifying as I'd imagined he'd be.

Heels clicked slowly over the garage floor. My stomach fell away as Feliks Zhirov stepped into a beam of dusky light. His smile was serene. Expectant. I could only shake my head. "No," I croaked. "I don't think so."

His smile opened wider, revealing straight white teeth. His

sleek, dark hair fell curiously over one eye. "And yet, you were following me. Why?"

"I wasn't—"

He held up a hand, his cuff links glittering in the low light.
"Let's do each other the courtesy of not wasting each other's time."
His voice was ominously soft, the tight muscle of his jaw hinting
at his impatience. "Yesterday, a blue sedan, with the same license
plate as the one you just parked, followed my limo on a little expe-
dition through Fauquier County. My colleague tracked that plate
to this garage." Feliks tucked his hands in his pockets, his elegant
gait and his words thoughtfully measured as he paced in front of
me. "Ramón and I had a little talk. He told me you'd be coming
to return the car tonight, so I encouraged him to take the rest of
the evening off. Which means we can stay in this garage as long as
necessary.

But I'm sure you'd rather be home with your children, Ms. Donovan." He let my name hang in the silence. Finding my home—my
children—would be easy, assuming he hadn't already . . . "So let's
cut to the chase. Tell me." He straightened his sleeves with a pinch
of each cuff as he sauntered closer. "Why were you following me?"

"I wasn't following you." Feliks paused in front of my chair, the
hard lines of his mouth tightening into a thin line as his eyes cut
to Andrei. Andrei's hot cigarette breath rolled over the back of my
neck. His knife bit my throat as his calloused hands pinned me in
the chair. All I could think of were the three men Georgia's friends
had found murdered in an empty warehouse, their throats cut from
ear to ear, left in a river of blood.

"I was following Theresa!" I blurted. It wasn't entirely a lie. Eyes
squeezed shut, I braced for death. When it didn't come, I peeled
one open.

Feliks cocked his head. Curiosity softened the sharp contours of his face as he regarded me the way a cat might consider its prey—uncertain if he wanted to kill me or play with me. "What exactly is your business with Ms. Hall?"

"She's engaged to my ex-husband."

His eyebrows rose with a hint of surprise. "And what had you hoped to gain by spying on our meeting?"

My mouth went dry. I tried not to think about the sting of Andrei's knife, or the cool trickle down the side of my neck that may or may not have been sweat. "Steven . . . My ex-husband thinks she's having an affair."

"So you enlisted the help of a police officer to catch her?" Feliks laughed quietly. He scratched the dark stubble on his jaw. "Don't look so surprised, Ms. Donovan. Detective Anthony and I go back a very long time. I may not have recognized the car, but I sure as hell recognized the driver." He leaned in, a wicked gleam in his eye. He smelled like expensive liquor, soft leather, and fancy cologne, what I imagined the inside of a limo must smell like. "I can safely assume you witnessed nothing worthwhile, since Ms. Hall and I share a purely professional relationship." The devious curl of his lip suggested we had different definitions of *professional,* and I recoiled as he brushed a stray lock of hair from my face with the tip of his finger. "But tell me," he said, slipping his hands back in his pockets, "what was the detective after?"

"Nothing," I said, my voice trembling. "He was just keeping me company."

"Am I to infer that you and Detective Anthony enjoy a . . . personal relationship?"

I nodded, mute as Feliks knelt in front of me. His dark eyes flashed as he took me by the face, jerking my chin up. His voice crackled over with ice. "If I discover you've been lying to me, I will find you. Do you understand?"

Heart pounding, I nodded into his hand.

Andrei watched him, knife held, waiting for a sign.

A siren wailed in the distance, drawing closer.

Feliks let go. He rose to his feet as a car skidded to a stop out front, flooding the high windows with swirling blue light.

"Thank you for your time, Ms. Donovan," Feliks said. "I trust I won't be seeing you again."

He motioned to Andrei, and the hulking man followed him to the exit at the rear of the garage. My breath rushed out on a shudder as the back door closed behind them.

"Finlay!" Nick's muted shouts echoed from outside. Doors rattled on their hinges, one by one, as he made his way around the building. Bells jangled in the office. I got to my feet, surprised my shaking legs would hold me up.

"Over here," I managed to say.

Gun in hand, his figure swept into the garage, his eyes darting to every corner of the room. He rushed toward me and jerked to a stop. His gaze fell to my neck, then quickly over the rest of me. "Are you okay? What happened?"

I swiped a sticky bead of blood from my throat. The red smear it left on my fingertips made me woozy. "Just a scratch," I assured him. "I'm fine."

He took a slow step closer, tucking his gun back into his holster. I flinched as he lifted my chin to check the cut on my neck. His hand lingered possessively on my jaw, his body a little closer than professional protocol probably called for.

"What are you doing here?" I asked.

"Vero called but I was in a meeting and couldn't pick up. She left a frantic message. All she said was that you were at Ramón's Towing and Salvage and you'd forgotten your phone, and you needed help. I got here as fast as I could."

Ramón must have called Vero. He must have told her Feliks and Andrei were here waiting for me. When she hadn't been able to get through to warn me, she must have realized she had my phone. And she'd been worried enough to call Nick.

"You mind telling me what the hell's going on here?" he asked.

"I had an appointment to pick up my van, but Ramón wasn't here. Feliks Zhirov was inside waiting for me with one of his goons."

Nick's hand froze where it cupped my jaw. His eyes skated back and forth over mine, the skin around them creased with worry.

"I'm fine," I insisted. "They ran out the back door when they heard your siren." His eyes leapt to the rear of the garage, as if he was ready to run after them. "Don't bother," I told him. "They're long gone by now." I hadn't seen Feliks's car when I'd pulled up. He'd probably parked on the next block. The last thing I wanted was for Nick to go looking for them.

Nick dragged the folding chair closer, holding it steady as I slumped into it. The adrenaline rush was fading, and exhaustion was filling the void.

"Tell me everything," he said.

"Feliks knew we were tailing him the other day. He got the tag number of the loaner car and tracked it here. My mechanic is Vero's cousin. He must have called her to let her know I was in trouble." I leaned my elbows on my knees, rubbing the tension from my temples. Not only was I on Feliks's radar now, but so was Nick.

He rested his hands on his hips and looked down at the floor. "I'm sorry I didn't get Vero's message sooner."

"It's not your fault," I said through a shaky sigh.

"What did Feliks say?"

"He wanted to know why I was tailing him. I told him I was following Theresa. But he recognized you."

"Shit." Nick scrubbed his face as he paced a slow circle around the garage. "How'd you explain that?"

"I told him you and I were . . . *involved*. And the fact that you were in my car had nothing to do with him. But I'm not sure he believed me."

Nick paused, amusement lurking in the suggestive lift of his smile. "If you want to try convincing him, I have a few ideas."

With a roll of my eyes, I stood up, turning my back on him as I strode to the office to recover my purse. All I wanted was to make sure Vero was okay, to peek in on my kids as they slept, and to kiss them good night.

"Finn, wait." Nick swore quietly, catching me by the elbow. "I'm sorry. I was only trying to lighten things up. I know you've had one hell of a night. And I feel terrible that Feliks roughed you up because he spotted us together." He shook his head, raking his hands through his dark curls and setting them heavily on his hips. "I should've taken my own car. I should never have brought you along. Georgia's going to strangle me when she finds out—"

"She won't find out," I said, ignoring the guilt that tugged at my insides. "I won't tell her if you won't."

A weight fell from his shoulders. He nodded. "Go get your things. I'll drive you home."

My knees were still wobbly as I retreated to the office, and I was grateful for the excuse not to drive. I bent to collect the spilled contents of my purse, scraping cosmetics and loose change from the floor and jamming my wallet back inside. Nick's footfalls grew louder as I reached for my wig-scarf. As he came up behind me, I pushed it deeper under the desk.

"I'm going to have an unmarked keep an eye on your house for a while." I stood up, ready to protest, but Nick held up a finger. "Just for a few days. Just until we know he's not going to try to come for you again."

I opened my mouth to argue, but he was already calling it in. By the time he dropped me off at home, a cop would be stationed down the street from my house, documenting my every move, watching me come and go. This was worse than Mrs. Haggerty. Much, much worse. I used my shoe to nudge the wig-scarf deeper under the desk; I didn't dare bring it home.

CHAPTER 35

Suddenly, plotting murder didn't seem so hard. At the very least, it seemed easier than figuring out how *not* to murder someone in real life. Because when the doorbell rang at eight thirty on Saturday morning, I was irritable enough to try.

Honestly, I was surprised Steven had bothered to use the doorbell at all. Maybe Vero's lecture had sunk in. Either that, or the key she'd thrown in the diaper pail had truly been his only one. I nursed a cup of coffee as I padded stiffly to the door.

"You're early," I droned into my mug as I drew it open. "The kids aren't—"

Nick leaned against the doorframe, freshly shaven and his hair still damp from a shower, a grin taking hold as he took in my disheveled state. "Good morning to you, too."

I smoothed a hand through my hair, then clutched the front of my robe to hold it closed over the same sweat-soured clothes I'd been wearing the night before. "Sorry, I thought you were Steven.

What are you doing here?" I pressed my mouth shut; I hadn't even brushed my teeth yet.

"Came to see how you're doing after last night." His eyes dipped to my neck, and I reached to cover the nick Andrei had given me. The tiny scab was hardly noticeable this morning, but I'd just as soon forget the whole experience. Nick's brow furrowed, his usual easy smile turning down at the edges. "How'd you sleep?"

"I didn't. Much." Under the pressure of my looming deadline and countless emails from my agent, I'd been up working until three. I'd hardly been conscious enough to remember to send my latest batch of work to Sylvia before crashing in my clothes.

Nick hooked a thumb over his shoulder, toward an unmarked car parked just down the street. "You can rest easier tonight. Officer Roddy's keeping an eye on the place. Feliks won't get within five hundred feet without me knowing about it."

Great. Just what I needed. Maybe Officer Roddy and Mrs. Haggerty could have tea and share notes.

Nick raised an eyebrow. He bounced lightly on the heels of a pair of dress shoes. He'd ditched his usual dark jeans and Henley for a pair of steel-gray slacks and a button-down shirt. "You up for a little field trip?"

"Is that a euphemism?"

"Only if you want it to be."

I rolled my eyes at him over my coffee and gestured for him to come in. He followed me into the kitchen.

"Good morning, Detective," Vero said over her reading glasses and her textbook. "Help yourself to some coffee. Mugs are above the pot." She checked him out under her long lashes and mouthed "so hot" to me while his back was turned.

"Where are we going?" I asked, feeling a little crotchety. I didn't care how good Nick looked. Every time he showed up on my doorstep, I was just grateful he wasn't holding a pair of handcuffs and a warrant.

Nick pulled a mug from the cabinet. "Got any milk?"

"In the fridge," Vero said, running a highlighter over her textbook page without looking up.

"I'll get it—" I held my breath as he beat me to the fridge, pausing in front of the open door.

"I got a call from a tech at the lab," he said, plucking the carton of milk from the shelf. I offered up a silent prayer of thanks that there hadn't been a bag of cash wedged under it as he splashed some in his mug. "I'm heading over this morning to pick up his report. I thought you might want to come along."

Vero glanced up at the mention of the lab. "You go ahead," she said. "I'll stay with the kids."

"But you've got your exams to study for."

"Steven's picking them up soon. The house will be quiet."

"But—"

"You really shouldn't pass up a visit to the lab," she said firmly. "You might learn something interesting. You know, for your *book*." She placed a particular emphasis on this last bit.

"Okay," I conceded, infusing each word with the same added weight. "I'm sure you'll be fine here, since Nick has *Officer Roddy* doing surveillance just outside."

Vero's mouth formed a soft *oh*. "That's so thoughtful of him." She glanced sideways out the window, lifting a little in her seat to see Roddy's car. "Why don't you go get ready? I'll keep Detective Anthony company." She shooed me upstairs, ignoring my protests.

"So tell me about this Officer Roddy. Is he single?" I heard her ask as I shut myself in my room.

Great. This was just great. Knowing Nick, he probably had an officer stationed outside Theresa's house, too. But Vero was right. I'd learn more about the status of the investigation sitting in his car than I would watching it play out from my window.

I hopped in a fast shower, towel-dried my hair, swiped on some mascara and gloss, and stood in my towel in front of the closet. My wardrobe consisted mostly of sweatpants and T-shirts, so I was surprised to find my only pair of black slacks, cleaned and pressed, hanging beside a crisp white button-down shirt that Vero must have washed and ironed for me. I dragged them on, nearly tripping myself as I rushed to sling on a pair of low heels. If we were going to a forensics lab, I should at least look like I'd arrived in the front of a police cruiser, rather than the back of one.

I descended the stairs, fishing around for the holes in my ears with the posts of the diamond studs Steven had bought for me on our first anniversary. I hadn't worn them since the divorce, and I was surprised to find the holes in my lobes hadn't closed completely.

Nick and Vero glanced up as my heels clicked into the kitchen. Vero looked confused. "I'm sorry. Do I know you? Because I thought I worked for a vampire in yoga pants."

Ignoring her, I turned to Nick. "Ready to go?"

He wore a crooked smile as he rose from his chair, his gaze falling into the deep V in my blouse. "Is that a euphemism?"

Heat bloomed over my chest and I turned sharply for the door.

Vero snickered into her textbook. "Have her home before dark, Detective. Finlay has a book to work on."

"We'll be back in a few hours," I called over my shoulder.

The children's duffels were already packed and waiting in the foyer. The sight of them left me feeling a little untethered. I was pretty sure I'd never get used to this. Nick waited as I pasted on a convincing smile and gave them each a kiss good-bye. Delia's peach-fuzzy hair was soft against my chin. Zach's pudgy cheeks smelled like Cheerios and warm milk and I breathed them in. "Be good for your daddy, and I'll see you on Monday morning, okay?"

I swiped my eyes. When I threw open the door, Steven was standing in front of me, his hand poised to knock. I darted a panicked glance into the windshield of his truck, thankful Theresa and Aimee weren't in it.

Steven's jaw tensed as he looked over my shoulder at Nick. Nick came around me and extended a hand. Steven took it reluctantly.

"Who's this?" he asked me.

"That's Nick," Delia answered from the living room, dragging her naked Barbie around by the hair. "He's a friend of Aunt Georgia's."

"Oh, yeah?" Steven's smile was bitter under his ball cap, his tight fists punching an outline through the pockets of his sweatshirt.

"He and Mommy are dating."

My eyes flew wide as I realized how this must look to him. I couldn't remember the last time Steven had seen me wear makeup. Or anything other than pajamas, for that matter. I gestured to Nick. "We're not . . . I mean, he's not . . ."

"This is the attorney?" Steven glowered, his blue eyes raking over Nick with a look of disgust.

"No," Delia said. "He's a policeman. Like Aunt Georgia."

I pulled Steven aside and said in a hushed voice, "You know Delia. She has no idea what she's saying."

"Why do you all keep saying that?" Delia huffed.

"Don't forget to feed Christopher," I called back to her.

"Christopher?" Nick asked, leaning close enough for his breath to warm the shell of my ear as Steven glared at him.

"Her goldfish," I answered.

Delia padded into the foyer and tugged on her father's sleeve. "Can we go get Sam today?"

Steven screwed up his face. "Who's Sam?"

"The doggy at the shelter." She gazed up at him with pleading eyes. "Aaron told me I could adopt him. But Mommy said since Christopher already lives here, Sam will have to live at Theresa's house."

Steven gritted his teeth. "She did, did she?"

"We should go," I said, surprised when Nick's hand found the small of my back on the way to the door. He smirked, making a grand gesture of holding it open for me as I blew kisses to my kids and told them I'd see them on Monday. I saw Steven's face watching us through the window as Nick opened the passenger-side door for me. In my rearview mirror, Mrs. Haggerty's curtains fluttered like a ghost. Nick got in and started the car.

"So," he said, "tell me about this attorney."

I spent most of the drive to the lab dodging Nick's questions about my love life. Everything that came out of my mouth was the truth; I wasn't dating an attorney. Not technically. Technically, I wasn't dating Julian *or* Nick. But knowing Nick, he would probably investigate my claims himself. And I hoped that investigation wouldn't take him back to The Lush.

By the time we pulled into the parking lot, I was grateful for the distraction. Nick clipped a visitor badge to the collar of my shirt, then clipped one to his.

"What are you expecting to find?" I asked as we crossed the bright two-story lobby of the regional forensics lab.

Nick headed for a set of long, winding stairs, nodding at the lab techs as we passed and greeting them by name. He waited until they were out of earshot before answering. "When we tailed Feliks and Theresa, they drove to four different properties without stepping foot on a single one of them. They never even stopped the car. But there was soil and grass stuck to the undercarriage of Feliks's Lincoln that day. Which means they'd been off-roading somewhere pretty recently." Nick's pace quickened as he climbed the stairs, his focus sharpening. "My guess is he's found a piece of land already, or at least one he's seriously interested in. If I can figure out where it is and how it's zoned, I can probably guess what he's planning to do with it. Or at least be one step ahead of him when he buys it."

"Why?"

"Feliks never records the deeds in his own name. He uses straw men or dummy corporations, which makes his holdings harder to find. If I know what name he's using as a front when he buys this lot, I might be able to use that information to track down a few others."

"And do what?"

"Raid them. See what kind of dirt I can turn up."

"What does that have to do with Theresa and Harris Mickler?"

"Maybe nothing. But I'd love to find a reason to bring Feliks into the station, stuff him in an interrogation room, and find out."

Nick's long legs ate the stairs two at a time, his pace eager as we neared the top.

"And the guys in the lab can figure all this out with a piece of dirt?" I asked, struggling to keep up.

"I wasn't sure. It seemed like a long shot, but the call I got this morning sounded promising." Nick pushed open a door and held it open for me. He led us to a lab at the end of the hall and rapped on the window glass. A tech in a white coat waved us inside.

"Hey," the tech said, meeting us halfway into the room and extending his hand to me. "Finlay Donovan, wow!" His handshake was enthusiastic and more than a little sweaty.

"I'm sorry," I said with a puzzled glance at Nick, then back at the tech. He was young, cute in a geeky, awkward sort of way. He pushed his glasses up the bridge of his nose. Even when I could see through them more clearly, I couldn't place how we knew each other. "And you are?"

"Oh, right!" He shook his head, giving himself a playful slap on the forehead. "Sorry, I'm Peter. We've never met. But Georgia's told me all about you. I'm a huge fan, actually." He wiped his palm on his lab coat, his ears flushing pink. He snuck a peek at Nick and leaned toward my ear, confiding in a low voice, "I've read your books."

"Oh! So you must be the one." I laughed as Peter's face fell. "I'm kidding." I pitched my voice to a conspiratorial whisper. "There are at least two of you." The corner of Peter's lip pulled up with an uncertain smile. "Seriously, I'm kidding."

He released a nervous laugh. "Nick told me you might be coming. I was wondering if you'd sign an autograph?"

"Sure," I said through a blush. No one outside my family had ever asked me for an autograph before. "Why not?"

Nick gave a reticent shrug, but I could tell he was anxious to get what we'd come for and his patience was wearing thin. Peter pulled a dog-eared paperback and a Sharpie from the pocket of his lab coat. Nick glanced at the bulging pecs of the model on the cover and heaved an impatient sigh as I scribbled a quick signature in it. Peter studied my face as I handed him back his book.

"You don't look anything like your picture," he said, thumbing to my bio page. "You know, the one in the back of the book? You're blond in your photo. And with the dark glasses, it's sort of hard to see your face." He held up the photo, scrutinizing my features against my headshot. My scalp itched, and I tucked my hair behind my ear. "If I didn't know you were coming, I totally wouldn't have recognized you." I avoided looking at Nick as he glanced over Peter's shoulder at my photo, then checked his watch. "You probably wear a disguise so you won't be recognized in public and get swarmed by your fans, right?"

"Right," I said with a nervous laugh. Or be recognized when I'm abducting scary rapists from bars, breaking into real estate offices, or taking contracts to kill problem husbands while eating cheesecake in Panera. Through all of this, I had never stopped to consider that my headshot—which appeared in every copy of my books—was now an incriminating piece of evidence against me. Or that Nick could use it to place me at The Lush.

"Georgia said you have a new book coming out. I can't wait to read it. If you ever have forensic questions, I'm your guy. I've always wanted to—"

"Pete," Nick barked. Pete turned, as if only just remembering Nick was there. "Do you have something for me?"

"Oh, yeah! You're not going to believe this." I released a held breath as Peter tucked my book back in his pocket and waved us toward a lab table. A wad of muddy grass sat in a specimen dish beside a microscope. He pushed up his glasses, his dark eyes brimming with excitement. "So, normally," he explained, "this would be a monumental feat you've asked me to pull off, and the best I would be able to do would be to narrow the sample down to a particular growing region—like, maybe a few counties, or even states—but *never* a specific piece of property. However," he said with a dramatic pause, "in this case, the grass you found is pretty rare."

Nick leaned in. "How rare?"

"Like . . ." Pete's eyes rolled up as if he were calculating in his head, the way Vero often did, "really rare. It's a variation of a popular fescue, but this specific variety is new, so it hasn't been widely used in this part of the mid-Atlantic. The sample you grabbed contained a layer of topsoil, and the combination of industrial-grade fertilizers and pesticides I found suggests it was professionally maintained. So I pulled up a list of seed distributors and used that to track down a list of companies in the mid-Atlantic that recently purchased it. There are three possible matches in Virginia. But only one of them hits all the criteria you gave me—west of the airport, east of Interstate 81."

Peter handed Nick a piece of paper.

Nick's brow pulled down, his posture becoming rigid as he read the report. He frowned, uncharacteristically quiet as he folded it and slipped it into the breast pocket of his coat.

"Wait," I said, curious about the reason for Peter's excitement. "What did it say?"

Nick turned me by the shoulders and directed me with a firm hand toward the door. "Thanks, Pete. Gotta go."

Pete's smile crumbled. "Wait, you're leaving? But there's more."

"I'll call you later," Nick said over his shoulder.

"Bye, Finlay!" Pete called after me. "It was great meeting you!"

I didn't get a chance to reply. Nick applied a steady pressure to the small of my back, ushering me to the head of the stairs.

"Where are we going?" I clutched the rail to keep from slipping on my heels.

"I'm taking you home. There's something I need to check out." His gait was tense and quick, his low voice rumbling like a revved engine.

"What did you find?" Whatever it was, it must have been important. "Why won't you tell me?" I asked, chasing him down the stairs.

"Because I've already told you too much."

I stopped in the middle of the lobby, arms crossed stubbornly over my chest as he barreled toward the glass doors, his car keys already in his hand. "If this is because of last night, I'm fine. You don't have to protect me from Feliks or his goons."

He doubled back and took me firmly by the elbow, hauling me toward the door. "You weren't fine. I'm taking you home. I made a mistake. I don't want you anywhere near this investigation."

I planted my heels, pulling him up short. "If you didn't want me involved, you wouldn't have brought me along." A muscle tensed in his cheek. "You found something in that report you don't want me to know. Didn't you?"

He raked a hand through his dark hair and swore under his breath.

"You've told me everything else about this case. Why not this? Why not now?"

He pressed a finger to his lips, casting anxious looks around us. "Because I thought we could help each other," he said, struggling to keep his voice down. "You wanted proof that Theresa is unfit for custody, and I wanted to arrest her. But this isn't just about Theresa anymore."

"You're right. It's not. And after what Feliks tried to do to me last night, I think I deserve to know."

He pinched the bridge of his nose and loosed a heavy sigh. "It's better if you don't."

"You can't shut me out! You said it yourself, I already know too—"

"Steven's farm," he surrendered in a low voice. "The grass on Feliks's Lincoln came from your ex-husband's farm."

I fell back a step. Of all the things I'd expected to hear, this wasn't it.

"There has to have been some mistake," I said through a tight throat. "Theresa would never have been stupid enough to take her fling to Steven's farm."

"You're assuming they were there for personal reasons. What if it was business?"

Ms. Hall and I share a purely professional relationship.

That's what Feliks had said. But that made even less sense. "Steven just bought the farm last year. It's not for sale."

"If it isn't for sale, what was Feliks doing there?"

I didn't have an answer for that.

"Now do you understand why I didn't want to tell you? If I can prove Feliks was conducting illicit business on Steven's farm, and if a lawyer can prove you or your kids stand to benefit in any way from that business, then your involvement compromises the whole case."

"My involvement already compromises your case," I argued. "No one has to know."

"Feliks knows, and he can use it against me in court."

"He can't prove I know anything about your case. I told him we were romantically involved."

There was a challenge in the dark shine of Nick's eyes. "Are you going to tell your ex the same thing when we roll up on his farm?"

So that's where Nick was going. To the farm. I could either let him drop me off at home and spend the rest of the day wondering what he'd found there, or I could make him take me along.

"He won't be there," I said, my legs a little unsteady at the thought. "He's got the kids."

Nick chewed his lip as he studied me, his knuckles white on his hips. He pitched his voice low. "I can do this without you, Finlay. The less you know, the better off we both are."

I wasn't sure who he was trying to convince, him or me. The only thing I knew for certain was that Harris Mickler was buried on that farm, and I couldn't let Nick find him. "I'm coming with you." I snatched the keys from his hand before he could object. If Nick was going anywhere near that farm, I'd be damned if he was going without me.

CHAPTER 36

"You're sure Steven isn't here?" Nick was wound tight as a drum as he turned down the long gravel drive into the farm. My own stomach was already tangled in knots, and the ruts in the road weren't helping matters. I swallowed the urge to be sick on the floor mats of his car.

"He has the kids until Monday."

"Is anyone else here?"

I recognized the red VW bug parked in front of the sales trailer. "Bree. She works in the office."

"Does she know you?"

"Yes."

"Then this'll be easy," Nick said, swinging his car into the space beside Bree's and slinging open his door. "Follow my lead."

A pit opened in my stomach as I followed him to the trailer. He held the door open for me, but I lingered just outside. "Should we be here?" I whispered. "I mean, shouldn't we have a warrant or something?"

"I'm just in the market for some sod." He pasted on a wholesome smile and directed me inside.

Bree looked up from her computer. "Hey, Mrs. Donovan! It's so good to see you. But Steven's not in." Her head cocked as if I should have known. "He's off today."

"I know. He's got the kids. They're probably at the animal shelter looking at puppies."

"Oh, that's so sweet." She clutched her heart. I could practically hear her ovaries exploding. Nick raised an eyebrow. I gave a short nod in answer.

He suppressed a wry grin and introduced himself. "I'm a friend of Ms. Donovan." He placed a particular emphasis on my honorific, his hand moving to my lower back, a little lower than it had before in the lab. Bree's eyes followed it, and I could see her tuck that morsel of information away. "I'm looking to dress up my yard, and Finlay tells me you've got quite a nice selection of sod."

"We sure do." She dragged open a file drawer. "I'd be happy to get you a brochure."

"Actually, a buddy of mine recommended something called Blue Sheep's Fescue. Do you carry it here?"

"We do, actually. But we've sold through our very first batch of it, so it's all been spoken for. A developer preordered the entire lot over the summer."

"So you all haven't sold any of it anywhere else?" he asked. I stepped on Nick's toe. Bree might be young, but she wasn't naive about everything.

"Not yet," she said. "But we'll be seeding another lot in the spring. I can get you pricing if you'd like to order some."

"Thanks, but I think I'd like to take a look at it first, if you wouldn't mind. You said you have some growing here?" His fingers curled around my waist. A bead of sweat trailed down my side, and I hoped he couldn't feel it through my shirt.

"We sure do. I'd be happy to take you out and show you. Let me just put a note on the door in case anyone stops by while we're gone." Bree opened her desk drawer and withdrew a pack of heart-shaped sticky notes before Nick stopped her.

"I can't ask you to do that. You're the only one here, and I'd hate to pull you away from your desk. If you tell me where it is, I can find it myself."

Bree seemed relieved. She dug around in her file drawer and fished out a photocopied map of the farm. I gnawed on my thumbnail as she marked the dirt road with a pink highlighter, pointing out the square of land Nick was searching for . . . the plot directly across the gravel road from Harris Mickler's body.

"Mrs. Donovan . . . err . . . *Ms.* Donovan knows the way," Bree said, correcting herself as she handed Nick the map. She turned to me and said, "You've driven past it before, Ms. Donovan. It's the very last field before the rear entrance, across from the big fallow plot. The grass you're looking for has a blueish tint to it. You can't miss it."

"Thanks, Bree. You've been very helpful." Nick took me by the hand and led me to the door. "I'll be in touch soon."

His shoes crunched over the parking lot in giant, fervent bites. I cracked the window as soon as we were in the car, sweat building behind my knees and under my arms.

"Your ex is a real piece of work." He glanced up at his rearview mirror, his eyes narrowing on something behind us. "I'll probably catch hell for this, and I should probably feel guilty about it, but I don't." He leaned across the console, took my face in both hands, and kissed me. It was the kind of quick, hot kiss that would have made my toes curl if I wasn't so busy wondering how I would look wearing his handcuffs and a pair of orange coveralls. I shoved him back with a firm hand to his chest.

"What was that for?" I asked, flushed and breathless.

"That was for Bree. Because she's watching out the window right now. And since Mrs. Haggerty hasn't seen anything quite so newsworthy, I figured someone should tell Steven we're involved and back up our story. As far as anyone is concerned, we were here on personal business." His smile was a little crooked. "Let's go pick out some sod for my house."

My chest felt tight as he put the car in gear, the air thin as his sedan bounced down the long dirt road through the fields, kicking up brown clouds of dust. Nick parked before we reached the end, just within sight of the line of cedars surrounding the property line of the farm. Behind them, I could just make out the narrow rural road Vero and I had used to get here the night we'd buried Harris.

Nick turned off the engine. He stared at the stretch of gravel in front of us, then at the fields, thoughtfully tapping the steering wheel.

I didn't dare look left, into the russet-brown lot of mounded dirt where Harris was decomposing. Instead, I stared into the swaying sea of hairlike blue fescue to my right. Nick didn't have a shovel, I reminded myself as my palms grew clammy. He wasn't digging anything up—at least not today. All I had to do was keep cool and determine his next move. Then Vero and I could figure out what to do.

"What do you think Feliks and Theresa were doing out here?" I asked in a shaky voice.

"I don't know. Let's find out." My pulse quickened as Nick got out of the car. He walked along the edge of the field where the fescue met the road, pausing to kneel beside a set of tire tracks that had

crushed a short path through the grass. The tracks had left deep div-
ots where they'd met the gravel, and a wide swath of grass had been
torn from the roots, as if the undercarriage of a car had dragged over
it. Feliks's Lincoln.

Too anxious to sit still, I got out of the car, arms crossed against
the biting wind that rolled over the endless acres of sod and billowed
the thin fabric of my shirt. I hovered behind Nick as he followed the
tread marks into the field. They stopped just a few feet into the
grass. "Feliks and Theresa probably entered the farm from the rear
entrance," he said, studying the direction of the tracks. "Looks like
they backed into the field, just enough to turn around."

"So they didn't stay?" I hoped this meant we didn't have to stay
either. "Maybe Feliks decided he didn't like this farm any more than
he liked the others."

Nick shook his head, hands on his narrow hips as he turned
between the tread marks, thinking. "Why would he look at a piece
of land that's not for sale? And why come through the back unless
he didn't want to be seen doing it?" He paced slowly between the
tracks, talking to himself out loud, as if he were trying to see this
place through Feliks's eyes. "If he didn't want to risk being seen
here, he wouldn't have come during the day. He would have come at
night, after the office closed, when the place was dark . . ."

He stood where the Lincoln would have been, his feet strad-
dling the gash at the edge of the field, his eyes seeming to follow the
path of the car's headlights to the precise spot where we'd dug our
hole. My breath caught as he stared at the dirt over Harris's grave.
"Zhirov wants this land for a purpose, and he doesn't care if it belongs to someone else, as long as no one sees him using it. So what's
he doing with it? And why involve a real estate agent if there's no
sale? Unless . . ."

Nick's voice trailed. He walked closer to the fallow field, dirt crumbling under his shoes as he paused at the edge of it. Wind howled in my ears. Or maybe it was my blood. I felt a little light-headed as his expression morphed from confusion to wonder.

"That's it," he said in a low voice. "He's not going through Theresa because she's an agent. He's going through her because she's about to become an owner. Legally, this whole farm becomes hers the minute she marries your ex-husband." He backed away from the field, his eyes lit with a wild intensity. "I can't believe I didn't think of it," he said under his breath as he rushed back to his car.

"What do you mean, *that's it*? Where are we going?" I hurried after him. The engine was already running as I stumbled into the car. He put an arm around my seat back, turning to see behind us as he backed up the car, the road through the windshield in front of us obscured by thick clouds of dust as he sped up.

"To find a judge who isn't already in Zhirov's pocket," he said. "Preferably one who'll issue a search warrant on a Saturday."

He wrenched the wheel, spinning us around. I braced myself against the dash. "A search warrant for what?"

His eyes narrowed as he hit the gas. "To dig up your ex-husband's farm."

CHAPTER 37

Nick hugged the far-left lane of the interstate, flashing his lights at the slower cars in front of us and leaning on his horn. His knuckles were white around the steering wheel, his attention squarely on the road. I could practically smell the rubber burning from the spinning wheels in his brain.

"I don't understand. Why is it necessary to dig up Steven's farm?"

"Feliks isn't looking to buy land. If he was, he would have come in through the front door, flashed his cash, and made Steven an offer he couldn't refuse. And if Steven did refuse, Feliks would have pressured him into selling it—probably under threat of violence. I'm guessing Feliks is just looking to use the farm for something shady, and he wants to keep it as quiet as possible. So he went to Theresa—someone he could easily manipulate with attention and money. I'm betting Zhirov is bribing Theresa to let him use the farm for a very specific purpose. Whatever it is, he doesn't plan to use it for very long."

I thought back to the cash Steven had found in her drawer. "Maybe Feliks is just meeting people out there."

"No," Nick said, growing impatient with the driver in front of him and passing him on the right. I gripped the door handle as we zigzagged between cars. "Zhirov owns restaurants and hotels all over the state. He can meet with people anywhere. If he was only meeting them, he wouldn't go to so much trouble."

"Then what do you think he's doing?"

"I don't know. But I'm guessing the answer is buried somewhere in that field."

I swallowed back a wave of nausea. "Why would you think that?"

"There was more than one set of tire marks. There were two other sets at the edge of that field."

"Two others?"

"All three vehicles came in through the back entrance. They all parked in different places, but all three of them stopped facing into that dirt field. Feliks's stash is probably buried under the intersection of those headlights."

"Maybe they were just . . . doing business there." I pressed back in my seat as six lanes of traffic closed in around me. "You know, on top of the ground. Covertly. In front of the headlights."

Nick shook his head. "The dirt was freshly turned. There wasn't a single footprint in it. Someone cleaned up after themselves. And I'm going to find whatever it is they're hiding."

Nick's jaw was hard set. I had no doubt he would tear this county apart until he got what he was after. "How long will it take you to get a warrant?"

"Maybe a day. Probably two. The farm isn't in my jurisdiction, so we'll need to coordinate with the guys in Fauquier County. I'm going to run you home," he said, his tone leaving no room for discussion. "I'll have to pull a few favors. Judges don't like being dragged off the golf course, and it's probably better if I do this myself."

He pulled into my driveway with a sharp jerk of the wheel. The car lurched to a stop, and I reached for the handle. "Hey, wait," Nick said. I turned, hoping he couldn't see the guilt and fear written all over my face. He cupped my cheek. Stroked it with his thumb. "I know today got a little crazy. How about I come by later and take you to dinner?"

"That sounds . . ." I cleared the tight knot from my throat. "That sounds really great, but I should probably skip dinner. I have a ton of work to do, and I've been gone all day. I've got some deadlines to juggle." And one very dead body.

Nick leaned in and stole a sweet, soft kiss that left me feeling even guiltier. I threw open the door and got out. Watched his car peel out of the driveway. He waved at Officer Roddy as he hurtled past his car.

Across the street, Mrs. Haggerty's curtains were hemmed open, her white hair hovering like a specter behind the glass. I'd had enough of the woman. That was it. I was finally going to give her a piece of my mind.

Her curtain fell closed as I crossed the street, my low heels clicking as I stormed up her front steps.

"Mrs. Haggerty!" I banged on the door. "It's Finlay Donovan, and I have something to say to you."

I had just raised a hand to bang on it again when it flew open. The rush of warm air from inside threw me off-balance.

"It's about time you came around." Mrs. Haggerty glared up at me over the gold rims of her half-moon glasses, her tawny-rose lipstick wobbling outside the natural lines of her wrinkled scowl. She wore too much rouge on her pasty cheeks, and her old-lady perfume was thick in my nose.

I gaped at her, breathing shallowly. She didn't make any gestures to invite me in, but she didn't shut the door in my face either. "What do you mean?"

"It's about time. I've been waiting for my apology for a year now. Now then, you said you have something to say to me?" She lifted her chin, the loose skin underneath wobbling proudly between the gold chains hanging from the tips of her glasses.

"That's why you wouldn't open the door for me last week? Because you were waiting for me to . . . apologize?"

I tipped my head, baffled, as she gave a tight, determined nod. "I knew you would eventually, since you probably want to know if I saw anything suspicious happen in your garage."

The ground bottomed out from under me. "You saw something suspicious inside my garage?"

"I'm not a member of the neighborhood watch for nothin'."

"You're not?" I caught myself, shut my mouth before I said something stupid, and shook my head. "I mean, of course you're not. And you're right, that's exactly why I came over. To apologize. For . . ." She raised the two pencil-thin eyebrows she'd drawn lopsided on her face. I had no idea what she expected me to atone for. She'd been the one to spy on my house. She'd been the one to tell on Steven and kick my marriage into a downward spiral. She'd been the one to blab it to the rest of the neighborhood watch. And yet, at the end of it all, the blame belonged squarely on one person's shoulders. And they probably weren't the bony, hunched ones in front of me now. She lifted her chin higher, waiting.

"I'm sorry," I said, swallowing the last of my pride, "that I yelled at you and called you terrible names. I was angry at my husband, and I took it out on you. And I shouldn't have."

Mrs. Haggerty wrinkled her nose, adjusting her glasses to peer at me through them, as if she were gauging my sincerity. With a satisfied grunt, she let them fall to her bosom.

"So, about my garage," I said cautiously. "What did you see, exactly?"

She reached for the bound diary on the hall table behind her. Thumbing it open, she licked a gnarled finger and fanned through the pages. She settled on one with a sigh. "On the night of Tuesday, October eighth, I saw you leave with the kids a little before six in the evening. And then I saw you come back without them at approximately six forty. I figured you'd probably be in for the night since you don't get out much." She looked down her nose at me, and I smiled tightly back. It was all I could do to keep from throttling the woman. "But then I saw you leave again, all dressed up like you were going on a date, I assume with that dark-haired policeman you've been entertaining lately." She raised a poorly drawn eyebrow, inviting me to elaborate on my relationship with Nick, but why bother? She seemed to have it all figured out. "I actually mistook you for Ms. Hall at first, to be honest. But then you tripped in your heels coming off your garage step and I knew right away it was you. You're clumsier than Theresa. And you have horrific posture," she added, scrutinizing my shoulders. "That's probably because of all the time you spend in front of that computer. It's unhealthy, you know."

I gestured impatiently for her to go on.

"Anyway, I guess that must have been just after seven," she said, returning her attention to her book. "After that, everything was quiet for a few hours. I watched my TV programs and had a slice of pie, which is how I knew it was about nine forty-five when I noticed the lights in your garage. You left your van running when you ran inside. I figured you were grabbing something you'd forgotten before going to pick up the children from wherever you'd taken them earlier."

"My sister's," I said, gesturing again.

"Your sister, the police officer? There sure have been a lot of them over there these last few days—"

"Yes, she was babysitting for me," I said a little too brusquely. "Did you see anything else?"

"Of course," she snapped, as if the very question of her vigilance was offensive. "I watched the house, to make sure nobody bothered your van while you were inside. I was irritable at first because you were taking a long while, and I was missing my late-night TV program on account of it. But then something strange happened." She adjusted her glasses, the thick gold chain catching on the shoulder pads in her sweater.

"What did you see?"

She leveled an arthritic finger at me. "I saw someone snooping inside your garage."

My breath rushed out of me. This was it. Mrs. Haggerty had seen the people who killed Harris. "Do you remember what they looked like?"

"It was hard to see clearly from here, especially so late at night. The headlights from the van were behind him, but I could tell he was tall. He had to bend down a bit to see inside the windows of your van. I thought he might be one of the hoodlums in the neighborhood planning to steal it, so I went downstairs to call the police. But by the time I got to the phone in the kitchen, you must have come out to the garage and scared him off. When I looked out my kitchen window, your garage door was already shut. As far as I could see he was gone." I glanced behind her, at an electric chairlift perched on a track at the base of the stairs. My grandmother had one in her house. They moved like molasses. Who knew how much time Mrs. Haggerty had lost? Or if she could even be considered a reliable eyewitness. She hadn't actually seen anyone close the garage door. And even if she had, the woman couldn't see her face in the mirror to apply her own lipstick. A judge might just throw her testimony out.

"You said it was a he?" I asked, making sure I'd heard her right.

She gave a confident nod. I raked back my hair, struggling to puzzle it out. Feliks was tall. I supposed he could have come here with Theresa. Or even with Andrei. But something about that scenario felt off. I'd had enough run-ins with Feliks to see how he operated. Feliks didn't do his own dirty work. That's what he had Andrei for. And Andrei wasn't subtle.

"Did you see who was with him?"

"I didn't see anyone else. Only the one."

But that didn't make sense. Someone else had to have been there to help the killer close the garage. Maybe they'd waited in the car, only emerging after Mrs. Haggerty was on her way down the stairs.

"Did you see what kind of car he was driving?"

Her eyes narrowed. "There was no car. Not anywhere I could see."

So the culprit had come on foot, as I'd suspected before. And without a description of a suspect or a vehicle—without proof that someone else had intentionally murdered Harris—I would become the prime suspect once Nick figured out that I was the woman at The Lush. My best hope was that Nick would hit a dead end. That Julian wouldn't identify me to the police, and that no one could prove Harris Mickler had ever been to my house.

"Did you . . . happen to see or hear anything else that night? Anything odd . . . in my garage?" I asked cautiously.

"No," she said. "I couldn't hear much of anything over the dogs down the street. They must have seen the thief and it got them going. They seemed to quiet once he was gone." She scratched her head, referencing back to her diary. "Let's see . . . I saw your babysitter let herself in the front door. I figured everything over there was settled, and I went to bed shortly after that." Mrs. Haggerty's nose scrunched up, pushing the wrinkles in her forehead together into a maze of thoughtful lines. "Come to think of it, I woke up before dawn to a horrible crashing sound, but I couldn't tell you what caused it." That would have been the garage door falling closed after Vero and I got home from the farm. Which meant she hadn't witnessed us coming or going in between.

"Good . . . I mean, thanks." My shoulders sagged with relief. "Did you happen to call the police? About any of it?"

"No." Her slack skin wobbled with the shake of her head. "I didn't bother. No point wasting anybody's . . ." Her thought broke off. She peeled off her glasses, staring up at me with her beady blue eyes. "Why?" she asked eagerly. "Did that man steal something? If he did, we can go down the street and talk to that policeman right now." She pointed at Officer Roddy's unmarked car.

"No, no. Everything's fine," I insisted, stepping back from her door. But it wasn't. Not by a long shot. By my best estimates, I had forty-eight hours to figure out who'd killed Harris Mickler before Nick dug up his body.

CHAPTER 38

I unlocked the front door of my house and let myself in, surprised by the silence inside until I remembered the children were with their father. Still, the quiet was unsettling. The TV was off. All the lights were out.

"Vero?" I called. Her name echoed back. Maybe she'd gone to the library to study.

My dress heels clicked loudly across the kitchen. I cracked the door to the garage. Vero's Charger was there, beside the empty space where I usually parked. I'd left Ramón's loaner car back at his shop after the incident with Feliks, and I still hadn't gotten my van back.

I shut the kitchen door, and as the sound was absorbed by the empty house I had the sudden heavy feeling that I wasn't alone. That I was being watched.

Something was definitely wrong. Something was very—

"Surprise!" My heart skidded to a halt. Vero jumped through the opening of the dining room with Zach on her hip. Delia jumped out after her. A bouquet of helium balloons had been tied to the buttons of her overalls with brightly colored ribbons that matched the spikes in her hair. A cake perched in the center of the cleared folding table where our bills used to sit. Streamers had been strung from the brass chandelier, and a bottle of champagne and two juice boxes were chilling in a bucket of ice.

Delia bounded into my legs, nearly knocking me over. I wrapped her in a tight hug, memorizing the shape of her—her slight weight, the feel of her soft skin against mine—wondering how old she would be the next time I saw her after Nick found Harris's body.

"I thought you were spending the weekend with your father." I pulled back to look in her big hazel eyes.

"Daddy had to go to work," Delia said, her tiny hands fiddling with the diamond studs in my ears.

"Steven showed up with them about an hour ago," Vero explained, rocking Zach on her hip. "He said there had been some emergency at the farm and he needed to go. Theresa was out showing homes and he couldn't reach her, so he asked if the kids could stay here tonight. And considering the amazing news, the three of us thought it would be a good excuse to celebrate!" Delia handed me a balloon. Zach blew spit into the plastic noisemaker in his mouth, his toothy grin wide around it.

"What news?" I asked as Zach reached for me and leaned into my arms. I squeezed him tight, pretty sure nothing was as newsworthy as Nick's discovery this afternoon.

Vero handed me a folded copy of the local gazette. "Bottom of the front page," she said.

I set Zach on the floor and he toddled off. My balloon thumped against the ceiling as I let it loose to open the newspaper.

There I was.

My author photo—me with my blond wig-scarf, my eyes obscured behind dark sunglasses—had been printed in black-and-white under a headline: *Local Author Scores Six Figures for Her Upcoming Crime Novel.*

My heart soared for half a second before it crashed in a burning pile of ash.

I was in the newspaper. My book was in the newspaper. What the hell had Sylvia done?

I skimmed the article, my pulse climbing.

An interview with Fiona Donahue's agent, Sylvia Barr, of Barr and Associates in Manhattan, revealed a sneak peek into Donahue's book, due out next fall.

When asked why she felt this book had made such a splash with her publisher, Mrs. Barr said, "Fiona is a real talent. This book will put her on the bestseller charts. It's fresh. It's hot. I smell a huge hit with this one!"

I let out a breath. Maybe that was all she'd told them. Maybe she hadn't told anyone what the book was actually ab—

I sank down into a chair, certain I was having a coronary as I read on.

When a professional hit woman is hired by a desperate wife to dispose of her problem husband—a wealthy accountant with ties to the mob—someone beats the assassin to the punch . . . and now the wife's gone missing, too. Determined to investigate her mark's mysterious murder before she can be framed for it, a sexy contract killer teams up with an unsuspecting hotshot cop to figure out what went wrong.

"You did it, Mommy! Vero says you're famous. Like a TV star." Delia squeezed my legs, looking up at me with the same doe-eyed, adoring expression she usually reserved for her father. "Can we have cake now?"

"Yes, this calls for cake!" Vero marched the kids to the kitchen as I read the rest of the article with my heart in my throat. A month ago, this news would have been every dream I'd ever had for myself. But if Nick secured a warrant to dig up that field, this press release could be the nail in my coffin.

Vero set a frosting-slathered chunk of cake on Zach's high chair tray, and another in front of Delia. "Can I talk to you?" I whispered.

"After cake," Vero said, carving herself a slice and dropping a dollop of ice cream on top.

I grabbed her by the elbow and dragged her with me, the ice cream scoop clutched stubbornly in her hand dripping a path into the living room.

"Ow!" She scowled at me as she adjusted her paper party hat. I resisted the urge to knock it off her head.

"Nick and I just left Steven's farm," I whispered.

Vero paled. "What were you doing there?"

"He found sod on Feliks's car and traced it back to the field. He's pulling a warrant to dig it up."

Vero looked down at the newspaper like she might be sick. It was one thing to have your fictional murder mystery featured in the local news. It was entirely another when someone actually found the body. "Why the hell didn't you stop him?"

"What was I supposed to do?"

"I don't know!" Drips of vanilla trailed down her hand and scattered across the carpet. "Distract him! Use your feminine wiles, like you did before!"

"For all the good that did me!"

We glanced back into the kitchen, both of us probably thinking the same thing.

"What the hell are we supposed to do?" she asked.

"I don't know." We could take Irina's money, pack up the kids, and flee the country. But where would we go? And how long would it take Andrei and Feliks to find us once Irina told them we'd stolen it?

"How long will it take him to get a warrant?" Vero asked.

"No idea." I couldn't very well call Julian and ask him. "Nick said it wouldn't be easy to track down a judge on a weekend. Maybe a day or two."

"Okay," Vero said through a deep breathing technique that reminded me painfully of Lamaze. "Okay, that's good. So all we have to do is move the body before he finds it."

A shrill laugh exploded in the kitchen. Vero and I turned to see Zach smearing cake frosting into his hair. Delia watched him with a look of mild disgust, her pout stained with blue food coloring. There had been enough sugar in that cake to keep them awake for the next forty-eight hours. This was not going to be easy.

"It could be worse," Vero said.

"Really? Tell me exactly how this could get any worse."

"They could have brought home a dog. Whatever you do, don't mention it to Delia. I just got her to stop crying."

"Why was she crying?"

"Steven took them to the shelter this morning, but Sam was already gone."

"Someone else adopted him?"

"That guy Aaron—you know, Patricia's friend. The shelter worker told Steven he took Sam home after work last week. She said it was odd, because he'd just adopted two dogs a few weeks ago, and three dogs aren't easy to travel with."

A sinking feeling dipped low in the pit of my stomach. "Travel? What do you mean travel?"

"He left that afternoon. Said he was going on vacation, but he never came back. No one knows where he's gone." Our eyes caught. Held. "You don't think . . . ?"

That must have been right after I'd met him, when I'd asked him all those questions about Patricia. I'd filled out the application using Theresa's address. Theresa and I lived on the same street. If he'd seen that street name before—like the night Harris died— Aaron could have recognized it and figured out who I was. And why I was searching for her.

Rescues make great companions.

Had that been it? Had Aaron closed the garage door, determined to save Patricia from her abusive home, just like he'd done for Sam and the rescue dogs at the shelter, not realizing she'd already made plans to handle it herself? Had I abducted Harris from the bar before Aaron had a chance? Had he followed me here, then taken the opportunity to finish the job I was too afraid to?

I couldn't hear much of anything over the dogs down the street . . . They seemed to quiet once he was gone.

Barking dogs. I'd heard dogs barking in the parking lot that night at The Lush as I'd loaded Harris into my van. And again later that night, while I'd been on the phone with my sister. According to the news report on the night she went missing, Patricia didn't own any dogs. But Aaron had adopted plenty.

Had Molly and Pirate been with him in his car?

I thought back to the brown Subaru I'd seen in Patricia's garage, with two human stick figures and two stick-figure dogs. In the photo in the break room at the shelter, Patricia had been sitting beside Aaron with Molly and Pirate, and she hadn't been wearing her ring. Had Aaron been more than a friend? Had he been a boyfriend? A lover? Had they planned a future together? Was that why they were both so eager to be rid of Harris? And if so, who'd helped Aaron shut Harris in my garage?

If he really had been alone, like Mrs. Haggerty said, how would he have kept the garage door from slamming closed without being close enough to . . . hold it?

I turned to Vero and took the ice cream scoop from her hand, dumping it in the ice bucket. "Give me your belt," I said.

"My belt?"

"Just trust me."

Vero unbuckled her leather belt and pulled it through the loops in her jeans. It was thinner than the one Aaron had been wearing the day we saw him at the shelter, but it looked just as sturdy. "Stay with the kids. I'll be right back."

I hit the remote button on the wall of the garage. Late-afternoon sunlight poured over the concrete and I stood in the middle of it, staring up at the tracks, searching for a way to use the belt to keep the door from falling, the way Aaron had used his to prop open Sam's kennel.

In the front corner of the garage, at the top of the tracks near the curve where they turned, two metal bars intersected. I grabbed the step stool, climbed up, and looped the belt around them, securing it just below the bottom of the open door. Then I moved the stool to the center of the garage, climbed up, and pulled the release cord.

There was a soft snap as the door disengaged from the motor. It sagged, suspended in place against Vero's belt.

Aaron had killed Harris.

Not Theresa and Aimee. Not Feliks and Andrei. Aaron had done it alone. He knew the door would slam and I would come running, the same way the self-closing kennels had wreaked havoc in the shelter when Vero set the animals loose and let the doors bang closed. Aaron had tied his belt to the track. Then he'd pulled the cord to free the door from the motor. Quietly, he'd unhooked his belt with one hand, and he'd gently lowered the door.

But if Aaron had killed Harris to be with Patricia, why bother leaving town now that Patricia was dead? I was the only person who knew the truth about Harris's death, and, as guilty as I looked, I wasn't any more inclined than Aaron to report what I'd uncovered. With Patricia gone, Aaron could just as easily have stayed here in town and moved on with his life. Unless . . .

Patricia Mickler no longer exists. I made certain of it.

I thought back to my conversation with Irina in the gym. She'd never come out and stated Patricia was dead. Only that there was nothing of Patricia Mickler left to find.

He has friends that can make almost anyone disappear . . . new name, new passport, and wipe them off the map as if they'd never existed.

What if Patricia Mickler wasn't dead after all? What if Irina had only helped her friend disappear? What if they'd dumped her car and her personal effects in the reservoir and staged her death? What if Patricia was just someone else now, living some*place* else, with *someone* else? Someone who would take care of her and make her feel safe.

The car I'd seen in her garage must have been Aaron's—the stick figures on the rear window must have been them and their family of dogs. What if they'd driven off into the sunset in his Subaru? Aaron and Patricia could be anywhere. Wiped off the map, as if they'd never existed. Which left me—soon to be the only suspect in Harris Mickler's death, my word against the mountain of evidence against me.

Numb, I stepped down from the stool.

My phone buzzed relentlessly in my pocket. I fished it out, surprised to see I'd missed a dozen calls: my parents, Georgia, Sylvia . . . All of them probably to congratulate me on the article in the newspaper. I couldn't stomach the idea of talking to a single one of them.

Tires screeched into my driveway. I whirled, flinching as a silver bumper stopped inches from my knees. Nick's face was furious through the windshield of his sedan. He pointed at me with a hard finger, then at the passenger seat. "Get in," he mouthed.

I looked longingly at Vero's shadow in my kitchen window before opening Nick's car door and sliding in. He put the car in reverse and hit the gas, fishtailing out of my driveway, silently seething as we peeled away from my house. He made a hard turn into a cul-de-sac down the street and jerked to a stop at the curb, refusing to look at me.

"Funny thing happened when I left your place. I called my commander," he said, "to tell him I was onto something big, that I had news. He informs me he has news, too. Then he tells me all about some press release in the local rag." Nick pulled a newspaper from the glove box and tossed it in my lap. "Apparently, *I'm* the unsuspecting hotshot cop, and my investigation has just been some big research project for your book."

"It wasn't like that . . . It's not what you—"

"I'm on suspension." The words stole all the air from the car. "Pending a review by my superiors. They took my piece. They took my badge. And now I have to wait until Monday to walk into my boss's office and explain why I let a novelist with a personal stake in the case work my investigation. By then, the whole damn thing may be over."

My mouth went dry. "What do you mean, over?"

"My boss took over my case. He's coordinating with Fauquier County PD to move forward with the request for a warrant. If they can get it tomorrow, they'll have that field torn open and have Feliks and Theresa in custody by the time I get my badge back."

"I'm sorry." My apology spilled out on a panicked breath. "No one was supposed to know what the book was about. I only sent it to my agent. She got carried away and—"

He turned to face me, rage and betrayal flashing in his eyes. "Did it ever occur to you that I was trusting you with sensitive information? That if anyone knew how much I'd let you see and hear, I could lose my job?"

"That was *your* choice, not mine!" I unlatched my seat belt, turning in my seat as my panic yielded to anger. "You came to me, remember? You offered to help me with research for my book."

"You used me!"

"And you used me! Because you wanted to nab my ex-husband's fiancée on some trumped-up kidnapping charge and you thought I could get you information you couldn't get yourself. Because you didn't have enough evidence to justify questioning her, much less search her office or her house. So don't talk to me about using people!"

He looked away, letting loose a long breath as he stared out his window. "Answer me one thing." He reached into his coat, withdrawing something from the inside pocket. He dropped it in my hands. My wig-scarf—the beautiful disguise I'd been hiding behind, the successful person I was pretending to be all this time, the identity that was supposed to keep me safe and out of trouble—was a tangled mess in my lap. The scarf was torn, the blond tresses coated in a layer of dust. Nick's eyes met mine across the car.

"What are they going to find in that field when they dig it up?"

He looked at me like he didn't know who I was, as if he were seeing me for the first time and he didn't like the face staring back at him.

When I didn't answer, he started the car. We didn't speak on the way back to my house. He didn't say good-bye when he left me in my driveway.

Vero was wringing her hands by the door when I finally came inside. "What's going on?"

A balloon drifted across the ceiling. The children played in the next room. Vero's uneaten ice cream had melted into a puddle on her plate.

"We have to move Harris's body. Tonight."

CHAPTER 39

Vero and I stood in front of the open trunk of Ramón's loaner car. The dim light illuminated the contents with an eerie glow that only made the surrounding darkness feel more sinister. At least this time, the kids weren't asleep in the back.

Getting past Officer Roddy hadn't been as difficult as it probably should have been. I'd begged my sister to take my children for a sleepover, explaining that I was behind on my deadline and needed a quiet night alone in the house to work. After a lot of whining and bribery on my part, she'd agreed. Vero had driven the kids to Georgia's apartment, slipping them casually out of the garage in her Charger while I stayed in plain view of the kitchen window, where Officer Roddy and Mrs. Haggerty could clearly see I was home. On the way back from Georgia's, Vero had swapped the Charger for the loaner car I'd left at Ramón's. The old blue sedan would be far less conspicuous than Vero's muscle car or my minivan, and if we made a crime scene of the trunk and had to scrap it for parts to cover it up, I was pretty sure no one would miss it.

Vero had then driven the loaner to our rendezvous point at the park down the street. Meanwhile, I'd fished a few Christmas-light timers from a dusty box in the basement, connected them to the lamps in my office, my bedroom, and the kitchen, and programmed them to turn on and off every few hours. After dark, I'd tied my hair back in a tight ponytail and changed into a pair of black yoga pants, black gloves, and a black hoodie. Then I'd drawn the curtains closed and snuck out the back door, praying my neighbors didn't catch the flash of my white sneakers cutting through their yards and decide to shoot me on my way to the park.

We'd made it to the rear entrance to the sod farm by eleven o'clock without a hitch.

The air was cold and dry. My breath billowed in clouds as I stood behind Ramón's car, taking inventory of our supplies.

"Why do we have three thousand feet of cellophane in the trunk?" I asked Vero.

"Costco was having a special."

I screwed up my face. "And you decided to stock up now?"

"You told me to bring plastic wrap."

"I told you to get plastic *sheeting*."

"Same thing."

"No, it's not. Plastic *wrap* goes around sandwiches. Plastic *sheeting* goes around dead people. It's bigger and sturdier. More like a shower curtain."

"You told me not to bring a shower curtain because it would make us look guilty!"

"Because nothing screams innocent like a rotting corpse in three thousand feet of Cling Wrap!" I grabbed the shovels and stuck one in Vero's hand. The slam of the trunk echoed for miles, the frost-crusted ground crunching loudly under our feet as we approached the edge of the field.

The headlights cut bright swaths across the dirt, stretching our shadows across it. Vero poked at the soil with the tip of her shovel.

"Are you sure this is where we left him?" She pointed a few feet to the right. "I thought he was farther that way."

"No," I said, standing beside her. "This is definitely it." I didn't tell her I wasn't one hundred percent sure. We'd been careful to leave the car on the gravel road this time, angling the headlights into the field rather than leaving another set of tread marks in the soft ground for the police to follow. Between the shrouding darkness and the eerie tunnel of light cast by Ramón's car, it all felt a little disorienting. But we had to start somewhere. And this seemed close enough.

She cast a longing sideways glance toward the hulking yellow tractor in the next field. "Are you sure you don't want me to bring in the heavy artillery? I watched some videos on YouTube—"

"We are *not* digging him up with a front-end loader!" The last thing we needed was a grand theft charge on top of everything else. "He's not very deep. We can do this ourselves."

Vero grumbled to herself as she stepped out onto the uneven surface of the field and thrust her shovel in the dirt. "Let's get this over with. It's freezing out here."

I switched off the headlights. Better to work in the dark so no one noticed the light from the road. I ventured a few feet from Vero, closer to where she had pointed before, in case she was right. My blisters had hardly healed into calluses, but at least we had two pairs of gloves and two sturdy shovels this time. Between all the digging and Spinning these last few weeks, I felt stronger somehow, capable of hefting more. Our shovels cut through the soil with a steady rhythm, our two holes widening, converging somewhere in the middle. The loose dirt formed mounded piles around us that made us feel deeper in the ground than we probably were.

"Where are we going to move him?" Vero asked through a puff of blue fog. "To a cemetery? Like in your book?"

I choked out a breathy laugh between shovels. If we did that, this damn book would probably be the reason we ended up in prison. "No. We'll hold on to him for a couple of days until the investigation wraps up, then we'll put him back in the same spot. The police aren't likely to get another warrant to dig up the same piece of land again. And the ground will be soft. Easy to dig. Easy to hide," I added between huffs.

"A few days?" Vero leaned on the handle of her shovel and dragged her sleeve across her brow, her disgust clear, even in the dark. "Ramón is going to kill me when I give him back his car. Do you have any idea how bad a decaying body's gonna smell? Cling Wrap may be a whole lot of things, but a giant Odor-Eater isn't one of them."

I drove the blade of my shovel deeper, the hole already up to our hips. "JCPenney is having a fall clearance sale on those big chest freezers. We can pick one up in the morning and put it in the garage."

She chuckled darkly. "And to think you were worried about a damn shower curtain. *Nothing* says 'serial killer' like a chest freezer in a garage."

"You have a better idea?" A thud resounded from the ground at my feet. I tapped it with the tip of my shovel and connected with something hard. Moving the shovel a few inches, I tapped it again, in case I'd hit a rock.

"Wait." Vero wrinkled her nose as she poked the ground a few feet away from me. She sniffed cautiously, the air suddenly pungent and sickly sweet. "I think I found him."

I abandoned my shovel for the flashlight in my pocket, aiming the beam at the ground by Vero's feet. I turned away from the smell. "How bad is it?"

"Um . . . Finlay?" Her voice rose with an odd lilt as she knelt to clear away the dirt. "Harris wasn't wearing jeans when we buried him, was he?"

I dropped to my knees beside her, frantically brushing dirt from a long denim pant leg. A Nike swoop appeared below it. "No." I swallowed the urge to be sick. "And he definitely wasn't wearing running shoes."

"Then who the hell is this?"

"I don't know, but it's definitely not Harris." Gingerly, I patted the pockets of the man's jeans, searching for a wallet, but they were empty. Head craned away from the smell, I scooped handfuls of dirt from the dead man's face. Saliva pooled in my throat. "Oh! Oh, no." I buried my nose in my sleeve.

"What is it?" she asked, crawling closer to see.

The man's eyes were clouded white, wide and open. His pale skin sagged, a hideous shade of gray, and his blue lips spilled dirt from the corners. A purple hole darkened his temple. "I think he's been shot in the head."

Vero jolted to a stop. She glanced down slowly, prodding the dirt beside her knees. "Finlay?" She brushed a handful aside, swearing in Spanish, her voice shaking when she said, "I hate to tell you this, but I just found another pair of shoes. And I'm pretty sure these aren't Harris's either."

I pushed myself to my feet, the ground unsteady beneath them.

The smell grew stronger. My eyes watered as we dug out two more pairs of shoes. Nick was right. Feliks *was* using Steven's farm for business. As a dumping ground for bodies. "How are we going to find Harris in this mess?"

"I don't know." Vero sounded on the edge of panic. Her flashlight skipped to my face.

"Point that thing down," I snapped, shielding my eyes. "I can't see."

"Point what down? I'm not pointing any . . ." The sudden break in her voice sounded all wrong. I held my arm above my eyes, blinking, but I couldn't make out her face against the light. "That's not a flashlight," she whispered frantically. "Someone's coming!"

We ducked, the shoes of the dead men digging into our shins as we peered out over the edge of the hole. Headlights bounced down the gravel road toward us. The lights were square and widely spread, the kind you never wanted to see in your rearview mirror at night.

"Crap! I think it's Nick." I should have known he'd be staking out the farm. There was no way he'd stand aside and let someone else take over his investigation without keeping one foot in it. He'd probably seen us pull in. He'd probably waited, biding his time until we were sure to be ass-deep in a hole full of evidence before swooping in to catch us. Hopefully, he hadn't called in for backup.

"What do we do?" Vero croaked as Nick's car rolled to a slow stop beside Ramón's loaner. It idled ominously, exhaust drifting over us like smoke, its headlights aimed right at us.

"There's no point hiding." This was it. There was no way out of the hole we'd dug that wouldn't involve handcuffs and a conviction. "He knows Ramón's car. He already knows we're here. I should turn myself in. Explain everything. I'll tell him it was all my idea." Vero hissed in protest, grabbing my elbow as I rose to my feet. I dropped my shovel in surrender, one arm shielding my eyes from the glare of his headlights.

Vero stood beside me, her hand shaking as she set her shovel on the ground. Arms raised, we waited for Nick to get out of his car and arrest us.

The car door opened. He left the engine running, exhaust chasing away the smell of rotting bodies as his boots crunched slowly over the gravel toward us. He paused in front of his car, his body silhouetted between the beams as he reached into his left pocket. Probably for his handcuffs.

The wheel of a lighter rasped once. Twice.

I lowered my arm, blinking against the headlights as the flame ignited and extinguished. The red cherry of Nick's cigarette glowed brighter with his long, thoughtful drag.

"I didn't know Nick smoked," Vero whispered.

"He doesn't," I said in a choked voice.

Vero tucked herself closer to my side. The man exhaled a long white stream that melted into the bright glow of the headlights and the blowing exhaust. A puffy jacket distorted the outline of his upper body. But it was his legs that drew my attention, spread shoulder width against the light. They were sturdier than Nick's, two solid tree trunks rising from the ground. My eyes climbed them, pausing at the disconcerting length of his right arm, which was suspiciously longer than the one his cigarette dangled from.

"Finlay—?" Vero grabbed my hand as the barrel of a gun caught the light. My heart stopped as he pointed it at me.

"I can explain . . ." I said, hoping whichever cop I was staring at knew my sister, or maybe could be bribed with an autograph. The weapon issued a soft click and I shut up. He approached the hole, his gun aimed at us, his backlit face indecipherable in the dark.

"Get out." His voice was low and rough, clipped at the edges like the rasp of his lighter.

"Aren't you supposed to read us our rights?"

"I said, get out!"

Vero clung to my arm. On shaking legs, we climbed out of the hole, holding each other for balance.

"Turn around," he demanded.

Vero and I turned toward the field. The officer's headlights cast our shapes over the piles of dirt we'd dug up. Over the dim ghosts of a pair of filth-covered sneakers and the hazy outlines of rotting faces in the dark. My pulse raced as the officer's shadow stretched closer.

"We didn't know these bodies were here," I sputtered. "My sister works for Fairfax PD. If we could just call—"

"Get on your knees," he barked. This was it. He was going to cuff us.

"Look, I think there's been a big misunderstanding. If I could just talk to—"

"I said, get on your knees!" He shoved the gun against the back of my head. I lurched forward, nearly tripping into the hole. Vero caught my arm, steadying me as I followed his orders and lowered myself to the ground. Resisting arrest was a charge we didn't need right now.

Vero knelt beside me, her hand clutching mine, both of us shaking, waiting for the clink of his cuffs.

Instead, the cold steel of his gun pressed against the back of my skull.

My breath hitched. I squeezed my eyes shut, voice trembling as I asked, "Aren't you going to arrest us?"

His gun shook with his deep, throaty laugh. It started low, then rose, climbing up the rough terrain of his throat and echoing back at us from the hole. He muttered something I couldn't understand. Something that sounded a lot like Russian.

Vero's nails dug into my skin.

Andrei Borovkov.

I looked down at the tips of the white sneakers in the hole. These were his bodies. This was his mess Feliks had been hiding. And we were going to be next.

"Wh . . . what are you doing here?" Were there more bodies in the trunk of his car? Was he here to bury someone else?

"You don't listen so well. Feliks told you he would be keeping a close eye on you. Your policeman—the one parked near your house . . . he was not such a good bodyguard."

Officer Roddy . . . Andrei had been watching my house. "You followed us here?"

I felt his shrug in the small movement of his gun. "I was curious to see what you were up to. And now I know. We were all surprised when Harris Mickler disappeared so suddenly. When he hadn't returned the safety deposit box key after making the usual deposits, Feliks was sure Harris had fled the country with his money." The small key from Harris's key ring . . . Patricia had taken it the day she'd met me in Panera. She must have used the money to escape with Aaron.

Andrei sucked in a thoughtful drag. "Me? I had my money on my wife. Irina never liked Patricia's husband. She said he was a disgusting piece of filth who deserved to die." I held my breath through a long pause as he blew smoke past my head. "Maybe I won't bother telling Feliks what you were doing here. I don't like losing bets."

My breath rushed out of me as he lowered the gun. Was he going to let us go? Was he going to blackmail us to keep us quiet?

I didn't dare move as Andrei's legs appeared beside me. He propped a foot on the mound of dirt at the edge of the hole, smoking as he peered down into it. A sinister smile curled his lip around the long ribbon he exhaled. "Looks like you've already done most of the work. That will make burying you much easier."

Vero made a strangled sound and my stomach fell away. Andrei was going to kill us. Right here. Execution-style in the back of the head. I was going to fall into that hole on top of all those other bodies. On top of Harris Mickler. Nick's boss would come with a warrant tomorrow and dig me up. My sister would have to ID my remains.

My head shook in silent protest. I'd had all I could take of Harris Mickler. There was no freaking way I was going in that grave without a fight.

Andrei took a last drag before flinging his cigarette butt in the hole, his shoe sending loose clumps of dirt cascading toward me as he turned away from it.

I stared down at my fist where it braced the ground. At the gritty soil dusting the top of my hand. I glanced up at Andrei through the blowing strands of hair that had come loose from my ponytail. The wind carried exhaust from his tailpipes over the hole. I watched as Andrei blew out the last of his smoke, angling his head so the breeze wouldn't throw it back in his face.

I blew my first traffic stop when some punk dumped his ashtray in my face.

I eased my hand from Vero's, sinking it into the soil. My fists closed around two dry handfuls of dirt, crushing them to a fine grit between my fingers. Andrei's shoulders shook with silent laughter, his head shaking as if he couldn't believe his luck as he turned back to face us.

"I'm ready," he said. "Let's make this quick."

I threw my hands up, tossing them high. Grit swirled in the

wind and sprayed across his face. He cried out, swatting violently at his eyes. The light from the headlamps glinted off his gun as he fought to scrape away the dirt with both hands. I waited for him to drop it, prepared to take his weapon and run, but he only held it tighter, the gun thrashing aimlessly while he shouted and swore at us. I ducked as it fired, the muffled shot scattering dirt beside my knees.

A silencer. He was using a silencer. No one would hear the shots. No one would come to save us.

Heart pounding, I grabbed Vero's hand, dragging her alongside me as I scurried for cover behind Ramón's car.

Andrei hollered, shrieking in pain, his boots stomping wildly against the ground as he dug at his eyes. Another shot. Vero and I huddled close behind the bumper, our hands pressed to our mouths, our arms wrapped tightly around each other. Another bullet pinged close to the hood. With a yelp, we scrambled to the far side of the car and crouched behind the back wheel, clutching each other's hands as Andrei flailed and screamed at us.

If we could make it into the car, maybe we could escape.

I reached over Vero for the passenger-door handle. Another shot rang out. I ducked, throwing my arms around Vero instead. A heavy thump came from the direction of the hole.

Then silence.

We pressed against the side of the car, waiting for him to fire another.

But the shooting had stopped.

The only sound was the soft hum of Andrei's idling engine. The wind rustled the cedars behind us. Shaky breaths steamed from our lips. Neither of us dared to move.

After a long moment, I peered around the hood of the car. Exhaust from his tailpipes blew over the hole. Andrei's legs sprawled on the dirt at the edge of it. The rest of him disappeared inside of it, as if he'd fallen in.

Vero clutched the back of my hoodie, hugging me like a shadow as I crept cautiously toward his body. Andrei's gun glimmered, limp in his hand. I lowered myself into the hole, towing Vero behind me, trying not to think about the sticky dampness soaking through the thin knees of my yoga pants as I crawled toward him. As we inched closer, we both flinched. Andrei's face had been blown clean away, a dark puddle fanning out from what was left of his head.

I took a deep, shuddering breath, fighting the urge to be sick. "He shot himself."

"On purpose?" Vero sputtered.

I blinked down at the gun in his hand. He'd been waving it around like a lunatic, thrashing and clawing at his eyes between his blind shots in our direction.

It hurt so bad, I couldn't think straight . . . I was lucky I didn't kill myself.

"I don't think so. I think it was an accident."

"What do we do now?"

The pile of bodies Andrei had buried loomed in the shadow of the hole. On top of them, the cherry of his abandoned cigarette dimmed and burned out.

"Turn off his car," I heard myself say as I patted his pockets, fishing out his wallet and stuffing it inside my coat. "Don't leave any fingerprints."

Vero scrambled out of the hole and ran to Andrei's car. The field went dark as she killed the engine. I took a moment to think. To breathe. To process what I knew, as my eyes adjusted to the moonlight.

The police were going to dig up this field in the next twenty-four hours.

They would find all of Andrei's victims inside it. Harris, too.

Nick had already assumed Feliks was connected to Harris's death. As far as they knew, Harris was just one more body.

"We're going to leave Harris here," I said, infusing the words with as much confidence as I could muster.

"Leave him?" she whispered, as if she were afraid he might hear us. "We can't leave him!"

"If we take him, the police will only keep looking for him."

"But if they find him with Andrei and all the others—"

"They'll probably assume the mob killed them all." It was a gamble, but moving Harris seemed far riskier. "Help me put Andrei with the others." I grabbed his corpse under the arms, Vero grabbed his boots, and with a grunt, we lowered the rest of him into the hole. When the police came tomorrow and found a mass grave, they would find his freshly smoked cigarette and his gun. It would look like someone—probably Feliks—had met Andrei here, watched him bury the bodies, then executed him and dumped him with his victims, ridding his organization of the sloppy enforcer who kept thrusting his dirty business in the public eye.

Nick wouldn't be here to take credit for the bust, but he would get the satisfaction of knowing he'd solved the case that finally put Feliks Zhirov behind bars. Patricia and Irina would be free of their husbands, Patricia and Aaron could come out of hiding, and Vero and I could get on with our lives.

Without a word, we shoveled all the dirt back into the grave and returned the shovels to the trunk, careful not to leave any traces of ourselves behind. When it was done, I got behind the wheel of Andrei's car, and Vero followed me in the loaner to an overgrown field about a mile down the road, where we abandoned Andrei's car and left his wallet in the glove box.

On the way home, we stopped at Ramón's garage, switched out the loaner for Vero's Charger, and headed the rest of the way to South Riding in silence, too shocked and exhausted to speak.

We reached the park just before sunrise. Vero pulled over, checking to make sure nobody was watching as I climbed into the trunk. With an apologetic smile, she slammed it shut, closing me inside.

Curled up beside the shovels, I listened to her tires roll back onto the road. Her engine wound down to a soft purr as she slowed past Officer Roddy's car, making sure he and Mrs. Haggerty both saw her return home alone.

I rocked as the car swung into the driveway. It idled while the garage door groaned open. The car pulled forward a few feet, then the engine died. Through the walls of the car, the motor hummed as the garage door lowered again. Vero's door slammed, her sneakers squeaking on the smooth concrete as she rounded the car. The trunk flew open to her weary, grime-coated smile as she reached in to help me climb out of the dark.

CHAPTER 40

Vero and I kept the news on, watching the changing headlines as the day waned into night. We had just tucked the kids into bed when the story broke.

Six bodies, including the remains of Harris Mickler, reported missing by his wife nearly three weeks ago, have been found buried at the Rolling Green Sod and Tree Farm in Fauquier County. One of the bodies has been identified as suspected mob enforcer Andrei Borovkov. Detectives with both Fauquier and Fairfax County police say the killings appear to have been executions related to organized crime. While the owner of the farm claims he had no knowledge of the events before tonight and police say he is not a person of interest at this time, suspected mob boss Feliks Zhirov and an unnamed associate have been detained by police for questioning. More as this story develops.

My phone buzzed. I fished it from the sofa cushions. Steven's name flashed on the screen.

"Finn? Are you and the kids okay?" He sounded frantic. I hated to admit it, but it was good to hear his voice.

"We're fine. I just saw the news. Are you all right?"

"I think so. But they took Theresa in for questioning. I don't know what's happening." I could hear the noises of the station in the background—walkie-talkies and buzzing doors, the booming voices of the officers ribbing one another in the halls. "Finn, I swear to god, I didn't know about any of this."

"I believe you." I hugged my knees. It was hard not to feel guilty for my part in all of it. But even if I hadn't buried Harris and Andrei in my ex-husband's field, there had been four other bodies hidden there, thanks to Feliks Zhirov. At least now they could be identified and properly laid to rest. "Do you think Theresa knew?"

"Honestly, I don't know. She swears she didn't. But I don't know what to believe anymore. I'm at the station right now. Your cop friend is here—Nick. He said I can stay until they're done with her, but it might be a few hours before she's released."

If she was released. If Nick or his boss believed Theresa had any inkling of what had been buried in that field, he'd book her and charge her as an accessory to the crimes.

"Take whatever time you need," I reassured him. "Vero and I will take care of the kids. Do you want me to ask Georgia if she can meet you at the station?"

Steven released a shaky sigh. "That'd be . . . really great. Give the kids a kiss for me. I'll call you tomorrow when I know more. And Finn," he said, "I'm sorry. About all of this."

"It's okay," I said. "We'll figure it out." He disconnected.

"Do you think Nick suspects anything?" Vero asked as I set down my phone. She curled on the other end of the couch in a pair of fuzzy slippers and warm pajamas, hugging a throw pillow. The news flickered on the muted TV. The headlines hadn't changed much in the last few hours.

"If he did, we'd already be in the back of a cruiser on our way to the station." Patricia would be a fool to confess anything now. If she was smart, she would come out of the woodwork, claiming she had suspected the mob was involved in her husband's disappearance and she'd gone into hiding, fearing for her life. She could provide eyewitness testimony of her husband's connections to Feliks's dirty business, collect Harris's life insurance policy, and go on to live a long, happy life with Aaron and their three dogs.

And Irina Borovkov was probably thrilled. Her husband was dead. Problem solved.

"What happens to Theresa?" Vero asked, resting her chin on the pillow, looking as tired as I felt. I doubted either of us would sleep much that night.

I tipped my head back against the couch, the events of last night finally catching up with me. "I guess that all depends on how much she knew. If she knowingly took bribes and allowed the mob to use the farm, she's complicit in whatever crimes were buried there. If the police can prove it, she'll probably go to jail."

"Would that be so bad?" Vero asked.

I sighed. Maybe that thought should've given me some petty sense of satisfaction, that after all Theresa had done to our family, she'd gotten her just deserts. But I couldn't make myself feel that way. Whoever Theresa had been to me, she was someone else to my children, and my heart hurt when I thought about what I would say to them if she ended up behind bars. I hoped, for her sake as well as theirs, that she'd had no idea what Feliks had truly wanted from her. And maybe part of me—the bigger part—hoped that for Steven, too.

"I'm pretty sure Steven's suffered enough."

She raised an eyebrow. "Do you think he'll come crawling back?"

I shrugged. "He can ring the doorbell and see if I answer, just like everybody else."

CHAPTER 41

Georgia showed up at my door the next morning with bags under her eyes and a box of glazed donuts under her arm. Apparently, she'd been at the station with Steven all night.

I put on a pot of coffee as she filled me in. The DA had offered Theresa a plea bargain: everything she knew about Feliks and his operation—and her association with it—in exchange for a lesser charge. She probably wouldn't keep her real estate license, but she'd never spend a night in prison. Theresa's decision had been easy, and she'd stayed through the night giving her deposition.

Georgia and I took our coffee and donuts into the living room. It would be easier to have this conversation side by side on the couch, rather than across a table. That way, I wouldn't have to look her in the eyes. She sank into the cushion beside me, sipping her coffee as she shared what she knew around a mouthful of donut.

According to what she'd read in Theresa's statement, Feliks had hired Theresa to find a plot of land. He'd told her he only wanted a lease, and she was never made aware of its intended purpose, only that he needed to bury something for a short period of time. She had assumed he was hiding drugs, and claimed she would never have agreed to let Feliks use the farm if she had known he'd intended to hide bodies there. She'd agreed to let Feliks rent the fallow field for a few months in exchange for a large sum of cash, the first deposit of which Steven had found in her underwear drawer.

Steven had assumed Theresa and Feliks were having an affair. And he hadn't been wrong. Theresa did, in fact, have an alibi for her whereabouts the night Harris Mickler was murdered. She had been consummating her agreement with Feliks over champagne in the back of his limo at the sod farm, which was how Nick had come to discover the soil and sod caked in the limo's undercarriage. According to the ME's initial report, Harris was probably buried that night, the other four victims a few days after that, and Andrei Borovkov as recently as thirty-six hours ago. All but one had been shot at close range.

Harris's death, Georgia explained, would take some time to sort out. But Feliks was expected to be charged with all six counts.

I picked at the edge of my donut. "What does Nick think happened?"

"The going theory is that Andrei was contracted to kill the first five victims for Feliks, and then Feliks had Andrei killed to cover his tracks. Andrei had been careless lately. Too many arrests and too many headlines made him a liability to Feliks's operation. Feliks probably wanted him gone. So he used him for a few quick jobs, then buried him with the rest of the trash.

"Nick's guessing Feliks never planned to exhume and move the bodies. Most likely, he'd planned to just leave them there, assuming they'd never be found." Georgia popped a huge chunk of donut into her mouth. Mine turned to a dry ball against my tongue.

"What's Feliks saying?" This was the sticky part. If Feliks admitted to killing the four unnamed men they'd found, but claimed he was innocent of Harris's and Andrei's murders, would the police believe him and open a new investigation? Or would they assume he was lying?

"Feliks hasn't made a statement yet. His lawyers are being cautious, taking time to come up with a game plan. With Theresa's deposition and testimony, Feliks is going to have a hard time walking away from this. As far as Nick can tell, every victim in that hole had a direct connection to Feliks's organization."

"What was Harris Mickler's?"

"Money laundering. Apparently, he was one hell of an accountant, but he must have done something to piss Feliks off." Feliks must not have told them about the stolen key and his missing money. Why would he? It would only provide the police with a motive to use against him.

"Did they ever find his wife?"

Georgia snorted around her donut. "They tore that field apart last night and never found her. Ironically enough, she called into the station early this morning after seeing the news. She said she'd left town, afraid for her own safety because she suspected the mob might have been behind Harris's death. She said she'd received a death threat at her house and she'd been too afraid to say anything to the police, because she didn't believe they could protect her. OCN sent someone over to her house to check out her claim, and sure enough, they found a knife mark in her back door, exactly where she told them to look. Apparently, her story checks out. Once she saw Feliks had been arrested and Andrei was dead, she said she finally felt safe enough to come out of hiding."

"I bet she did." Because now that Feliks had been set up to take the fall, she didn't have to worry that I would rat her out.

"And," Georgia added, "she offered to turn over everything she knew about Harris's laundering activities in exchange for immunity from any obstruction and withholding charges. She agreed to come in later today to give a statement and bring in Harris's files."

"I'm glad she's okay," I said through a forced smile. Though I guess it was mostly true.

"And get this," Georgia said eagerly. "Andrei Borovkov's wife offered her full cooperation with the police. She agreed to give a statement about her husband's involvement with the mob. Her attorney worked out a deal with the prosecutors. Immunity for dishing dirt on Zhirov."

So, the whole thing wasn't exactly neat, but I was guessing Irina was happy. As far as she was concerned, the job was done, and I could wash my hands of her.

"Nick must be pleased with the way things turned out."

Georgia licked sugar from her fingers. "Nick's on cloud nine," she said with her mouth full. "Between Patricia Mickler's testimony, Irina Borovkov's statement, and Theresa's depositions, he should have enough to shut down Feliks's operation for a long, long time. Nick might even come away with a promotion after this one."

"So he's not in trouble?"

"What? Because of your book?" Georgia made a face. "Nah. He'll get a slap on the wrist for too much pillow talk—"

"It wasn't pillow talk!" She raised an eyebrow, and I threw the rest of my donut at her. "It wasn't like that! There were no pillows involved!"

"Whatever." She pulled my cruller from her lap and dusted it off. "Back seat of his car then."

"Front," I corrected grudgingly. She smirked. "Is he still mad?"

Georgia shrugged. "He'll get over it. But if he does come back, I wouldn't make it too easy for him. Make him work for it."

Mostly, when I'd imagined seeing Nick again, it involved an arrest warrant. All I could see when I pictured his face was the disappointment in his eyes after he'd tossed my wig-scarf at me.

"How's Steven holding up?" I asked, changing the subject.

Georgia gave a slow shake of her head. "Not gonna lie. He was pretty torn up. Nick says he overheard Steven and Theresa arguing after her deposition. Steven told her he planned to move out. I'm guessing the engagement is off." Georgia watched my reaction out of the corner of her eye. "If he asked, would you take him back?"

"I'm not in the business of plea bargains," I said, wiping the glaze from my hands. "I'm moving on with my life. Steven's a big boy. He'll be fine."

"Moving on, huh?" She raised an eyebrow. "You and Nick?"

"No." I rested my sock feet on the coffee table, crossing them at the ankles as I considered the possibilities. It felt good, to have possibilities. "No. Just me. Me and Vero and the kids. We're going to be okay." The bills were paid, my van was back, and there was a little wad of cash under the broccoli in the freezer. I was pretty sure I knew how my story was supposed to end.

Georgia put her feet on the table, too. She leaned back and closed her eyes, wearing a contented smile. "Good. I guess I can finally stop worrying about you."

CHAPTER 42

Picking up the mail wasn't as daunting as it used to be. The box was usually empty now, with the exception of a few catalogs and coupon books, and the occasional insignificant bill. I crossed the lawn just before dark, hunched into my jacket, my hands jammed in my pockets against the cold as I dodged the paper skeletons hanging from the tree out front and the Styrofoam gravestones peppering my front yard. The air was redolent of chimney smoke and carved pumpkins, the misty night shimmering with the promise of Halloween.

Crisp blades of frozen grass crackled underfoot, and I waved at Mrs. Haggerty's kitchen window, certain she must be watching me. I didn't mind her nosiness so much anymore.

The hinge on the mailbox creaked as I fished out a short stack of envelopes. I thumbed through them mindlessly as I crossed the lawn back to my front door. Electric bill, water bill, internet and phone, the usual . . . I paused over a fat envelope from Steven's attorney, which probably contained the new joint custody agreement he'd proposed this week.

As I flipped to the next envelope, my feet jerked to a stop. The thin letter had no postage. No return address. Just my name written in stark bold letters across the front.

I looked both ways down the street. No strange cars lined the sidewalk. No one was standing out on their lawn. Officer Roddy had been dismissed days ago, as soon as Feliks had been taken into custody, and I glanced back at Mrs. Haggerty's window, wondering if she might remember who'd delivered it.

The house felt overly warm as I dropped the bills on the side table and kicked the door shut behind me. The foyer was thick with the heavy smells of bubbling cheese and pasta sauce spilling over from the kitchen. I tore open the envelope, slowly unfolding the paper inside.

PANERA. 10 A.M. TOMORROW.

"What's that?"

I started as Vero peered over my shoulder. "You scared me half to death."

"A little jumpy?" Vero studied the note. "You think it's Patricia Mickler?"

"Who else could it be?" I shredded it as I carried it into the kitchen and stuffed the pieces down the garbage disposal.

"You're not gonna go?"

"No. It's over. I'd be happy if I never saw Patricia Mickler ever again." That was exactly how I felt about Irina Borovkov, too. I'd been dodging her calls for days. I didn't want any more of her money. No matter how it might look to her, I wasn't the one who'd killed her husband, so there was no reason for me to accept payment for it. As far as I was concerned, our business was over. I was ready to put this entire disastrous chapter of my life behind me.

I cracked open the oven, relieved to see my lasagna boiling, the noodles at the edges a light golden brown. Vero reached around me to lift the foil, and I smacked her hand away.

"It's my turn to cook. This is your party." I closed the oven and pulled down two glasses for wine. Vero had passed her accounting midterm exams, and tonight, the four of us were celebrating.

Vero grumbled as she set the table. "Well, I might have a few things to say to the woman if I were you."

"Who? Patricia?" Oh, I wasn't without things to say. I could go on for hours about her little disappearing act and what her boyfriend had pulled in my garage. I turned on the faucet and flipped the switch on the disposal, letting the last of Patricia Mickler and her crazy husband slide away as I washed the pots and pans I'd used to prepare dinner.

The doorbell rang. It had only been a few days since the police had dug up Harris's body, and Vero and I still held our breaths a little, every time. I turned off the disposal. Vero's eyes met mine.

"You expecting someone?" she asked.

I shook my head. "Probably just Steven coming to talk about the new custody agreement. It came in the mail today."

Vero crept to the door. The lock snapped and the door swung open, letting in a rush of cold air.

"Hey, Vero. Is Finlay here?" My spine drew up tight when I recognized the gravelly voice outside.

"Detective Anthony," Vero said loudly enough to give me fair warning. "We weren't expecting you."

Georgia hadn't mentioned any new developments in the ongoing investigation when I had talked to her earlier. As far as I knew, the depositions had gone well. And Feliks had pled not guilty on every count, so Harris's death didn't necessarily stand out from the others. Nick and I hadn't talked since the day he'd seen the press release about the book. So what reason did he have for coming here now?

I stood frozen in the kitchen through Vero and Nick's awkward pause.

"Can I come in?"

"Sure, yeah, sorry," Vero sputtered.

Steeling myself, I came out of the kitchen. Nick stood close to the door wearing a grim expression. His dark brows pulled lower when he saw me, and he held something behind his back. I hoped to hell it wasn't an arrest warrant. "Hey, Finlay."

"Hey," I said, one eye on his hidden hand.

"What's *he* doing here?" Delia asked, peeping around the stairs in the pink satin princess costume she'd been wearing all week. Vero and I looked to Nick for an answer, waiting through the tense silence. The shadow of his jaw was freshly shaven, the dark waves of his hair neatly combed back. He wore his signature black jeans and a hunter-green Henley, and through the open lapels of his leather jacket, I could just make out his sidearm in its holster. I couldn't tell if he was dressed for work or a date, or if there had ever been any difference for him.

"I just came to visit your mom," he said.

"Oh." She fidgeted with her plastic tiara, her scrunched-up face the picture of bemused innocence. "My daddy says you're an asshole."

Vero expelled a hard cough into her hand. She pressed her red lips tight.

"Delia Marie!" I pointed with a hard finger to her room. With a huff, she tromped up the stairs. Nick took the hit with a self-effacing smile, wincing as if maybe it still stung a little.

"I'm sorry," I said.

"Don't be. Her dad's probably right." He cleared his throat, looking down at the floor.

"I . . . should check on the kids," Vero said, disappearing up the stairs.

Nick didn't speak for a painfully long time. "Is everything okay?" I asked. My gaze slid purposefully to the hand behind his back. If he was serving me a warrant, there was no sense dragging it out.

"Oh, I almost forgot." Every nerve in my body sagged with relief as he pulled a bottle of champagne from behind his back. "I never told you congratulations. For your book."

Guilt gnawed at me as I reached for the bottle. "I should have congratulated you, too. Georgia told me you earned a promotion."

"Yeah, well," he said, scratching the back of his neck. "I didn't exactly do it alone." His eyes lifted to mine. I studied the bottle, feeling my cheeks warm. It wasn't a cheap brand. He'd gone all in for the good stuff.

"You didn't have to, really."

"No, I did." He rubbed his empty hand, as if he weren't sure what to do with it now that the bottle wasn't there. "I'm sorry for the things I said. I was just . . . caught off guard by the article in the paper. And you were right. About everything. It wasn't your fault. I was the one who got you involved."

"Still," I conceded. "I should have told you about the book."

He shrugged, in dismissal or acknowledgment, I wasn't entirely sure. "We did sort of use each other, I guess. But I was thinking . . ." His dimple flashed with his tentative, crooked smile. "If you'd like to use me again, maybe I could take you to dinner sometime."

It was tempting. Nick was attractive. Steady, reliable. And my toes curled a little at the prospect of making out with him again.

But I'd made more than my fair share of impulsive choices lately. And I'd spent a lot of time trying to be someone I wasn't. Nick had never seen me in my wig-scarf or a dress. He'd never known me as Theresa or Fiona, or anyone other than Finlay Donovan. He'd been inside my house and met Vero and my kids. He'd seen me in my bathrobe and slippers, and yet . . . Nick didn't really know me. Could never really know me. Because if he did, I'm guessing he wouldn't like what he saw.

Like Steven, sometimes it felt as if Nick only saw the parts of me he wanted to. For once, I just wanted someone who saw and appreciated what was really there all along.

I touched the label on the pricey bottle of champagne cradled in my arm. "Can I think about it?"

Nick's face fell. He quickly picked it up again. "Sure, absolutely. I understand," he said, trying not to look surprised as he took a step back toward the door. "You know, call me. Anytime. If you change your mind."

"Thanks again for the champagne. And good luck with the trial." I hoped he'd be able to put Feliks away for good, for both of our sakes.

We said an awkward good-bye at the door, me inside and him outside, and I sighed as I closed it behind him, hoping I wouldn't regret this in a few hours when I was lying in bed alone, staring at the ceiling.

Vero leaned around the corner. I held out the bottle of champagne. "Is it over?" she asked with a sympathetic smile. I wasn't sure if she was talking about the investigation or my relationship with Nick.

"For now."

She wrinkled her nose. Tipped her head toward the kitchen.

"The lasagna!" We ran to the oven as tendrils of smoke slipped out through the seams in the door. I flung it wide and dragged on my baking mitts, dropping the smoking casserole on the stove top. Vero opened the windows, waving at Mrs. Haggerty as a cold wind blew through the room.

"Pizza goes better with fancy champagne anyway," she said over the blare of the smoke detector.

I leaned a hip against the counter, fanning smoke from my eyes as it billowed through the kitchen. "Pizza sounds perfect. I'll buy."

According to our agreement, Vero was entitled to forty percent of the large supreme with extra cheese we shared that night, but neither of us bothered to count the slices this time.

CHAPTER 43

A few hours later, after Vero and I had polished off all the pizza, an order of hot wings, and the last of the Oreos in the house, I carried my beer upstairs to my bedroom. The champagne had given me a headache after the first glass, and I'd poured mine down the drain, washing away the stubborn remains of Patricia's letter.

Licking pizza grease from my fingers, I fell back on my bed. The ceiling was low and close, the house too quiet after the kids had gone to sleep. I swiped at a tomato stain on my T-shirt. The fabric was loose and stretchy, the color dull from years of washing. The graphics had peeled away in so many places, they were impossible to read. I didn't feel like a soon-to-be bestselling author. But I guess I hadn't felt much like a killer-for-hire either. I stared up at the ceiling, wondering who I was now that the nightmare was over, with my kids soundly asleep in the rooms beside mine and Vero settled across the hall. With Steven living alone in the trailer on his farm, and the threat of a custody battle finally behind me.

I leaned back against the headboard with my beer in my lap,

peeling at the sweating edges of the label, thinking about Julian and what he'd said the first night we met at The Lush. How he'd seen right through my disguise.

What's my type then?

Cold beer and takeout pizza. Barefoot, jeans, and a loose-fitting faded T.

I set the bottle on the nightstand and reached for my phone, my index finger hovering over his number. It was nine thirty on a Tuesday night.

You know where to find me.

I texted Vero across the hall.

Finn: *You okay with the kids if I go out for a while?*

Vero: *Thought you'd never ask.*

I swung my legs over the bed and dragged on my sneakers and a hoodie. My bedroom door creaked open as I threw on a baseball cap. Vero peeked around it.

She gave my jeans and T a pained once-over. With a resigned shake of her head, she tossed me a small Macy's bag. "At least put some makeup on if you're meeting with your attorney. I want to hear all about it tomorrow over coffee when you get home. I won't wait up," she said with a wink.

My door closed. I opened the bag and looked inside, expecting an explosion of color, surprised to find a tube of clear lip gloss and simple brown mascara. I leaned into the mirror and swiped them on, self-conscious but satisfied that the woman I saw staring back at me was someone I recognized.

On instinct, I reached for my diaper bag. Then set it down as I realized I didn't need it. Not tonight. Instead, I took a small stack of cash from my desk drawer and stuck it in my purse. Something soft tickled my hand when I reached inside. I pulled out my wig-scarf.

It was torn and tangled, the long blond tresses matted in clumps. I ran my fingers through it, smoothing over the wrinkled silk. With a sigh, I left it on my desk.

It was three minutes to ten when I parked beside Julian's Jeep in the near-empty lot. The windows of The Lush were dim, the chair legs rising up from the tops of the tables silhouetted against the whisky-gold lights behind the bar. I cupped a hand and peeked through the door, surprised when it opened.

Julian stood with his back to me, restocking bottles on the liquor shelf above his head. His crisp white sleeves were rolled to the elbow and his collar was unbuttoned, as if he'd already clocked out for the night. "Sorry. Bar's closing," he called over his shoulder.

"I'm not exactly a top-shelf customer." Julian's hand stilled, his eyes finding mine in the mirrored wall. I set my purse on the bar and perched on a stool. "Am I too late for that beer?"

"Bottle or draft?" he asked quietly.

"Bottle's fine."

He reached into a fridge under the bar. Air rushed from the cap as he broke the seal and rested the bottle on a napkin in front of me. He slung a rag over his shoulder and leaned back against the counter behind him, taking me in as I sipped it. A curl hung over his eyes, their color decidedly gold against the amber glow behind him.

"Don't take this the wrong way, but we don't normally get your type in here."

"Yeah? What's my type?"

He pushed off the counter and stood in front of me, his hands braced on the bar. "Unassuming famous authors. The kind who use fake names and wear terrible disguises."

I set down my beer and extended a hand across the bar. "Hi.

I don't believe we've been properly introduced. My name's Finlay Donovan."

He gave me a wan smile. "Not Fiona Donahue?"

"I can show you my ID, if you want to card me."

He seemed to consider that. When he finally took my hand, it felt nice in mine, and I let it linger. Or maybe he did. "It's nice to finally meet you, Finlay Donovan."

I hid a blush behind my beer, liking the sound of my name when he said it.

"You doing okay?" he asked.

"Yeah," I said, surprising myself. For the first time in a long time, I felt like I meant it. "I think I am."

"You want to talk about it?"

I picked at the edge of my napkin. "It's kind of a long story."

"I'm not in any rush." He reached into the cooler and popped a cap off a beer, his eyes never leaving mine as he took a long, slow sip.

I glanced up at him from under from the shadow of my baseball cap. "Would our conversation be protected by our attorney-client privilege?" My teasing lilt suggested I was flirting, but the question danced around the edges of my very real fear. No one but Vero knew my whole story.

He watched me over another sip of his beer. "I'm not an attorney yet. And you're not a client. But any bartender worth the salt around his glass will uphold a solemn unspoken oath with the customers who frequent his establishment." He leaned forward, his arms folded over the bar, his voice falling soft as he toyed with the neck of his bottle. "Call it a duty of confidentiality."

The bar was empty. The lights over the booths in the back switched off in sections, until all that was left were the soft glow behind Julian's head and the bright white light through the swing door to the kitchen, where glassware clanked and dishes clattered, the sounds muted under a high-pressure spray.

I took off my baseball cap and set it beside me on the bar, raking back my hair as Julian's eyes moved over my face. I fortified myself with a long, slow breath, and then I started where every story truly starts—not on page one, but at the very beginning. I told him about my family and my childhood, about Georgia and my parents and my marriage to Steven. I told him about my job as an author and the books I'd written that no one had read. I told him about Theresa and how my marriage had ended. About Vero and my children and the day the electric company turned out the lights. About my meeting with Sylvia at Panera, and how my life had spiraled out of control after that. I told him everything, holding nothing back, watching his face for reactions as I recounted the night I'd slipped out the back of The Lush with Harris slung under my arm. Julian listened, looking away only once to replace my empty beer with a new one. There was no disapproval on his face, no judgment in his eyes. The quickening beat of his pulse in the tight, tanned skin above his thumb as I recounted our escape from Andrei at the farm was the only clue to his thoughts.

When I reached the end, our beers were empty. He didn't offer me another. I let out a long, shuddering breath as I opened my purse and laid a twenty on the bar. "Thanks for the drinks. And for listening. I should probably go—"

Julian's hand closed over mine as I reached for my hat. "My shift's over. Feel like grabbing something to eat?"

My heart hitched. "I'd like that."

Julian held my stare, his gold eyes warming as he called out to his boss, "Hey, Les, I'm heading out. See you tomorrow." He set his rag on the bar and shrugged on his coat, meeting me on the other side. I felt his eyes trail over me, a smile creasing their edges when they fell on the long T-shirt peeking out from under my hoodie. He held the door open for me, raising an eyebrow when I pulled my keys from my purse. "Where are we headed?" he asked as he followed me to my van.

Sometimes, I decided, you just had to sit down in front of a blank screen and start typing. My minivan was clean. My alternator was fixed. I had a babysitter and plenty of cash in my pocket.

"I don't know yet," I said. But I had a pretty good feeling this chapter would have a happy ending. "Get in. We'll figure it out."

CHAPTER 44

It was nearly ten o'clock the next morning when I reluctantly tumbled out of Julian's apartment. Barefoot and shirtless, he'd backed me to the door, his jeans riding low on his hips and his hands knotted in my hair, whispering good-byes between kisses I felt everywhere. Wearing a stubborn smile, I sat at a red light, singing along to the radio and raking the tangles from my hair, wondering what I would tell Vero. Technically, I only owed her forty percent of the story. But it was nice to know there was someone there waiting, eager to know what happened, when I got home.

Across the busy intersection, the parking lot of the Panera was lightly peppered with cars. I checked the time on my dashboard clock. Patricia Mickler was probably already inside waiting for me. But why? What could she possibly have to offer me except an explanation? Or an apology?

The light turned green. The Mercedes behind me leaned on his horn. Instead of proceeding straight across the intersection, I put my foot on the gas and cut the wheel hard, crossing two lanes of traffic and sliding into Panera's lot. Idling in front of the restaurant, I stared through the tinted glass windows into the dining room, but I couldn't make out the faces in the booths inside.

Maybe Vero was right, and I did have a few things I needed to get off my chest. I pulled into a parking spot, slung my purse over my shoulder, and crossed the lot before I changed my mind.

The line at the counter was short, and the heads behind the registers all looked up as I blew in. Frankly, I didn't care if Mindy the Manager happened to recognize me. The worst she could do was ask me to leave or call the police. Let her try. Head held high, I strutted into the dining room with all the confidence of a woman who'd just spent the night with a pretty fantastic attorney.

I skimmed the faces, searching for Patricia's, stopping short when Irina Borovkov waved casually from her booth.

She sat alone in the far corner, watching me over her coffee, her crimson-lipped smile curling up at the edges as I gaped at her. She gestured to the empty seat in front of her. I hitched my purse higher on my shoulder, steeling myself as I crossed the room.

"Ms. Donovan," she greeted me as I slid into her booth, "I'm glad to see you got my note." A cold shiver trailed up my spine. The way she spoke my name—the subtle way she had of making it clear that she knew exactly who I was and where to find me—reminded me a little too much of Feliks and our conversation in Ramón's garage.

Irina traced the lip of her mug with a long manicured nail. Her other hand was concealed under the table, and I stiffened as it occurred to me that she might be armed.

"I thought I was meeting Patricia," I said.

Irina nodded, a thoughtful dip of her head. "Patricia's given her statements. By now, she and her young companion are on a flight to Brazil, to start their new life someplace warm."

"You're happy for her."

"Of course," she said, her raven-black hair falling over her eyes. "Otherwise, I never would have arranged for her to leave."

"And what about you?" I asked. "What will you do now that . . . ?" I shuddered at the memory of Andrei's bloodied face. At the heavy, hollow sound he'd made when Vero and I dropped him in the ground.

"Now that my husband is gone?" Irina gave an elegant shrug. "Someone needs to stay and make sure Feliks ends up where he belongs. He will not be happy once he figures out how Andrei died. You and I have cost him too much, and Feliks is no fool. It won't take him long to figure it out."

It was a sobering thought. "You think there's a chance he'll walk?"

She raised a perfectly plucked brow as she sipped her coffee. Her hand was steady as she set down her mug. "I suppose there's always a chance. But your detective friend is quite determined. And as Patricia suggested, you were very neat." She appraised me with the same amused expression she'd worn in the Spinning class at the club. "I must admit, I was pleasantly surprised." She pulled her hand from under the table and dropped an envelope on top, sliding it toward me.

"What's this?" I asked, seized by a sudden suffocating case of déjà vu.

"This is the balance I owe you. The job was completed, exactly as we discussed." I resisted the urge to look at it. "Don't worry. It's washed—unmarked and untraceable." It felt wrong to take Andrei's money. Money Harris Mickler had probably laundered—and Feliks had probably used to pay Irina's husband.

Something hardened under her easy smile. "If you do not accept my payment, I might worry about your reasons. Perhaps you've grown too close with Detective Anthony? Or is it your sister you're worried about?" She pushed the envelope closer. "Georgina, is it?"

I snatched up the package, checking the dining room to make sure no one was watching as I drew it to me. A skinny boy in a Panera uniform swept crumbs from the rug with his head down, and a gray-haired woman hunched over her soup a few tables away. No one cared as I stuffed the envelope of dirty money into my purse. No one but me.

Irina dabbed at her mouth with her napkin and tucked her Prada handbag under her arm. "Good. I'm glad our business is concluded to our mutual satisfaction. I will be in touch if I find myself in need of your services again."

"No, I don't—" Irina reached inside her pocket and pushed a thin white envelope across the table.

"A letter from Patricia. I did not take the liberty of opening it, but if I'm not mistaken, I believe it's a referral. Before she found you, she spent some time lurking on an internet forum—a site for women like us." At my baffled expression, she explained, "Women in difficult situations seeking a specialist with a certain skill set." Irina's conspiratorial wink made me feel like I needed a shower. "Patricia seemed to think this particular job might interest you. She asked me to make sure you received this."

Irina left the envelope on the table. She extended her hand. It hung in the space between us for an uncomfortably long time. Every cell in my body recoiled as I shook it once, quick to let go.

Exhaustion set in as I watched her go, the absolution I'd found after my confession to Julian last night suddenly buried under a mountain of fresh guilt. Patricia's letter felt just as heavy as the brick of cash Irina had paid me. I turned it over in my hands, grateful to find the envelope sealed shut. If it was sealed, I wouldn't be tempted to open it. And I couldn't be accused of knowing whose name was inside. Or how much their life was worth.

I tucked Patricia's letter in my purse and walked out of Panera, grateful when no one stopped me. I got in my van, grateful when the alternator started. Grateful for the night I'd spent with Julian. Grateful that Patricia was alive, that Irina was out of my life, and that Feliks was behind bars. But mostly, I was grateful to get home to Vero and my kids, and that the nightmare of the last few weeks was over.

EPILOGUE

The house was quiet. Vero was downstairs watching reality TV, and the kids were asleep for the night. I carried a mug of hot chocolate to my office, set it on the coaster beside my keyboard, and stirred the mouse. The screen came to life.

I braced myself as I stared at the face of a new blank document. The screen was bright, empty, and more than a little terrifying. I had turned in my finished draft to Sylvia last night, and my editor was already wanting to know the plot of the next one.

I cracked my knuckles and started typing.

BOOK 2: Untitled First Draft by Fiona Donahue

My hands hovered over the keyboard as I waited for divine inspiration to strike. I stared at the screen for what seemed like an eternity, but I hadn't the foggiest idea what to write.

I slouched back in my chair. Took a sip of my cocoa. The last story had begun with Patricia Mickler's note . . . a slip of paper on a Panera tray.

I slid open my drawer, peeking at the sealed envelope at the bottom of it. Vero and I had sworn we would never open it. And yet, neither of us had volunteered to throw it away. Instead, I'd kept it, telling myself it was a cautionary reminder of the Pandora's box we'd opened before.

I picked up the envelope and held it against the light of the screen, but the ink was too faint and the envelope too thick; I couldn't make out the letters through the creamy textured stationery. The cursor blinked, ticking away the seconds. And here I was, wasting my few precious hours of solitude staring at an empty screen.

All I needed was an idea. A spark of inspiration.

I tore a tiny hole in the edge of the envelope and stuck a finger inside. The paper made a loud shushing sound as I slid it along the seam. I paused, listening for Vero's footsteps in the hall, certain the rip had been loud enough to incriminate me. A TV laugh track rose up in the background, and I pulled the letter free.

All I needed was a name. The name of some terrible, horrible man whose life I could pick apart online until I came up with a story of my own.

I unfolded the paper from the envelope, skimming Patricia's note.

I FOUND THIS JOB POSTING ONLINE, ON A WEBSITE
FOR PEOPLE LIKE ME. I WASN'T SURE IT WOULD
INTEREST YOU, BUT I THOUGHT YOU SHOULD KNOW.

I glanced down at the name and froze. I read it again, then the dollar amount, certain I must have misread it the first time.

STEVEN DONOVAN

$100,000 CASH

The address was my ex-husband's farm.

ACKNOWLEDGMENTS

This book was born in a crowded Panera in 2017 over lunch with my longtime critique partners, as we were talking through some particularly challenging plot holes in a particularly bloody story I was writing under a particularly tight deadline. The diners around us had given us some rather odd looks, and later that evening, we'd laughed about how lucky we were that they hadn't gotten the wrong idea about who we were and what we were (and were not) plotting there. In that moment, the inspiration for this book nearly knocked me off my feet, and by the end of the night, the three of us had hashed out a very rough character sketch for Finn, as well as a pitch for her story. As with every book I've ever written, I am deeply grateful for Ashley Elston and Megan Miranda. Thank you for your support, encouragement, and the countless laughs we've shared through it all. This story is yours as much as it is mine. You remain the very best part of this wild ride, and I would bury a body with either of you.

I would never have found these two amazing friends had it not been for my superhero real-life agent, Sarah Davies. Thank you for introducing the three of us all those years ago, thank you for your unwavering faith in me since, and thank you for loving Finn. I am grateful for all I've learned and all the ways you continue to support me.

Finlay's story is the first book I've written for an adult audience. I cannot adequately express in words how thankful I am to Kelley Ragland and Hannah Braaten for their willingness to take a chance on me and Finn. Thank you for making me feel so at home at Minotaur.

So many people have contributed their talents and strengths to the success of my books. Enormous love for the entire team at Minotaur and St. Martin's Press, including Catherine Richards, Nettie Finn, Laura Dragonette, cover artist David Baldeosingh Rotstein, John Morrone, Allison Ziegler, and Sarah Melnyk. I couldn't imagine a more wonderful home for Finn's story.

And thanks to everyone working behind the scenes at Greenhouse Literary, Working Partners, and the wonderful folks at Rights People. A million thanks to Flora Hackett at WME for pitching Finlay with such amazing enthusiasm. I'm grateful for all you do.

Stretching wings and writing a new kind of book involves a leap of faith, as well as a steep learning curve. I'm grateful for the keen eyes and open hearts of writer friends who offered to read very early versions of this story. Tessa Elwood, Megan Miranda, Ashley Elston, Chelsea Pitcher, Romily Bernard, and Christy Farley—you all helped make Finn's story so much stronger. And your enthusiasm early on, while my confidence was still a bit shaky, meant the world to me.

I owe a huge debt of gratitude to Ashley Elston's family, specifically Jim and Mary Patrick, who hosted us for dinner. We were all sitting around the table, laughing about our working lunch at

Panera, when John and Sarabeth Ogburn first posed the question, "Wouldn't it have been hilarious if those people in Panera thought you were contract killers?" That question started me down a path I never could have expected!

My mom has always been my biggest cheerleader, and during the writing of this book was no exception. Mom, thanks for all the ideas you jotted on index cards. Your excitement for my stories is unflagging and keeps my fires lit on my hardest days. I'm lucky to have an "idea person" like you. Also thanks to my mom, my dad, and Tony, for their endless patience and willingness to jump to my rescue when I need time to write my books. I could not do this job without my family's steadfast confidence in everything I do.

Finn's character and voice emerged from the deepest parts of myself. Maybe because we're both authors (and therefore, always struggling), but mostly because we're both moms. Just like Finn, there's nothing I wouldn't risk or give of myself for my kids. Connor and Nick, in so many ways, every book is for you.

And last, for my readers, old and new. Thank you for embracing Finn, and thanks for being such a wonderful part of my story.

1. *Finlay Donovan Is Killing It* takes a slightly different tone than many crime and thriller novels. How does Finlay's character contribute to this tone? Did you appreciate this twist on the genre?

2. Were you surprised that Finlay is so intrigued by the note that she actually decides to scope out Harris Mickler? Why or why not?

3. The lines between fiction and life are slightly blurred in this novel: Finlay is a character, but she is also a writer herself, and later in the story she uses the crimes she's been involved in as inspiration for her new book. What does this book-within-a-book setup add to *Finlay Donovan Is Killing It*?

4. As early as chapter 6, the Russian mafia is mentioned. When did you put the pieces together that Finlay's accidental hit/well-planned murder by others was connected to organized crime? How does their involvement affect the story?

5. Vero and Finlay's relationship is central to the story—how does it change throughout the novel?

6. How does Finlay's relationship to her motherhood (and especially single motherhood) play out throughout the novel?

7. Finlay catches the attention of two very different potential romantic partners: Detective Nick Anthony and bartender/law student Julian Baker. In what ways are these men different or similar to each other? What unique heroic traits, character flaws, or potential challenges does each man present? Do you agree with the romantic decisions Finlay makes through the course of the book?

MINOTAUR BOOKS

8. In chapter 32, Julian recites a quote inspired by the principles of Hanlon's razor: "Let us not attribute to malice and cruelty what may be referred to less criminal motives." He tells Finlay that he "makes it a point never to assume the worst about people." How does this idea reflect what we know of his character? How does Finlay's response reveal more about hers?

9. Consider the theme of women supporting women. What examples of this did you see in the story? Did any of these instances surprise you? Why?

10. During several scenes, Finlay wears a wig-scarf and sunglasses to hide her identity or masquerade as her ex's fiancée, Theresa. She wears the same wig-scarf and glasses in her author photo, which appears in the books she's written. What do you think the wig-scarf represents to Finn, and how does her attitude toward it change throughout the book?

11. Finlay's view of her career is often self-deprecating, reflecting the various attitudes of her agent, her family, the market, and her ex toward her work. How do these attitudes change after Finn is awarded a lucrative book deal? How does Finlay's attitude change toward herself? What role do you think money plays in how society values women's contributions at home and in the workplace?

12. Finlay toes the line between right and wrong throughout the book, yet she somehow manages to stay on the right side of that line. Though she's tempted by the money—and curious about the potential victims—she never actually commits any of the murders herself. How would your feelings about Finlay have changed if she had killed Harris Mickler or Andrei Borovkov? Does her identity as a woman and a mother influence your answer?

13. Were you surprised by the note Finlay received from Patricia Mickler at the end of the book? Do you have any predictions about who the guilty party might be?

MINOTAUR BOOKS

CHAPTER 1

Christopher was dead. They'd found him bobbing on the water's surface, his eyes bulging and empty, just after dawn. While I couldn't honestly say I'd ever killed anyone before, this time, there was no denying I was 100 percent responsible.

"It wasn't your fault." Vero gave my arm an encouraging squeeze through the sleeve of my long black sweater. I hadn't had anything else appropriate to wear; it's not like I'd woken up expecting to attend a funeral. And yet somehow, my children's young and ultra-hip nanny had managed to pull off a pair of formfitting slacks, a killer updo, and a designer blouse. She offered me a wan smile. "It's not like you meant to do it."

My daughter's hand was frail in mine, her body tucked close to my other side, her eyes red from crying.

"In your defense," Vero whispered, "the instructions were in very small print. And at your age—"

"I'm thirty-one."

"Exactly. No one would expect you to be able to read those tiny letters clearly. You just gave him too much. That's all."

"He looked hungry." The excuse sounded weak, even to me. But every time I'd stepped foot in my daughter's room, Christopher had looked up from his bowl with those round, pleading eyes.

"I know." Vero's glossy lips pursed as she patted my shoulder. "You did your best, Finn."

My daughter's goldfish drifted in the cloudy water, his bloated belly pointing at me like an accusatory finger. Christopher had been a gift to Delia from her father, though I was certain Steven had bought the fish just to spite me. To pile one more responsibility onto my overflowing plate, just so he could watch me fail and then rub it in my face as he challenged me for custody. After he'd left me for our real estate agent and they'd gotten engaged, he was determined to demonstrate that I was less fit. It had become a competition for him, one that only became worse after he and Theresa split. I'd been bent on keeping the damn fish alive, to prove to my ex I was capable of providing for our children—and their pet—on my meager writing income without him. That I could feed and care for Delia, Zach, *and* Christopher on my own. Or at least, with Vero's help.

Christopher had survived in my care for less than a month. And while Zach wasn't old enough to rat me out to their father, Delia couldn't keep a secret to save her life. There'd be no keeping the news of Christopher's death from Steven. He'd gloat about it to Guy, his sleazy divorce attorney, and probably bring it up in court. *Your Honor, I'd like to call your attention to the fish in the evidence bag marked Exhibit A. The deceased went belly-up after a mere three weeks in my ex-wife's care. Clearly, she's unfit to parent our children.*

If Steven had any clue about the *human* who'd died while in my care over the last month (or where Vero and I had disposed of the body), he'd probably have a coronary—a possibility Vero had gleefully considered until she calculated the narrow odds of the news actually killing him. A month ago, after a woman named Patricia Mickler had overheard me plotting a novel with my literary agent in a crowded sandwich shop, she'd offered to pay me fifty thousand dollars to murder her husband, a horrible man who happened to launder money for the Russian mob. How Harris had come to be drugged in my minivan had been an accident, and though I wasn't the one who'd actually murdered him, his wife had been certain I had. She'd passed on my name to her friend Irina, whose husband was an enforcer for said very scary mob. Irina's husband's death had also been an accident. Regardless, both women had expressed their gratitude by giving me copious amounts of cash. And a tip: that someone had posted an ad online, searching for a willing party to murder my ex-husband for money.

Vero held the green plastic net out in front of me. "Care to say a few words?"

Zach toddled toward the fishbowl on pudgy legs, the frilly ends of his diaper sticking out from under his black shirt. His sticky fingers clamped around the edge of the dresser as he pulled himself onto his toes to see. He touched a finger to the glass, drool spooling from his chin. Delia's breath hitched, her upper lip shiny with snot as she looked up at me expectantly. I took the net from Vero. "What am I supposed to say?" I whispered.

She nudged me toward the bowl. "Just say something nice about him."

I held the net to my chest, struggling to find the words that would calm my grieving five-year-old, who'd been hysterical since she'd awoken and found her pet floating in his bowl like a Cheerio. I was a writer, for crying out loud. I strung words together for a living. This should've been easy. But every time I looked at Christopher, all I could picture was my ex-husband's face. Not because I wanted to kill Steven. I mean, I did, I guess. Some days. Most days. Definitely whenever he opened his mouth. But no matter how contentious our relationship had become since he'd left me for our real estate agent, Steven loved our children, and they loved him. And I would never do anything to hurt Delia or Zach.

Someone wanted Steven dead. And it wasn't me.

"What can I say about Christopher?" I glanced back at Vero for inspiration. The corner of her mouth twitched as she gestured for me to go on. "He was a good fish. A loyal and steadfast friend to all of us, he . . ."

There was a forceful tug on my yoga pants. "Tell them about his smile," Delia said, wiping her nose on the sleeve of her black leotard. "And how he blew the best bubbles." She crumpled into my side, burying her face in the folds of my sweater. Zach's tiny forehead creased with concern. I was grateful he was too young to really understand what was happening as I echoed Delia's sentiments and dipped the net into the water, scooping Christopher out.

She held my leg as we marched solemnly to the bathroom across the hall. Zach perched on Vero's hip behind us, marking the end of our procession. We stood around the open lid of the toilet, paying our last respects as Christopher fell into the commode with a soft *plink*.

Delia grabbed my arm as I reached for the handle. "No, Mommy!"

"Sweetie, we have to. He can't stay in the potty forever."

"Why not?" she whimpered.

"Because . . ." I threw Vero a pleading look. This chapter was definitely not in my copy of *What to Expect When You're Expecting*. I wanted my money back.

"Because," Vero supplied helpfully, "he's going to start to stink—" I stepped hard on her foot.

"But I'll never see him again," Delia sobbed.

A bubble swelled from her nose and I wiped it on my sleeve. "We'll always have his memories." And the dozens of photos she'd made me post on *#goldfishofinstagram*.

"Maybe we could go to the pet store and get another one." The words were out of Vero's mouth before I could stop her. Delia erupted in a fit of keening wails. Zach's lower lip began to tremble.

"I don't want another fish!" Delia shrieked. "There are no other fish like Christopher!"

"You're absolutely right," I said, raising my voice as they both began to howl. "There will never be another fish like Christopher. We should honor his memory with a moment of silence."

Delia's mouth pinched shut. The bathroom fell quiet except for my children's shuddering sniffles. I lowered my head, jabbing Vero in the ribs with an elbow until she bowed her head, too. I waited a full minute before reaching for the lever. This time, Delia didn't try to stop me, and with a swirl of orange scales, Christopher was gone.

Vero gently ruffled the tear-soaked spikes of Delia's hair. "Come on, Dee. I'll make you some cookies."

"Not too many," I reminded her. My mother was preparing enough turkey and stuffing to feed an army, and she'd murder me if I spoiled the children's appetites before dinner.

Zach squealed as Vero scooped him up and carried him downstairs. Delia lingered, giving the toilet one last look before following them to the kitchen.

As I reached for the light switch, I paused. Turning back to the toilet, I flushed it again. Because I'm not the luckiest person in the world, and I know better than to assume the dead don't come back to haunt you.

CHAPTER 2

An hour later, Vero and I buckled Delia and Zach into their car seats. Vero wiped cookie crumb evidence from their cheeks as I hauled two small Rollaboards into the back of my minivan and slammed the hatch closed.

"What's the luggage for?" Vero asked.

"I got an email from Steven this morning. He's moved into his new place and he wants to take the kids for the weekend." He'd attached photos of the restored farmhouse he'd rented in Fauquier County, careful to point out that the children's bedrooms and toys were already unpacked, and the kitchen was stocked and ready for them. He'd cc'd his attorney, Guy, who had replied to both of us, congratulating Steven on finding such a "great place for the kids," which was clearly lawyer-speak for *you have no grounds to fight this.*

It had been easy to keep the kids away from Steven's farm since his ex-fiancée's arrest. After five bodies had been found buried there and Theresa Hall had been implicated in the ensuing investigation, Steven had called off their engagement. He'd moved out of her town house within hours and had been sleeping on the sofa in the sales trailer on his farm since. He and his attorney had both agreed it would be best for the children to suspend their overnight visits until he was back on his feet. But they didn't know what Vero and I knew. That someone had posted an ad on an online forum, offering a hundred thousand dollars to anyone willing to dispose of Steven Donovan. As far as Vero and I could tell, the forum was an online cesspool, thinly disguised as a mom's support group—an anonymous gathering space for hundreds of disgruntled middle-aged women to bitch about things that bothered them, namely their husbands, bosses, and boyfriends. Apparently, for those with means, it was also a way of getting rid of them.

Vero looked aghast as she slid the van door closed, shutting the children inside. "You're not actually going to let them stay with him, are you?"

"Of course not. I called my mom and asked her if the children could stay with them. Then I emailed Steven and told him the kids already had plans."

A wicked smile pulled at her lips as we climbed into the van. Her voice dropped to a conspiratorial whisper and she wagged an eyebrow. "Three whole days without the kids? I can spend a few nights at my cousin's place if you want to invite Julian over to play house for the weekend."

My face warmed when I pictured Julian in my kitchen. Or my bedroom. I snuck a shameful glance in the rearview mirror, but Zach's head was already drooping against his car seat, and Delia's red-rimmed eyes were drifting closed. "I don't have time to play house." As tempting as it was to spend a weekend alone with the sexy young law student I'd been seeing, I had far more important things to do. "I have to figure out who posted that job offer. I won't feel safe letting the kids spend the weekends with Steven until I'm sure nobody's trying to kill him." And if that wasn't enough, I had a pitch due to my agent by nine A.M. Monday morning.

I turned the key in the ignition, wincing when the engine protested with a sputter before groaning to life.

Vero made a disgusted sound. "We're going car shopping on Monday."

"The van's fine. Your cousin just fixed it."

"No. Ramón put a Band-Aid on it. Face it, the van is toast."

I threw my aging Dodge Caravan in gear, praying nothing shook loose and fell off—at least nothing important—as it rattled down the driveway. "I can't afford to buy a new car right now. Not with Steven and his attorney scrutinizing all my expenses."

"You could if you took that job on the forum. One hundred Gs would buy a pretty sweet car."

"We are not killing my ex-husband for money," I whispered, glancing back at my sleeping children.

"How much do you think we could get for his lawyer?" Vero suggested. I threw her a withering look. "Calm down. I'm kidding. But that transmission isn't going to last much longer. You'd better get busy writing that book Sylvia thinks you've been working on."

"I know. And I will." My literary agent, Sylvia Barr, had been hounding me for sample pages of a novel I had supposedly started a month ago and my editor was expecting before the end of the year. "I'll work on it this weekend. I'll be at the library anyway." Vero and I had been taking turns rotating among nearly a dozen branches of our local county library system, careful to delete our search history each time we used their computers to check that no one had accepted the job offer on the forum. A month had gone by without a bite, but that didn't change the fact that someone wanted to murder my children's father, and now that Steven had a place of his own, I had no reasonable excuse to keep the kids from him. I'd spend the entire weekend at the library if I had to. I'd scour that women's forum until I figured out who posted the ad—probably one of countless women

Steven had either scorned or managed to piss off. Then I'd make an anonymous call, report her intentions to the police, and hope like hell this was the end of it.

Powell Woulfe Photography

ELLE COSIMANO is the award-winning author of several acclaimed young adult novels, including *Nearly Gone, Holding Smoke, The Suffering Tree,* and *Seasons of the Storm.* Elle's debut, *Nearly Gone,* was an Edgar Award finalist and winner of the International Thriller Writers Award and the Mathical Book Prize recognizing mathematics in children's literature. Her more recent young adult thriller *Holding Smoke* was an International Thriller Writers Award nominee and a Bram Stoker Award finalist. In addition to her novels, her essays have appeared in *HuffPost* and *Time.* Elle lives with her husband and two sons in Virginia.